THE HOLLYWOOD HIGH CHRONICLES

book 2

Dark Water

by **Melissa Velasco**

ISBN 978-1-960378-05-7   (paperback)
ISBN 978-1-960378-06-4   (eBook)

1ˢᵗ Edition

Models contracted through DMe Talent Agency:
Deidre Michelle (Agent) @dmetalentagency11

Front Cover Models: Maddie Dawn Cordero, Julian Gopal, Zane Barber, Justin Graham, Mike Prince

Back Cover Models: Maddie Dawn Cordero, Julian Gopal, Zane Barber

Makeup and Hair: Xavier Visage
Costume Concept: Melissa Velasco
Cover Concept: Melissa Velasco
Photography: Tino Duvick @brokenchainphotography
Front Cover Design: Tino Duvick and Anna Hall
Editor: Kyle Fager
Proofreader: Doris Nehrbass

Dedicated to Carol, Jordan, and Brian.

*Boots on the ground, you're my collaborative warriors.
With bleary eyes, honesty, and fresh pots of coffee, you
read well into the night so many times. I thank you for
selflessly helping me realize my dreams!*

DARK WATER

I close my eyes and breathe in the cool air wafting through the open window next to my seat on the school bus. A smile graces my lips. Technically it's fall, but you'd never know it. Southern California has four seasons: summer, kind-of summer, windy season, and nearly summer. After moving to Los Angeles when I was six, I remember how odd this buzzing metropolis felt. Now that I'm fifteen, I'm a Cali girl through and through.

Most of the other kids on this bus dread the long ride, but I love it. My pickup time is so early that I get to watch the sunrise every morning as we drive slowly through the Valley, Studio City, and Hollywood. In a city like LA, there's something rare and magical about getting to sit calmly in my seat, drinking my coffee and basking in the quiet of early morning.

My life's changed so much these past few months. A new school, an amazing group of friends, a new boyfriend . . . a new me. I've blossomed from a mousy caterpillar into who I'm meant to be—at least the version of me I'm meant to be right now. I don't know what I'd do without Hollywood High for the Performing Arts.

Granted, it hasn't been all rainbows and roses. It's been one horrific thing after another, actually. At the start of my freshman year, I asked the universe for a new reality where I could be strong, have a voice, finally come into my own. But I guess it's like what my stepfather, Rich, always says: "Be careful what you ask for; you just might get it." The universe granted my wish but balanced it out with a nightmare in the form of a group of evil bullies that we call the Drones.

Bullies . . . Right! Understatement of the freaking year!

Let's have a rundown, shall we: the Drones blackmailed, attacked, and emotionally tortured just about every other student on campus. Apparently, the attempted rape of quite a few girls, including me, wasn't enough for their leader, student council president Joel Stamp. He cut loose, letting his freak flag fly, as he dangled me over a three-story balcony, with murder in mind.

I can still see Joel's face as he stared down at me while I hung there. I thought I was going to die. Honestly, I *should have* died.

If Trey hadn't dropped into my life, things would be different. Our soulmate connection started as a gentle, synchronized hum and quickly grew to include pain and emotional thought sharing. It's been a wild ride.

My coffee and the sunrise isn't helping to sooth my nerves this morning. I take a shaky breath and wonder why.

Oh yeah. That whole trial-for-attempted-murder thing.

My hands get clammy like they always do when thoughts of Joel haunt me. I squeeze my eyes shut, willing my racing heart to calm. My mom thinks I have PTSD from all of it, but I'm still not up for therapy. *Not yet anyway. For now, I can deal with it on my own.*

The bus wheels down Hollywood Boulevard, then left onto a side street, where the football field at Hollywood High comes into view. The driver expertly makes the sharp final turn and slows to a stop at the curb. I wind up my headphones and shove my Discman in my backpack before squeezing into the aisle, which is crowded with kids slowly heading to the door. Through the window, I spot Trey lounging against the block wall. His gorgeous tan is made even more perfect by his carefully styled, wavy raven hair.

I hop off the bus and into the waiting arms of Trey.

"Good morning, gorgeous," he says, but then his golden-brown eyes pierce with concern. "You okay?"

There's no point in downplaying what I'm thinking. Our soulmate connection is open, and so he already knows. "Just pondering the whole Joel mess. I had nightmares most of the night."

"You should've called me."

"You can't save me from my own mind."

He scoffs. "I can, and I will. That's what we do, Melanie. I'm your other half."

When he laces his fingers through mine, our energies wrap and braid together, and it sends a calm synchronicity through me. My anxiety fades.

My promise ring glints in the sun, the little black and silvery gemstones shining and flashing. I haven't taken it off since Trey gave it to me at the homecoming dance.

"What are you grinning about?" Trey asks, looking relieved at the sudden calming of my energy he senses through the connection we share.

"My ring's pretty in the sun. I love it." I rise up on my toes and kiss him good morning.

"Don't you two ever get sick of greeting each other like long-lost loves from a fairy tale *every single* morning?" a familiar voice hollers from a distance.

It's Presley. She and Marcus are crossing the street from the student parking lot and heading toward us. Trey and I laugh at how our sappy romance is always such ready cannon fodder for our more cynical friends. Presley Verelle and Marcus Vinsky are two of our best friends, and together we're a part of a student council that, after the insane events with Joel, is now run by our group. These days, we're a real who's who of the school.

As they approach, it's obvious why Marcus and Presley are one of the most beautiful couples at Hollywood High, a place with no shortage of fly people. Marcus is wearing a white T-shirt with the sleeves rolled up, perfectly broken-in blue jeans, black sunglasses, and Doc Marten boots. He's always drop-dead gorgeous, but this James-Dean-inspired look makes him just about breathtaking. Today, Presley's blond hair wafts loose around her shoulders, her heart-shaped face breaking into an ear-to-ear smile. Her black denim pleated miniskirt and her white Nirvana T-shirt ensemble stretches tight around her curves. None of the boys are likely to complain because Presley has the figure of Jessica Rabbit. How she keeps from getting a big head about her bombshell good looks is beyond me, but she's one of the most down-to-earth people I know. When I started at Hollywood High, Presley quickly became one of my best friends.

When they get to us, Marcus assumes an over-the-top haughty debonaire pose. He pulls his sunglasses down a touch, peeking seductively over the top, and sarcastically says to Presley, "My dearrrrrr, I'd buy you the world if you hadn't already given it to me when you said yes to my promise of forever . . ."

In turn, Presley pops one foot, cocks a hip, and slants down one shoulder, looking like a pinup model. She tosses her hair over her shoulder and responds dramatically, "My loooooove, I see the world in your eyes, and our hearts beat as one."

Trey and I crack up, but the truth is that their silly impression of the two of us isn't that far off the mark.

"We can't help it," Trey says. He gestures to Presley and me and says to Marcus, "I mean really, dude, you have to admit that we're lucky guys."

Presley and I exchange a look, a silent plan sparking between us. Simultaneously, we strike terrible supermodel poses. Both guys crack up as they steer us through the alley gate.

"Anyone have an update on the trial?" Presley asks.

My mood takes a nosedive.

Trey frowns. "Bad timing, Pres."

Presley glances my way. "The nightmares again?"

I nod and take a shaky breath. "If I don't get a good night's sleep soon, I'm gonna lose it."

Trey puts his arm around me. "She really can't handle much more."

Marcus checks his watch. "We better get to first period. You two have tests in Mr. Martinez's class."

We herd ourselves through the crowded walkway.

Marcus managed to test out of algebra class last week, and Presley and I couldn't be more jealous. He's right that we need to be on time. An *F* on the test would put a real damper on our eligibility for the school musical, and we don't want to jeopardize our chances of getting cast. Not to mention that shitty grades would add a whole new layer of anxiety to my already fragile state.

We get to the door outside Mr. Martinez's upstairs classroom. Trey squeezes my hand, and I hang on a little tighter as he pulls away. He raises one eyebrow, and with a smoldering expression, backs me against the lockers. He puts his hand on the locker behind me, cups my chin, and gives me a kiss that leaves me gasping. The universe narrows to just the two of us, right up until Presley's voice breaks into our dreamy existence.

"Why don't you ever kiss me like that, Marcus?" Presley huffs, and Trey and I start grinning mid-kiss. "I want sexy movie star kisses! Your idea of romance is giving me snacks."

Marcus, always good-natured, bows a bit at the waist, his hand circling comically to take Presley's. He backs her into the lockers and performs a perfect imitation of Trey's hand-on-the-locker move.

Presley laughs and shoves him away. "I don't know how you can take all that smoldering mystery guy stuff so seriously, Mel! When Marcus does it, it's hilarious."

"What can I say?" Trey says with a smirk and a shrug. "When you got it, you got it."

"Never mind," Presley says to Marcus. "I like our snack-sharing love way more."

On cue, Marcus produces a Twizzler from his backpack and hands it to her with all the gallantry of a courtly knight.

She takes the Twizzler and smacks him on the ass with it. "You two better get to class!" she tells the boys. "You're gonna be late."

Trey sends a pulse of love through our soulmate connection before letting go of my hand.

The boys wave goodbye, and Pres and I watch them walk down the hall, our heads tilted together. We sigh at the same time just as Surfer Guy Tad cuts off our view. Tad's still in his swimming trunks and surf shirt from his usual early morning ride on the waves. He looks us up and down and whistles before hitting us with a dopey grin.

"Ew, Tad!" Presley says with a grimace. "I've known you since we were in diapers. Beat it."

Unfazed by Presley's brush-off, Tad says in a surfer drawl so stereotypical it's sometimes hard to deal with, "I might not, like, have a membership to the store, but I still like to, you know, window-shop the merchandise."

We nearly gag. With his sun-bleached hair and tan muscles, Tad's cute, but there's something so friend zone about him.

"Hey, Tad!" Trey's voice growls, loud and threatening, from the end of the hall. "It's hard to balance on a surfboard with two broken legs!"

"Yeah, duuuude," Marcus chimes in. "Get to stepping."

Evidently, our guys turned back to make sure we got into the classroom and noticed Tad's little performance. Alarm bells must have started ringing in their heads as soon as they heard Tad's voice. Tad slinks down the hall, totally oblivious to how close he just came to ending up in urgent care. Our guys wave a second time, then round the corner out of sight.

Presley raises an eyebrow at me. "They're so hot."

We link arms, giggling, and duck into class to face our dreaded test.

CHAPTER 2

As Presley and I leave first period, she asks, "Am I crazy, or was half of that test about a bunch of stuff we haven't even been taught yet?"

It's not just me, apparently.

"The whole second half of the test was a complete mystery," I agree, panic rising to the point where I nearly double over. A cold sweat breaks over my brow, and my breath catches in my throat. Suddenly, I can't take another step. I stop in the middle of the hall, forcing the throng of other students to dodge around us. Here I stand, with the rational part of my brain at war with the irrational. Panic attacks have taken me by surprise more and more frequently since my near-death Joel incident, but so far, they've usually happened at night or when I'm alone. If I'm this over the edge about a math test, right here in the middle of the crowded hall, then things are clearly escalating.

Presley's eyes widen as she watches my internal struggle. "Breathe, Mel." She frowns, scans her study guide, and says, "I'm telling you, Mr. Martinez is evil. I've heard from upperclassmen that he does stuff like this on purpose because he's a miserable little man. *None* of the second half of that test is on this study guide." Suddenly, her face is a mask of rage. "You know what? No! You don't need this stress, and I'm pissed. Come on."

Presley grabs me by the arm and stomps back down the hall into the classroom we just departed. Mr. Martinez looks up from his grading and hits us with an exhausted stare. Presley waits for a greeting, and when she doesn't get one, says, "You do realize that sabotaging already distraught teens makes you evil, right?"

My eyebrows shoot into my hairline. *Presley strikes again.*

Mr. Martinez stares at her blankly.

"The back half of our test wasn't part of the unit you taught," Presley says. "None of that's on the study guide." As if to prove her point, she waves the study guide in front of him. Even the rustling paper sounds irritated.

"You're responsible for what's on the test," Mr. Martinez answers tonelessly. "Maybe you should spend more time studying and less time being rude."

My eyes widen, and Presley's mouth drops open.

She sets her hands on the stacks of paper on his desk and leans into him. "I've got you figured out," she growls. "You fail students because it's the only control you have in your pitiful life. You're pathetic, Mr. Martinez. I mean, is shit at home really that bad?"

Mr. Martinez's expression becomes so intensely pained that I gasp out loud. I can feel his tumultuous emotions for a moment before he steels up again. The energy exchange shuts down so fast that it leaves me reeling. I blink, trying to verbalize how sorry I am for him, but no sound comes out. Presley and our teacher glare at each other for a few solid seconds before, finally, I manage to choke out, "Mr. Martinez, you need help."

He looks at me with curiosity. It's the most expressive I've ever seen him. "You can sense that, can't you? I've heard that about you. How does it work?"

Presley is so thrown off by his sudden humanity that she glances, confused, between him and me.

"The intuition is a little different than what just happened," I explain, "but they're linked. I know things are going to happen sometimes before they do. But this time, I felt what you're feeling. How do you live with that pain?"

Mr. Martinez's eyes suddenly fill with a hurricane of emotional turmoil. His whole inhuman robot façade cracks around the edges, revealing the real Mr. Martinez. The transformation is so stark, he almost looks like a different person.

"What happened to you?" I ask, my heart breaking for him.

His eyes fill with tears as he whispers, "She died."

"Who?" Presley asks softly.

"Martha Stamp, my fiancé." He looks between me and Presley. "You two are lucky. Enjoy every minute with Trey and Marcus."

This is the last thing I expected him to say. "I'm so sorry, Mr. Martinez. When did she die?"

"A year ago today."

"Is she by chance related to Joel Stamp?" Presley asks.

A surge of dread passes through me at the sound of that name. I take a laborious breath and try to shiver it away.

Mr. Martinez nods. "His aunt. The whole family fell apart. His mother's been at a loss ever since. No one knows how to cope. Honestly, none of us are right anymore." His face somehow falls further. He ages twenty years in front of us as a tear slips down his cheek.

Without warning, he turns his head and clamps down on his expression. "Out. I'm busy."

"Please don't shut down, Mr. Martinez," I plead. "We'll help you."

He points to the door. Presley and I exchange a glance. I shrug, unsure what to do. Presley grabs my elbow and pulls me through the door, closing it after her.

We stare at each other.

"What I felt . . . the pain he's living with . . . Presley!"

"We need to talk to Ms. G," she says with concern pressed on her pretty, heart-shaped face.

We walk briskly down the stairs, through the double doors to the quad, across the quad to another set of stairs, which we take two at a time down to the basement level. We run down a checkered hallway and into the Magnet office. There, we find the cheerful secretary on the phone. She motions for us to hang on a moment.

We take a seat in the row of hard plastic chairs. I like coming down to this office because it's like time stopped in this room. The furniture and décor are exactly what students must have seen forty years ago.

It's 1992, Melanie. Be here in the present. Focus. The thought stands completely out of place with the intuition nagging persistently at the back of my mind. Seeds of panic have been planted in me, making it hard to breathe, but I can't quite tell if they're the result of the emotional shitstorm Mr. Martinez just shared with me unintentionally, or they come from my own ever-present anxiety. This ability to share in other people's emotions has been building slowly within me since I first learned I was an energy worker, but up to now, it has only ever happened with close friends and family. For my intuition to be affecting me so deeply, something must be very wrong with Mr. Martinez. He's not just sad; he's in trouble.

The secretary hangs up and greets us with a rosy-cheeked smile. "Good morning, girls. It's so nice to see you. What can I do for you today?"

"Good morning, Ms. Austin," Presley says. "We need to speak to Ms. G please."

Ms. Austin picks up the phone and pushes a button. "Ms. G, Presley and Melanie are here to see you." She listens for a moment before hanging up. "Head on in, girls. Ms. G's happy to speak with you." She holds out a piece of hard candy in each hand and winks.

"Girls, bring me one of those candies!" Ms. G yells from behind the closed door to her office.

Presley and I can't help but giggle as we accept an extra candy for Ms. G.

"Hello, gals," Ms. G says with a warm grin as we enter. "What's up?"

Her ample personality matches her ample form, and she always radiates positive energy. I love her. I hand her the candy, which she unwraps and pops in her mouth.

We take a seat. Presley looks at me, and I take a deep breath.

"Mr. Martinez has lost it," I say, cutting straight to the point.

Ms. G rolls her eyes. "I can't say I'm surprised. He's an underpaid, overworked teacher who isn't particularly liked."

I shake my head. "No, you don't understand . . ."

Presley takes up the thread. "He gave us a test today, and literally half of it was never taught to us. The whole class is going to fail, and let me tell you, none of us need help getting crap grades in that class. We can do that perfectly fine on our own!"

Ms. G snickers.

"Anyhow," Presley continues, "we went in to confront the sniveling robot, but it got weird."

The counselor looks contemplative.

"You need to check on him," I implore. "It's the one-year anniversary of the death of his fiancé, and he's not okay. I could feel what he's feeling. Ms. G, I'm telling you he's in trouble."

Ms. G snorts. "You could *feel* it?" She continues in a sarcastic tone, "That's a touch melodramatic, wouldn't you say?"

Presley jumps in. "You don't understand, Ms. G. Melanie isn't making this up. She really can feel what other people feel. I can't tell you how many times she's showed up at the right time or known exactly what someone else is feeling. It's linked to her intuition. I swear to you."

Ms. G snorts again. "Oh, now there's intuition also?"

Exasperated, I say, "Please, Ms. G. You don't have to believe me about the intuition thing! Just check on him."

"I'll look into the issue," she says. Then she makes a motion to dismiss us.

"Promise?" Presley prods her.

"Frankly, I think you're both misguided. I've never seen Mr. Martinez crack a smile, let alone feel heartbroken, but I'll check on him when I have a moment."

Presley looks my way as if to confirm that I'm satisfied with this answer, but I'm at a loss. "Thank you," she says finally.

We stand to leave.

Ms. G seems to be studying me. "You're really serious, Melanie?"

I nod. "There's nothing Presley and I can do. He hates most of the students. Maybe he'll listen to a colleague. You need to help him."

Ms. G nods and bids us farewell.

CHAPTER 3

I wipe sweat from my eyes and glare at Trey. "Enough."

Trey shakes his head. "I'm sorry, but you've got to learn these defense tactics. After everything that happened with Joel and the Drones, we can't take chances."

Mr. Isley grins at me from his spot leaning against the wall in the dance studio. "You're doing surprisingly well, Mel. Keep at it."

I'm surprised Mr. Isley has agreed to being a part of this little demonstration. Mr. Isley has a Broadway and film career that's jaw-dropping. He now runs the dance program at Hollywood High. He rarely wastes time, and his presence makes me nervous.

I huff and square off against my boyfriend again. Trey feints right and I block, but I realize too late that it was just a distraction.

He gets an arm around my neck and twists me around. "Now what do you do?" he demands.

I try to twist away, but he tightens his hold. I throw an elbow, but he wrenches his body, and my attack meets nothing but open air. I attempt sweeping his leg from behind me, but he traps my leg between his thighs and starts to lower me to the ground. Using the momentum in my favor, I snake my left arm over his neck, pulling hard and dropping to the floor. It sends him over my shoulder and to the mat.

Trey, flat on his back, grins up at me. "That's my girl."

Suddenly, the lights go out, and I hear rustling in the dark. Megadeth's "Skin O' My Teeth" blisters through the speakers. "Trey!" I yell.

"Think through it, baby," he calls out over the racket. "Your sight and hearing are now compromised. What do you have to work with?"

I feel a breeze to my right just before I'm grabbed from behind. Arms lock around me, and I'm overcome with irrational panic. I know I'm in the dance studio, and this must be some kind of test, but the person who grabbed me doesn't feel like Mr. Isley or Trey. I wrench my shoulder low and slip from my attacker's grasp, spinning and backing away.

"She slipped away from me," comes the familiar voice.

It's Arch.

"Good, Mel." Arch leads our group of misfits. He's cool, calm, and takes readily to being the boat captain of our Titanic-doomed group.

I'm met by lightning-quick movement to my left just before a strong hand snakes out and snatches my wrist. I kick high and twist. My shin makes contact, and Tanner squeals, letting go of me.

"Damn! That hurt."

I need to be careful. Tanner's gorgeous, even on an average day. He's the resident David Bowie of Hollywood High, and striking that pretty face would require additional work to his over-the-top makeup jobs.

Mr. Isley turns the music down some and announces, "I don't want anyone to actually get hurt."

Still disoriented, I rush back and bump into someone.

I try to duck, but Adam's sultry voice returns me to reality. "Uh-uh. Not so fast."

I chuckle. Adam is my ex-boyfriend. I can't see his ocean-blue eyes and blond hair in the pitch-black, but I can feel his muscled arm around my waist.

He spins me around, and my tension melts away. I giggle as he slides his hands around my sides seductively. I run my hand down his impressive chest, and he inhales sharply. Adam and I have a never-ending supply of sexual tension. We both enjoy this game more than we should.

"Think you can get away?" he drawls gravelly.

"Maybe," I answer in a suggestive tone.

"Good answer." He pretends to bite at my neck, setting me into a giggling, girly fit.

"Holy shit, Adam!" Trey says with exasperation. "Seriously? Just let my girl go."

Adam laughs, giving me a love tap on my tush, and announces, "Oh, look at that. She got away."

I whip around, expecting the assault to be over, but another pair of arms wrap around me suddenly. My face crushes into a wide, T-shirt-clad chest. The scent of Drakkar cologne fills my senses. I giggle and hug my newest attacker. "Hi, Demitri."

Chuckles ring out all around the room.

"Told you she wouldn't find Demitri menacing," Adam says.

Demitri . . . Lord help me. He's the heartthrob of the dance department. I've never seen someone who can affect a room quite like him. He's built like a dance God, with his perfect six-pack. Add to it his stunning eyes and charisma, and every girl within a fifty-mile radius melts into a horny puddle when he smiles.

"Demitri, what the hell is she doing?" Trey asks. "She's clearly not fighting back."

Demitri laughs. "She's hugging me."

I run my hand along Demitri's impressive stomach and chirp, "Now I'm fondling his abs. I like this game. Leave the lights out for another ten minutes, and I'll be in a great mood." I don't usually flirt with Demitri. In fact, I avoid him, mostly because he's flirtatiously harassed by every girl who lays eyes on him. It's so base, and I refuse to pander to his charm like a pathetic Normal. Today seems to be an exception.

"I didn't know that was a part of the master plan," Demitri quips, "but I'm game."

More laughter belts from all my would-be attackers.

"Don't be a sleaze, Mr. Honest!" Trey says.

Demitri rubs my shoulders flirtatiously. "I'm a team player. Melanie's safety is my utmost concern."

I purr, "Aren't you sweet!" I bite my lip in the dark, secretly enjoying the rare moment with Mr. Wonderful.

"Wait a minute!" Adam scoffs. "Seriously, Mel? You'd pick Demitri over me?"

"Would you two stop!" Trey barks.

"I didn't know we were supposed to play slap and tickle with her," Arch says. "Send her back this way."

Everyone laughs.

"Demitri!" Trey snarls. "Would you please attack her before she mounts you like a sleazy koala bear?"

"If I must."

Demitri grabs my shoulders and spins me around, twisting my arms overhead before sweeping my legs. I drop to my knees, jokingly purring, "Ooooh, kinky."

He leans, attempting to pin me in the dark. I giggle and untwist, managing to yank my right hand free. I feel his breath on my cheek as he whispers flirtatiously for only me to hear, "Damn, girl."

I giggle and reach up, tickling Demitri's side.

He squirms, announcing, "Your little vixen just tickled me. I'm the wrong brute for this job."

I crabwalk away, bumping into an unexpected pair of legs. A hand reaches down and grabs the back of my shirt as I try to roll out of reach. I'm lifted off the ground and left to dangle like a toddler.

Bear's big laugh booms. "Turn on the light."

I can't help but squeal happily. Bear is my personal Yoda and the spiritual guru of our group. Mountainous, he effortlessly holds me up with one arm.

The lights blaze on.

"Look!" Bear says. "I caught a flirtatious fairy."

I lean into the toddler act by swinging my legs. "Weeeeee!"

Trey hits me with a scathing glare. "This is serious, Melanie. Joel's in prison, but his Drones are still out there somewhere. You *have* to be able to defend yourself."

I sigh happily as Bear sets me on my feet. "I'm amused, if it helps," I chirp.

Mr. Isley beams at me as he pauses the CD player.

"What do you suggest, then?" Trey asks me with disgust. "Clearly, my idea has failed."

"I don't know," I say with a shrug. "I kind of like your whole 'groping hot guys in the dark' scheme." When I side-eye Demitri mischievously, he silently chuckles. I make a show of scanning the room, then make a pouty face at Trey. "You forgot to invite Drake. He's hot too."

Trey glowers at me while my friends crack up. He gestures to Darren, who steps forward looking like a caged animal. He's long and lithe, easily a foot taller than me. He reaches out lightning fast, but I battement my right leg to my ear, hooking his shoulder with my leg as it descends. I pull him in, taking him off-balance.

As he falls to the side, I tweak his nose.

From the floor, Darren laughs. "Her methods are unconventional," he informs Trey, "but they're effective. Let her giggle, grope, and nose tweak her way to safety."

The bell rings and I grab my backpack. "Are you walking me to class, Trey?" I ask jokingly. "Or do I get to pick a special friend from your fine selection?"

Trey drapes an arm over my shoulder and hauls me out the door.

CHAPTER 4

We're ten minutes into fourth period and I'm staring off into space, worrying about Mr. Martinez. My intuition has quit nagging at me, and I'm scared about what that means.

"You're missing the show," Presley whispers.

Mr. Bentley's sitting all red-faced at his desk as he plows through a heated debate with Susan about her grade on a paper we handed in last week. That girl's impossible. If it's not one thing, it's another with her. The whole class tried to politely ignore the exchange at first, but now everyone's openly listening.

"Susan, the bottom line is that your research paper wasn't up to snuff," Mr. Bentley says. "I'm sorry, but it's just not an *A*-standard paper. You got a *B*, and a *B* is a perfectly fine grade."

Susan stomps her patent-leather-clad foot and balls up her fists like a toddler. "Buuuuuut, Mr. B-B-B-B, it's not fair!"

At this point, it's becoming hard not to laugh. We've all got our hands over our mouths, and we're turning various shades of red and purple.

Marcus can't take it anymore. "Give it a rest, *Susan*! The most interesting thing about you is that you finally got a *B*. Welcome to the Land of No One Cares, where *B*'s are *A*'s, those shoes of yours are awesome, and *everyone* agrees with you." His words are uncharacteristically mean, but none of us can deny that they're also hilarious.

Susan turns her beady eyes his way, and if looks could kill, Marcus would have expired in an instant. She stomps up to the table I share with Marcus and Presley, leaning aggressively toward Presley. "I don't know how you can date him! He's terrible."

Presley leans in fast, closing the gap, and hisses at Susan like a cat. Susan jumps back into the table behind her and nearly falls. I put my head on the desk to keep from laughing. I give Presley a thumbs-up, obscured from Susan's sight under the desk. Presley guffaws.

Mr. B's standing at the front of the room, eyebrows arched, his hands on the top of his head. As the favorite Magnet school teacher, he rarely has trouble with the students, so this whole episode with Susan seems to have him flummoxed. She's sulking in her chair, close to tears. Everyone she makes eye contact with rolls their eyes.

The door opens, breaking the silence. Tanner enters the room with Trey behind him. I cock my head to one side in confusion. Trey isn't in this class. Tanner is, but he rarely makes an appearance.

"Hello, boys," Mr. Bentley says. "I might thank you for your charmed timing. It's been an exciting class period thus far. Trey, to what do we owe the pleasure?"

Tanner and Trey exchange a glance before Trey says, "Tanner and I decided to ditch fourth period. We were down the hall in the two-story building when Tanner remembered he had to hand in an assignment to Mr. Martinez."

The look Trey gives—eyes glazed over, distress thrumming off him—causes my mouth to drop open. My boyfriend is one of the badass protectors of this place. Nothing fazes him. For him to look like this, something has to be very wrong. I try to garner details through our soulmate connection, but he has it walled off on his side, leaving me in the dark.

"Are you okay?" I ask, rushing to him.

When his gaze shifts to me, it's clear that he's been completely traumatized.

"Tell us what happened, Tanner," Presley insists in a panic.

Tanner's usually gorgeous face is pale and slack, devoid of his trademark spunk. He takes a shaky breath. "I opened the door, and we walked in. I put my assignment in his intake box, and we turned to leave. That's when we noticed Mr. Martinez on the floor behind his desk. He wasn't breathing."

When Trey takes my hand, the image of Mr. Martinez rips through our connection before he can stop it. I hear a rush in my ears as the blood wooshes and swirls in my head. I gasp and double over at the waist from terrible stomach pain.

"DAMN IT!" Presley exclaims. "Me and Melanie told Ms. G to check on him!"

Panic takes me down to my knees. Everything is swirling.

Faintly, I hear Mr. Bentley ask, "What do you mean you told Ms. G?"

Presley's voice fades away as my thoughts tornado.

My intuition about him dissolved. That was when he died. I'm sure of it. He's dead and I tried to tell them! What's the point of having this intuition if no one listens? I can't take any more of this.

"Was the office notified?"

"I called the office on the classroom phone while Trey started CPR," Tanner informs. "Principal Walker and the police took over, and we came here. Mr. Martinez still wasn't breathing when we left his room."

Everything comes crashing in at once. A tidal wave of my ever-present anxiety mixes with my fear about Joel's impending trial and my guilt about not being able to save Mr. Martinez. I try to inhale, but nothing happens. Once, when I was eight, the air was knocked out of me when I fell on the playground. This is worse.

I can't breathe!

The wall in the middle of my soulmate connection with Trey falls, and in an instant, his alarm shoots through. He now knows I'm physically and emotionally cratering.

"Melanie?" He kneels next to me just as my knees collapse and I fall flat. "Call an ambulance! NOW!" He grabs my face. "Melanie, you're turning blue. You need to breathe."

Weakly, I shake my head and try, but nothing happens except a slight rattling sound in my throat. I've had panic-induced asthma since I was little, and it gets bad, but never anything like this.

Mr. Bentley rushes up, hovering above me. "Marcus," he calls across the room, "use your cell phone and dial 911! Dante, call the office on my classroom phone."

Marcus is one of the only kids at the school who has a cell phone. They're new and really expensive. Somewhere in the back of my mind, the amused thought floats up just before I lose consciousness: *Thank God Marcus comes from money. I might make it because he's a rich boy.*

My vision goes spotty just as I feel Trey's lips over mine as he starts CPR for the second time today.

CHAPTER 5

I'm swimming in a gray void.

Think, Melanie . . .

But I can't. Thoughts don't connect. There's something blocking logic. I know this, but somehow, I can't make sense of all of it. It's like I have pieces floating past me that come and go, just out of reach.

I drift away from myself again, unable to make the connection.

———

When I hear a familiar voice, I float back up into the gray.

"What's wrong with her?"

My mom's here . . . but where is here?

"We believe she's in shock from a nervous breakdown. We have her sedated while we try to figure this out. Has she had any trauma to her head?"

Who's she talking too?

"No."

"Any emotional trauma she hasn't dealt with?"

"She was attacked and nearly died. Her attacker has a pending trial for attempted murder, but we thought Melanie was okay. She's got friends, a boyfriend, she went to the homecoming dance . . ."

I drift off again, carried away into the dark on a tide I can't control.

⸺

The black abyss opens above me, and I float almost to the surface again, nearly close enough to touch, but maddeningly out of reach.

"You can't keep her on those sedatives! I'm ordering you to take her off them."

Trey! I try desperately to speak, to move, but nothing. I want to scream. I'm trapped.

"Son, you have no authority to order a change in her medical protocol. We're doing what we need to for her. Every time we lighten the dose, she has a seizure."

"What do I need to be to have authority to change her medical protocol?" Trey asks in a tone somewhere between a threat and a whimper.

"You need to be a parent or her husband."

"Fine, get a minister. I'll marry her now."

"How old are you, Trey?"

"Sixteen."

The disembodied voice chuckles, and I'm sucked back down into the dark.

⸺

I'm stuck in the gray water as Trey floats down. I gasp at the sight of him. He strains, trying to swim through the bizarrely thick liquid. He reaches me and wraps his arms around me. I feel more solid than usual as he gets a grasp on me.

"You have to come back, Melanie. I'm lost."

I don't know how! I'm trapped!

"I know you are. I'm working on it."

You can hear me?

"I can hear you."

Trey launches away, out of sight, cast out by an unknown force. My heart nearly explodes. The quaking starts again.

— —

Everything's dark gray.

There's no time here. I'm disappearing.

— —

The world quakes and rattles for the hundredth time. Everything shakes, and I feel like I'm falling.

I have to find solid ground!

"Dose her! Do it now! She's spiking another fever and seizing."

"No! Please! I'm begging you. Give her a chance to come out of this."

"Wait outside, Trey!"

"I'M NOT LEAVING!"

Trey's upset! Have to get to him!

The world keeps throbbing and quaking. I can't get my feet under me.

There's no solid ground!

"Call security!"

"I'm leaving! Just don't kick me out for good. You don't understand!"

I fall, shaken back into the black abyss.

This time, when Trey floats down, I gasp and reach, kicking against the oily black water that holds me hostage. He reaches me and takes what should be my face in both hands, but instead, it's Disembodied Me. He stares into my eyes and wraps around me. He feels solid, but I'm nothing but a ghost. He grapples, trying to get a grasp, panicking. Suddenly, just like before, he's pulled back up through the dark water, and he soars out of sight.

I hear him scream before the dark water pulls me deeper down.

The black, oily abyss turns gray.

"So, this is the little bitch, huh?"

"That's her."

The male voice is familiar . . . but who is it?

"She doesn't look so scary."

"She's definitely scarier than she looks. If you're going to do it, do it fast. We're gonna get caught."

STAN! That's Stan's voice. Who's the woman, though?

Memories of Joel and his best friend, Stan, chasing me maniacally down Hollywood Boulevard make me shudder in the water.

"Hang on, I've got the syringe in my purse. If we get rid of her, Joel's got a shot. We have to off them one at a time, but it has to look like an accident."

Off us? Panic screams through me, and I try desperately to move my body to no avail.

"Can I help you?"

I know this voice. Every time he comes in, I get sucked back into the abyss.

"Our apologies, Doctor. We're just visiting a friend."

"This room is off-limits. You must be on the visitation list for entry. What are your names?"

"We apologize. We're leaving . . ." Then his tone changes like he's speaking to the woman. "Come on. We'll think of something else."

Stan's voice fades away, followed by the cold wash that always sweeps me into the dark.

— —

"It's been two weeks! This is madness. It has to stop!"

Trey's voice brings me out of the dark water, sending me drifting closer to the reality I can't ever reach. I've gotten good at listening when I'm in the gray water, but I can't ever speak or move. It's mind-numbing.

There's nothing left of me.

"Trey, I've told you over and over that she spikes fevers and seizes every time we try to bring her back."

"You don't understand. I know what's happening!"

"Okay, kid. I'll humor you because at this point, we have no clue what to do. What do you think is happening?"

"She's trapped in there. She's fighting to get out, and every time the sedatives start to wear off, she tries to break free. She's panicking!"

"How do you know this?"

"You don't understand us . . . what we have. I have nightmares where I'm trapped in dark water with her every time I sleep."

Yes! He's got it figured out!

My mom's voice joins the conversation. "I know that must sound insane to you, Dr. Bryant, but they can feel each other's physical pain. If he says it's happening, I wouldn't be surprised."

Rich's voice adds to the confusion in the gray water. "I can vouch for it also. Trey and Melanie aren't your average teen couple."

A chuckle, then, "He asked me to get a minister to marry them so he could change her medical protocol."

A contemplative pause stretches long.

"You feel that strongly about this, Trey?" Rich asks.

"I'm telling you that I *know*," Trey insists.

"If we do this," the doctor says, "it could kill her."

"I'll hold her," Trey implores. "I can get her through the seizures."

Rich's voice floats past again. "Let him try. We have to do something. Nothing else has worked."

"We'll consider it tomorrow," the doctor says hesitantly.

"I'm skipping school then," Trey insists. "I need to be here."

"Would you like to stay the night and keep watch over her, Trey?" Rich asks. "Her mom and I are exhausted. Honestly, we could use the help. We don't want to take a chance that she'll wake up alone, but we have to sleep at some point."

I'm sucked back down by the relentless dark water.

— —

I'm exhausted and worn to a sliver. *I can't keep doing this, but I have no choice.*

"Melanie, I need you to listen. It's just you and me. Everyone else is gone."

Trey!

"I know you can hear me."

I can hear you! I try again to speak, but nothing. *Please, Trey, get me out of here.*

"I've been tracking the dreams I keep having and the reaction you have when the sedative is wearing off. I know what's happening. You should be in the gray water now. The dark water sucks you down when they fully dose you."

Yes! He understands.

Disembodied Me starts to cry, and I hear Trey gasp.

"Melanie, you're crying. I'm right, aren't I?"

Yes!

"I've watched how the sedative machine works. They have you hooked to an IV drip. I know how to lessen the dose."

Do it!

"You're crying harder . . . Melanie, I know you can hear me. Listen, I'm going to lessen the dosage, but I have to do it slowly. It's late at night, and there aren't as many doctors and nurses on duty. I checked your chart, and we have four hours before Dr. Bryant makes his early morning rounds."

I hear him take a raking gasp.

"They keep saying it could kill you because of the seizures, but I know what we need to do. I need you back. I'm lost."

My heart's breaking. *I'm lost too.*

The sound of three beeps floats by in the water.

"I just turned down the drip. I'm going to lie with you and hold you while you try to come back."

The gray water's warmer suddenly. Heavy water on the right. *It's perfect.* I sigh. Finally, almost content.

"You sighed."

I sighed! I thought it was only Disembodied Me.

The water starts to turn a lighter gray. I drift away on what feels like a wave of real sleep.

Beep, beep, beep.

— —

"I love you, Melanie."
I love you too.

— —

Beep, beep, beep.

— —

The water is light blue. I'm so close to the surface. The shaking starts as a vibration that grows into a full-blown earthquake. My soul rattles. I pitch and flail in the water.

"I'm here. Melanie. Listen to my voice."

Trey. Clearer this time.

"You can do this, Melanie. Remember what Bear says about you being an Aries? You put on your armor and fight every time. I need you to fight through this."

The quaking gets worse. I feel like I'm shredding apart.

Trey gasps. "Melanie, stay with me!"

Suddenly, everything stops, and I feel myself pulled gently to the right toward a bright spot in the water.

Trey whispers, "No, no, no! Baby don't do this!" I hear him sob.

I'm so tired! I drift farther to the right, untethered.

"Melanie, please. Damn it!" Trey's voice shudders as if he's crying. "I don't know what to do. I'm getting the doctor on duty."

NO! If you get the doctor, I'll be sucked back into the dark water. I feel Trey holding my hand, and finally, I manage to blast an emotional thought bubble through our connection.

He whispers, "I got the pulse, but you aren't breathing. Come on, Melanie!"

I stop in the light-blue water, feeling something new surge up. *This isn't how this goes.*

"Breathe, Melanie! Please!"

Suddenly, images flash like a movie on fast-forward. I see it all just on the surface of the water, close enough to touch.

Trey waking up in a sweat-drenched fit, over and over. Trey crying, grabbing his pillow and screaming into it. Trey throwing up in the bathroom at school with Tanner standing at the stall door. Demitri and Adam with Trey while he cries at the lunch table.

I AM DONE! This is the only shot I'm going to get . . . I kick as hard as I can, straining against the water that holds me . . . And suddenly, just when I think I can't go any farther, I break the surface, inhaling a gasping breath.

———

My eyes open. Trey gasps along with me. He's lying next to me. The blanket on my chest is soaked through to my skin with my sweat and his tears. He's gripping my hand so hard it hurts, and his eyes are full of enough shock and relief to break my heart.

"You got me out of the water."

He whispers, "I was right?"

I nod. "You were right."

"I was in the water with you."

"I know."

Trey's face crumples. He sobs, his body shivering. It's gut-wrenching. I pull his head down on the wet blanket and hold him while he works through the trauma. My hands are shaking.

When he calms, I say, "I love you."

"You have no idea how much I love you. I was so lost. The seizure stopped, and you weren't breathing."

I can't help but laugh, the sound harsh from my vocal cords, left dormant for however many days I've been stuck in the hospital. "I was lost too. You have no idea."

I reach over and pull the IV out of my hand, letting it fall to the floor.

CHAPTER 6

The door closes, dragging me from my deep sleep. I blink and try to clear my blurry vision. Trey's sound asleep, his head on my chest. A doctor is staring at me with his mouth hanging open as his clipboard slumps slowly to his side.

"Dr. Bryant, I presume?" I ask quietly.

"You're awake!"

"I'm back. For the record, Trey was right. I screamed myself sick in the dark water trying to get you to listen to him."

Dr. Bryant rounds my bed. "He pulled out your IV?"

"No. He lessened the sedative dose in stages all night until I could break free. I pulled out my own IV."

"I should be upset, but I'm so relieved to see you awake that I can't be mad at him." He checks my temperature, heart rate, and other vitals. "How are you feeling?"

"Exhausted and thirsty, but I think I'm okay."

Dr. Bryant gives me a cup of water from the table. He smiles softly at Trey, curled up against my side. "That boy nearly drove us crazy. He loves you."

"I know. I was listening."

The doctor gives me a searching look. "When you're fully recovered, do you think you might be willing to answer some questions for a case study of mine?"

"I'll make you a deal."

"Hit me with it."

"If you're willing to let me and Trey catch up on some sleep together, I'll answer any questions you ask." I look down at my boyfriend and lightly rub the back of his head. "He spent every sleeping moment fighting to get to me in the dark water. We're both exhausted."

Dr. Bryant squints at me. "He really found you there?"

"He really found me there."

We're interrupted by the door opening. A nurse steps in and stares at me wide-eyed. "Well, my dear! Look at those big brown eyes. I prayed every night before I went to bed that those eyes would open and look at me!"

I grin.

"Trey's out cold," Dr. Bryant says. "I know it's against the rules, but these two have earned a good long sleep."

The nurse raises an eyebrow. "You want me to leave two teenagers in one bed, unsupervised?"

The doctor laughs. "They're both exhausted. I'm not worried. Feel free to check on them regularly, but let the other nurses know not to be disruptive. Sleep is the best thing for Melanie right now, and frankly, it wouldn't hurt Trey to rest either. I've nearly admitted him for exhaustion twice during all of this."

"No hanky-panky," the nurse says to me with a wink.

I laugh weakly. "I promise there will be none of that."

In his sleep, Trey inhales deeply, his reach snaking around the blanket in search of my hand. I lace my fingers through his.

He murmurs a "love you" in his sleep.

The nurse's expression softens as she gazes down at Trey.

As she turns to leave, I ask, "How long have I been in here?"

"Three weeks today, baby girl. Welcome back." She smiles and pulls the door closed behind her.

I wrap my arm around Trey's back, and he sighs again as I drift off into a sleep that, for the first time in three weeks, isn't heavy with oily dark water.

CHAPTER 7

My intuition stirs. Groggy, I try to get a grasp on it. I open my eyes, blinking in the dim light cast by the moon through the window. I look up at the clock on the wall, but all I see is a blur. My eyes droop closed. You would think I'd be rested, given the coma I was in for three weeks. Apparently, that wasn't a legit sleep state because I'm exhausted down to my soul.

Suddenly, my intuition rages. Pain swells in my chest like it always does when things are about to be bad. I inhale sharply, and my own rattling gasp causes my eyes to fly open. My throat still hurts from being dry for so long. I croak out, "Trey!" There's no response, and my gaze snaps to the chairs in my room.

There's no one there.

WHERE are Rich, Mom, and Trey?

I'm seized by panic as the intuition pain strengthens. My heart races. I don't know what's coming, but I can sense that something is definitely coming. I blink rapidly, attempting to gather more information in the engulfing dark of my hospital room. It does no good.

No more lights out when I'm alone!

Another pulse of panic breeds in me. I'm sure my family thinks I'm safe in the hospital and they needed a break now that my condition is improving, but the reality is that I'm helpless and trapped in my current state.

Tears well up and spill over my cheeks. Suddenly, I feel very little—just broken and lost.

I need my people!

I reach for the phone on the rolling table, wincing as the IV-line shifts. They insisted on putting the line back in, and I despise it. My hand is sore from the tape holding the needle in place.

I get hold of the receiver and dial Trey's bedroom phone number. After four rings, I stare at the receiver in dismay as his answering machine picks up. "Yo. It's Trey. Leave a message. Or don't. I don't care."

A fresh bout of tears pours over as I hang up the call. Obviously, that brash message wasn't intended for me, but it feels like it was. What's the plan? I could call my parents, but I know they need a break. They've spent a month sleeping in the uncomfortable hospital chairs.

I sigh.

I've put everyone through so much.

I steel myself, resigned to a new route. I need a fresh helper who can handle whatever my intuition pulse is nagging about. I quickly dial Adam's number before I lose my nerve.

He picks up on the first ring. "Hello?" He sounds wide awake.

My voice quavers as I meekly say, "Adam?" I sound like a terrified mouse.

Adam's voice registers alarm. "Melanie, what's wrong?"

"Something's coming, and I'm alone. My intuition is raging!" I gasp under the weight of my tightening chest.

"What do you mean you're alone?"

I whimper, "I woke up, and there's no one here. I'm scared."

"What room are you in?" he asks calmly.

"Two twenty-four."

"Keep your eyes open and stay alert. I'll be there in fifteen minutes."

"Are you sure? I'm sorry, Adam."

"Hang tight, love. I'm on my way."

When he hangs up, I squeeze my eyes closed. Relief floods through me. As much as Adam and I have a messy past, no one gets through him. Calling my ex-boyfriend for help wouldn't normally be on my radar, but my life isn't exactly normal right now. Besides, he's not exhausted from this ordeal, and he can handle this.

I wait, my eyes fixated on the door with my heart pounding. I hear the occasional voice of a nurse passing by outside, but no one opens the door. I glance at the clock, my vision having adapted some to the dark room. It's just after eleven at night.

Only a few more minutes and I won't be alone.

My legs hurt when I move them. Lying dormant in a hospital bed for so long has likely caused muscle atrophy. Pain throbs up and down my legs, causing me to gasp. Sweat starts to bead on my forehead. Then come the shakes that always accompany my panic attacks. I sag back against the pillows propping me up. My hand meets the remote control attached to the bed by a long cord. I push the button that raises the head of the bed so I can sit up easier. My arms work better than my legs right now. If trouble saunters through the door, I'll have a better attack angle sitting up.

Just as I get everything adjusted, there's a soft knock on the door. My heart jumps, suddenly pounding a million miles an hour as the door handle turns. Light streams in from the hall, and someone steps in.

It's Adam. Relief floods through me, the surge so strong that it leaves me breathless. My chin shakes, and tears well in my eyes. *I'm safe.*

My relief is short lived, as a nurse rushes in, flipping on the bright overhead lights as she enters. I wince.

The nurse glares in Adam's direction. "Who are you?" she asks frantically.

An exasperated look hangs on Adam's face as he turns to her. "I already told the lady at the desk. I'm Adam Stone."

"You aren't on the authorized visitation list. You must leave."

Adam's mouth parts in that joyfully sarcastic way of his. It's something we share. I laugh quietly, knowing that whatever he's going to say will likely be a doozie.

"I assure you, Nurse Rule Enforcer, that I'm on Melanie Slate's authorized visitor list. With just the slightest coaxing, I suspect she'd authorize me to visit *whatever* I pleased."

The nurse looks my way, and I nod through my laughter. Even with as tacky as Adam's sexual inuendo was, I've missed his particular brand of mischief.

The nurse starts to argue that I'm underage and can't add visitors to my list, but I raise a hand and kindly interrupt. "A quick call to my parents will clear this up."

I lean for the phone's receiver and dial my parents' number. Rich picks up groggily on the third ring, and I put the call on speaker phone.

"Hi, Rich. I'm sorry to wake you," I say sheepishly.

Suddenly awake, Rich barks, "Melanie, what's wrong?"

"I woke up alone with my intuition raging—"

"What do you mean you're alone?" he cuts in. "Trey was supposed to be staying the night with you!"

Suddenly blazingly irritated, I huff. I look Adam's way and deadpan, "Get ready for that visit to my *anywhere.*"

Adam chuckles.

"Trey's not here," I inform Rich.

My stepfather's sigh is heavy with exhaustion. "Hang tight, kiddo. I'm on the way."

"No, no. No need. That's why I'm calling. I didn't want to wake you. I know you and Mom haven't hardly slept in a month." I bite my lip and glance Adam's way, suddenly unsure. Finally, I admit, "I called Adam to come stay with me, but the nurse is upset because he's not on my authorized visitor list. That's why I had to call you. Can you please give your authorization?"

"Of course I'm fine with Adam being there," Rich says, "but I'm still on my way."

Adam jumps into the conversation. "Rich, don't do that. You need rest, and I've been beside myself worrying about Melanie. I'd really like to hang with her. I'll deal with whatever has her intuition flaring. You have my word that everything will be fine."

"Are you sure? This is a lot to ask." Rich grumbles for a moment. "Apparently it's a whole hell of a lot, because Trey couldn't handle it."

Adam snorts. "I'm not Trey. Yes. I insist that I can—and want—to handle this." He takes a gander around the room before asking, "How long have you and Carol been sleeping in these hospital chairs?"

"Most nights since Melanie was admitted," Rich says, sounding exhausted. "It got easier when we worked Trey into the rotation, but now I'm wondering how often Melanie has been alone on the nights he was supposed to stay with her."

Nurse Rule Enforcer makes a show of examining the visitor log she's clutching in both hands. "Trey generally leaves around eleven and returns early the next morning. We notate when he leaves and keep an eye on Melanie while she's alone, sleeping."

"Are you serious?" Adam growls. "Let me see that, please." He looks over the log and confirms for Rich, "There are three nights notated just like she described."

Rich huffs. "He's only stayed a total of three nights! I thought I could trust him. Looks like Trey's off the overnight shift list. I should've just toughed through."

"I'd like to take Trey's spot in the shift, if I could," Adam says. "Pulling all-nighters is no big deal for me. I won't even leave to get a soda from the vending machine. You and Carol need the help, and I promise you can trust me."

"As much as I hate to admit it, I'm completely exhausted. I have to get a solid night's sleep once a week or I'm going to be in the hospital myself. You sure, Adam?"

"Positive."

"All right. Please have the nurses' station add Adam Stone to the authorized list."

The nurse assures that she will before taking her leave.

Rich pauses before barking, "Adam, don't leave Melanie alone with Trey until I personally speak with him. Got it?"

Adam grins. "Yes, sir. It would be my pleasure to inform him of that." After a moment, he adds sincerely, "You should have called me sooner, Rich. There was no need for you to exhaust yourself like this. I would have been in the rotation a lot sooner had I known you needed the help."

"I wasn't about to put Melanie's ex-boyfriend on the sleeping rotation when her current boyfriend was so dedicated to the task. Now that I know Trey's not dedicated, I'm happy to toss you into the mix. Trey has earned this demotion."

Adam chuckles. "Before you ask again, Melanie will be fine. I won't abandon my post, and nothing will go wrong. I've got this. Legitimately get some sleep. She's in good hands."

Rich sighs but relents. "Thank you, Adam. This means a lot."

"You're welcome. Good night."

When I hang up, silence invades the room.

Adam stares at me. Now that he's not distracted by nurses or phone calls, it's like he's taking in my condition for the first time. He looks stunned. I shy away from his gaze. I haven't seen myself in a mirror, but I'm suddenly blazingly uncomfortable about how I must look. I glance back at Adam, regretting my decision to call him here.

His expression morphs to one of careful control. He softly says, "Hey, hey. You're okay, Melanie."

I shake my head, dejected and embarrassed. "I'm a mess."

Adam crosses with purpose, disappearing into the bathroom across the way. He emerges with a wet washcloth in his hand. "Is it okay if I turn on the reading lamp by the chairs and turn off the fluorescents?"

I nod meekly. He clicks on the lamp and digs through my bag that's sitting by one of the chairs.

He stands and crosses to the light switch, flipping it off. Now he makes his way toward me before setting a brush and the washcloth on the rolling table by my bed. "Let's get you fixed up."

I know my eyes are huge as I look up at him, mortified.

He gives a soft, quirky smile. Gently, he wipes my wet cheeks with his thumbs. "I think you might be prettier without makeup."

Taken by surprise, I laugh weakly. He does something that allows the bed rail to drop. He settles gingerly next to me on the side of my bed, and I adjust to give him more room.

He stares into my eyes, saying nothing.

After a long stretch, I whisper, "Don't let anyone hurt me, okay?"

Adam inhales sharply and tips his head back, closing his eyes. It takes him a moment to steady whatever he's feeling. When he looks at me again, it's obvious that what he's experiencing is a whopper. "No one is going to hurt you." His expression shifts to pondering. "What happened?"

"My intuition woke me up. I'm not safe here."

He considers this thoughtfully, not questioning what I've said because my intuition has proven itself to Adam more than once. "Remind me to thank Trey for bailing. I've been worried sick and wanted to check on you."

I break into a bright smile. "I've missed everyone. Thank you for coming to see me."

Adam enthusiastically informs, "I've got some big news."

I look at him expectantly, enjoying the promise of a moment of normalcy.

"I have an old friend named Michael who's an actor. Nothing fancy. He's not well known, but he needs a stunt double for several fight scenes in a movie." He waggles his eyebrows, causing me to laugh. "Guess who's also blond with blue eyes and built just like me?"

I bite my lip and nod, radiating excitement. "So, you're finally getting your big movie debut?"

Adam grins. "Sure am. I had my first fight scene practice this afternoon. It went well, but I have brushup to do on a few skills. I'm going to work with Darren and Mr. Isley on it."

"You might want to include Trey at that practice," I suggest. "As much as you two don't get along, he's got all that bodyguard training under his belt." I tip my head, admiring Adam. I love when his guard is down. He isn't *all of him* with many people, so I count myself lucky to be a trusted ally. "I'm proud of you," I say. "This is a big deal."

Adam smiles as he grabs the hairbrush. "Welcome to Pascal's beauty parlor," he says in a humorously horrendous rendition of a French accent. "We shall start with a gorgeous updo."

I crack up. He grins and starts brushing my hair. My eyes close. There has always been something about someone else brushing my hair. It makes me feel loved. My dad used to brush my hair whenever I would visit him in the summers when I was little. I exhale and feel Adam shift. Adam guides my forehead down to rest on his shoulder. He continues the brushing until every tangle is gone. It takes a long time, but there's something about it that makes me feel human again. I sync my breathing to his, slow and rhythmic. My heart rate drops, and a deep calm spreads through me.

Adam shifts, and I open my eyes, watching as he grabs the washcloth. He wipes down my face and neck before joking. "Want a full-body sponge bath?"

I give him a patronizing look, then decide to answer honestly. "Yes, but no."

He laughs and reaches behind me, gathering up my hair in a high ponytail.

An idea sparks. "Think you could get another hair tie from my bag?"

"Why?"

"I want pigtails."

Adam laughs. He grabs a handful of hair ties and does a surprisingly efficient job of whipping my hair into two bouncy high pigtails. When he's done, he says, "My turn."

He takes his hair out of its usual low ponytail and sets two hair ties on my lap. He kneels by my bedside, and I grin while I fashion his hair into pigtails that match mine. He turns and winks at me, leaning his elbows on my mattress. His ocean-blue eyes are alight with humor. I giggle and tweak one of his pigtails.

"Feel better?" he asks.

I nod. "Thank you. With you is the first time I've laughed since I woke up."

Adam smiles sincerely at me. "Good. My mission is complete."

I wobble my head right and left. "Almost. I'd like to go to the bathroom and brush my teeth." I grimace. "A warning that I haven't walked since all this started."

Adam hops up and grabs my toothbrush and toothpaste from my duffel bag. He takes them into the bathroom and flips on the light. He peeks around the bathroom door and dramatically announces, "Now competing in our five-yard dash, Olympic reigning champion, MELANIE SLATE!"

I laugh boisterously while he crosses to me. He rolls my IV drip stand out of the way and takes me by the arms. My sock-clad feet touch the floor, and I take a determined breath before standing. I feel a little unsteady, but Adam assures me. "I've got you. I'll wheel your IV stand with us. Take your time."

He walks backward, letting me set the pace. I discover that my legs do indeed still work. I hang on around his neck as he guides me into the bathroom. He gets me settled at the sink before sliding behind me with a solid arm around my waist. He holds me steady as I take my time washing my face and brushing my teeth.

When I'm done, I stare at our reflections in the mirror. Adam and I look insane with our bobbling pigtails.

He makes a smolderingly sexy face and jokes, "Come here often?"

I giggle and he grins mischievously.

When he gets me back to the bed, I'm suddenly exhausted. I slump a little against the pillows as he pulls over a chair. He starts to ask me something when the door opens. Adam stands, his energy suddenly menacing. I shrink into myself and squeeze my eyes closed as my heart starts hammering again.

"She's asleep," I hear Adam say. "Please come back later."

A woman's voice answers hesitantly, "I just need to give her a quick shot in her IV."

Adam answers with a no-nonsense tone. "Now isn't a good time."

"No problem. So sorry."

I hear the door click closed before I open my eyes and look up at Adam.

He shrugs. "Just a nurse. We're good." His expression shifts curiously. "I brought something."

I hit him with a big, hopeful gaze, and he smiles softly.

"I love when you look young like that." He takes a *Sweet Valley High* book out of his back pocket.

I grin happily. "You read *Sweet Valley High*?"

He laughs and shakes his head. "Nope. My cousin left it at my house when she came for dinner." He shrugs. "It's girly crap. I thought you might like some girly crap."

I give him a jokingly offended look. "I will have you know that *Sweet Valley High* is the pinnacle of teen girl entertainment. The girls are gorgeous, get all the hottest guys, and their lives are a dream."

Adam settles in the chair and scoffs. "Sounds like someone I know."

I nod sarcastically. "That's me! Living the dream." I gesture grandly with a sweeping arm to the hospital room.

Adam chuckles before opening the book. He starts reading aloud. "Chapter one . . ."

I wake with a start to the sound of the door opening. I blink away from the bright sunlight shining through the window. Trey is standing by the foot of my bed, surveying Adam. Adam is sound asleep, leaning awkwardly, still sitting in the chair with his head resting on his arm, which in turn rests on my mattress. He's loosely holding my hand.

Adam groans as he wakes. He stretches his stiff neck right and left. He looks at Trey and then me. "Well, lookee here!" he crows. "Trey Valdez makes an appearance!"

Trey winces. "What are you doing here, Adam?" His expression shifts to one of bafflement. "And why the hell do you both have pigtails?"

Adam grins sarcastically while he whips his pigtails about. "I like my ex-girlfriend to smile." He smirks, clearly enjoying the jab about how he and I once dated. "My presence though . . . Yes, let's discuss that. You see, Melanie's intuition flared, and your girlfriend woke up terrified and alone. Rich got me on the visitors' list when you weren't available." He nods grandly. "Rich would like to know why the hell you weren't here with his stepdaughter, as you promised. Good luck with that convo! We're all fully aware that you were assigned three nights and left *all three nights*." Adam leans his elbow on the mattress and hits Trey with a gossipy, girlish expression. "Whatcha been up to? Huh? Inquiring minds wanna know."

Trey appears mortified as he murmurs, "Shit." He shakes his head but doesn't enlighten us. Instead, he looks Adam's way and quietly says, "Thank you for staying with Melanie."

Adam nods boisterously. "Nice evasion tactic, stealth mode. Rich is taking you off the sleep-rotation schedule. Now, whenever Rich and Carol need help watching over Melanie, I'll be the one staying with her."

Trey turns a touch pale, but still doesn't fill us in.

Adam surveys Trey. "You look like shit."

Trey sighs and rubs his face hard. "It's been a rough few weeks." His gaze shifts to me. "I apologize, Melanie. You were in a deep sleep, and I decided to go handle a few things. My plan was to get back before you woke up."

I glance at the clock. It's a little after six in the morning. I nod, but I feel unsettled. Trey's acting weird. "Seems to be a pattern," I say softly.

"I'm not allowed to leave you here with Melanie until Rich chats with you," Adam interjects. He nods toward the door. "Go home and get some rest." He grins and picks up the book from the bed. "Besides, I'm not going anywhere until we finish this girly crap. Mel fell asleep during an exciting car chase scene. I need to find out how the twins are going to solve the mystery."

I side-eye Adam. "Told you this series is awesome."

Trey looks at Adam like he's lost his mind. "You're reading *Sweet Valley High*?"

Adam grins and nods slowly. "Melanie loves to read, and I brought a book. Turns out she likes being read *to* even more."

Trey rolls his eyes. "Well played." He smirks. "I didn't even know you *could* read, jackass."

Adam laughs. "Chicks dig big words. I know a few." He waggles the book Trey's direction. "Not even one picture in the whole thing."

Trey's gaze slides my way, and there's a mournful quality around the edges. He sighs. "I'm incredibly sorry, Melanie. I promise that I'll talk to Rich."

I rally, attempting a sincere smile even though fear of Trey slipping away is nagging at me. "It's okay, Trey." I nod encouragingly. "I know this has been a lot."

He smiles softly. "I'll make it up to you."

After he takes his leave, my gaze lingers on the closed door.

After a long moment of contemplation, I ask Adam, "I'm screwed, aren't I?"

Adam appears confused. "Literally or figuratively? I need context."

I jut my chin toward the door. "He's slipping away."

Adam hits me with the full weight of his serious eyes. "I honestly don't know, Melanie. It's no secret that he and I don't always get along, but I'm going to wingman for him on this one." He gestures to the door. "From what I've seen, at least up until the news of him leaving at night surfaced, that guy's been a champ through all of this. He was so dedicated, it was scary. Crying, falling apart, rallying, insisting on leaving school to be with you while you were in a coma." He raises his eyebrows and gives me a bright look. "He loves you. I think he's finally allowing himself to be exhausted now that you're awake again. It's all hitting him, and he just needs a minute. Cut the guy some slack until we know more. Realistically, he left when you were asleep. It's entirely possible that he just needed to deal with some stuff."

I shake my head at Adam, and he pats my knee. "There's no sense in worrying about it, Melanie. It'll shake out. You'll either be relieved because it's all okay, or I'll get to kick his ass. Either way, I've got your back."

I gulp and attempt to ignore my nagging worry as Adam begins reading where we left off.

CHAPTER 8

I wake up all at once, gasping. My entire body is racked with fear, and my hands are shaking uncontrollably.

Adam has gone, and Trey's sitting in a chair next to Rich. They both jump to their feet, rushing to me.

"Hang on, Melanie," Rich says, looking to Trey. "I thought the seizures would stop once she was off the medication."

The convulsing intensifies.

Trey throws open the door, yelling into the hall for help.

The nurse and Dr. Bryant race into the room.

"We need to take her for an EEG and MRI—now!" Dr. Bryan shouts. "Something's not right."

My neck convulses and wrenches backward. I can't control anything that's happening. My hospital bed starts moving, and Trey and Rich are running next me.

Dr. Bryant says, "You two stay here. I've got her!"

My neck is bent back at an angle that leaves Trey and Rich upside down in the hall behind me. Trey has tears rolling down his cheeks as Rich puts a hand on his shoulder. We round a corner, where double doors close behind us.

The shaking stops just as Dr. Bryant wheels my bed up next to a giant white machine. I close my eyes, trying to catch my breath. The doctor scoops me up and places me on a cold table. He starts sticking sensors to my head. The sensors are attached to a bunch of wires that seem to snake in all directions. I panic when I realize that he's about to put me in that tight machine.

"I can't go in there! Please, NO!"

"Melanie, calm down. The machine won't hurt you."

This has all been too much. The panic is irrational, but it's where I'm at right now. I scream and beg.

Dr. Bryant's head drops back, eyes closed as he sharply inhales. When he looks at me again, his expression says that he's managed to curb his irritation with me. "What are you afraid of, Melanie?"

"I'm terrified of tight spaces. PLEASE!"

"Get Trey," Dr. Bryant says to the nurse.

My breathing calms.

Trey's still wiping tears from his cheeks, trying to pull it together for me as he comes through the door. He strides over and takes my hands in his.

"She's terrified to go into the MRI machine," Dr. Bryant explains. "Something about tight spaces. The scan won't give us the information we need if she isn't calm."

Trey nods. "She's insanely claustrophobic."

Dr. Bryant gives him a look behind my back before Trey turns to me.

My soulmate puts his hands on either side of my face and says, "You can do this. I want you to get in the machine, close your eyes, and breathe." He turns to the doctor. "Can I stay in here and hold her hand?"

The doctor shakes his head. "I can't allow it, but there's another option. You and Rich can stand with me in the room next door."

He points at a big window and says to me, "You see that window?"

I nod.

"Rich and Trey will be able to see you the entire time."

"You promise you'll watch the whole time?" I ask Trey.

He snorts. "I literally found you in the dark water in my sleep. Standing in that room is easy. Promise."

The nurse we love so much comes over and squeezes my arm. "You've got this, baby girl. It's going to be okay. The machine is loud, but it's a rhythmic hum. It's not scary."

"I'm cold."

"I'll make you a deal. If you get through this, I'll run you a hot shower."

I haven't had a hot shower in over three weeks, and even though they must have given me sponge baths, it's not the same. I exhale. "You've got yourself a deal. That sounds amazing."

She exits just as the machine hums to life. It's louder than I expect, and my heart beats hard. I close my eyes as the table is slowly sucked into the machine.

The sound becomes overwhelming after a long moment, and I make the mistake of opening my eyes. The machine is around me, close enough that my nose almost touches the roof. I begin to panic.

A voice comes through a speaker. "Melanie, it's Dr. Bryant. I need you to calm down."

I can't! I start to hyperventilate.

I faintly hear Dr. Bryant say something before Trey's voice comes through the machine. "Melanie, you're okay. Remember, I'm out here watching with Rich."

My heart rate slows.

"Look at how the electricity in her brain shifts when you speak to her," Dr. Bryant says. "I specialize in this. Watch."

There's a pause, and then the nurse's voice comes through. "You're doing great, baby girl. Hang tight in there."

The speaker clicks off, and after a long moment, Trey's voice comes back. "I love you."

Dr. Bryant says, "Did you see how her brain responded differently to your voice compared to Nurse Foster's? It's fascinating. If you ever doubted whether she loves you, you now have proof."

Trey says softly, "I didn't need sensors and computers to tell me that, but thanks for showing me."

CHAPTER 9

"**W**ell, the problem isn't in her brain." Dr. Bryant comes in with a stack of paperwork and graph charts.

Trey nervously asks, "What is it then?"

"I have a suspicion. I need to take some blood work to the lab. We're putting a rush on it."

Nurse Foster says, "I promised Melanie a hot shower after her MRI."

Dr. Bryant nods. "I'll make this quick, and we'll have the results within a few hours. Hopefully, Rich will be back soon in case we need to make any decisions. He said he was going for a quick bite to eat. Trey is staying with her in the meantime."

Nurse Foster shakes her head. "You know, you two really are more like adults than kids."

Trey looks down, smiling. "When you got it, you got it, you know?"

I side-eye him with a grin as Nurse Foster laughs.

"Melanie," she says, "do you trust Trey to make your decisions, in case something happens and you're not able to help make them?"

I nod. "He already told Dr. Bryant that he'd marry me if that's what it took to make medical decisions for me. I trust him."

Dr. Bryant's eyebrows rise. "You were unconscious during that conversation."

I shake my head. "No. I was trapped. Big difference. I heard a lot. I just couldn't respond."

Nurse Foster says, "I'm just putting him down as having spousal privilege on her chart. I'm sick of fighting it."

"You kids are odd," Dr. Bryant says flatly, "but it's rather charming." He wraps my arm with a stretchy rubber tube. Then, without hesitation, he puts a needle in my arm. "You're doing great."

I laugh. "I'm only scared of four things, and this needle isn't one of them."

"I'm dying of curiosity. What scares Melanie Slate?"

"Losing Trey, being abandoned, tight spaces, and fighting alone."

Dr. Bryant looks at me quizzically. "You're really young to fear things like that."

Trey pipes up from his spot in the corner of the room. "We've been through a lot." He fuzzes out his side of our soulmate connection as I glance his way. His expression is so haunted that it makes my heart race.

Dr. Bryant undoes the plastic tubing and pulls the needle from my vein. "Get your shower. I'll be back."

Nurse Foster grins at me. "I'm going to help you, okay?" She turns to Trey. "She'll be a while. I don't want to rush her."

Trey smiles and settles into one of the chairs. "I've got so much schoolwork it's like I'm being buried alive. I'll stay chastely busy."

Nurse Foster shakes her head. "Schoolwork. It's hard to believe you two are in high school." She guides me into the bathroom attached to my room and turns on the shower. She pulls the curtain so the water doesn't splash all over the tiny room. "Think you can get undressed and in the shower on your own?"

When I nod, she leaves the bathroom, cracking the door just enough so she can hear me. I undress, leaving the awful hospital gown in a pile. I slip past the plastic curtain, step into the steaming water, and draw a sharp inhale. *I feel almost human again.*

The water's so scalding hot, it nearly burns. I bask in the heat and grab a bar of soap. Suddenly, the water shifts to lukewarm, and with the change comes panic. This is the exact temperature of the gray water. The lights flicker before I'm plunged into darkness. An emergency light comes on faintly on the other side of the curtain, but it barely creates enough glow for me to see my hand in front of my face. Terror roars through me. I scream.

"We must have lost power," Nurse Foster says outside the door. "The backup generators will kick on shortly. Let me go in. You need to stay out here."

The door opens and a rush of cold airs wooshes over the top of the plastic curtain. I scream again as the water and air mix, creating the temperature of the dark water.

"Move please," Trey says.

"You aren't going in the bathroom while she's undressed," Nurse Foster says sternly.

Trey snorts. "It's nearly pitch-black in here. Seeing Melanie naked is the least of my concerns. I'm trying to help her. I know what's wrong."

My hands start quaking, and my legs drop out from under me. I fall, pulling the shower curtain down from the metal rod above. I collapse into the full-body quaking. Water hits my face. The shower curtain clings and pulls at my body.

I'm trapped! I'm back in the dark water!

My world goes black.

CHAPTER 10

"**H**eavy metal poisoning."

"You want to run that by me again? Heavy, huh?" Trey sounds skeptical.

"I'm with Trey on this. Please elaborate." Sounds like Rich is confused too.

I open my eyes, listening as they hash out the latest in a long string of awesome news. The lights are back on, and I see wet blotches on the front of Trey's red shirt. *Apparently, he carried me out of the bathroom.* The tiniest twinge of panic wells up as I close my eyes. *Somehow, he keeps handling every new catastrophe, but no sixteen-year-old boy needs this drama. What if he gets to the point that he can't take it anymore?*

"Melanie's metal numbers are off the charts," Dr. Bryant says. "Enough that I think she's being poisoned."

"Who could do that?" Trey asks. "Someone's usually here."

Rich shakes his head. "Not always. There was a consistent gap each day while I was at work, her mom was gone to handle things at home, and you were at school. The weekend that you were gone, I was too, and her mom could only be a here a few hours each day."

Trey shutters his side of our connection. I look his way. He appears mangled with guilt. An intuitive pulse tightens my chest but gives me no details. Trey turns his back and drops his head.

Something's wrong.

"We ran a full blood panel on Melanie when she first arrived," Dr. Bryant says. "Her metal numbers were normal. Everyone has a little in their system from the environment. Here are those numbers."

He sets a paper down on the rolling table. They all lean over, studying the page.

Now Dr. Bryant sets down a second paper. "These were the numbers from nine days ago, when the seizures became worse. You see here." He points to the papers, comparing the two. "The metal levels are going up, but we didn't catch the rise. I was still focused on brain activity problems."

Rich nods. "This doesn't explain her initial breathing issue at the school or the first seizure before she was sedated."

Dr. Bentley shakes his head. "I don't think they're related. Melanie arrived here because she had a nervous breakdown. I think the emotional trauma she hasn't dealt with from her near-death experience finally took her down. It happens. I also think the early seizures after sedation were from her body trying to handle the lack of sedative when we lowered the dose each time. The sedative is addictive."

He sets down a third paper. "This is her workup from today." He points at the numbers, comparing the three.

Rich whistles. "That's bad. How high can it get before it's deadly?"

"It depends on the person. She's tiny, and I would normally say that it's already past the point of deadly. If she gets another metal dose, it might be lethal." He shakes his head. "Someone's poisoning her, likely through injection. Do you know who this could be? Injecting into an IV port is quick and easy, even if you aren't trained."

I clear my throat. "I know something."

They look at me expectantly.

"Hang on . . . It's fuzzy." I close my eyes and dive back into the dark-water memories, trying to sort through the moments I can recall. They blend and swirl in a nonlinear loop, twisting and swooping around. The memories from sedation aren't like normal thoughts. Finally, I swirl to the right moment. "Stan was here with a woman! I know his voice. She said she had a syringe in her purse, and she needed to 'take us out one at a time' to save Joel." I glance at Dr. Bryant. "Your voice floated in and asked who they were."

Dr. Bryant nods. "That was only a few days after you got here. The woman was in her forties. I'll have security check all the surveillance footage." He looks at the paperwork on the table. "Your numbers weren't bad then."

"They got caught before they could finish," Trey says with certainty. "They probably planned to kill Melanie with one shot, but then had to switch gears when you walked in." He looks my way, his gaze edged with panic.

"When Adam was here," I interject, "a nurse came in and said she needed to inject something in my IV really quick." I meet each set of eyes with suspicion in my gaze. "I didn't get a look at her, but Adam did. She sounded really hesitant. Now that I think about it, it was weird. Maybe it explains my intuition that night."

Rich sneers. "I'm so sick of the Drones. Every time we think we're done with them, something new happens. I'll talk to Adam and get a description of the nurse. Could be nothing, but I doubt we're that lucky."

Dr. Bryant sighs. "The surveillance cameras only pick up visitors at the entrance. We won't have footage of the nurse who entered Melanie's room. But I can tell you with certainty that I ordered no injections on the night in question." He pauses to study his paperwork. "The numbers got worse that weekend when all of you were gone. That clearly rules out the three of you." He flips a page. "It has to be someone who works at the hospital. I know it's not me or Nurse Foster, but everyone else is fair game." He looks back at Rich. "Find out what this Adam guy knows."

"It'll be someone connected to Joel Stamp," Rich says.

"In the meantime, she's leaving," Trey demands. "Now."

Dr. Bryant shakes his head. "She can't, Trey. We need to monitor her."

Trey slides a deadly serious gaze Dr. Bryant's way. "The only place we can keep her safe is at home."

"How about we bring her back anytime you need to do a new workup on her?" Rich offers.

Dr. Bryant stares pensively at the floor, the silence stretching as he thinks it through. Finally, he says, "I'll give you my beeper number. I want to see Melanie every day for four days, starting tomorrow. After that, we'll reassess based on what her numbers do in her blood panels. It'll take a few days to see the numbers drop. If *anything* happens, you call me immediately."

CHAPTER 11

The familiar scent of my house comes as a welcome relief. Rich closes the door behind Trey and locks the bolt. My muscles are so weak from nearly a month stuck in the hospital bed that it was hard for me to walk all the way from the car to the house. I've lost twenty pounds, and I didn't have any extra to start off with.

"Where would you be most comfortable?" Rich asks.

"The den. I want to be by the TV."

Mom is drying her hands on a dish towel as she comes around the corner from the kitchen. She looks at me, her face alive with worry and relief. "I'm so glad you're home, but I'm also worried. I don't know what we're up against."

Trey picks me up and carries me into the den. He sets me on the couch, then leans down to kiss my forehead. "I'll be right back." He disappears around the corner.

Mom and Rich smile softly at me.

"We've agreed to let Trey stay here until we're sure you're okay," Mom says. "Is that all right with you?"

I nod, relieved.

Trey comes back with my favorite fuzzy blanket, the book I was reading before this nightmare started, and my stuffed elephant.

I grin and shake my head. "You always know."

He nods, sits down, and grabs the remote before putting his hand out toward me. I lie down with my head in his lap, clutching my elephant while Mom puts the blanket over me. Trey clicks on the TV and scrolls through the channels. He settles on an old episode of *I Love Lucy*.

Minutes melt into hours as the four of us settle into a routine. I drift in and out of sleep, my life becoming a mixture of eating, showering, napping, going for blood work, and waking up drenched in sweat from nightmares of Joel, the dark water, and suffocation.

I like having Trey here, but I live in fear of the day he goes back to his house.

My blood panel numbers steadily improve, and there are no more seizures.

I wake with a start, gasping. The lights are on because waking up in the dark is still terrifying.

Mom's sitting in the recliner. "You're okay, Mel," she assures me.

"What time is it?"

"Just after midnight."

"Where's Trey?"

"He went home. You're out of the woods, kiddo. His parents wanted him back now that the worst has passed."

My heart hurts, and my chest tightens. A lump rises in my throat. This is the moment I feared. Trey keeps me tethered to sanity, but I know he has put so much on hold—school, baseball practice, his family, his friends. He has catching up to do, and I'm still stuck here. The doctor won't clear me to return to school until Monday. *Five more days*. "When will he be back?"

"He plans to make it for dinner. He's going to school and baseball practice tomorrow."

I bury my face in the blanket as tears silently slip down my cheeks. I realize that my fears are coming true. I'm codependent, while he's slipping back into independence.

Trey hugs Mom before crossing to me. "You're dressed in real-life clothes *and* you're up and moving?"

I smile and nod. "It's time. I'm feeling a lot better."

He cups my chin and kisses me. "You almost look like my Melanie again. If we can just get your weight back where it needs to be, no one will even know anything was wrong."

I duck my head, suddenly shy and insecure. I look like a skeleton. All my usual curves and muscles have withered away from so long without solid food and exercise. I'm pale, my face gaunt, with dark circles under my eyes. My hair is stringy and lifeless from a month of the awful dry shampoo they stock at the hospital. I look like a shell of myself.

Trey smiles at me genuinely. "I thought I'd bring a few visitors by."

He opens the front door, and Presley, Adam, Tanner, and Marcus troop through. They hug Mom and Rich, but all of them stop short when they see me. Everyone's breath catches in unison. None of my friends except Adam have seen me since I collapsed in Mr. Bentley's class.

I smile meekly before halfheartedly joking, "You should've seen me a week ago."

Adam crosses to me first and wraps his arms around me. He gasps at the touch of my skin-and-bones condition under my shirt. I've lost more weight since he saw me at the hospital. He presses his cheek against the top of my head and holds on. I'm hoping Trey doesn't get mad at this attentive reaction.

Finally, he releases me, and Presley steps in to gingerly hug me. We all stare at each other, but I don't know what to say.

Marcus grins and holds out a bag for Mom. "Leave this to me," he says.

Mom opens the bag and pulls out my favorite candy, some donuts, and a bag of chips. She laughs. "Anyone want snacks?"

I grin at Marcus. "A donut please."

Marcus steps up and hugs me. "We'll get you right back to the old Melanie." He pauses before saying softly, "I'm glad you're okay."

Rich turns to Adam. "Would you come chat with me? I need to find out what you know about a nurse who visited that night you stayed with Melanie."

Adam's eyebrows rise. "Sure." He follows Rich into the den.

Tanner clears his throat. "My turn." He pulls a handful of makeup brushes out of his side satchel bag and grins at me, raising his eyebrows.

I laugh and nod. "I definitely need a makeover."

He crosses the short distance to me. "I'm all over it." He studies my hair for a moment. "To the kitchen sink," he orders.

Tanner leads me to the sink, where he deep-conditions my hair with something out of a packet that smells like flowers and sugar. I inhale, feeling happiness blossom. Tanner finishes the conditioning and sits me down in the dining room. He hits my hair with a blow dryer while my friends all chat in the living room.

The sound of laughter makes me close my eyes again, grateful for normalcy.

"Makeup time," Tanner says once he's done surveying my hair.

I grab his hand and squeeze before he turns to get his bag.

He smiles at me. "You're welcome."

He finishes my makeover just as I start to wilt around the edges. I still get tired so quickly.

He smiles gently. "You wearing out?"

"Yes, but it's worth it. I've missed everyone."

Tanner turns to call out, "Trey, I think Melanie might need a lift to the bathroom mirror."

Trey stands up from his spot on the living room couch. His mouth drops open as he looks my way. "You're beautiful," he breathes. He looks at Tanner, his expression melting around the edges, and every emotion we've faced flashes through his eyes. Everyone smiles softly as Trey says, "Thank you, Tanner."

Tanner smiles. "I just wanted to help Melanie feel like herself again, but that look on your face . . ." He clears his throat and pulls himself together. "Let's just say I didn't understand how deep this all got. I'm glad you feel better too, Trey."

Instead of carrying me to the bathroom, Trey returns to the couch, plunking down with his hands over his face. Marcus sits next to him with his hand on Trey's back.

I can just barely hear it when Trey murmurs, "I've screwed up."

Marcus looks up at us. "Give us a minute."

My intuition nags at me, but I don't have time to pry into what Trey thinks he screwed up about.

Adam steps to me and gingerly picks me up. "How about I take you to the mirror?" He carries me down the hall to the bathroom and turns me to the mirror. Staring back at me is someone who looks almost like the old me.

CHAPTER 12

I close my eyes, trying to rally. My backpack feels like it weighs a hundred pounds as I step onto the sidewalk and close the van door behind me. *I don't know if I can carry this backpack all day . . . Hell, I don't know if I can make it through first period.* When I head up the sidewalk and spot my friends, I feel a little better. A grin spreads on my face.

Arch throws up devil horns.

I laugh and flash devil horns back at him.

Bear scoops me up in a gentle but enthusiastic hug. "Kitten Little's back!"

I wince. "Kind of. We'll see how this goes." I glance past my friends. "Where's Trey?"

Hiram flashes his meerkat smile. "He had a meeting with the varsity team this morning."

Not good! I haven't seen him since Friday. He was busy on Saturday, and Trey's family had a birthday celebration for his aunt on Sunday. Now he's not here to see me on the day I return to school. *He's slipping away.* The thought nags at me from the corner of my mind.

I shake off the thought when Darren presents me with a beautiful hematite ring. "For strength, blood healing, and resilience." The ring is gorgeous, a shiny oval hematite dome set in ornate silver.

I inhale and look up into Darren's wise brown eyes. "Thank you."

He smiles at me. "I did some energy work with it, so it should help you get through the day."

When I slide the ring on my finger, it gently hums through my hand like sunlight. My fingers are so gaunt that I have to move it over to my thumb.

Arch grins and says, "Badass."

The first bell rings. My friends surround me as we walk down the alley. Heads turn and whispers waft by in a tenor similar to the nonsensical thoughts of my time in the dark water. I close my eyes and inhale a shaky breath as we pass through Quad One.

My friends peel away from our group as their destinations arrive, each giving me a quick hug goodbye. I'm left making it the rest of the way with Presley.

We stop at our classroom door. Presley puts a protective arm around my shoulder and says, "Things are a little different in here now."

I inhale sharply, suddenly remembering how Mr. Martinez passed away. *It feels like a hundred years ago.* "New teacher?" I ask.

Presley shakes her head. "An endless stream of substitutes, each one shittier than the last."

We walk through the door together, all eyes turning my way as the room drops into hushed silence.

Fantastic! Let the gossip games begin . . .

The substitute teacher barks, "Seats. Now. You're late."

I shrink inside, feeling my chest cave a bit as the harsh tone deflates what little resolve I have. Presley hits the substitute with a death glare. Drake crosses to the desk at the front of the room and leans down to have a quiet but pointed conversation with the sub.

The teacher's eyes soften as he looks to me. Drake turns on his heel and marches over to me with purpose. He takes my backpack and puts his arm around me, escorting me to my seat at the far row by the windows. He sets down my backpack, looks me in the eyes, and says, "We've all got your back. Welcome home."

CHAPTER *13*

I *can't walk anymore.* I plop down on the closest bench. Tears well up, but I don't bother hiding them. It's lunchtime, and my friends in fourth period jogged off, each with a different place they had to be. I'm alone and don't have the strength to make it anywhere. Our usual lunch table might as well be a million miles away.

My vision swims. I feel like I'm falling even though I'm sitting still. Hopelessness overtakes me. My friends are across campus. I haven't seen Trey all day. He's been gone on some tenth-grade field trip. I'm literally a forgotten no one.

I spent all my junior high years trying to be invisible. My private joke was that I was "Ghost Melanie," but I had no idea what being a ghost really meant. I wasn't a ghost then; I was just a shell of what I could be because of fear and insecurity. Now, I'm truly a ghost.

A girl walks past. She gives me a haughty look before snooting rancidly to her friends, "Who sits on a bench at school and cries?"

The girls all laugh. I can't even muster up the energy to be embarrassed.

Just as I slip fully into despair, I hear Hiram. "She's over here!"

Footsteps rush my way as my friends round the corner on

Hiram's heels. Adam reaches me first and drops to his knees in front of me, wiping away my tears. It does no good because a never-ending stream cascades down my cheeks.

"Melanie, look at me."

I look into his ocean-blue eyes.

"I'm so sorry. I forgot that the tenth graders were cn a field trip. I figured Trey was getting you. We didn't realize you were having trouble."

I drop my head.

He mutters to himself, "I screwed up."

Adam stands and hands my backpack to his girlfriend, Valerie, who swings it over her shoulder. I look up at gorgeous Valerie and am overcome with insecurity. Val is an intimidatingly tough bombshell with a wicked temper. She's one of my close friends, but I worry that Adam's attentiveness will spark a blowup I don't have the will to face.

She looks down at me and smiles gently. "It's okay, Melanie."

I exhale, relieved, and hit her with a pathetically grateful look. Her expression morphs softly as she stares into my eyes.

When Adam picks me up, I feel small and broken in his arms. He carries me across campus to our lunch table. I close my eyes to block out the stares from everyone we pass.

Students flood off the field trip buses, and others step on, everyone rushing here and there to get home at the end of the school day. I search for Trey, but I'm not tall enough to see over the crowd.

Bear keeps an eye out. "Here he comes."

The crowd parts just in time for me to see Trey turn into the alley with a gorgeous blond who I vaguely remember as Tiffany.

He doesn't look this way. My friends all stare in his direction, slack-jawed. Bear puts his arms around me as shock bubbles in my chest.

Adam pushes away from the block wall and stalks indignantly through the crowd. My friends all follow. Bear guides me into the crush of students passing us on their way to the buses.

We turn into the less crowded alley just in time to hear Adam loudly call, "TREY!"

My friends part, making room for Bear to guide me through. We stop just behind Adam. Tanner's eyes widen as I pass, and I can feel his misgivings about not having a chance to touch up my makeup before I confronted Trey. I'm suddenly blazingly aware of my sunken cheekbones and the dark, exhausted circles under my eyes.

Adam steps up to Trey aggressively. "Where the hell do you think you're going?"

Trey blinks rapidly like he's clearing his head. "I've got baseball practice."

"You're supposed to drive Melanie home," Adam hisses.

Trey's eyes flick my way, and he grimaces. "Melanie, I'm so sorry. I completely forgot. Coach called a practice for the team at our meeting this morning. He wants to get me brushed back up before our next game." His eyes subtly flick to Tiffany, and worry crosses his face before it settles into a carefully controlled expression. He has me so blocked off that I can't tell what he's feeling.

Tiffany gives me a baffled look laced with pity. "Who are you?" she asks haltingly. There's confusion written all over her face when she turns to Trey.

He doesn't answer.

She bats her eyes flirtatiously. "Dinner tomorrow night?"

Trey turns pale and doesn't answer.

She glances back my way, looking me up and down, bewildered, before turning on her heel. "I'll find you after cheerleading practice and we can go do something," she says to Trey as she sashays away.

Presley crosses the distance and grabs her by the arm, spinning her around. Tiffany hits her with a snotty look, but it doesn't faze Pres. "Who do you think you are?" Presley demands.

Tiffany barks out a laugh and rolls her eyes before prancing down the alley and turning onto the field where the cheerleaders are gathered for practice.

Presley turns on Trey and snarls, "You spent an awful lot of time with Tiffany while Melanie was in the hospital, but I didn't realize it was a *thing*, or I would've kicked her *and* your asses on Melanie's behalf!" Her eyes narrow. "You wanna fill us in on what exactly has been going on?"

Trey turns a touch paler as he glances from Presley to me. He loses control over his blockage and starts blasting everything he's feeling in tidal waves down our connection.

He's guilty in spades!

I look at Bear and Darren, and their jaws are slack as they stare at Trey.

"Is this what he meant back at my house when he said he screwed up?" I ask softly of Marcus.

Marcus shrugs. "He wouldn't fill me in."

Darren says to Trey, "You have GOT to be kidding!"

Everyone takes in Darren's reaction with disappointment, because we all know that Darren's capable of reading things without being told.

My friends all circle around Trey, radiating anger.

"This is insane," Adam says. "She can't handle this right now."

All eyes turn to me, and my friends' faces slump into pitying expressions.

My mind sputters as I try to grasp the realization that on top of everything else, I now must come to terms with Trey cheating on me. I'd thought that he might slip through my fingers, but not because of someone else. Trey's watching me with a mournful expression. I start to crumble, unable to hide the heartbreak welling up inside me. I know he can feel it as it reverberates down our connection. Trey closes his eyes.

His tone full of conviction, Adam says to Trey, "Do you have ANY idea what Melanie's been through today?"

Trey squares up, suddenly defensive, and snarls back, "Do YOU have any idea what I'm dealing with? I've missed weeks of baseball practice. I'm one more missed practice from being launched from the team."

Adam blinks rapidly, ferocity blasting out of his mouth. "BASEBALL? You're worried about BASEBALL?" Adam whips around and points my way. "Are you LOOKING AT HER?"

I shrink into my shell, deflating with humiliation.

"Yes, Adam," Trey spits. "I'm aware! I've spent the last month praying like hell that she'd make it! I completely lost it."

I can't take any more of this. Spinning on my heel, I rush down the alley while my friends are distracted by Adam's rage.

"NOW ISN'T THE TIME TO DECIDE YOUR BOYFRIEND DUTIES ARE DONE!" he yells. "What happened with Tiffany?"

I turn the corner and get to my bus just before it pulls away from the curb. I slump into the first empty seat and collapse, the last dregs of my energy used up on the trot over here. Desperate tears roll down my cheeks.

CHAPTER 14

A tap on my bedroom window brings me out of another bout of crying. I haven't heard from Trey since school, and I couldn't sleep if someone paid me a million dollars.

I cross to the window, alive in the knowledge that this might be danger come to call, but I can't muster up the will to care. I peek through the sheer white curtains at Trey. He motions for me to come outside.

A glance at the clock reveals that it's just after midnight. I let go of the curtain, my head dropping back. I consider my options and finally decide that I need to talk to him. At this point, it would be better to know what I should be worried about than to keep avoiding the answers. Finally decided, I shutter my side of our connection, slip into my robe, and step into the hall. My parents are asleep, so I move as quietly as I can to the front door. Trey's on the porch, and he's wearing the same guilty expression he had when first confronted.

My heart seizes a beat. *This would be easier if he was a better liar.*

I step outside, steeling myself for what's to come. The best advice my stepfather has ever given me is, "The first one who speaks in an argument loses. Sometimes you need to say nothing."

Carefully, I avoid opening my yap-trap. Instead, I level him with a look that radiates exhaustion.

After the tense silence finally becomes too much for Trey, he begs, "Say something. Please."

I blink but say nothing. He leans on the ornate railing and squeezes his eyes shut.

I let the silence stretch long. "Let me be abundantly clear," I say finally. "I'm exhausted. I don't need this right now, but I get it. You were faced with watching me nearly die, and it was too much . . . I don't think that's what drove you to Tiffany, though. I think what sent you fleeing was me wasting away to nothing. I went from being someone you were attracted to, to a giant mess. Tiffany's gorgeous, and she comes with none of my baggage. She's not skin and bones. She doesn't have dark circles under her eyes. She doesn't have sleepless nights of panicked terror. She doesn't always need to talk about her problems. On one hand, I can't blame you. On the other hand, I thought what we had was deeper than this. You showed your true colors on this one."

Trey shakes his head. "That's not it, Melanie," he assures me. He looks down, and the slightest wave of emotion drifts through our connection. It confirms, to a certain degree, that what I said is part of it.

At least he feels bad. I guess that's something. I scoff at the thought. Trey winces at the sound.

"Just be honest with me, Trey. I can feel it when you lie."

He exhales. "Fine. Tiffany was intriguing. As shallow as it is, yes, I admit that Tiffany being hot without baggage was appealing. I almost lost my mind, and Tiffany caught me at a vulnerable time. In her defense, she had no idea about us."

My eyebrows rise. "Oh, I see. Defending Tiffany is where we're at? Good to know."

Anger starts to burn through the exhaustion. I close my eyes and welcome it. The dark water that lives in my mind roils, spreading the anger into the cracks and crevices in my psyche that were left behind by everything I've dealt with recently.

I snap my eyes open, leveling Trey with my newfound anger.

He cracks his neck, like he sometimes does when he's nervous. "I know you're mad."

"Very good, Trey," I croon sarcastically.

He sighs.

"All of it," I order. "Now."

"What do you want to know? Ask me and I'll tell you."

I guffaw. "Wonderful! Instead of you just spilling it, I get to play *Where's Waldo?* while I dig through your tacky affair." I clap my hands once, and sarcastically say, "Question number one. When did this start?"

"Two days after you were taken to the hospital, but it was just a little flirtation then."

"Two days. I'm impressed. Didn't take you nearly as long as I expected. I thought you'd give me at least a week of being in a medically induced coma before you accepted an invitation to slutsville."

He sighs.

"Question number two. How far did it get?"

Trey shakes his head, unwilling to answer.

I let lose an anguished laugh. "Fantastic. I'm sure rolling around in your back seat was exactly what you needed to get over all this pesky 'soulmate unconscious and seizing in the hospital' drama." I narrow my eyes at him. "Remind me to thank her for seeing you through this."

He shakes his head, defeated. The silence is deafening. Finally, he looks at me, softly saying, "I'm sorry, Melanie. You have no idea."

"I'm fully aware of what a sorry shit you are, Trey." I pause, gather myself, and ask, "Did you tell her you love her?"

He shakes his head. "I don't love her, Melanie. She was just a distraction."

"Seemed like she was pretty enamored with you when she asked if you two could have dinner. You've clearly been on dates."

He closes his eyes but doesn't answer.

"It doesn't matter anymore," I disgustedly tell him. "I don't need further details."

I pull my promise ring off my finger and take his hand. He mistakes the touch of my hand for forgiveness, and his eyes snap open. His face falls as I set the ring in the palm of his hand and step back.

"Maybe that'll fit Tiffany's finger," I say. "It's too big for me now, anyway, what with my life-and-death weight loss."

CHAPTER 15

I stare in the mirror at my heavily lined eyes. The bathroom reeks of teenage funk, but I'm desensitized to the point of not caring. I take out my blood-red matte lipstick and add a fresh coat. Closing my eyes, I thrill at the welcome adrenaline coursing through my veins. Maybe I'm running on borrowed energy, but I feel like a superhero. I look back at my reflection . . . harsh.

Good. I like it.

It's easy to pop another of the uppers from the bottle I bought from Tad. No need to even swallow it down with water.

Here goes nothing.

My new tight red-and-black chevron print minidress and black high-heeled motorcycle boots feel better because they fit. I'm down from my usual size two to a double zero. Everything I own hangs on me. I close my eyes and take one last breath before surveying my slicked-back chestnut hair in the mirror and pushing through the door.

Outside the music building, all my friends have gathered at our usual lunch table to pass the time waiting for the first school bell of the day to ring. Adam sees me, and shock flashes across his face.

Tanner whistles low. "Damn. That's aggressive."

Trey's brow wrinkles as his eyebrows raise. I glare at him as he makes his way toward me.

"Melanie, talk to me."

"Talk to Tiffany."

Trey shakes his head. "Nope. Not happening. We're *not* doing this. I've been waiting for you so I can apologize again and try to fix this."

I glare at him and drop my backpack.

He stares at me, waiting, but when I don't speak, he says, "Tiffany was a colossal mistake. You have no idea how sorry I am."

"Tiffany's a snotty bitch who's going to get her ass whooped the next time she slides those prissy eyes my way."

Presley grins as she takes a handful of pretzels from the bag Marcus is holding. "Hell yeah, she is. I'll help you kick her ass. Melanie's back!"

Adam softly responds, "This isn't our Melanie."

"I like this Melanie." Presley crinkles her nose at me playfully. "This Melanie's a little evil."

I slide harsh eyes Adam's way. "I'm doing what I need to so I can get through this."

He nods. "So I see. What exactly are you getting through, though? The rest of us are in the dark about the details." He rolls his eyes toward Trey. "Captain Wonderful over here didn't do much to fill us in after you disappeared down the alley."

As I scan my friends, a sarcastically bright expression graces my face. "Well, let's see . . . Trey came a-knocking at my window last night to have a chitchat. He told me how sorry he is that he worked out his devastation over my impending hospital death in the back seat of his fancy car with Tiffany."

Everyone's mouth drops open.

My phony grin grows wider. "Indeed. He also enjoyed a few dates with Tiffany." I bend a baleful gaze at Trey. "I told him I understand, though. Considering how long it took for me to return to the land of the living, I couldn't *possibly* expect him to wait it out with me."

All eyes turn to Trey, and Adam growls, "Please tell me you aren't serious. I figured you flirted with the bimbo, but you slept with her?"

Trey meets Adam's piercing stare. "I cratered."

Adam's brow furrows with deadly appraisal. "I can't wait to kick your ass over this."

With a roll of his eyes, Trey cracks his neck. "If it helps, I'm already doing that to myself." He turns back to me. His voice is gravelly as he says, "You have no idea how sorry I am."

"Melanie," Adam says, "come here. I want to talk to you."

I stalk Adam's way, and the moment I'm standing in front of him, the old attraction between us blazes to life unexpectedly. His energy shifts in response to the aggressively flirtatious undertones projecting from me. He smolders down at me, his breath coming in slightly ragged waves. His eyes morph a stormy blue as his lips part.

I smirk and gaze up at him through batting lashes. *What an unexpected and incredible distraction!*

Adam closes his eyes, his face almost painfully tensing as he tries to curb the sudden rush of hormones. When he looks down at me again, his expression is carefully caged. Neither of us speak . . . We don't have to.

Maybe I should've stayed with Adam a little longer!

"Thank God Valerie's not here yet," Marcus says. "Holy crap! I felt that insanity from over here."

I close my eyes, finding this newly minted side of me basking in the dark water of my mind. The pills have fixed my exhaustion. There's no holding back now. Might as well let the new side take control. Granted, I'm totally unaware of the extent of the abilities awakening in me, but . . . *Let's have some fun.*

Suddenly, waves of aggression roll from me. I snap my eyes open just as Trey pushes past me and rushes at Adam. It throws me off-balance.

"Watch it," Adam snarls as he steadies me on my feet.

"What the HELL WAS THAT, MAN?" Trey growls.

Adam takes a deep breath. "Honestly, I don't know."

Trey's voice is gravelly, edged with fury. "You better figure it out and check yourself."

"Or you'll do what?"

Oh, goody! This is interesting . . .

Trey shoves Adam hard, sending him stumbling back two steps. Adam rushes Trey and hits him with a right hook. Trey counters, gut punching him.

Arch, Kenji, Bear, and Marcus jump between both guys, holding them back.

A vicious grin spreads slowly across my face as the adrenaline rush burns through every muscle. I luxuriously roll my neck, feeling alive for the first time in a month.

Presley and Finley stare at me with their mouths open, eyes wide. They're both intuitive enough to know something's up.

"Oh boy . . . ," Finley says nervously.

Trey shakes free of Marcus and turns, stalking the couple of paces to stand in front of me. He starts to speak, but I cut him off.

"We're done, Trey."

Trey stills. "Melanie, we can work through this. I've never been sorrier about anything than I am about this. Tiffany means nothing to me. I screwed up royally, but I followed you into darkness when I slept. That alone is proof of how much I love you."

"Follow me into this darkness," I snarl. I turn on my heel, grab my backpack, and strut away, leaving my friends behind me in a bewildered huddle.

I saunter across campus, my heeled boots clicking on the pavement in time with my swaying hips. Up ahead, I see Tiffany talking with Victoria. *YEEEESSSSS! Two birds with one boulder.*

They notice me, and Tiffany says, "Here she comes."

I mimic her loudly enough for everyone in the quad to hear. "Here she comes!"

Victoria's eyes widen as she watches me stalk their way. When I draw close to them, she raises both hands and steps back in submission.

I smirk. *Why are all of Trey's bimbos so weak? Victoria and Tiffany are both pathetic.*

Victoria is a stunning sleaze. Nothing but dramatic curves and catty bullshit from that one. She dated Trey before me, and I despise her nasty snark.

"Clearly, you've been screwing around with Trey," I say, turning on Tiffany. "How about you fill me in."

Trey's latest mistake turns bright red as she glances at someone over my shoulder. I look that way just in time to catch the pleading expression she levels Trey with as he approaches. All my friends are following him pensively.

Fantastic. I roll my eyes at them, then turn back to Tiffany. "Prince Charming," I snarl.

Suddenly, Tiffany seems a bit frantic and scared. "I didn't know about the two of you. Victoria just filled me in."

I smile maniacally and tip my head to the side, contemplating my options. "You're clearly a slut. How about a game? Play with Trey. Let's see who wins."

Tiffany radiates shock, and she takes several steps back in retreat. She turns bright red, blasting mortification.

Awwww. She doesn't want to play. I turn, glowering, and scan my group of friends until my eyes meet Trey's.

He's standing statue still. "Melanie," he says softly, "we need to talk."

"About what?" I snap. "I already know everything I need to know. You cracked under the pressure and screwed around with Tiffany. The only thing left for me to do . . ." I shift a threatening gaze Tiffany's way ". . . is make sure she's aware that I'm pissed."

The gathered crowd of curious students rumble a low, "Ooooh!" My reputation at this school precedes me. It's no secret that I'm a rattlesnake.

From the front of the bystanders, Dante shakes his head. "This is gonna get good!"

I smirk Dante's way. He grins back at me as he cracks his knuckles. I don't know him well, but I like him. He's in a rock band and has a cool, appraising calm that I admire.

My friends all look at Trey, their disapproval hanging heavy in the air.

"What the hell were you thinking?" Adam asks him, glaring. "If you didn't care enough about Melanie to avoid all this, then you should've at least considered Tiffany." He levels Tiffany with a pitying look. "You're an idiot. Melanie's a beast on a good day, and this is clearly a very bad day."

As if driven by instinct, Tiffany rushes around my friends and hides behind Trey. Victoria must have done a thorough job of filling her in about me because Tiffany's so scared that she's close to tears.

Through our connection, Trey's guilt rolls to me in waves.

I snort. "Hiding behind Trey isn't going to help you," I

announce to Tiffany. "I'll kick his ass before I put you through the floor, bitch."

Tanner shakes his head Trey's way. "This is universally stupid, man. Of all the times to be a spineless jackass, you chose when Melanie was in the hospital?"

Having heard enough, I turn and head to the two-story building on the other side of the quad. Every pair of eyes in the quad follows me. My friends pick up the pace, staying quick on my heels. I feel the energy that's distinctly *Adam* before he races up behind me. He grabs me by the shoulders and tries to stop me long enough to talk. I pull up short, catching him off guard, and press seductively into him as he bumps me from behind.

This is a terrible idea. What are you doing? Valerie's one of my best friends.

The thought is washed away on a wave of rage-laced seduction.

Adam gasps, taken off guard. I smirk back at him before continuing my trek.

"What was that?" he calls after me.

"Can you PLEASE not touch her right now?" Trey snaps at him.

I turn, excited to watch them go at it again, just as Adam whips around and snarls, "Maybe if you'd touch *her* instead of Tiffany, none of this would be happening!"

Meeeeowwww. Potential for some fun. I narrow my eyes at Trey. "Good point." Without waiting for a reply, I whip back around, stretch my arms out to the sides, and bound up the steps into the two-story building. *Tad was right about these pills. I feel so much better.* Through the other side of the building, I hit the exit hard, shoving open the double doors to the outside world. I tip my head back, breathing in the fresh air as I exit the school building.

Trey calls from somewhere behind me, "Melanie! MELANIE!"

I shake my head and keep walking. *Shopping time on Hollywood Boulevard!*

CHAPTER 16

I glide through the front door of the school just as the lunch bell rings. The security officer attempts to stop me, but I breeze by. *No more jumping through hoops and following nonsense rules.*

My shopping trip was stellar. I picked up a new black minidress and an insane pair of burgundy Doc Martens. I wanted to shop longer, but I suddenly remembered that packets are being handed out during lunch for our auditions on Friday. The performing arts building is all the way across campus, so I have to hustle because I don't want to miss out on a packet.

Security follows me. "Come with me," he demands.

"I don't think so."

He looks perturbed by my lawlessness.

I take three giant steps back, my arms wide. "I'm in school. Isn't it your job to keep kids from leaving? I'm not leaving now, am I?"

I turn on my heel, stalking out of the two-story building and cutting across the faculty parking lot. Along the way, I swing my shopping bag, happily contemplating the upcoming fall musical, *The Pajama Game.* We've been anxiously waiting for months for auditions to start. Not only is it an awesome Fosse musical, but these shows are the whole reason most of us applied to the Magnet program. The school's divided into two sections, the Magnet program for performing arts kids who apply for a spot, and the Regulars who live in the area.

I arrive sweaty and winded, but I feel so alive!

Just as I start up the staircase, Bear's booming voice stops me. "Melanie, I have your packet."

I glance over the railing to see Bear holding a stack of packets. He gives me a thumbs-up.

Everyone stares at me anxiously as I approach.

Valerie pushes away from the table and struts aggressively toward me as I round the bottom of the staircase. "I heard about this morning."

I glower. "And?"

She gives me a calculating look. "I get it, Mel. You've been through hell, so you get a pass this time."

I laugh. "Gee, thanks."

She squints appraisingly. "We're friends, and I'm going to ride this out with you whether you like it or not." She gives Trey a harsh side-eye, warning, "If you ever touch Tiffany again, I assure you that the girls in this group will flatten you. Melanie doesn't need this shit right now."

When Valerie turns back to me, my mood shifts with unexpected appreciation. "I apologize, Val. Thank you for having my back."

She nods.

I hold out my hand to Bear. He passes me a packet and gestures toward an empty spot at the table next to Trey.

"Thanks." I avoid the spot and lean on the bungalow building instead, flipping through the packet.

I feel my friends' eyes on me, but I'm not interested in any further chatter. My entire body is buzzing from the pills, and it's a little distracting. I close my eyes and inhale, trying to calm the jitters. It doesn't help. Somewhere in the back of my mind, I'm panicking. *You're being an idiot. Those pills are screwing you up.* When I open my eyes, Trey's standing in front of me, and I jump, my heart racing out of control.

He's looking down at me, worry pouring off him.

My body thrills with a million bolts of unexpected hormonal energy as I meet his gaze. I can't think past the rush.

He presses two fingers to my neck, and his eyes widen. "Your heart's racing," he whispers.

My breath catches as he takes my hand unexpectedly. The energy that usually hums with synchronicity between us is jagged and uneven on my side. He closes his eyes, his forehead crinkling as he studies the shift.

I snake my hand around his neck, pulling him in to kiss me. He radiates shock through our connection. Unsure what to do, he finally gives in, and his lips meet mine. Everything explodes from me on a bolt of energetic lightning. I gasp as all the pain, fear, adrenaline, insecurity, rage, and sensuality I've kept tethered tight suddenly blast through our connection.

He pulls away, gasping, and stares down at me. The heated look he gives is laced with an emotion that slams me back to reality so hard it nearly knocks the air out of me . . .

He's scared. My heart nearly explodes. *He hurt me yesterday, but this isn't how things work with us. What am I doing? We don't passive aggressively play with each other like this.* I gasp, but it comes out as a dry, racking sob. I look past his shoulder to find all my friends on their feet, staring at us.

Adam takes two steps toward me. "Melanie. Come with me. We need to talk."

I shake my head a little too frantically. "Stay away from me right now. I'm in a weird place." The last thing I want to do is stir up a hornet's nest with Valerie, and I have zero control of myself right now.

"We're friends, Mel. This needs an 'us' talk. I'll help you figure it out."

Trey turns and meets Adam's gaze over his shoulder. "You don't want to go near her right now. There's a lot happening."

I press against the wall and close my eyes tight, trying to shutter the raging hormones and drug high.

Adam implores, "Melanie, what's happening?"

I feel Trey's fingers on my pulse again. "Melanie."

I look at him.

"Your pulse is off the charts. I've never seen anything like this."

I swallow hard, the energy thrumming off me. I lean into his fingers, and Trey freezes. His gaze heats up as his hand runs suggestively down my neck. His eyes are unfocused in a way I've never seen from him in the middle of a crowd. He traces my collarbone, more prominent now because of my emaciated weight loss. I can't help but close my eyes and shiver. The dark water rises in my mind, and I snap my eyes open.

Don't close your eyes, Mel!

Trey inhales sharply and drops his hand. His eyes are squeezed shut. He whispers just for me to hear, "I don't know what's happening with you, but I feel it, along with a whole lot of other things."

I don't respond.

"I'm at war with myself," he says. "I need to take you to the hospital, but I can't be alone in my car with you right now."

I smirk the slightest bit and whisper, "You sure about that?"

He averts his gaze. "You're killing me right now."

He inhales, hard and fast, and pushes away from the wall,

walking quickly to the end of the bungalow. The distance between us helps, but his reaction leaves me insecure and angry.

Why was it fine for him to be with Tiffany, but he runs from me every time things get heated between us? I close my eyes and press my hands as hard as I can against the wall as the dark water in my mind roils. *The wall is solid. You aren't in the water.*

I gasp, my whole body practically collapsing as I double over from the sudden bolt of terror that rages through me. Having to fight the dark water while in a coma, and then later in dreams, was one thing, but now it's there every time I close my eyes.

I feel a presence, my eyes open to Adam's Vans standing in front of me. I gasp as the adrenaline and hormone cocktail shoots back through me. The look I give him causes his eyes to widen.

"Holy crap, Melanie. What's happening?"

I turn my head and close my eyes, pressing my hands as hard as I can against the wall to avoid touching Adam. I whisper quietly enough that only he can hear, "Please don't touch me, Adam. I'm in a lot of places right now, and some of them are dangerous."

"So am I all the sudden," Adam whispers.

I open my eyes as he turns and walks away. He stands by Valerie with his back to me.

She looks between him and me and says, "Melanie, come here."

"Hell no."

Valerie crosses the distance. I press my hands against the wall again as I stare up at her, wondering anxiously if the hormonal rush will happen when she touches me.

She checks my pulse. "We need to take you to the hospital."

Nope. Didn't flare with her. Looks like it's just with Trey and Adam. That's both good and bad. "Back up, Val. Please."

She steps back, her expression lined with worry.

I pick up my discarded audition packet from the pavement and shove it into my backpack.

"No seriously," Valerie says. "You need to go to the hospital."

"I can't."

Trey returns, and he has his hands in his pockets to avoid touching me.

"Why?" Valerie asks. "I don't understand."

I shake my head, tears rushing up on a wave of panic.

Trey clears his throat. "She's worried about going back. Someone was poisoning her in the hospital. Whoever it was must know the Stamp family, and they're gunning for her."

Everyone looks shocked.

"Why didn't you tell us this before?" Finley asks.

Trey shakes his head. "There's a lot you guys don't know."

"We can go right now to Smokers' Corner," Bear says, "and you can fill us in."

A torrent of conflicting emotions blazes in white-hot circles through my rushing veins.

"Let's go," I say, turning to Trey.

He looks confused. "Are we back together?"

When I shake my head, he lets his head drop back. He cracks his neck as I take off walking toward the alley.

I hear Adam ask Trey, "Can you handle this?"

I stop with my back still turned and wait.

"Depends on what she has in mind," Trey says.

Adam scoffs. "Some of it might be a good time."

"That 'some of it' is new for her, and this isn't what I had in mind. I need to try to fix things with her."

"This might be your best shot. Good luck."

Trey's footsteps approach from behind me.

CHAPTER 17

As usual, I don't sleep. Three days and counting. I heft myself out of bed, pulling the curtains aside to let in the rising sunlight. There on the outside of my window is taped another note.

Here we go!

My pill bottle is in my backpack. I pop one, then slide on my shoes. I grab a pen off my desk before heading down the hall and through the front door. The early morning air clears my head a bit. I skirt the front of the house and stroll across the lawn. I take a deep breath before pulling the note off the glass and opening it.

I'M WATCHING YOU.

I roll my eyes and snarl to myself before taking the pen out of my back pocket and writing . . .

Bring it!

I tape the note back on the window, sure that whoever it is will come back again.

A knock on the front door jars me out of my room. I get into the hall just in time to see my mom greeting Trey. He smiles and gives her a hug before surveying my new black minidress and burgundy Doc Martens. He looks concerned.

Mom follows his gaze and looks me up and down. "A little aggressive with the burgundy lipstick, don't you think?"

"I have bigger issues than lipstick, Mom."

Her eyebrows rise. "I think it's time for the therapy we've talked about."

I glare at her. "Weren't you supposed to drive me to school?"

She looks surprised by my tone. "I asked Trey to take you. I thought you'd like spending some time with him. Is everything okay?"

My parents don't know how complicated things are between Trey and me. I sigh, not wanting to get into it right now. *Might as well accept the ride.* I grab my backpack from the kitchen table. "I'm good." I ease past Trey and head out the door.

"She isn't 'good,'" I overhear Mom saying to him.

"I know," Trey says, not softly enough. "I'm working on it."

"Come on, Mr. Fixit," I snort. "We must dutifully go to school."

Trey moves past me to unlock the passenger door of his black Z28 Camaro. He turns to let me into the seat, his eyes narrowing as he stares at my house. As he stalks quickly across the yard, my eyes alight on the note taped to the window.

Shit! I mentally prepare for the inevitable fight.

Trey grabs the note, reading both sides as I approach him. He looks at me like I'm insane. "When were you planning to tell me about this?"

"I wasn't."

He looks baffled. "MELANIE! You didn't think that maybe I should know?"

I glare at him.

He throws his hands in the air, hissing, "Breakup, or not, I'm still your other half, remember?" Trey freezes when my expression melts dejectedly.

It's time for a heart-to-heart. "Do you think I don't know what all this has done to you, Trey?" I ask. "You went from being the best baseball player on the varsity team, having close to straight *A*'s, no issues, and suddenly everything's gone to hell in a handbasket!" I stop and lean against the tree, my heart jackhammering against my rib cage. It almost hurts. After a long pause, I say, "I know you're sixteen and suddenly strapped with problems because of me. I know part of you is relieved to be done with me. I feel it . . . I just . . . I know." I look down, considering my next words carefully. "What you don't know is that something got blown wide open in me when Joel held me over the balcony. It just took a while to figure out. When someone around me feels something strong enough, I feel it. The closer I am to the person, the stronger I feel it. Darren and Bear worked with me on it for a while before my coma. They call it 'being empathic.' I almost had a grasp on it, but apparently when I was in the dark water, the ability went haywire. I feel like I'm losing my mind!"

Trey's expression remains impassive, but I feel waves of fear rolling off him. *He's scared I'm going to know how he feels.*

"Why haven't you talked to Bear and Darren about this since you got out of the hospital?" he asks.

I shrug and shake my head. "What's the point? I can't ground and center well enough right now to even handle the basics. I'm projecting every desire, every emotion, all over everyone."

Trey's brow furrows with suspicion. "The fight between Adam and me was fueled by you?"

I nod.

Insecurity ripples off Trey. "What about your attraction to Adam?"

I shrug. "I'm not sure. Adam and I have always been well matched in the attraction department."

After a long pause, Trey sighs. "I've screwed things up further because of the Tiffany mess. I want you to really understand how sorry I am. I was a panicked disaster the whole time. I knew, without a doubt, that I was making the stupidest mistake of my life. I shouldn't have even talked to her."

I hit him with mournful eyes. "Let me guess. The best thing that could've happened was me dying so you wouldn't get caught?"

Trey gapes at me slack-jawed. "That's the last thing I wanted, Melanie." He stares off into space. "I knew I'd get caught but I couldn't seem to untangle from what I was doing."

I take a deep breath. "Will you answer some questions honestly?"

Trey takes my hands. "Ask me anything." Through our connection, he sends his relief that I'm at least talking to him.

I take a shaky breath, realizing that I don't want the answers. Curiosity gets the best of me, though. "The night Adam came and stayed with me at the hospital . . ."

Trey looks to the side, avoiding my gaze.

"I called your bedroom phone, and your answering machine picked up," I continue. "Were you with her?"

Trey closes his eyes before softly answering, "Yes."

My heart clenches. "What about the next morning when Adam sent you away to get some sleep?"

Trey shifts his dejected gaze my way. "Yes again."

The sadness in me can't be contained. "I never thought this would happen to us."

Trey shakes his head. He looks lost. "I didn't either. I NEED to fix this with you."

My eyes flutter closed. *It's time to ask the big question.* "Why do you shut down every time things get heated with me, but you're perfectly happy to jump at the chance with Tiffany?" I open my eyes and they're shiny, but I will myself not to cry. My voice quivers betrayingly as I ask, "Why is she so special that she deserves all of you?"

Trey's head drops back. It takes him a long time to answer. "You've got this all wrong. Having all of me doesn't make her special. It makes her insignificant." He mutters to himself, "I used Tiffany."

It takes him a minute to work past the wave of guilt and shame that grace his pinched face. I study the sentiment as it breezes through our connection. He's humiliated that he hurt me and embarrassed that he put Tiffany in this position.

Finally, he levels me with a sincere gaze. "I care about you and didn't want to move too fast."

He's being honest. Don't blow this chance to talk while his guard is down. Still, I roll my eyes and exhale hard. "Every time you pushed me away, I felt unwanted and humiliated."

Blinking rapidly, Trey rushes to say, "That's the exact opposite of how I wanted you to feel."

I hit him with the full weight of my conviction. My anger and hurt peek through my tone. "You being ice-cold with me, then heating up with someone else, is supposed to make me feel special?"

Trey rubs his face. "I didn't think of it that way. That wasn't my intention." He blocks off his side of our connection so tight that I can't tell what he's feeling.

Damn it. He's shut down. Finally, I give up with a sigh. "If I can't trust you, then what's the point? None of this matters anymore."

"Melanie, I love you," he implores. "I truly mean that."

My eyes fill with tears for the thousandth time this week, but I blink them away. I say nothing.

"I was beyond selfish," he admits. "And terrified of what was happening with you in the hospital. Obviously, I didn't handle it well. I truly don't understand why I turned to Tiffany."

I have no clue what to say.

He cracks his neck. "Can we please work on getting back together?"

My expression crumples. I unblock my side of our connection and send him a pulse laced with humiliation because he chose Tiffany over me. Once he's had a chance to study the sentiments, I say, "I'm fully capable of knowing what I'm ready for, and I don't need a partner who second-guesses me or finds me unattractive. I'm also sure as hell not going to play second best to a snotty bitch like Tiffany. I have my own shit to work through. You made your choice when you cheated on me with Tiffany, and we're through."

"I have no interest in Tiffany," Trey gasps, his eyes watering. "I'm floored that you think I find you unattractive. My hesitancy was meant to be chivalrous, not a self-esteem grenade."

My eyes narrow. "Then open up and send that sentiment. We can't lie mind to mind."

Trey stares at me and doesn't drop his barrier.

My eyes narrow. "Actions speak louder than words, Trey. It's pretty clear that you're a lot more interested in Tiffany than you are in me."

As he stands there speechless, I grab the paper from him and tape it back on the window before turning and walking to his car.

CHAPTER 18

I flip through my nearly forgotten packet. Attempting to ignore Trey hovering over my shoulder, I scan Poopsie's audition page. As a Regular at the school, Trey has little interest in auditioning for the Magnet show, but he has offered to read the other characters' lines to help me rehearse my scene. He's doing everything he can to get back in my good graces. It's confusing.

I close my eyes and try to slow my racing heart. *That last pill was a bad idea. I'm losing it, one little fancy pill at a time.*

Trey's fingers find my pulse yet again. I glare at him and lean into it. He meets my gaze with concern written all over his face, but we're interrupted by Bear before he can ask me what's going on.

"Okay. Who's auditioning for what?"

Arch usually leads our friend group, but when it comes to the acting stuff, Bear's in charge.

We all announce our prospective roles. The competition's going to be stiff.

"I might not audition," Hiram says. "The set pieces are going to be so much work to design, I'm not sure I can do that and also keep up with this rehearsal schedule. I mean, look at this."

Hiram drops a sheet of paper on the center of the table. It's the rehearsal schedule, and it lists Monday through Friday from 3:00 p.m. to 5:30 p.m.

While everyone discusses the logistics, I feel Adam side-eying me. My dark-water side is intrigued. The attraction sparks between us, and he smirks the tiniest bit as he subtly runs his thumb along the inside of my wrist.

My breath catches. *What is he doing?*

"We're going to be stuck in rush hour every day after rehearsal," Presley says. "This is gonna be rough. By the time we get home and get homework done, we may not have any time left for sleep."

Good. Sleep is bad.

"We'll have to keep our student council meetings at Melanie's house and just hold them once a month," Arch says, looking pensive. "Damn. I was hoping to shift the meetings to school hours. There's no time left in the week if we do the show."

"Let's get down to business," Bear instructs. "Auditions are after school tomorrow. Everyone divide up and start rehearsing."

We pair up and spread out down the length of Actors' Alley, the area where the Magnet kids all hang out. Everywhere you look, there are auditionees working through the material. It's times like this when I love it here most. I wish I could really enjoy this, because as far as the eye can see, it's like a scene from the TV show *Fame*.

I walk into the dance studio at the end of the day and lean against the wall, watching Adam's training session. There's a man I don't know standing with Mr. Isley. He's watching appraisingly as Adam squares off against Darren. Darren lunges and Adam feints right before roundhouse kicking. Darren counters and Adam whips into a backbend. Adam hits a muscled shoulder-stand before dropping into a defensive crouch.

The mystery man nods. "That's better. Nice work, Adam." He looks Darren's way. "We have another stunt role we need to fill. Any interest?"

Darren's handsome face lights up enthusiastically. "Absolutely. I'd be honored."

The man shakes hands with Darren and thanks Mr. Isley. He takes his leave, hitting me with a slightly sleazy look as he passes. I cringe internally, and the hair on the back of my neck rises. *Gotta love a dirty old man. He's old enough to be my grandfather.* I fight the instinct to yak up a furball.

My attention is drawn back to the exercise at hand as Adam says, "Trey, think you can run me through that hand-grab slip-away again?"

Trey steps up quietly. He's been withdrawn ever since our talk on my front lawn this morning. He turns away from Adam, who grabs Trey's wrist and wrenches it behind his back. Trey twists and unwinds enough to toss Adam up and over, onto his back on the tumbling mat.

Adam hops up, and they switch places. After two failed attempts, Adam gets Trey up and over, dumping him on his back, but it's messy.

"You have to cock your hip," Trey informs him. "It'll give the other stuntman leverage to get over your back. The camera angle will hide it."

Adam nods, and they try again successfully. Satisfied, Adam crosses to his backpack, grabs a towel, and wipes his face. He looks up from his kneeling position and says to the guys, "Thank you for helping me. I have to get this right."

Mr. Isley grins. "I'm really excited for you, Adam."

Adam smiles thoughtfully. "Me too. This is a big deal. I've always dreamed of doing this." He stands, and Mr. Isley claps him on the shoulder.

I turn as movement catches my eye. In walks a tall, blond-haired guy led by Isaac. Isaac's an enigma. He's been well acquainted with the Drones, but when their reign of terror as the student council ended, Isaac found himself in an odd situation. He's a Regular at the school but didn't fit in with his neighborhood crowd. The Magnet kids took him in. Turns out, he's a nice guy and has even started taking the acting electives at the school.

I smile warmly at Isaac. "You planning to audition for *The Pajama Game*?"

He nods enthusiastically. "Think I've got a shot?"

"Definitely."

Isaac announces across the room, "Yo, Adam. I found your twin wandering around in search of the dance studio."

Adam grins and crosses the room, where he fist-pounds his friend. "Thanks, Isaac." He addresses us. "This is Michael." He glances Michael's way. "Meet Mr. Isley, Trey, Darren, and Melanie."

Michael greets each of the guys before looking down at me. He surveys me appreciatively before saying to Adam, "You're a freaking moron."

Adam rolls his eyes. "Don't start. Trey and I are finally getting along."

"Yeah, I heard about all of this drama," Michael says as he surveys Trey. "You're a moron also."

Trey gives him a dirty look as I giggle, enjoying this new guy putting my two exes in their place. *He really does look like Adam.*

Michael looks back at me in response to my giggle. "I'm glad you're okay, Melanie. It sounds like you had a hell of an adventure."

I nod. "Thank you. It's never dull around here."

Michael asks Adam, "Any luck with the training?"

Adam grins and motions Michael over to the tumbling mat. "Wanna see what all us morons have worked on?"

"Did you date her too?" Michael quips to Darren.

Darren laughs and shakes his head. "Nope. She's like my little sister. I don't see her that way. Even the thought of it makes me shudder."

I narrow my eyes as humiliation bubbles in my gut. "You and Trey finally have a shared sentiment to bond over."

Darren looks confused. "Trey thinks of you like a little sister?"

Trey winces and murmurs something I can't hear in Darren's direction.

Darren appears stunned. "I wasn't saying you aren't hot," he says defensively. "You just aren't my brand of sizzle."

"Please don't help, Darren." Trey looks my way and attempts to assure me. "You sizzle, Melanie."

I roll my eyes. "Can it, Trey."

Trey bends at the waist. "Please don't lump Darren's comment into the general fuckery I'm trying to extricate myself from with you."

I hit him with a deadpan expression. "Don't you have coaching to do?" I'm blazingly irritated at being insulted yet again about not being attractive enough.

Trey steps closer to me. "Why did you come to Adam's training session?" he asks softly.

I hit him with a steely glare. "A soft spot for you weaseled up in my soul. I thought you could drive me home, and we could fix things." I raise an eyebrow in response to Trey's hopeful expression. "It's sizzled out."

Darren makes a tragic face as Trey appears defeated. Adam's

grinning, doing nothing to hide his elation at this unexpected little exchange. He basks in Trey's misery on the regular.

Trey motions Adam over, attempting to get everyone back on task.

"I'll drive you home, Mel," Adam offers. "Hang tight a few."

Relief and a wave of excitement zip through me. *Adam's a terrible idea.* Another round of bubble guts flares, and I hightail it to the ladies' room.

CHAPTER *19*

It's been the longest day ever. I've spent the day dodging everyone and everything. I'm avoiding Trey like the plague, and the rest of my friends are maniacally hunting me. They mean well, but what I really need is to be left alone. The only person I can tolerate right now is Adam, but it's for all the wrong reasons.

The moment the door to Mr. Bentley's classroom closes behind me, I hightail it down the walkway. I asked if I could use the restroom, intentionally timing the request to happen five minutes before the lunch bell. Granted permission, I slipped my backpack on my shoulder and scuttled out subtly. My goal was to dip out before Tanner, Presley, and Marcus could scoop me up. I've hit the phase where I'm being babysat laboriously, and I despise it.

I make it around the corner and into the restroom. Unfortunately, I'm not alone. There's another girl in here, her gorgeous raven curls shining in the light from the dingy window. She leans on the sink, surveying me. I don't know Deb well, but she's in a few of my classes. She smiles warmly, her expression out of place with her tough-girl black leather motorcycle jacket. Deb is feared by most, but I'm intrigued by her. She rides a Harley and rivals me with the cussing and no-shit-taking.

"Hey, Mel," she says.

I choose not to respond, instead turning to survey myself in the mirror. My eyes are sunken in, my exhaustion apparent. "I look like death warmed over," I mutter to myself. I take out my lipstick, touching up.

Deb moves closer, leaning on the sink next to me. As she stares at my profile, I'm blazingly uncomfortable under her scrutiny.

I side-eye her, asking, "What the fuck, Deb?"

She smiles playfully. "I love that about you. Everyone else fears me, but not Mel."

I snort. "True."

"I know what you're doing," she murmurs.

I turn to her, guarded but curious. *Looks like she's not going to take my rude brush-off easily.* "Do tell."

Deb smiles softly. "You're avoiding your keepers. You're avoiding your reality. You're avoiding your past. You're attempting to determine your future."

My eyebrows rise. "For a Normal, you seem rather intuitive." My tone holds a touch of sarcasm, but she seems unfazed.

Deb nods. "That's the problem with you metaphysical freaks. You become convinced that you know shit and the rest of us are oblivious." She wobbles her head and gestures to the door. "In your defense, most of those assholes out there are useless lumps, but not all of us."

A genuine smile graces my lips. I turn and look at my reflection in the mirror again. Deb steps up next to me, and I study her in the mirror as she stares back at me.

"I like you, Melanie. You're one of the few people around here I trust. If it came down to the nut-cutting, you'd be the first person I'd find to fight next to me."

I nod my appreciation. "That means a lot. I could say the same about you." I tip my head, studying her. "You know, you'd fit right in with my group."

Deb smiles genuinely. "I'd love that."

A thought occurs to me and my eyes narrow. "My turn."

She looks at me curiously.

"You don't have patience for bullshit," I say. "That's why you're always alone."

Deb nods. "For me, friendship must be genuine. I despise most of the people I deal with here, and they aren't worth my effort."

I look down, feeling at home in this brief moment of reality. I exhale hard. "Thank you, Deb."

She bumps me affectionately with her shoulder. "You're welcome." She takes a breath. "Your friends torture you with all this coddling because they love you. What do you say we go introduce me to your friends? Meeting me might be the perfect distraction from their maniacal helicoptering."

I laugh. "Deal, but on one condition."

"Name it."

An evil grin spreads. "We have to pass Tiffany in the cheer-leaders' bunny hutch corner in the quad, and you must glare at her with me."

Deb cracks up. "Deal. She's insufferable." She raises an eyebrow. "Bet you money I can make her cry with just a look."

We both laugh as we exit the bathroom together.

Trey struts up as Deb chuckles at Finley's story. As usual, Finley takes readily to the new addition. She's excellent at that. It's one of the reasons we've deemed her our resident mom. While the others get acquainted, Trey grabs my arm and drags me away from the group. His back is to our friends, and he doesn't realize that Deb has intentionally sauntered our way, motioning for everyone to follow.

I glare at Trey as he accusingly hisses, "What did you do to Tiffany?"

Deb loudly answers on my behalf. "Mel did nothing to her. I, on the other hand, gave her the look she deserves." She chuckles. "Your side-ride is pathetic. Instant waterworks. Hell of a shame. I prefer a challenge."

She grins at Trey as he turns and glares at her menacingly.

"I don't need you stirring the pot," he growls. "Who the hell do you think you are?"

Deb holds her hands wide as her lips curl with a devastatingly vicious smirk. I grin at her from behind Trey's back.

"I'm Mel's new friend that's been silently watching this charade of *yours* for months," she crows at him.

Trey assumes a haughty expression. "Is that so?"

Deb nods exuberantly. "Sure is, Sir Screws-a-Lot. Let's recount, shall we?" She holds up a finger. "First, there was Victoria, and what a waste of air *that* one is. Always preening and yapping about a big bunch of nothing. Can't stand her." She crinkles her nose up at Trey. Now she holds up her middle finger, shooting Trey the bird. "Second, there's Tiffany. That girl is worse than Victoria because at least Victoria KNOWS she's a tart. Tiffany, on the other hand, thinks she's God's gift. It's revolting."

Unfortunately, Victoria of all people chooses to sashay past during Deb's proclamation. She whips around and strides up, stopping nearly nose to nose with Deb. "Who the hell do you think you are?" she barks.

The way her question mimics Trey's has everyone snickering.

Deb is totally at ease as she loudly announces, "I'm the gatekeeper of hell, Victoria. Your social hell, to be exact. I don't give a damn that you think you're special. Run along and jiggle your cans at some horny unwashed scrub." She makes a shooing motion at Victoria while my group all gapes in disbelief.

Oh yes! I can definitely work with Deb!

Victoria sputters with offense before glaring at Trey. She gestures to Deb and says to him, "Well?" as if she expects him to defend her. He glances my way, and I give him a challenging look. Unsure what to do, Trey stares off into space, ignoring Victoria's request for a hero.

Victoria spits out, "You're a real sack of crap, Trey."

I crack up. "Amen and hallelujah! We finally agree on something!"

"Eat shit, Melanie." Victoria hits me with a death glare.

I nod at her enthusiastically. "Chop yourself up into bite-sized pieces, and I'll have at it."

With an obnoxious huff, Victoria turns and flounces away at a heel-clacking clip.

Next, Tiffany shuffles up with a tear-streaked face.

Arch breathes out, "Oh boy."

"Round twoooo," Tanner crows.

Adam chuckles and takes his Zippo lighter out of his pocket. He strikes it and asks Trey, "I don't suppose we could move this little farce out to Smokers' Corner so I can enjoy it properly?"

Trey glares at him, but his attention is brought back to Tiffany as she quietly murmurs, "Trey, can I talk to you?"

I study Tiffany. She's oddly pale. Her big, pretty eyes are sunken in.

Trey sighs, and his head drops. Suddenly, I feel bad for him. I realize he created this mess, but he despises public displays of drama.

Deb jumps to the rescue, saying to Tiffany, "No. You can't." Her expression morphs into amusement. "Lesson time, Tiffany. You're supposed to use your powers for good, not evil." She gestures grandly toward Tiffany's cheerleading skirt. "Your Venus flytrap mustn't eat the taken bugs. Go find a cockroach that's single and nom-nom until your soulless heart's content."

I crack up, resting my forehead on Adam's shoulder. Adam tips his head back and howls with laughter.

Tears pour down Tiffany's cheeks. She drops to her knees, clutching the edge of our group's lunch table with one hand and her stomach with the other. Finley kneels next to her and whispers something I can't hear. After a moment, Tiffany nods and Finley guides her away with a comforting arm around her shoulder.

There's something about her reaction that strikes me as more dramatic than it needs to be—like there's something else bothering Tiffany. Still, I roll my eyes, point a thumb toward Finley, and mutter, "Group Mom strikes again."

Deb watches Finley as she walks away. "Yeah," she says with a note of compassion. "Finley's a sweetheart." She looks my way with a slight shrug. "The world needs nice girls to counterbalance assholes like us."

I chuckle quietly.

Trey inhales sharply and hits Deb with a blistering gaze. "You aren't welcome in our group," he says with his trademark no-nonsense tone.

I square off opposite Trey. "On the contrary, *mon frère.*" I grin at Deb. "Welcome to student council, Deb. Unofficially, of course. Meetings are at my house."

Deb makes an overly delighted face. She scrunches her shoulders. "I'd be honored."

We shake hands joyfully, to the delight of many in our group, and to the dismay of Trey.

CHAPTER *20*

I'm dripping sweat. Mr. Isley is relentlessly drilling me on a piece from jazz class, and I have no idea why. He called me in to join his sixth-period advanced class that just ended, and I have thirty minutes until *Pajama Game* auditions. I'm exhausted, but it's nice to have a distraction. I'm always most comfortable in the dance studio.

When Trey and Adam walk into the studio, I sigh. Doing this piece in front of Trey is the *last* thing I'm interested in.

"Demitri, Melanie," Mr. Isley calls out. "Come here."

I cross to Mr. Isley in my sports bra and black leggings. I'm suddenly blazingly uncomfortable with the amorous looks that both Trey and Adam are hitting me with.

"I want you two to try the 'In the Closet' piece," Mr. Isley says.

Confusion must be alive on my face because the dance instructor grins.

"I thought it was choreographed as a solo," I say.

He shakes his head. "It's a duet. Now that I've had a chance to test your limits, I'm considering pairing you with Demitri. I think you two are well matched."

My mouth drops open. "Demitri's the best dancer at this

school," I say bluntly. "I assure you I don't have a shot of keeping up with him."

It's uncomfortable, the way Mr. Isley hits me with the weight of his stare. He's a mountain of a man with a Broadway and film career full of jaw-dropping credits. Seeking his approval drives the dance kids nearly to madness.

"I'm going to give this to you straight," Mr. Isley says. "You tried a duet with Javier, and he can't handle you." He turns to Demitri. "I know you know her as a friend, but as a dancer is a different story. She's a powerhouse. Don't let her size fool you. She doesn't hesitate, she launches hard, she muscles through movement, and her center of gravity is low because she's bottom heavy."

My head drops back before I tip it to the side and give Mr. Isley an exasperated look.

He shrugs. "Sorry, Mel, but it's true. Demitri's tall and has twice Javier's muscle mass. I need a big guy who can handle you. You're tiny, but you have no fear of hitting the floor, and it makes you a challenge to partner."

"What about Kendra?" Demitri asks. "I've been partnered with her for a year."

"I need someone to put with Gabe next year because Jamila is a senior, and there's zero chance Gabe can handle Melanie." Mr. Isley looks my way. "Melanie's my next female dancer coming up the line as long as I can figure out who to put her with."

My eyes snap wide, and I glance Demitri's way.

Demitri grins at me. "You're good, Melanie. Everyone was wondering if you were coming up in the ranks."

"She has a hip-hop background and can pop and lock, and slide and glide," Mr. Isley continues. "She has a jazz background, as you know from assisting in her jazz class. She also has belly dancing training."

"That could come in handy in this piece."

Mr. Isley grins. "So, will you give it a shot with her?"

Demitri shrugs. "Sure."

My potential new superstar dance partner turns to me, and we mark through the timing of the piece with our hands. When he finishes explaining the lifts, I squeeze my eyes shut, suddenly nervous. The prospect of dancing with Demitri has me spun out. He's the resident heartthrob in the dance department, and he's unreal talented. I'm hoping like hell that I'm not about to humiliate myself.

"Try the waist wrap into the backbend so Demitri can get a feel for you," Mr. Isley instructs. He smirks at Demitri. "It'll be different. This is the moment when Javier dropped her."

I back up and prep, turning rapidly three times. I leap up and wrap my legs around Demitri's waist. I backbend over, and my head arches through Demitri's knees.

"Holy crap!" Demitri says. "You're insanely flexible, Mel."

I rise back up, and he sets me down.

He turns to Mr. Isley and nods. "We're good. I've got her. I'm more concerned about how bendy she is than I am about her center of gravity. I'm not used to that." He looks back at me and says, "Torch lift next? I need to see how you hold your weight."

Hesitant about all this, I scrunch my face up, but he gets under me anyway and lifts me. He straightens his arm, pressing me high above his head. I'm shockingly uncomfortable with his hand nearly up my ass.

As Demitri lowers me, Mr. Isley nods, pleased.

"Is there any way this could be a private event?" I ask. "Because right now, it's more of a public demonstration."

Mr. Isley glances to Trey and Adam and chuckles. "Nope. Adam's one of my advanced dancers, and I want him to take a look at this pairing. He's a senior and won't be here next year, or I would have paired you with him." Curious, he points to Trey. "Aren't you dating him?"

I keep my expression carefully caged. "No. I'm not."

Mr. Isley chuckles as he crosses to the sound system.

My dark-water side blazes to life unexpectedly, sending an unchecked blast of energy through the room. I close my eyes, trying to calm this side of me that I still have no control over.

I look Demitri's way, and he has his back to me. Mr. Isley's glancing between Demitri and me. He looks surprised. Suddenly, Demitri bends at the waist and gasps.

Fantastic. He must be intuitive. Either way, he's freaked out by my energy.

There's no time to ponder it either way because the seductive intro of Michael Jackson's "In the Closet" slides through the speakers. *If I have to do this piece in front of Trey, then I'm going for it.* I flex my back, pop my vertebrae all the way up my spine, and hit Demitri with a suggestive gaze.

Demitri and I jazz walk to each other and start the sexy piece. We hit the first quick hip-hop section right when the beat kicks in, and we nail the timing.

"YESSSS, girl!" Demitri says. "You hit hard. Let's do this."

I grin at him as we turn into each other. Demitri slides his hands around my waist while I snake my arms around his neck and swivel my hips dramatically right, then left. We're facing the mirror, and I see Trey's eyebrows rise as Demitri and I body roll together. He's pressed against my back, and he looks suggestively down at me, in character.

I smirk up at him.

He picks me up. I wrap my legs behind me and around his waist. I drop down and snake up, per Mr. Isley's graphic instruction.

Demitri sets me down and grabs my crossed hands. He spins, and my feet leave the ground. After two revolutions, he lets go of one hand and I grab his shoulders, wrapping my right leg around him. He lunges, and I slide down his back before slithering through his legs.

I stretch into a split as he lowers himself down. He rolls me over, still in my split. I grip my ankle by my ear, and my toes touch the floor.

Demitri chuckles. "I've never seen anyone as flexible as you are," he says as he lies down on me. "Do you even have bones?"

I giggle and blush. This is awkward, what with me in a full split against him. We roll twice before he pulls me to standing.

Back on my feet, I can feel Trey sending shock down our connection. Apparently, he was unaware I could do any of this. There's a clear sense that he feels like an idiot for not going with my amorous suggestions back when we were dating.

Demitri slides both of his hands onto my sides, and I lean back against him as I work through the more-than-suggestive belly dancing section that Mr. Isley put into the piece specifically because of my training. Demitri's eyes widen as he glances at me in the mirror. A nervous flash of anticipation trembles through me as Demitri gives me a flirtatious look before sliding to the floor. I step over him, smirking down as I meet his gaze. My dark-water side gets a mischievous idea.

"Nope," Mr. Isley instructs. "You're supposed to drop into a right split."

I raise an eyebrow, glancing Mr. Isley's way, and laugh seductively as I continue a controlled center split. Demitri's eyes snap wide before he hits me with a sexy smirk. Feet pointed, I touch down, but I'm polite enough to drop onto Demitri's stomach instead of his crotch. I put my hands on the floor by his shoulders, and he gets a grip on my hips as I pike and rise into a handstand. He shifts his grip, wincing a touch. I hold my weight while he adjusts his hands. My abs shake with the effort, but I've got this.

Demitri nods at me when he's set, and he muscles through lowering me slowly down to almost lying on him.

"How's your shoulder, D?" Mr. Isley asks.

"Fine. She holds her weight. It's easier than I expected. I had to shift my grip because she's so little."

I jokingly chirp, "Tee-hee."

Demitri grins.

I slide to the side at the last moment and whip around, crawling away. I glance over my shoulder to Demitri. It's in the choreography, but Demitri looks baffled and laughs a bit. I get the giggles at his expression, and he cracks up.

"Pull it together, you two," Mr. Isley barks. He can't suppress his own laugh, though.

Demitri shakes his head. "Sorry. She's a lot."

I roll my eyes. "Mr. Isley wants seduction, but I'm apparently amusing. So sorry."

Demitri jazz walks my way and dips me into a layout. "You're seductive, all right. Laughing through it is easier than melting into a puddle."

Suddenly, I'm putty. *God, he's sexy.*

We get through the rest of the piece, and as it ends, Demitri slides me out of the torch lift, down his front. I melt against him, but quickly disengage as the magical music moment fades. Panting and sweaty, we take a few steps away from each other and look at Mr. Isley.

"You two are magic," Mr. Isley says. "That was everything." He looks to Demitri. "Well?"

"I can definitely partner her." Demitri rattles his head and turns without warning to Trey. Demitri's usually very calm and quiet, but he blurts out, "You gave her up for TIFFANY?"

Trey and Adam are staring at me with their mouths open.

Adam snorts and says to Trey, "You have to be the biggest idiot on the planet!"

Trey just stares at me, dumbfounded.

I blush and shake my head.

Mr. Isley cackles. "Melanie, be prepared to be on my all-star team next year. You have to be a sophomore to be eligible, but you've got a spot."

I nod my appreciation. "Thank you, sir. This has been incredibly awkward, but I'm glad you're pleased." I turn to Demitri. "Thank you for hefting my bottom-heavy ass through that piece. It's been a pleasure."

Demitri rubs his forehead with his thumb. "I'll partner you in a New York minute. Damn, girl. I didn't realize you had that in you."

I roll my eyes. "Apparently that side of me is rather ignorable." I smack Trey with a nasty glare.

Mr. Isley releases us, and I gather my stuff.

"Can I walk you to auditions?" Demitri asks.

An unexpected romantic interest in Demitri sparks within me. I can't help but smirk as I feel it accidently slide down my connection with Trey. My ex-boyfriend sends back an undeniable sense of alarm.

"I'll walk you too," Adam says.

He and Demitri exchange a look.

"Didn't you leave Melanie for Valerie earlier this year?" Demitri asks suggestively.

Adam narrows his eyes. "Well played."

I look up at Demitri flirtatiously, and he winks at me, amused.

"Melanie, I'll be the one to walk you to auditions," Trey says.

The sarcasm must be dripping off my expression. "Suddenly, you're interested? Fascinating."

"I was always interested. Soulmate connection and all."

I tip my head to the side and hiss back, "I guess I should have done the splits in your back seat. That would've fixed everything."

Demitri and Adam's eyes widen.

Trey grabs my backpack, but I snatch it back from him. "We'll see you over there," he says to the other boys. "Melanie and I need to talk."

I huff as Trey guides me out the door.

CHAPTER *21*

Susan's sitting at a table in front of us with Mandie. *Ugggghhhh.* These two are by far the most annoying students in the Magnet program, with their butt-kissing, know-it-all nonsense. My jittery irritation starts to climb, which brings my dark-water side writhing to the surface.

"Melanie!" Susan cheerfully says, leaning over the table and air-kissing me. "I wondered where you were! Hi, girl!"

Who does that? Sigh . . .

Susan's wearing one of her trademark middle-school-cartoon-inspired outfits. I guess she thinks she's being cute and trendy, but her rainbow-striped leggings and purple dress make her look like a Chucky doll.

I better get this over with. "Susan, I see you and Mandie are special helpers. How nice."

Presley's leaning against the wall in the audience aisle, and she snorts at my comment, rolling her eyes.

I stifle a laugh as I lean down to fill out the form that Susan spastically flings at me. *I hope these two aren't in the cast. I don't think I can handle hanging out with them every afternoon.*

Susan reads my form as soon as I hand it to her, which irks me because I don't want her to know my phone number. Calls from Susan would be the worst. She's an insufferable gossip and a relentless stage-five clinger.

"Looks like you're all checked in," she says cheerily. "I'll come and get you when Ms. Ferry's ready for your audition. "*We . . .*" She proudly gestures between herself and Mandie. " *. . .* are the assistant directors."

Mandie beams pridefully from ear to ear.

Oh no! They're going to be ordering us around. That's worse than having them in the cast!

It takes me by surprise when Susan looks from me to Trey and says, "I thought you two broke up?"

I hit her with a death glare. "How about you mind your business?"

"Come on, Mel, we better find a seat," Trey interjects, rescuing me from any further conversation with the Dynamic Duo.

We head to the center bank of audience seats and get settled.

"Those two are going to be a disaster," Trey whispers. "You sure you still want to do this?" He pauses, studying me. "We could always slip away after school every day, just the two of us. That would give us lots of time to fix things."

He raises an eyebrow at me suggestively, and I can't help but laugh. His flirtation is flattering, but it's too little too late.

His expression softens. "I miss your laugh."

My heart breaks a little. I take a breath and try to slow its rapid pace. *These pills!* I'm starting to hate them, but I can't function without them. "Sorry, Trey," I say finally.

His face falls, disappointed. "Where do you stand with Demitri?"

I look at him like he's lost his mind. "Not that it's your business, but I don't stand anywhere with Demitri. I was just forced to roll around with him while I was in the splits, in front of both of my ex-boyfriends. It was freaking awkward. Considering that you and I just had a humiliating conversation this morning, and I feel like a rejected tragedy, I truly hope today ends soon so I can go home and die of shame."

"Clearly, I misjudged things with you. Your whole vibe in the studio proved that. I'm sorry I held you off. It didn't have the respectful effect I was aiming for."

"Thank you for that."

"I have to admit that seeing Adam and Demitri's interest in you was eye-opening."

I sigh. "Trey, other people's interest in me isn't your concern."

Auditions are suddenly in full swing, and when Ms. Ferry calls Arch's name, it mercifully ends my awkward conversation with Trey. Arch strides to center stage, his wide shoulders confidently back. He's wearing his trademark trench coat with a red hand-painted anarchy symbol on the back. His audition for the role of Prez kills.

"He's amazing!" Trey whispers as he leans into me. "I think he just sealed the deal on that one. Hope the other guys have a backup plan."

I'm halfway through another silent read-through of the Poopsie lines when I'm interrupted by Susan's shrill hiss. "Mel, you're up next."

My palms break out in a nervous sweat, and my racing heart nearly leaps out of my chest. Trey's eyes widen, but there's no time for another round of, "Honey, I'm so worried." He surprises me by taking my hands and wiping my sweaty palms on his jeans. Clearly, he knows that moments like this get to me.

I'm torn apart for a second. *I love when he does stuff like that.*

When Ms. Ferry calls my name, I head to the stage. Our school has a policy to run these things like professional auditions to prepare us for future professional acting careers. Normally, the formality would stress me out, but Bear coached me on what to say.

I stop center stage, and suddenly it's like there's a war going on inside me between the recently destroyed Melanie and the dark-water Melanie. "Good afternoon. My name is Melanie Slate, and I'm auditioning for the role of Poopsie."

Ms. Ferry is sitting in the first row of the audience at a table full of papers and headshots. She flips through a stack and pulls out my form and picture, stapling them together. "I'm so glad you chose to audition today. I'm curious, though . . . you don't sing. Do you think you can handle a musical?"

Her question throws me off, but I quickly rally, thinking past my racing heart. "Yes, ma'am. I'm an alto, and not so bad in an ensemble. Poopsie doesn't have a vocal solo. Plus, I can dance. I've given this a lot of thought and really researched the show. I've chosen the role carefully."

Ms. Ferry smiles and writes a few notes on my page before looking up and saying, "When you're ready."

Good. The pills aren't so obvious. I still pass for normal.

I turn and nod to Isaac, who's auditioning for the role opposite Poopsie. He says his first line, and suddenly, I realize that I've got this if I can just keep it together. Poopsie's a giggly, ditsy stereotype, and not all that difficult to play. I just need to make her three dimensional and interesting.

As I work my way through the audition, Isaac improvises, sneaking around behind me and playfully putting his hands over my eyes.

Darkness! My breath catches and I panic. The dark water sloshes ominously in my psyche. I drop to one knee as my heart nearly explodes. *I can't see!* The dark water rises in my mind.

I try to shake loose from Isaac, but he clamps down, not realizing what's happening.

NOOOOOOO! I scream in my head. Then, to my horror, I realize I also screamed out loud.

I hear snickers, gasps, and Trey yelling, "Let her go!"

My heart is beating so fast it feels like I'm going to shred apart.

Isaac releases me just as Ms. Ferry calls, "Hold."

"I'm so sorry," Isaac says to me.

I open my eyes and exhale hard.

Ms. Ferry's on the edge of the stage in front of me. "Are you okay?"

"I don't know."

"If you ever want to talk, I'm here," she offers.

I nod.

"Your audition's done. I already know what you can do. Go get yourself together, okay?" She turns to the crowd and announces, "Everyone take ten."

My head sags as I relearn how to breathe. My whole body feels like Jell-O.

Adam kneels down next to me. "Can I help you up?" he asks softly. When I nod, he jokingly whispers, "You aren't going to light my libido on fire again?"

I laugh half-heartedly. He grins and helps me up cautiously. We're both relieved when that familiar surge of firework hormones gently pulses between us only slightly. Together, we head for the backstage hallway.

Adam exhales. "It's there," he says. "But it's lighter this time."

"That's just our normal attraction that's always been there. What happened the other day? *That's* what I'm dealing with right now."

He sighs, stopping for a moment in the hallway. "That insane energetic explosion was from you?"

I nod. "I'm having a hell of a time not projecting what I'm feeling onto others. I'm freaking losing it!"

Adam looks me in the eyes seductively. "I should have stuck with you a little longer."

I laugh. "I just thought the exact same thing about you the other day."

Adam raises a suggestive eyebrow at my statement. My heart starts racing. My dark-water side studies Adam in my mind's eye, and she's intrigued again. I lightly trace the edge of his angular jaw. He picks me up before slowly backing us into the empty dressing room. He gently kicks the door closed.

He closes his eyes, his hands tightening on me, and I gasp. My barely held control blasts open. My heart pounds a million miles an hour as the latest pill I took in the bathroom on the way to auditions surges to life on the seductive wave.

The energy slams into Adam, and he looks at me with heat in his eyes. "You're trouble," he breathes.

The energy hums and dances electric as he starts to lean down. *If he kisses me, it's over. We'll destroy everything with our entire group.* "If you kiss me," I whisper, "all hell breaks loose."

He clenches his jaw as if trying to hold himself back for a moment. "I know."

I close my eyes, willing the energy to slow, but my galloping heart is causing a lot of problems for me lately.

Adam's voice brings me back out of the dark water that lives in my mind. "I'm having a hard time caring about consequences right now. I can't resist bad-girl energy. Add to it what I just watched you do in the dance studio, and I'm thinking I've met my perfect match."

Dark-water Melanie's sitting in the driver's seat. *Let's play.* I glance up through my lashes at him, and my energy floods the room, nearly suffocating us this time. I close the distance, my lips almost touching his. "Your choice," I whisper.

Adam's voice is gravelly. "Don't put this on me."

"Tell me what you want. Kiss, or no?"

Dark-water Melanie is alive, humming with anticipation of what he's going to say. He doesn't respond, his face contorted as if he's conflicted about what to say.

After a long pause that's pulsing with tension, I get control of myself and take a step back. "I know you, Adam. You love to walk on the wild side. With that said, I'm a disaster right now."

He's holding his breath.

"Breathe, Adam."

He takes a gasping breath and I smile. I reach out, running my finger lightly on his wrist, mimicking his secret flirtation from yesterday. He closes his eyes, interest radiating from him in waves.

"Turn around," I breathe. *This dark-water side is trouble.*

Adam's expression projects an odd combination of curiosity, flirtation, and caged guilt, but never one to run from danger, he turns his back to me. He puts his hands on the table and stares into the lit mirror in front of him. I meet his ocean-blue gaze in the mirror and gently place the tips of my fingers on his shoulders. I run my fingers slowly down his back, featherlight. He closes his eyes and gasps, the muscles in his back tensing.

I get to his waist and run my hands along his sides until they clasp in front of his stomach. I put my cheek on his back and hug him. "Thank you for getting me off that stage." I let go, meeting his gaze in the mirror again.

His jaw is slack, his eyes a stormy blue.

I grin seductively, my dark-water side loving this. "How's your resolve holding up?"

He squeezes his eyes closed and exhales.

I laugh.

He turns and leans on the vanity counter, meeting my gaze. "What's the deal with Demitri?"

I laugh softly. "Trey asked me the same question. Demitri's just a friend. Why?"

Adam appears relieved. "Because of earlier."

I shrug. "He's gorgeous. He's intimidating. He can have anyone he wants, and I guarantee I'm off his radar."

Adam furrows his brow. "What's the deal with us?"

"You're gorgeous." I shake my head. "You're a terrible idea. You're on my radar when you shouldn't be."

"This is going to be bad."

I raise an eyebrow. "Or good, depending on your perspective. I'm going to leave the decision up to you."

"Why is it my choice?"

I hit him with serious eyes. "You're the one who's in a relationship, not me."

Adam runs his hands down my arms, watching my face as my eyes close. My dark-water side is elated by the chaos rolling off both of us in waves. He gets to my hands, lacing his fingers with mine. He kisses my neck lightly, and my arms goosebump.

"I've told you before that I made a mistake letting you go," he says. "I meant it."

I open my eyes, and he's gazing at me.

I murmur, "Hurting Valerie is a terrible plan."

He nods. "You read my mind." He hesitantly takes a step back, letting go of my hands, and the distance helps. He turns his back, takes a shuddering breath, and softly says, "Don't tell her about this."

"Tell her about what? That we talked and I hugged you?"

He laughs. "Oh, you're good." He breathes a warning. "I don't know how long I can resist the energy that rolls off of you."

"What's happening with me is a disaster."

Adam steps up to me and traces the line of my jaw. "Do you think I can help?"

I nod and look up at him. I know my eyes are huge and scared.

Adam's expression morphs serious. He pulls me in and hugs me. "I'll help you."

My cheek is pressed against his chest, and I grip the back of his shirt in my balled-up fists like a scared toddler. "You're going to destroy your relationship if you do that."

Adam's chest heaves. "Who else do you recommend to help you? You and Trey are a wreck."

I smirk up at him. "Demitri?"

"Screw that!"

"Why are you and Trey so threatened by him?"

Adam's expression is strained. "Because he's Mr. Perfect. He's also single." He pauses before adding, "I need to be the one that helps you. I've felt like you were mine from the first day I saw you. I screwed up terribly when I stood you up. It's eaten me alive ever since."

With monumental effort, I let go of Adam's shirt and take a step back. "Can you keep things in the friend category while you help me?"

He looks down at me with smoldering eyes. "I hope I can, but I also hope like hell that I don't."

I raise an eyebrow.

We leave the dressing room, head down the hall, and walk out the alcove into the audience. Trey's waiting for me.

The energy is still whooshing from me in time with my

heartbeat. The moment we get to Trey, he cracks his neck and glares at me.

"This again," he says, turning to Adam. "I know you feel it."

You have no idea.

Adam gives him a serious look. "I respect you too much to lie to you. Yeah, it's there between Mel and me." He pauses. "Are you mad?"

Trey shakes his head. "I can't be mad. I don't have much ground to stand on lately."

"She needs help."

Trey nods. "Your thoughts on what we should do about this?"

I have some ideas.

An amused expression spreads across Adam's face. After a pause, he glances Trey's way. "I think you need to ride that wave every chance you get. It's what I'd do."

Precisely.

Trey chuckles darkly and shakes his head. "I'm more concerned that she's going to energetically burn herself out or have a heart attack."

I roll my eyes. *Yet again, Trey fails to entertain my attempts at flirtation.*

"You need to get Bear and Darren on this," Adam informs. "They'll know what to do."

When I shake my head to refuse the idea, Trey sighs in frustration.

"Why are you being so stubborn?" he asks. "You keep isolating yourself from the people who love you! The only reason you even talk to me and Adam is that you have these insane carnal instincts with both of us."

I side-eye them flirtatiously. It can't be helped. All the bad ideas, bad plans, all the bad bubbles in me—the pills make it fun to shove all the rules aside. I intentionally let just a touch of my throbbing seduction waft out of what little control I have, like smoke from a blown-out candle.

Adam squeezes his eyes tight and starts rubbing his forehead.

Trey groans. "We need to get this fixed."

Ms. Ferry calls my competition to the stage, and we turn to watch the audition.

"I'm going to head out," Adam says softly. "I can't take much more of Mel's energy. I need to cool off."

Trey nods. "I get it." After Adam is gone, Trey leans over to me and whispers, "Anyone else it fires up with?"

"Just you and Adam."

"Of all people . . . why does it have to be him?"

Before I can answer, the girl auditioning for my once-coveted role announces, with a bit of a sneer, that her name is Jessica.

"I don't believe I've met you," Ms. Ferry says, politely but a little skeptically.

"I'm new here," Jessica says flippantly.

Ms. Ferry seems to accept this explanation because she gives Jessica the green light to start her audition. Her version is shockingly different from mine. Where I portrayed my Poopsie as a ditsy, sexy goofball, hers is more of a tough girl who's run out of patience.

"What do you think?" Trey asks when her audition is done.

"It was weird. Whatever, though. At this point, I don't even care."

There's worry written all over his face. "You've been talking about wanting this role for months!"

I shrug.

Jessica turns slowly, scanning the crowd. She pauses on me, her eyes narrowing. "Watch your back, Melanie," she announces across the auditorium.

"Ah, so *she's* been leaving the window notes," I growl to Trey. "Mystery solved."

After several aggressive steps forward, I level Jessica with an evil grin, waiting for her to clue me in on how far she wants to take this. Everyone in the auditorium is switching their gaze rapidly between Jessica and me.

This girl has to know me. Why else would she leave the notes? She's ballsy to be threatening me in front of everyone. I rack my brain, but I can't figure out who she is. *It doesn't matter . . .* The thought makes me laugh deeply, the sound bubbling up from my dark-water center.

Jessica takes two hesitant steps back as I radiate the insanity that's been living in me lately.

"She looks evil," comes a voice.

I turn to see that Adam has returned and is talking to Trey.

"I know," Trey agrees.

Before I get a chance to chime in, Jessica cuts in loudly with a singsongy, "I'm waaaatchiiiing."

"I'm waaaatchiiiing," I mimic.

Everyone scoffs and grins.

My eyes narrow. "Game on," I growl.

"Shit," Trey says. "Don't do it, Mel."

"Hell yes!" Adam cracks his knuckles. "Let's do this!"

"You two are like the angel and the devil on my shoulders." I raise an eyebrow at Adam. "The devil wins this time." I spin around and stalk toward Jessica. Vibrating with malice, I stop and slowly raise my left hand, pointing at her without a word. Violent waves roll off me, my heart screaming as it nearly pounds out of my chest.

The students within my line of sight shiver, though most are unaware of the very real energy rolling off of me. Few people that I meet get it, which is one of the reasons my group of intuitive friends are so appealing. My friends are scattered around the audience seating area, and it's clear that they feel it.

The boys follow me.

"She just called her shot," Adam hisses.

"We have to stop this," Trey whispers back. "I'm worried Melanie's going to kill her."

"What makes you so sure? If you won't tell the whole group, then just tell me."

"A lot happened while she was in the hospital. I'll explain later, but she was trapped in this dark water in her mind when she was under sedation. She didn't come out of it right."

"How do you know?"

"I was there with her every time I slept."

"This is more than some metaphysical PTSD trip, Trey. Something else is up."

The silence stretches between Jessica and me.

A thought occurs to me. "Hey, Jessica. You're clearly one of the Drones. Wanna fill me in on who Joel's mother hired to kill me at the hospital?"

Gasps ring out all over the auditorium.

Jessica's mouth drops open.

"Oh, yes," I say with a smirking nod. "I know what you people are up to."

I glance Ms. Ferry's way, thinking she might offer some help, but she's apparently occupied in the corner. If she heard my question, she gives no indication. Judging from her murmured conversation with Mandie and Susan, she's missed this whole exchange. I roll my eyes about the obliviousness of some Normals.

I turn my snarling attention back to Jessica. "I'll offer you a warning. You have no clue who you're fucking with."

I shine a comically pleading glance toward Ms. Ferry, but still nothing. If she didn't hear me drop that particular word, then she definitely isn't paying attention.

"You people will need to get creative now that I'm not sedated in the hospital," I say to Jessica. "Bring it! Anytime, anyplace."

CHAPTER 22

As I stride across Arch and Hiram's yard, my tight red dress and heels draw attention from the usual hangers-on that always gather on the lawn. A few catcalls and whistles pierce the air.

I roll my eyes. *So base.*

My bloodstream is quaking from the fresh pill I popped before I left my house. The bottle's almost empty, and I've already made a mental note to talk to Tad at school on Monday. I'm scared that if I run out of pills, I'll finally slip into a much-needed deep sleep, and the dark water will be waiting. Fear bubbles up from my gut, but I shove it aside as I strut up the long, three-story staircase to the balcony.

I stop dead in my tracks as the balcony looms into view. Panic uncoils from deep in my gut. This is where I almost died by Joel's hand. I close my eyes tight, and I'm engulfed by the dark water in my mind. I double over, panic at war with my resolve for control of my psyche. My legs start to shake, and I feel the edge of a seizure coming. I clamp down on it, willing my body to hang on while I mentally work through this.

Joel's evil face flashes through the dark water.

Noooo! Not Joel! Anything but that.

The dark water whisks his image away, what's left of my rational mind protecting me from the trauma I haven't been strong enough to deal with yet. A racking sob blisters from me. Crippling terror tornadoes through my bloodstream, riding the roaring bullet train of the uppers coursing in my blood.

I have to stop taking the pills! They might kill me if they don't drive me insane first!

An arm snakes around my shoulders, and I open my eyes with a gasp. The dark water retreats as reality floods in, and I'm left mentally reeling from the relief and fear. My hands are shaking as I look up and find Arch standing next to me.

Arch's arm tightens around my shoulders. "You okay, kid?"

I look down and wait for my heart rate to slow. The pounding vein in my neck is throbbing so hard that I can feel it in my right ear.

"You're scaring me," Arch says.

That's bad news. Arch is never scared. This is worse than I thought. The dark water's waiting for me when I close my eyes. I snap them open. *You can't find respite in your mind, Mel! You know that.* I rally and pull up through the swirling chaos, the only thing I can count on right now. "Looks like I'm legit good," I lie, forcing a grin. "You got a stepladder?"

Arch shakes his head rapidly, clearly baffled by the swift change in topic. "Yeah. Why?"

I hold up a grocery sack. "Install these for me in the living room, would ya?"

He takes the sack, opens it, and laughs. "Red lightbulbs?"

"Let's have some fun."

Arch guides me through the door. The happy sounds of Ace of Base's "The Sign" beat through the town house.

Nope. This won't work.

It's usually one of my favorite songs, but not today.

I survey the room with my friends all speculatively watching me. After what happened with Joel, only the inner circle is allowed in the house this time, so I'm safe here. I'm surprised to find Isaac here with a date. I grin at him. It looks like he's officially one of us now. I scan the room further and am delighted to find Deb flirting with Adam's friend Michael in the corner. Michael flashes a winning smile, and I'm taken aback again about how much he's like Adam. He slides an arm around Deb, and she glances my way with a baffled expression. Clearly unaccustomed to being flirted with, Deb's tough girl façade cracks a bit around the edges. She looks up at Michael with big, girly eyes and says something that makes him laugh. He tips up her chin and leans down, kissing her. My mouth drops open as I watch Deb sink into the couch. Michael pulls her into his lap. She wraps her arms around his neck, and the vibe gets personal.

I avert my gaze. *Get it, Deb.* I tip my head to the side contemplatively. *He's a little old for her, though.*

While Arch changes the lightbulbs on the ceiling fan, I grab a pen and a piece of paper from the table. I jot down a song request on the paper and pass it to the deejay.

The deejay's eyebrows rise when he reads it. "This is a little aggressive."

I smirk. "It is."

He shrugs and sets down the paper, then turns to search his CD stack.

Arch flips the switch on the ceiling fan lights and turns off the lamp. The room washes in red. I saunter to the girls, who are bunched together in the middle of the room.

"You good?" Valerie asks.

I nod as the energy I have no control over uncoils from my gut. The red light brings my new seductive edge to the surface.

Presley grabs my hand. "We're worried about y—" She must sense my energy because she stops, and her eyes snap wide. "What was that?" She lets go of my hand.

"That's what I'm dealing with."

Presley shakes her hand before rubbing it on her jeans.

"What are you two talking about?" Finley asks.

"Grab her hand."

Finley delicately takes my hand and closes her eyes. She inhales sharply. "God, that's intoxicating." She looks at me with something bordering between awe and worry. "How do you sleep?"

"I don't."

When Bear steps up, we spread our tight circle so he can join us. "Whatever's happening is affecting the entire room." He looks at me. "Spill it. Now. What's going on with you?"

I shake my head, unwilling to discuss this with Bear because he possesses the level of wisdom that's likely to unravel my whole world in an instant. I'm not ready to face the countless demons in my mind.

"Grab her hand," Presley tells him.

Bear reaches down and takes my hand. At first, he gasps, but his initial shock is replaced by irritation. "You KNOW how to shield your energy! Darren and I have worked with you for months on this."

I crack around the edges and look at him pleadingly. "I didn't come out of the dark water right, Bear. Something's very wrong."

It looks like Bear has been waiting for this opportunity. "What dark water?"

My gaze flickers away because I'm not sure how much to tell him.

Of course, Bear's having none of it. He grabs me by the shoulders, practically yelling, "Don't shut down! Tell me. I'll help you."

This isn't the time. Everyone wants to have fun. I glance over my shoulder at the guys, who are huddled together watching us.

Darren pushes away from the wall and walks over. "What's wrong?"

"Grab her hand," Bear orders. He pulls Darren over to me and forces our hands together.

Darren's eyes narrow as he gently holds my hand. His eyes widen as my erratic energy pulses through. "Oh. My. God." He looks at Bear before turning back to me.

With two fingers, Bear reaches out and touches my pulse. "You need to tell us what's happening."

Shouldn't have taken that last pill. I quake on the inside. *I can't tell them. Not now. Not until I have enough control to avoid completely losing it.*

"What did she say?" Darren asks Bear.

"She said she didn't come out of the dark water right."

Darren looks down, contemplating. "Adam mentioned something about that."

Bear doesn't have time to answer because the throbbing, pulsing beat of my Nine Inch Nails selection, "The Only Time," pounds from the speakers. The music engulfs me, and I suddenly feel juiced in a way that makes me wonder how I ever do anything but worship those pills. I roll my neck slowly, luxuriating in the thrill.

The girls are watching me.

Valerie holds out her hand. "I'm more intuitive than these two." She gestures to Finley and Presley. "I want in."

I grin, my expression laced with daring, and hold out my hand.

She takes my hand and soaks in my energy. She closes her eyes and takes a deep breath. "I'm jealous. I could ride that wave every minute."

I shake my head. "It's fun at first, but I'm losing it."

Valerie grins down at me, her expression full of barely leashed conviction. "You can lose it later."

I smirk evilly at her as she turns, sauntering slowly toward Adam, her hips swaying in time to the music. I lock eyes with Adam, my smile carrying a suggestive edge. His eyes narrow at me before shifting to watch Valerie's approach.

When he glances back at me, I yell over the driving beat of the music, "You're welcome."

"What's happening?" Darren asks Bear from behind me.

"Melanie's got zero control over her empathic side. She's taking in everything around her while simultaneously blasting everyone with her energy. What's fueling the energy is the part I haven't figured out yet."

Bear's onto me.

Valerie reaches Adam and takes his hands, pressing them against the wall above his head before kissing him passionately. The guys watch her little show and turn to look at me suspiciously.

Presley steps up next, her gaze hopeful and expectant. "Juice me."

My eyes lock with Trey's. I can't tell if he's worried, intrigued, or both. I hold out my hands to either side and say to Finley and Presley, "Help yourselves. There's more where that came from."

Both girls grab my hands at the same time. More than I hear it, I *feel* them gasp as my dark-water seduction fills them. They saunter toward Marcus and Tanner.

"She's unleashing chaos, and they're loving it," Bear says.

"We have to stop this," Darren answers.

"No question," Bear replies frantically. "We have a lot of work to do getting Melanie through a shitload of trauma before we can help her control that energy."

As the music throbs through me, I strut toward Trey, leaving Bear and Darren to their spiritual discussion.

"What the hell are you doing?" Trey hisses at me when I stop in front of him.

My eyes narrow as disappointment creeps up. "Seriously? Do you *ever* just give in and make spontaneous decisions?"

Trey grabs my wrist and pulls me out to the balcony, leaving the seductive fun behind. "You're affecting everyone in that room!" he admonishes.

I rattle my head, baffled. "Everyone in that room is well acquainted with their partners. All I did was give them a boost." I glance back through the open door, and my gaze lights on Deb and Michael. They're all over each other. I wince, muttering, "Well, most of them, anyway." I take a nervous breath before leveling Trey with a look that holds far more pleading than I'm comfortable with. "I'm standing in front of you, quaking with seductive energy, and you're *still* overanalyzing?"

Trey closes his eyes. "I'm not giving in to this side of you while we're in a house full of people."

My vibe shifts rapidly under the weight of the rejection I've become all too familiar with.

When Trey feels it down our connection, he starts to explain himself, but I cut him off. "Did it ever occur to you that I need to give in to this side? Maybe this side is the heat we need."

Trey is too stunned to reply.

Before I can say anything else, I notice movement from down on the lawn. It's Demitri.

"Mel, wait!" Trey calls after me as I head down the stairs.

I ignore him and finish my quick trot to Demitri.

"Hey, Melanie," Demitri says, concern in his tone. "Are you okay?"

"Honestly, you don't want to go upstairs right now," I say with a sigh. "Hate to ask this, but would you be willing to drive me home?"

Demitri glances up at Trey on the balcony. "Did he hurt you?"

"Not in the way you're thinking."

He thinks about it for a moment. "Of course I'll take you home, but why do I want to avoid Arch's house?"

"This'll sound insane."

"Would it help if I told you I'm also an energy worker and I've got it figured out that you have a lot going on in that department?"

I close my eyes. "Yup. That helps a lot." A soft chuckle escapes my lips. "I just juiced the room with seductive energy, and now everyone is all over each other."

Demitri raises an eyebrow and looks up at the balcony. I follow his gaze to find Bear, Darren, and Trey all staring down at us.

"I take it Trey didn't wanna play," Demitri says.

I roll my eyes. "Nothing new there."

In that very *Demitri* way of his, Demitri says nothing. Instead, he turns and puts his hand lightly on my back, guiding me to his black Jeep. He opens the passenger door for me, and I slide in.

He gets into the driver's seat and turns to me. "I don't want to overstep, but it's like you're rattling out of your skin. Will you let me help you?"

"What's that expression about?" I ask, noticing how his forehead creases.

He smiles softly. "Your big eyes make you look really little and scared."

"I *am* really little and scared." I look down at my hands. "Please help."

Demitri laces a hand with mine and sends a wave of calm

through to me that makes my head slump. I close my eyes and hang on to Demitri's hand like it's a lifeline to sanity.

It takes me a moment to realize I should let go. I open my eyes and unlace my fingers.

"Better?" Demitri asks.

I nod. "Thank you. I'm sorry. I'm a mess."

Bob Marley's "Three Little Birds" drifts happily through the speakers when Demitri starts the engine.

"That's a welcome surprise," I say, exhaling with relief.

As he pulls away from the curb, he asks curiously, "What does Trey play when you ride with him?"

"Heavy metal."

"I take it you don't like it?"

"Eh. It's all right, but it's hard to count eight counts to. I prefer music that's danceable." I pull my heels off and slide my feet under me, sitting on them in my sleazy dress. "I feel like I can breathe again." I tip my head back and take a deep breath.

Demitri watches me out of the side of his eye. "What do you need?"

My chin tilts down as I look at him cautiously through my eyelashes. "Out of this dress. I need to be me." I wince and add, "That didn't come out right."

"Yes, it did." Demitri smiles softly. "What time do you need to be home?"

"Trey was supposed to drop me off by one."

"If I promise that I totally get what you just said, will you tolerate a detour to my house?"

I side-eye him curiously, but somehow, I'm sure I can trust him. We drive the ten minutes to his house, listening to Bob Marley all the way. When he pulls into his driveway, I slip my heels back on. We get out of his Jeep and make our way up the front walkway.

Demitri opens the door, and the gentle sounds of Beethoven's "Funeral March" engulf me. The energy gathers in my chest, threatening to build to an uncontrollable level.

A man gets off the couch and walks over. He and Demitri watch me.

"I can't ground it out," I say desperately to Demitri.

"Let it go," the man says.

I shake my head frantically.

"I'm Mr. Cantrell. Demitri's dad." The man holds out a hand for me to take.

Demitri takes my other hand.

"Now, let it go," his dad says.

I scrunch up my face and fight to let go. I drop my shields all at once, and all the tension I've held through my hospitalization, everything Trey put me through with Tiffany, and all my rejection and despair, release on a massive energy wave that rocks the house with a silent boom.

When it's over, I exhale hard and open my eyes. My breathing is shallow but unexpectedly calm.

"I'm sorry," I whisper.

Mr. Cantrell's expression holds an edge of wonder. "Don't be. Do you feel better?"

I nod.

Beethoven's "Moonlight Sonata" comes on next.

"Can I take these off," I ask, gesturing to my heels.

"Of course," Mr. Cantrell says. He looks curiously at his son as I pull off my heels.

Suddenly, I'm a little uncomfortable about how skimpy my dress is.

"I brought you here to get you something to change into," Demitri says as if reading my mind. "Is that okay?"

I nod shyly.

He takes my hand and guides me into a bedroom that holds the calmest energy I've ever felt. Demitri pulls sweatpants and a T-shirt out of a dresser and hands them to me. He closes the door as he leaves.

I change quickly and come back out with my folded dress in my hand. I drop it on my heels and bourrée halfway across his hardwood living room floor.

Demitri smiles. "Ballet too?"

When I shrug, he comes to me. He takes me by the hips and dips me into a deep penché before guiding me up, taking my hands, and promenading me around.

I smile and exhale. I développé my leg and thread it through our arms before stepping onto relevé and following Demitri's lead as he turns me around him and guides me into an arabesque just as the musical piece ends.

With a broad smile, I glance at the CD player as the next track starts. "'Adelaide,'" I say.

Mr. Cantrell looks at me appreciatively. "You know your Beethoven."

"You have no idea how charmed the classical music timing was." I smile softly at him. "I apologize for coming into your home, dropping an energy bomb, and dancing in your living room."

"I'm glad you did," he says with a soft smile. "But I'm afraid I still don't know your name. You are?"

I beam. "I'm sorry again. I'm Melanie Slate."

"Melanie's being partnered with me," Demitri explains. "It was supposed to happen next year, but Mr. Isley's testing us out in *The Pajama Game* as partners this year." He looks my way. "Long story short, Melanie needed to leave Arch's party, and I happened to walk up just in time. I figured out pretty quick that she needed a breather and to change."

I look down at the oversized T-shirt and sweatpants. "Thank you for this, by the way. I promise to get your clothes back to you."

Mr. Cantrell hits me with a serious gaze. "You're a vibrant little meteor."

There's no disagreement from me as I exhale hard. "Unfortunately, things are a little out of sorts lately."

"A little out of sorts is a way to put it," Mr. Cantrell says with a laugh. He takes my hand and assesses my state. "You feel more leveled out."

"Think we can grab a joint and my boombox?" Demitri asks his dad. "She needs to decompress."

Mr. Cantrell heads to the end table and pulls open a little drawer. He hands me a joint.

"Thank you."

Meanwhile, Demitri's coming back out of his room with a boombox. "You up for some calm?"

"Yes, please." My smile fades as I think about it for a moment. "I feel bad taking you away from the party."

Demitri shakes his head. "Don't. I hate those things. Only reason I go is to fit in."

My eyebrows rise. "*You* want to fit in? You do realize you're one of the most popular guys at school, right?"

A flicker of sadness pulses from him. "Not for the right reasons."

I look at him quizzically.

He rolls his eyes. "I don't want to get into it."

"Then we don't get into it."

"Just like that?"

I make a cartoonish face at him. "Just like that."

Demitri laughs and returns my silly expression.

"Look at you," I say, studying him thoughtfully. "A clandestine side to Mr. Perfect."

"What if I said I'm not Mr. Perfect?"

"I'd say, 'Thank God, because I'm the Hot Mess Express and Mr. Perfect would get sick of partnering my nonsense really quick.'"

Demitri laughs.

Mr. Cantrell raises his eyebrows at his son. "I like her."

Suddenly, I'm feeling bouncy and happy.

"Cactus Cooler for the road?" Mr. Cantrell asks.

"What's that?" I chirp.

"You're adorable. It's a soda."

I nod enthusiastically. "Yes, please."

He leaves for the kitchen and returns with two sodas, handing them to Demitri and me.

I pop the top and take a sip. Pleasantly surprised, I bob my head. "So good! Nom-nom-nom."

Demitri laughs. "Ever seen the Fraggles?"

With a grin, I sing the start of the theme song of *Fraggle Rock*.

His mouth drops open. "You, Melanie, are Red the Fraggle."

I tip my head. "That's so sweet of you."

"Yowzers!" Mr. Cantrell says. He juts a thumb my way as he looks to his son. "You found the girl version of you."

"She has to be home by one," Demitri tells him with a grin. "You good if I get home at one-thirty?"

Mr. Cantrell nods. "It was nice to meet you, Melanie." He hands me my dress and heels.

"Thank you, sir. It was nice to meet you too."

Demitri opens the door, and I walk out onto the porch. I stop at the top step and say, "Boing, boing," as I hop down the two steps to the walkway.

Mr. Cantrell chuckles, and Demitri is grinning as he opens the passenger door for me. I climb in happily.

Demitri stops by the front of his Jeep, where he and his dad talk for a second before he gets in and starts the engine.

"You good with a joint?" Demitri asks me while we're still idling. "I should have asked if you smoke."

Excitedly, I hand the joint to him. "Definitely."

He sparks it and takes a hit before slipping it to me. He backs out of the driveway, and we pass the joint back and forth as Bob Marley's "No Woman, No Cry" sways out through the speakers. My high builds slowly, and I discover too late that my eyes have been closed for a long time as I dance gently in my seat.

When I open my eyes, I catch Demitri stealing a glance at me. He wheels the Jeep into a parking space, and I smile as I realize that we're at a park. He pops his Bob Marley *Legend* CD out of the car stereo and gathers up the boombox. We get out of the Jeep, and I follow him to his chosen spot in the empty park. The grass under my bare feet grounds me. I sigh happily.

Demitri puts the CD in and turns the volume up just loud enough for us to hear. I suddenly feel like I'm in my own world. He skips forward to "Stir It Up," as I lie down in the grass. We rest in silence, just listening for a long stretch.

Finally, he asks, "What makes you happy?"

The unexpected question brings a smile to my face. "I don't know if anyone's ever asked me that."

"Guess I'm just curious. You aren't what I expected."

"What did you expect?"

Demitri shakes his head. "I don't know how to put it. You've always seemed reclusive and mysterious. You hugged me during the attack simulation, and you were suddenly flirty. When you got sick, you were destroyed. Then you showed up after the Tiffany mess and were a brass-balls, vibrating alley cat. At my house, you suddenly became a Fraggle. Clearly, you have layers."

"My life's complicated, I guess. But to answer your question about what makes me happy: dance, music, reading, and learning about history."

"That's the last answer I expected," he says, looking baffled.

"I'm actually rather quiet when I'm not a disaster." I roll slightly toward him and look up at him curiously. "Same question. What makes you happy, Demitri?"

"Getting to be who I really am."

"Who are you?"

"Goofy. Silly. Like a big kid."

I sit up and grin at him curiously. "Let me guess . . . that gorgeous face and chiseled body get in the way of you being seen for who you really are."

He chokes on his soda and sputters. After he's done coughing, he says, "No one has ever realized that."

"I'll make you a deal."

He looks at me, his gaze totally open and trusting.

"I'll let you be who you are, and you let me be who I am. We're both trapped in the same vortex, although the catalysts are different."

"What traps you?"

I give a sad smile. "I'm tiny, have nightmarish metaphysical abilities that are completely out of control, and I'm almost constantly misunderstood. I need to be a silly little girl, but I also need to be trusted that I can handle my own shit."

"That, I can do." He side-eyes me. "I need a friend who overlooks my outside and appreciates who I really am."

I smile. "Would it help if I said your silly chill side is a lot less intimidating than your whole Greek god outer covering?"

"You can overlook that?"

"Honestly, you look different to me now that we've gotten to know each other a little better." I shrug. "I wasn't all that caught up in your looks before, to be honest. I'm no stranger to mind-bendingly hot guys." I pause with a contemplative half smile. "I was secretly amused by all the lollygagging girls. You can't go anywhere without drama. I mean, do *any* girls ever finish a sentence around you?"

Demitri shakes his head. "Not really."

"That was the reason I suddenly started talking to you. Seemed like I needed to redeem the female half of the population."

Demitri laughs. "I was floored when you sat down next to me in the studio a few months ago. You asked what I was working on, without hitting on me, and it took me a second to verbalize. I spend a lot of time alone in a crowd."

"Me too." I hold out a hand. "Friends?"

Demitri shakes my hand. "Definitely."

He hauls me up and starts dancing with me to Bob Marley's "Jamming." I'm elated by the freedom of dancing with Demitri. He dips me and I giggle.

Demitri laughs and spins me around him. When the song winds down, he checks his pager. "We need to head out."

He gathers up the boombox and guides me back to his car. I settle contentedly in my seat. The contentment doesn't last long, chased away by the realization that this is the only time in the past month when I've been truly happy, and the moment is about to end.

Demitri starts the car, searches for a CD from a soft case holder he keeps in the back seat, and then pops his selection into the stereo. He skips several tracks until he lands on Wham!'s "Wake Me Up Before You Go-Go." I beam at him as the song bubbles and bounces through the speakers. He cracks up at the sight of me wiggling to the beat.

"You like this song?"

I giggle.

He starts singing the lyrics. We shimmy our shoulders at the same time, and I laugh boisterously. Demitri hits a perfect falsetto note.

"Yes you did!" I crow. "Damn, D!"

He grins at me as I kick my feet to the rhythm.

My guard is completely down as I smile at him. "We've got to choreograph a duet to this song together!" A wave of insecurity washes through my gut as I realize that I just suggested something that he may view as insulting. He's way out of my league as a choreographer. He's created pieces that are artistically mind-blowing, and I might as well be a no one in the dance department.

Demitri's expression lights with joy. "Are you serious? I would love that."

I shrug one shoulder and hit him with big, happy eyes. "Really?"

He nods, clearly thrilled. "I love to choreograph. Let's do it."

The song winds down, and I realize that his CD is likely homemade when "Black Velvet" by Alannah Myles comes on next. The mood suddenly shifts sultry as the lyrics flow from the speaker. I gasp at the weight of the shift. Demitri is side-eying me, his expression open and slightly stunned. Apparently, he feels the looming "ooh la la" also. His lips part, but he's not wearing his usual charming façade. I realize that I'm seeing his genuine romantic side, and I'm blazingly interested.

I close my eyes as a dejected pulse swells in me. Things are a tragedy with Trey, and firing up with Demitri while I'm vulnerable would be disastrous. I already have Adam creeping about on the sidelines. I sigh dejectedly, overwhelmed by all of it.

Demitri's hand lands on mine. "Melanie . . ."

When I glance his way, his lips part again. He can't seem to hold his usual chill together. I watch as everything he's experiencing morphs across his expression. Interest, worry, and appreciation seem to be at war in him. He's so gorgeous, it's brain liquifying. My thoughts are a jumble, but then all at once, they're taken over by the realization that Demitri is so far out of my league, it's laughable. The thought blazes through on a roaring flame of insecurity.

Determined to avoid the temptation, I turn my attention straight ahead and stare out the windshield. I clamp down on my expression, aiming for something that looks at least neutrally polite. *The last thing I need is another guy getting trapped in the complicated web that is my current life.*

He seems to get the message. I can feel the disappointment. It's surprising, and I'm confused by the possibility that he could be interested after all.

We spend the rest of the ride engulfed in the seductive song while I awkwardly navigate him toward my neighborhood.

As we get within a few blocks of my house, he breaks the tension, quietly asking, "Would you tolerate a little advice?"

My head drops, even though the question brings relief. *At least we're speaking again.* "I'm so lost that I'll take any advice I can get."

Demitri smiles gently. "I met Trey last year. I don't know him well, but I know enough to realize that he's handling things with you far differently than he has with other girls he's dated. I really think he's trying to look out for you because you're dealing with so much."

When I look his way, I know my eyes are big and childlike.

His forehead furrows with worry.

"His Tiffany affair wasn't exactly what I would call looking out for me," I retort pathetically.

Demitri rushes to clarify. "I get that. I was referring to him taking things slow with you."

My head bobbles. "That goes back to the discussion we had earlier. He's catering to the whole tiny girl side of me, instead of the entirety of who I am. He gives me no say in my choices. I dislike that a great deal. I don't want a father figure. I want a partner."

"That's fair."

We pull up to my house and park by the front curb.

I get out of the car, turn back toward him, and lean into the open windowsill. "Thank you. Tonight meant a lot. I desperately needed a breather. I'm sorry I dumped so much on you."

Demitri smiles. "You didn't dump anything on me. I needed a breather too. I got to be me."

I nod and tap the windowsill twice before turning and heading up my brick walkway. The house is dark. My parents aren't home, so I decide to sit on the front porch. I've always done my best pondering here.

Suddenly, I realize that Demitri's waiting for me to go inside. When I plunk down on the porch, he shuts off the Jeep's engine and gets out.

He heads up the walkway and stops in front of me. "I don't want to leave until I know you're locked safely inside the house."

I laugh the slightest bit. "This is my favorite place to sit and think."

He looks around. "Fresh air. View of the moon. Railing to lean on. It's a good spot."

I gesture to the spot next to me on the porch. He takes off his flannel and drapes it over my shoulders as he sits. The night has gotten chillier. I scoff at how perfect it is to suddenly find myself in his warm flannel. Unexpected tears fill my eyes. I put my head on my knees as they roll down my cheeks. I want to die of humiliation. The brief magic of knowing Demitri as nothing more than a normal guy has dissolved, and he's stunning again. *The most gorgeous boy in school is sitting on my porch, watching me fall completely apart.* I shake my head, suddenly mortified that I revealed so much to him.

"A thought made your energy shift," he observes. "What was it?"

I wipe the tears from my face, my mood lilting to one of curiosity at his unexpected inquiry. "You sure you want to know?"

"Rule number one about me. I don't ask unless I want to know."

Slightly amused, I look down at my hands. "The thought was, *The most gorgeous boy in school is watching me fall apart.* As usual, I want to die of embarrassment because I'm a hot wreck all the time." I chance a glance at him. "I feel ridiculous. I revealed a side of me to you that I would normally never show Mr. Perfect."

Demitri nudges my shoulder with his. "Don't get all confused now. We already established that I'm not Mr. Perfect. You promised to actually be my friend."

I roll my eyes but can't help grinning at him. After some thought, I quietly change the subject. "Can I offer you some advice?"

He looks at me curiously. "Yes."

"Stay away from me. I'm a train wreck."

Demitri smiles and glances away, but only for a moment. "My turn to offer advice."

I nod.

"Take it one day at a time. Most monumental problems need time to resolve. The desire to fix things quickly can create unnecessary anxiety."

I close my eyes and inhale deeply. "Thank you. I needed that."

He smiles softly at me as he helps me to my feet. I hand his flannel back to him.

"Thank you for everything, Demitri."

"You're welcome."

I turn, unlock my door, and slip inside. I lean against the coat closet door and try to make sense of my bizarre evening. A minute later, I hear Demitri's Jeep pull away.

CHAPTER 23

The air is cold. I inhale deeply, waiting. It's three in the morning, and I'm nervous . . . *and excited. Don't lie to yourself.* Shortly after Demitri dropped me off at home, Adam called and asked if he could come pick me up. Everything within me screamed that it would be a terrible idea, but I still agreed to his questionable plan.

As Adam's Harley pulls up, I push away from the ornate iron railing and step off the porch. He's radiating anticipation as I make my way toward him on the brick path.

My dark-water side drifts to the surface. *Every time he's near me, this other side of me roars up.*

Without a word, I swing my leg over the back of his Harley. He waits as I get settled and holds both hands behind his back. I put my hands in his, and he wraps my arms around him, placing my hands on his chest.

He glances over his shoulder and says, "Good morning," before he takes off down the road.

My dark-water side whispers in my head, *Don't think. Just enjoy the ride.* I gladly take her up on the offer. We make the twenty-minute drive to a quiet spot overlooking the city lights.

After Adam stops on the dirt overlook and cuts the engine, I swing my leg over the bike and move out of the way to make room for him to stand. He pulls a Discman and a little speaker out of his motorcycle side compartment. He pushes *play*, and Nine Inch Nails' "Something I Can Never Have" oozes from the little speaker.

As we listen, he leans on the side of the seat with his eyes closed, thinking. I stare out at the city lights in the distance. Suddenly, his fingers are featherlight as they run slowly from my shoulders to the small of my back. I gasp, shuddering as the energy I've barely gotten in check surges to the surface. I don't fight it this time. With Adam, the energy feels right. He runs his hands along my sides, pulling me back against him before clasping his hands in front of my stomach.

I tip my head back, resting it on his shoulder as I stare up at the moon. "Nice music choice."

"You played NIN at the party, so I pulled out the album. It's crazy accurate lately."

I nod and relax against him.

After a long pause, Adam says, "I don't know what to do. I don't want to hurt anyone, but the connection we have . . . How do we not explore that?"

"I don't know what to say except that my only hesitation is the fear of hurting Valerie. Trey and I are done."

Adam's breath is on my neck, and I shiver. After a long moment he says, "You don't have much else to say. It makes this more difficult."

"You've always just *known* with me. I don't really have to say anything with you."

"I didn't realize you'd noticed that."

"I notice everything about you."

Adam rests his forehead on my shoulder and sighs. "Tell me. I need to know what's happening with you."

I ignore his request. "Tell me what you're thinking. Right here, right now."

Adam inhales sharply. "All right . . . I'm scared. I've never met someone who can affect me like you do lately. I don't know what's changed—with you, with us—but I can't ignore it. I can't think about anything else."

"What, specifically, are you scared of?"

"I'm scared I'm going to burn down everything in my life, and it'll be worth it."

My dark-water side roars up, and the energy starts rolling from me in waves.

Adam gasps. "That's what I can't ignore."

I turn to face him, his hands sliding into the back pockets of my jeans. He stares into my eyes. I wait, saying nothing, my arms around his neck while he thinks.

Finally, he says, "This will cannonball what you have with Trey. You must know that. Without me in the way, you two are likely to fix things."

I laugh softly. "Honestly, I should just let you listen to this song. It says everything."

"Tell me. I can listen to the song at the same time."

"When I was sedated, I was in this dark water in my mind. It's complicated, and one day, I'll fill you in on the details. But every time I close my eyes, a new side of me is waiting in that water. It's like part of me woke up that I didn't know I had. It's there every time I sleep, every time I blink, every time I try to collect myself. That side of me is a lot. She's bold, dangerous, brave, sexy, challenging, and full of baaaad ideas that are perfect . . . At first, I couldn't figure it out, but I've come to realize that she's the voice in my head that counters the cautious part of me. Angel and devil, yin and yang. Does that make sense?"

"Perfect sense, actually." Adam closes his eyes, contemplating. "That's what you've been fighting so hard against?"

"Yes. Fighting this part of me is exhausting. When I'm with you, just us, I don't have to fight it. This side of me fits with you. I need to be able to embrace her."

"Do you think she's going away?"

"No, I think she's who I'm becoming."

"How does that side fit with Trey?"

"It doesn't."

"Why?"

"He doesn't seem to 'approve' of that side, if that makes sense. I'm worried I'll break him. He's just not daring enough. When it boils down, if I can't be all of me with my other half, then what's the point?"

"Are you worried you'll break me?"

"Nothing breaks you, Adam. This side of me can't leave you alone. You're her match."

He slides his hands up my back and pulls me against him. He leans in, our lips almost touching. "That, I can't resist." He kisses me as the lyrics of the song he chose swirl around us.

Waves thrum from me as my entire universe spins into a free fall of electric energy. He moans against my lips. I give in to my dark-water side. Her eyes snap open within my mind's eye. She knows something is about to happen, something she's been waiting for. Suddenly, a matching energy rolls off Adam, and it sends my dark-water side reeling. The perfection that melds between us is the synergy of everything I've ever wanted, and a whole lot that I never dreamed of.

The kiss slows, but neither of us want to end it.

Finally, he pulls away. My eyes are still closed as I bask in the dark water, without fear, for the first time since it started existing in my mind.

Adam breathes, "Melanie."

I open my eyes to the storm raging in the depths of Adam's ocean-blue eyes.

"You made the dark-water part of me into something that's *right*." I close my eyes again, testing the waters. Relief radiates through me. "When I'm with you, I'm . . ."

"You're what?"

I grapple for the words. "I'm . . . complete. The raging, massive, heart-stopping parts of this dark-water side become something I can welcome. You make me safe in my own mind."

Adam's expression wars between fear and hope. "That's worth destroying everything and everybody for."

I lean in, and he kisses me again. Fire seethes.

CHAPTER 24

I hop off the bus, the Monday morning sunshine a bit hazy with LA smog. The girls have gathered by the back-alley gate, all excitedly chattering. We find out during sixth period who got cast in the show, and apparently, it's going to be agony for everyone while they wait for the posting.

I'm so over the school-day charade. I'm wearing the hematite ring Darren gave me, and I'm dressed for the appearance of normalcy—a pair of black jeans, a button-down fire-red blouse, and my motorcycle boots. "Where are the guys?" I ask. *I need to talk to Adam.*

"They'll be back," Finley says with a sparkle in her eyes. "They have a plan to head to Ms. Ferry's office to see if they can wrangle some early information about the casting for the show."

I roll my eyes. Apparently, the girls aren't the only ones on pins and needles.

"You look fab, Melanie," Valerie says with an appraising glance.

Be normal. "So do all of you!" My racing heart is going to pound out of my chest. *Almost out of pills. I need to ditch the girls and find Tad. But first, Adam.*

"Anyone else so nervous they can't eat or sleep?" Finley asks.

You have no idea.

Everyone's hand but Kelsey's goes up. Kelsey is Trey's sister, and as a Regular, she doesn't audition for the shows.

Chitchat. Kill me.

"Are we really going to act like everything's hunky-dory?" Presley asks. "We still need to talk about Saturday night."

Something real out of one of them. Finally!

My dark-water side reminds, *All of this is real for them.*

Whatever.

"What happened on Saturday?" Kelsey asks.

All eyes turn to me.

Valerie shakes her head. "You missed a hell of a party."

Kelsey glances around the circle of girls. "Makes me wish I hadn't been sick."

Presley locks eyes with me. "It's Arch who missed out."

I laugh inwardly. "I owe you all an apology."

Presley scoffs. "No you don't. We had a blast." She pauses to think about it. "What you owe us is an explanation."

With a thoughtful nod, I turn to walk away. "I'll give you one soon. Catch you later."

Before they can object, I stalk off and around the corner. Adam's leaning against the wall at the end of Actors' Alley. I cut across, headed his way. He pushes away from the wall, puts his hands in his pockets, and rounds the edge of the building out of sight. I pick up my pace and turn the corner.

He's waiting for me. "You okay?" he asks.

"No."

"Tell me what you need."

I grin. "To get out of here."

"Let's go."

We turn to leave, but just as we round the edge of the bungalow alongside Actors' Alley, the guys hop down the staircase. Arch spots us just as the girls bound up to them.

"Damn it," Adam says.

"I don't think I can do this today," I whisper.

"I know. If I swear you can trust me, will you finally fill me in on everything?"

Our whispered conversation is cut short when our friends join us.

"It's a no-go," Arch says. "We tried to get a look at the list, but Ms. Ferry was onto us."

Bear glances at Trey. "Smokers' Corner. Now."

"Fantastic," I say under my breath.

"Let me talk to Melanie alone for a while first," Adam says. "I don't think she can do this with everyone."

Bear levels him with a weighty look. "No."

Adam tries to communicate to Bear silently, but it does no good. Bear turns on his heel, and everyone follows. Valerie hugs Adam and pulls him ahead. Curiosity and anxiety roll off my friends in waves as the group moves briskly through Actors' Alley toward Quad One. My gaze stops on Isaac. He's glancing between Adam and me with a curious expression. He's new to my drama, and I don't want him here.

I can't do this.

Trey stops abruptly and turns to his sister. "Kelsey, I need you to listen to me." Her expression morphs to one of concern, and he continues, "I don't want you involved in what we're about to discuss. I'm asking you to go to class."

Kelsey's face falls. "These are my friends too."

Trey nods. "I know, but what Melanie's about to discuss is dark. Some of the details . . ." He looks down, thinking before he finishes. "You don't want to know everything, and we're going to have to tell it all."

"I don't want to tell any of it right now," I indignantly inform.

Trey turns to me. "You have to."

"Why?" I hiss. "Because you and Bear have decided it's time? Let me guess. You two have a plan."

"We can't keep doing this," he implores softly. "We all need you back."

"What if this me *is* me?"

He looks baffled. "The real you is this energy-blasting, sensual, cynical bitch?"

"That's how you see her lately?" Adam asks.

Demitri's standing across from me in the circle of friends. He looks from Trey to Adam, concern rolling off him.

"Yeah, Adam!" Trey snarls. "You don't?"

Adam looks at me. "No, I don't. I see it as Melanie embracing *all* of who she is."

Trey scoffs. "You've GOT to be kidding!"

"Why?" Adam asks with a glare.

"You're trying to tell me that this mean, snide, raging, antisocial version of Melanie is the real her?"

Adam cocks his head to one side. "Do you really think people stay the same forever? You think she wasn't going to shift as everything in her life changed? She went from her biggest problem being loneliness and social anxiety to being nearly raped numerous times, almost killed, having PTSD, having empathic abilities rage up completely unchecked, losing her boyfriend to a bimbo, and now she has this dark-water side trying to meld with the rest of her psyche."

Everyone looks confused. Demitri's mouth falls open, and he looks at me with extreme worry.

Trey whips his gaze my way and exasperatedly asks, "You told ADAM details about the dark-water side?"

Adam answers for me. "Who else is she supposed to tell? All of them?" He gestures to our friends. "They're obsessed with the musical, with school, with student council, parties. There's nothing wrong with that, but what's happening in Melanie's world doesn't fit with the happy high school daily giggle fest."

He completely understands everything.

"What are you saying?" Trey growls. "That it fits with YOU?"

Yes.

"I'm not done," Adam rages back. "You're so busy trying to drag her out of this that you never stopped to think about how it's making it worse. What if what she really needs to do is embrace it?" He takes slow, menacing steps toward Trey. "What if she has a dark, dangerous, aggressive side? What? You can't handle that side, so you're hell-bent on your tunnel vision mission to *fix* her. To turn her back into the sweet, nervous, sweaty-palm girl she used to be?" He spits out venomously, "Did any of that occur to you, or was it too much to consider because you have baseball practice?"

Trey looks like he's been punched. His face goes slack.

"Can we leave now?" I ask Adam.

He nods, and we both turn to walk up the alley.

"Stop," Demitri calls after us. "Both of you."

We halt and glance over our shoulders at him.

"Are you sure you've got this?" he asks Adam intensely.

"I'm positive," Adam says.

Demitri closes his eyes and shakes his head.

Valerie crosses the short distance and hugs Adam. "Take care of her, okay?"

Kill me!

"Melanie," Trey implores, "don't leave with him. If you need to talk, I'm here. *I'll* leave with you." The desperation in his tone is thick.

"I've tried to talk to you, Trey, but it's always on your terms, with your narrow understanding."

Almost frantically, Trey insists, "I'll listen. I'm sorry. I didn't understand until Adam's little speech just now."

I shake my head and continue my brisk journey down the alley with Adam.

As soon as we get out of earshot, I say, "I can feel their eyes on us."

"I know," Adam breathes.

"Do they know about us?"

He laughs. "No. They're still trying to comprehend *you*."

———

Adam's Harley slows to a stop in front of a gift shop on Pacific Coast Highway. He cuts the engine and I get off the back, letting him swing his leg over the side.

He kisses my forehead. "I'll be right back."

I turn to the ocean across the highway and watch the waves glimmering in the sun. *Everything's better with Adam.*

When he returns, he's carrying a bag. He hands it to me.

I glance at him, amused, and look inside. "Flip-flops, sweatpants, and a 'California Dreaming' tourist T-shirt?"

He grins. "You need to be comfortable for this."

I mouth a "thank-you" at him.

"You're welcome." He gestures to the shop. "Head in. The salesgirl says you can change in the fitting room."

CHAPTER 25

Adam's Harley rumbles to a stop. The ocean shimmers below the cliff where we've parked. Adam gets off the motorcycle and scoops me up. He carries me as he descends a craggy, treacherous, path, but his steps are sure. He sets me down on the sand. We're alone on a little beach, a tucked-away haven hugged on three sides by the tall cliffside.

We take off our backpacks, and he sits next to me. "This is the spot that inspires my beach drawings."

"It's beautiful here."

We watch the tranquil water for a while.

Finally, he says, "Before you tell me everything, I have two conditions."

"Name them, and I'll see if I can agree."

His smile is rueful. He glances down and picks up a handful of sand that he lets run through his fingers into my hand. "First condition is that you tell me everything. The second condition is that you tell it with the understanding that I won't judge you. I don't want you omitting important details because you're worried about what I'll think."

I'm lost in my own thoughts.

He touches my chin, drawing my gaze from the sand to look at him. "What are you thinking?"

"That you're perfect. You just said exactly what I needed to hear."

His hands settle in his lap. "I don't want to be arrogant enough to think I know what you need, especially when things are so intense with us under the surface. I know it's complicating all of this for you. But I've been paying attention." He smiles and traces the edge of my jaw. "I brought you here because it's one of my favorite places, and I want to share it with you. I've never brought a girl here. Also, I've never been interrupted when I'm here. It's hard to get to, and few people know about it. I want you to take as long as you need to tell me everything."

He takes off his leather jacket and puts it over his lap. He stretches out his legs before pulling me down and laying my head on his lap. His jacket smells like warm sunshine and his cologne. He waits patiently while I listen to the sound of the ocean.

Finally, I say, "Here goes nothing." Suddenly, I'm a nervous wreck.

Adam puts his hand over my pill-racing heart.

"I know, I know, my heart's racing," I say with exasperation. "It's scary, and you're worried."

Adam scoffs. "I'm not Trey. I'm putting my hand over your heart to keep you grounded. I do energy work with Bear and Darren too, remember?"

More perfection.

My heart slams into his hand, and the harder it beats, the more pressure he puts on my chest. He projects nothing but calm. I close my eyes, willing my heart to slow.

Once my heart has returned to its normal pulsing, Adam asks, "Better?"

"You have no idea."

"I have every idea. I've wanted to do that every day since this started, but we had to get past the initial honesty about the attraction between us first. Your heart wouldn't have slowed with that looming between us."

My heart starts sledgehammering again. He laughs softly, the sound oddly intimate.

Slowly, I sit up. His hand slides up the center of my chest, coming to rest on the side of my neck. I shift, straddling his coat over his lap.

He looks into my eyes and smiles. "If we get this out of the way, will you be able to focus on telling me what's happening?"

I murmur, "I hope not."

Adam smirks, and I kiss him. My energy boils over, mixing and melting with his energy.

When the kiss ends, Adam says, "I don't want you to take this the wrong way, because I care about what you're going through, but I'm thinking we skip the story of doom and I fix you my way."

I laugh and wrap my arms around his neck, resting my head on his shoulder.

He lifts me slightly so he can cross his legs under me. He sets me back down and holds me. "Tell me," he implores.

I pause in thought. *He said he wants to hear it all.* "Trey explained his part of all of this to me, and so I'm going to have to tell you. Is it going to make you mad?"

"No," Adam responds simply.

"Okay. According to Trey, I got to the hospital and was unconscious that whole time. The nurses raced me from the ambulance into a hospital room. At that point, I had a seizure. They couldn't get it to stop. Finally, they decided to sedate me. The medication worked and the seizure stopped, but the sedatives had a trapping effect in this dark-water portion of my mind. I couldn't talk or move my body in reality, but after a while, I could hear sometimes."

I close my eyes to regroup, but the dark water's there, and it's roiling, violent.

Adam feels the shift. "What just happened?"

"When I closed my eyes, the dark water was churning."

"I'm not going to let anything happen to you."

I take a breath. "While I was sedated, the dark water was terrifying. There was nothing solid. It took what felt like eons to learn how to think straight. At first, thoughts and sounds would drift by, just out of reach."

The memories are flooding back, and my heart is racing again. Adam puts his hands flat on my back and radiates calm. I take a deep breath.

"Better?"

I nod and continue. "After a while, I had more cohesive thoughts. I heard things here and there, but I've never been that alone in my life." *Here we go. Let's see if he can handle this.* "Just when I thought the darkness would swallow me up, Trey appeared in the water. He said he missed me, and then he was swept away." I take a shuddering breath. "Seeing him, and then watching him fade away, was one of the worst moments of my life."

Adam seems to contemplate this.

"Do you remember when Trey really started to fall apart?" I ask him.

"When his panic attacks started while you were in the hospital?"

I nod against Adam's shoulder. He slides his hands along my back, hugging me again.

"That's when he found himself in the thick, dark water," I explain. "It happened every time he tried to sleep. He'd find me, but he couldn't figure out how to stay with me." I pause, insecurity bubbling up. "I know that sounds crazy."

Adam shakes his head. "Not at all. What you're describing is called astral projection. I'm floored to hear that Trey can do it."

"Explain."

"It's a whole spiritual New Age practice. Sounds like science fiction, but it's actually possible, as you found out firsthand. The idea behind it is to get yourself into a meditative state that allows your spirit to leave your body. In Trey's case, I think it was a combination of desperation and luck that allowed him to do it."

"Trey and I have an energy connection. It's been out of whack since the Tiffany drama, though. We can send these emotional thought bubbles back and forth."

"How do you feel about that?"

I sigh. "It's hard to have lost so much with him, but he made that choice. I'm exhausted enough that I don't have the gumption to try to fix it. If what we had meant so little to him that it was worth giving it all up for Tiffany, then maybe it wasn't what I thought it was."

"I'm sorry."

Quiet takes over for a moment while I stare at the rocky cliff.

"We've pieced together a few things," I say. "The deeper the sedation, the deeper I was in the dark water."

"Your mind tried to make sense of something that was nonsensical. This all tracks. I've read studies on dreams and sedation. Your mind created a world where it could try to make all the pieces fit."

I swallow down a pang of fear. "That makes perfect sense, except that the dark water is still in my mind."

What Adam says next floors me. "I want you back."

I freeze. "You're sure about that?"

Adam drops his carefully controlled shields, and I feel an intense love emanating from him. "I don't drop my guard for anyone," he says earnestly. "No one knows this but Bear and Darren, but I'm the most solid energy worker of the three of us. You have an ability, Melanie, and I think your potential to master this ability is similar to mine."

"Will you teach me?"

A smile of surprise crosses his lips. "I would be honored." He kisses my forehead before putting my head back on his shoulder. "First, continue the story of doom."

I laugh. "At some point, I also heard Stan and a woman talking over me while I was sedated. The Drones plan to take all of us out to clear the witness list and free Joel of the attempted murder charges."

Adam snarls, "I'd like to see them try."

"Me too," I say, my grin laced with evil. "I'm looking forward to it."

Adam squeezes me tighter. "I love that about you."

"Anyhow, every time they'd try to take me off the sedatives, I'd have a seizure. Finally, Trey formed a plan. He spent the night at the hospital. As soon as the nurses left him alone with me, he started lowering my drip dose until I finally had a whopper of a seizure. I stopped breathing and died in his arms."

Adam's breath catches.

I lift my head to look at him. "I'm okay, Adam."

He drops his head on my shoulder and holds me tighter. "If I was there, I could have stopped all of this sooner."

"I know. Trey tried, but he doesn't have the energy control you do."

"Keep telling me the story. I'm okay."

I kiss his neck, and he rubs his cheek against mine. "I love you," he whispers, and my heart nearly explodes.

There's no way to curb what I'm feeling. "I love you too."

"I know." He kisses me, his usual control lost on the dark-water wave that rolls from me. He flips me over, gently landing me on my back on the sand. He collapses next to me and laces our hands together. All thought disappears.

He ends the kiss with a gasp. "I will leave every friend we have, destroy Valerie, and throw everything away to be with you again."

I gaze up at him. "Then your fear has come true."

He nods, his expression faraway as he sorts through his feelings. I consider each new emotion that drifts from him. Fear. Worry. Heartbreak. Finally, he settles on irresistible, earth-shattering love.

I trace his jaw lightly with my finger as he looks down at me. "What do we do?"

He grins. "Right now, we let you finish your story."

I settle back in the sand and stare up at the clouds floating across the sky. I fill him in on the seizures and blood tests. He listens patiently.

"After they finally let me go home, things got bad in a new and exciting way." I take a shaky breath, careful not to close my eyes for too long because I sense the black water rising. "Every time I try to sleep, I'm back in the dark water. Every time I close my eyes to think, the water engulfs me. The water is full of all these swirling images of Joel, the upcoming trial, being alone, pretty much all my fears that I've suppressed. I haven't really slept in two weeks. The only time the water's calm is when I'm with you or Demitri."

Adam rolls his eyes. "You can forget about Demitri."

"Oh, is that so?" I ask flirtatiously.

He smirks. "Definitely."

He kisses me and I melt.

"So, we need to deal with the insane empathic energy issue," Adam says. "We need a plan to deal with the Drones attempting to take us out. And we have to make sure you can sleep. Does that sum it up?"

Time for the big reveal.

I sit up and reach for my backpack, dragging it to me. I unzip the front pocket and take out the bottle of pills. Adam's emotional shields slam back in place in anticipation of what's coming. Without a word, I hand him the pill bottle.

He reads the bottle. "The racing heart."

I nod and swallow hard.

"These are highly addictive," he says softly. "They could've killed you."

I sigh. "I was more scared of the dark water than I was of dying."

"Does Trey know?"

"No one knows but you."

He tips my chin up, looking me in the eyes. "Who sold them to you?"

"Tad."

Adam's eyes turn a deadly steel blue. "I'm going to kill him."

My head drops as I panic about what he's going to say next.

He brushes my hair from my cheek. "It's too soon after kicking the hospital sedatives for you to be on something this addictive. We need to tell the others and devise a plan for you to get away from these things. Make up a girls' camping trip or something so you can spend three days at my house. I can get you through it, but it's going to be ugly."

"I've only taken them for a few weeks."

"You were on the sedatives for weeks before that. I'd love to say that the three days is going to be a romp through romance-ville, but it's not. I'm going to see the very worst in you. I've dealt with this before. It gets bad."

"Why not just send me back to the hospital then?"

"Too dangerous with Joel's poison buddy hanging around. I don't trust anyone but me to get you through this."

A sigh escapes my lips.

"I assume you took them this morning?"

I nod.

"So . . . is that all of it? The whole story, I mean." He chuckles when I nod again. "Pills?" he says as he puts the bottle in his backpack. "I feel like such an idiot. I should have figured that out a lot sooner." When he's finished chastising himself, he cups my jaw. "Will you trust me?"

"I think that's a given at this point."

"You okay swimming in your underwear and bra?"

I laugh. "They cover more than my swimsuit."

"Would you be mad if I said that was a shame?"

My dark-water side sends out a seductive pulse.

Adam's eyes turn a deeper shade of blue, and he smirks. "I think I have an idea about how to fix this dark-water thing."

He stands, pulling me to my feet, and takes off his shirt. The sight of him sends me tumbling into a teen girl moment. He turns and raises an eyebrow as I secretly admire his perfect six-pack.

"You okay?"

I smirk. "You're mind-bendingly hot."

Adam throws back his head and belts surprised laughter. When I take off my shirt and sweatpants, he says, "You aren't so bad yourself." He steps to me and puts his forehead on mine. "You ready to let all of this go?"

"Parts of it, yes. Some of it, no."

"Like what?"

"You."

He smiles and picks me up, carrying me to the water. He wades us in chest deep. The cold ocean makes me gasp and hang on tighter around his neck.

"Breathe, Melanie."

I exhale and give in to the water. I wrap my legs around his waist, and he holds me as I look over my shoulder at the ocean waves. When I close my eyes, the dark water is calm.

"Every time the dark water becomes too much," Adam says, "I want you to remember that I've got you, and the water isn't scary."

I exhale hard, so relieved to be okay in the water that it nearly makes me dizzy. "Adam?"

"Yes."

"I'll give up everything for you. Heart and soul, I'm yours."

"Are you sure?"

"Absolutely."

He exhales hard. "Then we make a plan to pour gasoline on our lives and light that shit on fire."

A dangerous grin spreads across my face.

"That look right there! God, that look is why I can't ever get you out of my mind. You get it every time you're about to punch someone, have a confrontation, or torch your universe."

I laugh.

"What's funny?"

"That's the look that scares Trey," I explain.

He tightens his muscular arms around me. "I'll follow you into hell every time you get that look on your face." There's heat in his expression as he adds, "I wonder . . ."

"You wonder what?"

He leans in, his lips nearly touching mine. When I close my eyes, he whispers against my lips, "I wonder if there's any other thing we can do that will put that look on your face."

His lips meet mine.

CHAPTER 26

Adam drops a quarter in a pay phone. A beep chimes out of the receiver, and then he enters a quick series of numbers before hanging up. I look quizzically at him.

"I paged Bear with our code for Smokers' Corner and fifth period. Bear will gather everyone."

My heart starts hammering again. "I don't want to go back to school."

He takes my hand and pulls me into a café called the Beach Bar, choosing a table outside overlooking the ocean.

A waitress comes over. "Hey, Adam. The usual?"

He nods. "The usual for me, but a margarita for Melanie. Blended."

The waitress nods and wanders away.

"She didn't card us," I say in disbelief.

Adam laughs and shakes his head without explaining. He goes silent, serious.

"Tell me what you're thinking," I request.

He pulls my chair closer. "Today, I have confirmation of something I've suspected for a while."

I grin mischievously at him. "What's that?"

He drops his energy shields and takes my hand, sending a pulse of love down the stronger connection that's formed between us.

My breath catches, my lips parting. I stare into his eyes, surprised. "There's no way."

He smiles. "I know everyone thinks you and Trey are soulmates, but when we were in the ocean, I confirmed that we have this connection too." He gives me a carefully weighted look and says, "We're both energy workers. Our energy is largely the same. I don't know what it means for you and Trey, but I do know that I'm your other half."

I smile ruefully. "What . . . the . . . hell are we going to do?"

He looks torn. "I'll figure something out. We can't avoid hurting Valerie, but I'll try to handle it as tactfully as possible."

"We don't just let this go between us, right?"

He gives me a baffled look. "Ummm, no."

I laugh.

A giant platter of nachos arrives, and the waitress sets down our drinks with a smile. "Need anything else?"

Adam shakes his head and thanks her. After the waitress takes her leave, Adam looks at me and motions to the plate. "Eat. It's my turn to talk."

It's been a long time since I felt comfortable eating, but now I'm eagerly reaching for a nacho.

"I'm also an empath, like you," he explains, "but the gift hit when I was little. I've had a lot of time with it. Unfortunately, your empathy opened up when you were faced with a life-and-death struggle. It's a lot harder to manage when you're under duress."

A confused look must cross my face as I chomp my nachos, because he takes a deep breath and starts over.

"Imagine it like this. You have a really full cup. If you aren't careful, it sloshes everywhere. If everyone you pass pours a little more liquid into that cup, it becomes impossible to manage. You take in other people's general vibe, and it affects you; except you don't have any more room for any outside energy because of everything you're dealing with emotionally. As everyone's emotional junk gets poured into the cup, it runs over, affecting everyone around you. It's a vicious cycle."

"How do we stop it?" I ask, fascinated.

"We don't stop it. It'll always be there, but you can learn to control it to where it's on your terms. Imagine if you had the cup inside your own house. You can choose to set it down, drink from it, pour it out. You can decide who refills it, and what you want in it."

"Right now, I want margarita in the cup," I say. Reaching for my drink, I take my first indulgent sip. *So good!*

Adam laughs and clinks his beer bottle to my margarita glass. "Cheers, my love." He gazes into my eyes. "I can, and will, help you."

I set my drink down and pick out another nacho. "Thank you, Adam. Today means more to me than I can say."

He checks his pager. "Bear paged back our code for 'yes.'" He checks the time and clips his pager back on his pocket. "We need to be back there in three hours."

"What time is it?"

"Ten-thirty."

"I swear time stops with you. We left school at seven-thirty. It's only been three hours?"

Adam laughs, but his response is cut off as his buddy Michael saunters up in board shorts. Adam boisterously fist-pounds Michael, and they chatter for a moment before Michael looks down at me and breaks into an enthusiastic grin.

"Good to see you again, Melanie."

I smile up at him.

He says to Adam, "She looks far happier than she did the first time I met her."

Adam nods appreciatively at his friend.

Michael's eyebrows rise, and his smile widens. "You look far happier, also." Before Adam can answer, Michael holds a hand down to me and asks, "May I have this dance?"

I grin and glance Adam's way. When he nods his approval, I take Michael's hand. Michael hefts me to my feet and guides me to the open space in the aisle where several other couples are dancing to the Ventures' "Pipeline." The song is fun and bouncy. I squeal as Michael lifts and turns me. Adam's smiling as he watches us. He polishes off his beer and eats nachos, totally at ease.

Michael turns me out before pulling me in. He laces his hands behind my back and dances close. "Adam's not going to be mad, if that's what you're thinking."

I giggle shyly and shrug the slightest bit. "I have no clue where he and I are at. Today has changed a few things."

"That guy has loved you from the moment he first saw you. I razzed him about it, but I get it now. You seem to be his perfect puzzle piece."

Curious, I tip my head. "Willing to explain?"

"Let's just say that you check all his boxes." He gives me a playful look. "I think he might check your boxes, also."

I give him a wry, searching look. "You don't know me well enough to be acquainted with my boxes."

Michael tips his head back, belting laughter.

I grin, satisfied about how well he handled my suggestive pun. *Points for Michael.*

"True," he says. "And I never will." He juts his chin Adam's way. "That guy has been a mini-me since we were little. We grew up on the same street, but there were no kids his age. I'm three years older than he is, but he always fit in with us. I know he seems older than all the kids at your school." He wobbles his head right and left. "My troublemaking friends are why."

I laugh and glance Adam's way. He's totally at ease, not at all worried as he watches my intimate conversation with Michael.

I glance back Michael's way, my neck crooked back because he's so tall. "Adam is rather grown," I confirm. "Most people at our school are scared of him."

Michael nods. "That tracks." He turns me out and then back in before he dips me at the end of the song. He stares in my eyes and adds, "I'll keep Adam's head on straight. He needs to do what he needs to do to be with you."

He lifts me to my feet as I ask, "What about Valerie?"

Michael trains his thoughtful gaze on the ocean in the distance. "I like Valerie, but those two are a hard-headed nightmare together. All they do is fight. Adam needs some calm and fun in his life." He shakes his head with a caged air that makes me wonder what he knows that I don't. Finally, he gazes down at me with a smile. "Adam needs someone who's up for adventure and who he can laugh with."

"I could use the same thing," I say with a grin.

Michael whisks me back to the table. "I like this one," he says to Adam.

Adam reaches for me, and I sit on his leg. "I do too," he says.

"Don't be late to set tomorrow," Michael instructs. "The schedule is packed. I was relieved to have a day off today. Really needed the recharge. This movie's been grueling."

Adam assures that he'll arrive early. Then he turns to me and smiles. "Want to have some fun?"

I grin. He pays the check. We say goodbye to Michael and leave the Beach Bar.

— —

We stroll down the boardwalk, the smell of kettle corn and cotton candy wafting by.

I'm smiling from ear to ear. *I haven't been this happy since homecoming.* The thought brings nagging guilt to the surface. *This is going to hurt Trey.* I shove the thought aside. "I've loved the Santa Monica Pier since I was little," I tell Adam.

He puts his arm around me. "I thought you might like this." He steers me to the roller coaster and pays for two tickets. We walk up the ramp, and there's no line. He gestures to the ride. "Your chariot, my lady."

I crack up and settle into the seat, pulling down the metal bar after he sits. The roller coaster starts clicking up the track to the top, and then we free-fall. Suddenly, I'm laughing and screaming. All the terror and insecurity finally leaves on a wave of happiness.

We get out of the roller-coaster car, and Adam takes my hand as we head through the exit turnstile. He guides me to the wood rail at the far side of the pier overlooking the ocean. He wraps his arms around me, holding me while we watch the waves.

The silence stretches, and I lean back against Adam, closing my eyes.

"Feel better?" he asks softly.

"You've fixed so much for me today."

"I know it's a little childish, but indulge me. I want to hear what I've fixed."

"You let me get my whole story out. You made the water something I can be content in. You stopped my maniacal heartbeat. You accepted everything I told you, without judgment. You taught me how some of this empathy works." I grin. "You balanced all the serious with the fun of the pier." I turn in his arms to look at him, raising an eyebrow. "You fixed the seething hormones that've been driving me bananas."

He blushes a touch.

"I'm sorry, am I hallucinating? Did Adam Stone just blush?"

He throws back his head and laughs. "Yes. I blushed . . . We both know I'm not exactly a stranger to amorous fun, but . . . you make me blush." He traces the curve of my jaw. "It's a good thing, for the record. It's different with you."

"I can't say it was different for me."

He looks shocked. "Wait . . . Are you saying that was your first time?"

"Yes, and I'm good."

"But Trey? I figured he eventually went for it."

I shake my head. "He never throws caution to the wind . . . at least with me."

"Yeah, the whole Tiffany situation floored me."

In agreement, I roll my eyes. "Everything's planned out, and yapped through, and contemplated a million times with him. It's freaking mind-numbing. So, to answer your question, no. Never with Trey."

He cups my chin. "You should have told me before. It's kind of a big deal."

I sigh. "I'm sorry, Adam. You had a right to know, but I'm tired of everyone trying to do what they think is right for me out of some sense of chivalrous obligation. I wanted to make my own decision without putting the pressure on you that you're standing here worrying about right now." I rise on my toes and kiss him. "I'm telling you that I'm legit good."

He exhales, relieved, but I can see the edges of guilt lacing his expression. "Trey's going to be pissed that I was your first."

This is uncomfortable enough that I decide to change the topic. "And . . . wait for it . . . this is the most important thing!" I grin. "You got me the most *fabulous* outfit I've *ever* worn." Gently, I push him back a step and pose like a ridiculous supermodel against the railing.

His surprised laughter belts again. "That is *definitely* what fixed things."

"Just imagine Tanner's face when he sees it," I joke. "The *jealousy*."

Adam is beaming as I turn around, and he wraps his arms around me from behind. We stare at the ocean.

He's radiating vulnerability as he says, "Don't leave me, Melanie. Be brave enough to destroy Valerie and Trey. If I lose you, I'm going to lose my mind."

CHAPTER 27

Everyone has gathered at Smokers' Corner behind the row of hedges that block the view from the school buildings. Darren lights up a smoke while Marcus passes out snacks from his backpack.

"That's not what you were wearing this morning," Trey says to me.

Adam smirks.

"No," I say flatly. "It's not."

Trey pensively says, "You smell like the ocean."

He hits Adam with a death glare, and Adam returns the sentiment. We're not going to make it five minutes before everyone figures out what's going on.

I take off my flip-flops and wiggle my toes in the grass.

Wistfully, Trey watches me. He scoots closer and asks, "Can I sit with you without creating an issue?"

When I nod, he reaches out to touch my arm. My darkwater side's calm. My gaze shifts subtly to Adam, who's watching us with a clenched jaw. The energy doesn't flare. Trey exhales. Unexpectedly, he wraps his arms around me and pulls me back against his chest. We've sat together this way a thousand times, but we're not dating anymore. I'm suddenly tense and uncomfortable.

Adam and I stare at each other from across the circle. Valerie and Trey are oblivious.

"Before we descend into hell together," Arch says, "Demitri, why don't you tell us what you know about Jessica."

Jessica? Who gives a damn? I've completely forgotten about Jessica and the Drone drama. I roll my eyes. *This is a waste of time.*

Adam grins and narrows his eyes. It's like he's read my mind again.

Or is he able to read more through the connection we have?

I send my curiosity down our connection, and he nods the slightest bit at me. He sends a less proper emotional vibe back my way. I bite my lip. He smirks at me before averting his eyes.

Hmmm . . . Interesting. It's not really like the emotional bubbles that Trey and I used to share. It's almost as if we can literally share our thoughts.

"Here's the scoop," Demitri says. "Jessica doesn't go to school here. She lied about that. She's dating—"

Trey cuts him off loudly. "JOEL! That's who she's dating! I knew I'd seen her! I was at a party this summer, and she was with him." He turns to Demitri. "I'm sorry for interrupting you. That's been nagging at me."

Demitri smiles. "Yup. She's Joel's girlfriend. She's also Stan's stepsister. That's how Joel and Jessica met. Jessica doesn't live with Stan's family most of the time, which is why she goes to another school. Anyhow, when Joel went to jail, Jessica was destroyed. The trial's coming up, and I knew there was trouble when I saw her confront Melanie at the auditions."

This sparks a memory. "All the insanity distracted me," I say. "I totally forgot to tell you guys! Marcus, have you told anyone about your dad's situation yet?"

Marcus shakes his head.

"Then do you want me to tell them what Bruce is up to?" I ask.

He sighs. "My dad got word that the state wasn't planning to prosecute Joel's case."

Our friends all holler in protest.

"But he talked to the attorney general," Marcus adds quickly, holding up his hands to calm the dissonance. "He and my dad went to law school together and have stayed close friends."

"Does that mean the trial's back on?" Hiram asks.

"Yeah, but the AG had one condition."

"What's that?"

Marcus sighs. "The AG has been trying to recruit my dad to run for district attorney for years. Our county had the position open up when the elected DA resigned. The AG told my dad that if he wanted to see Joel prosecuted, then he was going to have to accept a temporary appointment to the DA role."

Now everyone is hooting with excitement.

"That's incredible," Hiram says.

"Yeah," Marcus says. "Dad left one of the cushiest firms in the state and took up a thankless government job."

"Nice to know he hates Joel as much as we do," Adam offers.

Marcus shrugs. "No question. But the change is only temporary. His firm's giving him a leave of absence, and he's only the acting DA until the next elections. He doesn't plan to run for the office. He'll just go back to his old firm."

We're all nodding appreciatively.

"Anyway," Marcus continues, "I filled Dad in on Jessica showing up at auditions. He's going to come to Melanie's house after our next student council meeting to talk to us. He says Jessica's digging her own legal grave because she's going to be in hot water for threatening a witness. She's already on the list of people that the defense plans to call as character witnesses on Joel's side. Her little performance at auditions just cannonballed her credibility."

The energy shifts, and all eyes turn to me.

Bear hits me with a weighty expression. "Your turn, Melanie."

I sigh, not really wanting to do this. Having Demitri here only makes things more uncomfortable. I like him, and I think he understands me, but then again, he's new to hearing my dark secrets. My gaze slides to him, and he meets it without flinching.

"I know you," I say to him, "but I don't 'know you' know you, you know?"

Demitri's eyes light up. "I know you don't 'know me, know me,' but I *know*. You know?"

Everyone cracks up.

Tanner throws his hands in the air, triumphantly exclaiming, "Melanie's speaking in witty riddles again! She's back!"

There's a part of me that wants to dismiss this idea, but here with my friends, I do feel a little like my old self again.

"Cactus Cooler, Fraggle," Demitri says as we study each other.

My attention snaps to Isaac, and my eyes narrow. I really don't know him at all.

Arch sighs exasperatedly, anticipating what's coming. "Can we not go through another round?"

I glare at Arch. "I'm incredibly private about my personal hell, Arch."

Arch gestures Isaac's way. "He was around through all the hospital drama, Mel. Isaac's been completely on board."

Trey jumps in. "Isaac helped me through the whole ordeal. He spent the night at my house several times to get me through the worst of it."

"Really?" I say to Isaac, my tone blazing with condescension. "How nice. Let me guess! You encouraged him to buy a season pass to Tiffany's amusement park since I was conveniently out of the way."

Isaac's eyes widen, and he shakes his head. "I'll level with you, Mel."

I glare. "It's Melanie to you."

He clears his throat. "My apologies." He gives me a pointed look and corrects himself. "Melanie." He raises his hands in a friendly gesture of peace. "I'm the only one in the group that knew about Tiffany. I tried regularly to steer Trey away from her. She's a nice girl, but she lacks the depth you have. I knew he was making a mistake."

I glare at Trey, who nods, radiating emotional exhaustion. "That's all true. Isaac was on Team Mel the whole time."

I survey Isaac before holding out my hand. When he hesitantly takes it, I smile the slightest bit. "Mel," I say, shaking his hand. "Nice to meet you."

Isaac smiles. "Thank you. I know I'm the new guy, but I've got your back."

This is all I need to hear to regain the confidence to do what must be done. I fill them in with just enough details to satisfy their curiosity, nothing more.

Suddenly, right as I get started on the explanation, an old enemy appears from behind the hedges. Victoria assumes a wide-legged stance, aggressively glaring at me with her arms crossed over her straining crop top.

Presley snorts. "Look! One of my biggest annoyances just popped up from the dark water."

Everyone cracks up.

Dark-Water Melanie rides in on a bitchy wave of the uppers as I glare at Victoria. My heart starts racing again as an evil scowl graces my lips.

"I know you love her," Victoria says to Trey.

Tanner rattles his head, his face awash with a hilariously baffled expression. He throws up his hands. "What in fresh *hell*! Thank you, Little Miss Random, for that fascinating tidbit!"

Victoria hits him with blazing eyes. "Can it, David Bowie. I'm trying to do something nice."

Marcus cracks up and waves a half-chewed Twizzler her way. "Obviously," he says sarcastically.

Victoria surveys my crowd. Her gaze stops on Isaac, and her eyes narrow. She skeptically asks, "What the hell are *you* doing here, Isaac?"

Isaac shrugs, refusing to answer.

Arch snaps, "Get on with it, or leave."

Victoria rolls her eyes. "Bring me Melanie's backpack," she says to Trey.

My ex-boyfriend looks baffled. "You have ZERO clue how bad your timing is, Tori."

Victoria levels him with a serious look. "I've loved you since the first day I saw you," she says with sorrow. "I miss you every single day, but I can see that Melanie's the one for you."

What does this have to do with anything?

Demitri stares at Victoria like she's lost her mind. "*Seriously*, Victoria! This isn't a good time."

"Let me finish!" Victoria snaps. She looks at Trey again like they're the only two people in Smokers' Corner. "I saw what happened to you when she was in the hospital, and I don't want her to die, because it'll destroy you. Bring it to me."

Trey glances from Victoria to me. Then, to my surprise, he stands, grabs my backpack, and hands it to her. I don't fight it because I have a feeling I know what she's doing. She opens each section, searching, but doesn't find what she's looking for.

Just as a look of disappointment crosses Victoria's face, Adam unzips his backpack, takes out the pill bottle, and tosses it by Trey's feet.

I send a pulse of irritation down the connection I share with Adam.

"Better to get it over with," Adam says aloud.

I sigh.

"That's why Melanie's been acting like such a crazed monster lately," Victoria announces. "Tad just told me he's been selling them to her. So, I came to warn you guys." She turns to look at me, her gaze intense. "Those things will kill you. My aunt's addicted to them. She's in rehab right now."

Shocked, Trey examines the bottle for a moment before turning a grateful gaze on Victoria. "Thank you, Tori."

"You're welcome." Her expression shifts, and she levels me with a snotty look. "Get your shit together, Melanie, so I can respect you again."

I glare at her but have nothing to say.

Trey says again, a little harsher this time, "THANK YOU, VICTORIA."

Tanner stands and dramatically bows in her direction. "You're dismissed."

As soon as Victoria leaves, Trey whips around and tosses the pill bottle in the grass in front of me.

"Mystery solved," Marcus crows.

Trey fumes at me. "Have you COMPLETELY lost your mind?"

"Yes."

Adam rubs his face with his hands to cover a laugh.

Trey radiates fury at me. "The doctor was CRYSTAL clear that you can't take ANY addictive substances!" He takes a giant breath. "YOU CAN'T EVEN TAKE COLD MEDICINE UNTIL HE CLEARS IT!"

Finley scoots over next to me and puts a comforting arm around my shoulders. She looks up at him and says, "This isn't the time, Trey."

"NOT THE TIME?" He hits Finley with a death glare. "When was the time, Finley? When she was sedated? During the, I don't know, DOZEN seizures she had? How about when she DIED in my arms in the hospital while I tried ILLEGALLY to get her out from under sedation?"

The difference between how Adam handled the news and Trey's reaction says it all. I raise an eyebrow and sarcastically snarl, "Perhaps the time was when you were screwing Tiffany."

He glares at me.

"When did you start taking the pills?" Finley asks.

"The morning after Trey filled me in that he was Tiffany's personal carnival ride."

Finley hits Trey with her infamous "disappointed mom" look.

Trey throws up his hands. "That's your excuse? REALLY!"

"We're all in this now," Arch cuts in. "You've shouldered a huge burden, Trey, but you don't have to do it on your own anymore. You got Melanie this far, and we're all going to help pull her to the finish line."

Um, Adam's already doing that for me.

"You have *no* idea how hard this has been," Trey says with teary eyes.

"You both just told us," Arch says. "We know."

You know nothing.

I accidently send the sentiment down the shared connection with Adam, and he coughs, covering a laugh.

I smirk.

Arch looks from Trey to me. "We've got your back."

I stand, intending to walk away. My intuition flares as I look past the hedges. Jessica's slinking across the expansive field like a mountain lion ready to strike. I grab the pill bottle, opening it and popping two of the evil little magic machines before closing the cap and tossing the bottle to Trey.

He catches the bottle. "Two for the road?" he asks sarcastically.

My heart starts racing with battle rage. "The last two I'll ever take. I need them right now, but I'm done with them. Toss the bottle. This is over."

"Thank God we're through," Trey says with condescending relief.

My heart constricts, but there's no time to wrap my mind around his statement because my intuition blazes again. I have to fight not to double over around the pain that comes with it. *This is about to be bad, and Jessica's the least of my worries.*

Having heard my thought, Adam side-eyes me and stands.

This connection's going to get messy if I don't figure out how to selectively send stuff. Two pills were a bad idea. *Too late.* My heart starts racing as my entire body seethes and churns. My hands shake as I slip on my flip-flops.

"Please sit," Bear says.

"I can't," I snarl. "Jessica's coming this way."

Everyone jumps up, turning to look past the hedges.

"I'm right behind you," Adam says as I start moving toward my enemy.

CHAPTER 28

"YOU DID THIS!" Jessica pulls a switchblade out of her pocket and snaps it open.

Wonderful.

Adam sends a nervous pulse down our connection. I ignore it.

"We talk first," I inform Jessica. "And if you aren't satisfied, then you get your way, and we fight. Something tells me you don't know the whole story."

"I know that you put Joel in jail," she spits. "He told me what happened. YOU hit on him and then tried to jump off the balcony when he said no. He tried to SAVE you, and you LIED ABOUT HIM."

You've got to be kidding!

Presley bursts out laughing. "Riiiight, that's why he was all black and blue from a fight. Think about it, chick. Joel's a lying sack of . . ."

Jessica cuts her off and points the knife at Presley, venom dripping from her voice as she screams, "LIAR!"

I gesture for my friends to quiet down, and in a calm tone, I ask, "Are you aware that Joel attempted to rape me?"

That's the end of the rational conversation. Jessica lunges at me. "Yeeessss!" I hiss as I side-skirt the knife.

From the way she tumbles past me, it's immediately clear that she has no idea how to use that thing.

Perfect!

My heart pounds like a semitruck speeding downhill. My poorly controlled shield drops, and every ounce of rage, frustration, fear, being in love with Adam, and my internal panic about Trey and Valerie roars to the surface with such ferocity that it makes me dizzy.

Focus!

I feel Adam doing something through the connection, and suddenly, everything I'm blasting is somehow blocked from everyone else feeling it.

No time to think about that now because Jessica barrels toward me with the knife.

I spin, grab her wrist, twist the knife from her grasp, and toss it down at her feet. "Your first mistake was threatening me with your pathetic little notes," I snarl at her. "Your second mistake was coming here. Your third mistake was not learning how to use that knife before you pointed it at me."

Before she can react, my self-defense training kicks in. I sweep her legs and dump her on her back. She hits the ground hard, knocking the air out of her. Before she can catch her breath, I lunge, kneel on her chest, and press hard with my knee.

She gasps.

I press harder. "I swear to GOD," I growl, "you have to be the stupidest girl on the planet! You have ZERO clue what lives in me!"

Her eyes are wide with terror. "Can we go back to talking?" she chokes out.

"Hell no. You wanted it this way, and you've got it!"

"I'm sorry . . ."

She loses her voice as I push hard off her and stand. Adam's behind me. He puts his hands on my shoulders. His matching rage fuels me.

"The next time you come for me, you better bring more than a knife." I point down at Jessica. "Remember my face! Memorize it, because it'll be the last thing you see if you come for me again."

Her mouth drops open.

"You thought you were going to prance in here and have a bullshit hair-pulling catfight? You've got the wrong girl."

My friends' faces are slack with shock at my death threat. Only Adam is grinning.

I take a few steps away before turning back to Jessica. "Pass on the message to Stan and any of the others trying to take us out. You tell them I'm ready anytime, any day." Just as I finish the threat, I catch movement out of the corner of my eye.

Marcus screeches, "Wait! Are the Drones threatening to *kill* us?"

There's no time to respond. Security, administration, and police are flooding the far side of the field. It takes me only a second to realize that it has something to do with me.

"What now?" My intuition blazes to life again, and my stomach knots with fear.

"What is it?" Adam whispers.

"Something bad is about to happen."

An ambulance pulls onto the field. Ms. G, Principal Walker, and Mr. Bentley rush toward us with Susan in tow. My heart is pounding almost out of my chest as I wait for the inevitable.

Ms. G reaches our crowd, draws a breath to speak, but then falters when she notices Jessica. "Who are you?"

"I'm not a student here. I'm sorry! I'll leave." Jessica rolls onto her knees in an effort to stand, and there in the grass beside her glints the knife.

"Did she hurt you, Melanie?" Ms. G asks me with wide eyes.

My laugh is laced with a sinister vibe. "She didn't stand a chance," I say with a glare at Jessica.

"Explain yourself," Ms. G demands of my enemy.

"My name's Jessica. If you let me leave, I promise I won't mess with Melanie again."

The dark water is raging. Jessica shrinks as I take two menacing steps her way.

"I wish you would," I tell her. "This isn't done. I'll hunt your sorry ass if I have to. But it's easier if you come to me."

Ms. G reaches toward me and sets two fingers on my neck, checking my pulse. "Your heart is racing."

I glower at her, all sense of rules and manners washed away on the raging adrenaline. Ms. G waits for a response, but I say nothing.

Finally, she sighs. "Susan overheard a conversation between Tad and Victoria, and she came to us with her concerns. Rumor is you're on drugs, Melanie. Judging from what I just saw, I'd say it's a distinct possibility the rumor is true."

I shift my gaze to Susan and say with a clipped tone, "You can't ever mind your own business, can you, you candy-ass nightmare?"

Susan cowers. "I was worried. I wanted to help."

"You need to think up a few ways to help yourself the next time I catch you alone."

Ms. G grabs my arms. "Look at me, Melanie."

My hard and unflinching gaze slides to Ms. G.

"We're sending you to the county hospital for evaluation."

The paramedics step forward as terror washes through me.

I shake my head rapidly. "You can't send me to county. *You don't understand!* I'm not safe at that hospital."

The second the words tumble from my lips, I know it was a mistake to speak them. My eyes snap to Jessica, and she's smirking at me. It doesn't take a genius to know that she'll tell Joel's family that I'm back at the county hospital so they can get their hired assassin back on her mission.

Being cuffed by the police doesn't faze Jessica a bit. She's escorted off as Adam loudly attempts to inform the police, "There are things you need to know."

The officers pay him no heed as they haul her away.

Ms. G thinks I'm just arguing because I'm scared of detox. She doesn't know there's an employee at county who's trying to kill me.

"It's school district policy," Ms. G explains. "I'm legally bound to send you, and the county hospital is the designated place we're authorized to use."

All hell breaks loose as I turn to run. Trey and Adam both reach for me, but the paramedics and two police officers grab me first, wrestling me to the ambulance.

I scream and buck. "You don't UNDERSTAND!"

One of the paramedics says, "Don't worry. It's going to be okay."

I turn just before the ambulance doors close and watch as Trey takes off running at full speed to the student parking lot with Adam on his heels.

CHAPTER 29

The door closes with a solid thud, leaving me alone. I turn, my heart pounding as I survey the room. White walls, a white bed with no sheets, and a tiny bathroom.

I sit on the plastic mattress in my hospital-issued white shirt, loose white pants, and slip-on white sandals. I'm not allowed shoelaces or sheets because I'm on suicide watch. I tried to explain that I'm not suicidal, but the nurse divulged that many patients become suicidal as they go through the detox program.

Adam said something similar. How could it possibly be that bad?

My head slumps. The pills are still racing through my system, but I've only been on them a few weeks. There's no way I'm that thoroughly addicted yet. I was off the sedatives for a full week before I started on the pills. I think I'm going to be okay.

Yeah, as long as Jessica somehow misses the opportunity to tell the killer hospital employee that I'm locked in here.

I allow myself a moment of hope that maybe she wouldn't have had a chance to get the word out after being hauled off to juvenile lockup. Then it occurs to me that she'd get at least one phone call . . .

I gasp, fear boiling up with the realization that I'm truly trapped in here. The walls are thick enough that, as the paramedics walked me to my new room, even though I could clearly see several other patients . . . *inmates* . . . through the little windows on each door, I couldn't hear them screaming at the top of their lungs.

I'm one hundred percent alone. My dark-water abyss has been replaced with a bright-white hell.

Overtaken by panicked gasps, I'm so scared I can't even cry. I lie down on the plastic mattress, trying to calm my frazzled nerves.

Think, Melanie. What's the plan?

Okay . . . let's consider this rationally. I need to worry about the person trying to kill me who works in this building. That means I can't sleep, but I won't be able to anyway until the pills wear off in my system.

Tears well up, spilling in long wet rivers down both cheeks. I double over and curl up in a ball, making a keening sound. My heart feels like it's going to explode.

I wonder how Adam and Trey are handling this.

I know they're both losing their minds.

Trey's voice sounds out in my head, a memory from when I was on the balcony after Joel tried to kill me. *Melanie, you're in shock. I need you to look at me. Breathe in . . . out . . . in . . . out.*

What am I going to do?

I cry until the plastic mattress runs wet from my tears.

The door opens, and a nurse enters. She hands me a little paper cup. "Pill time. We're giving you something to take the edge off so you can sleep."

I take the cup and thank her politely, then put the pill in my mouth and let it tuck into my cheek by my teeth. I take the water cup she offers and sip. She checks under my tongue to make sure it's gone, then leaves.

It's only the first night, and I'm already sick of this.

I walk into the bathroom and close the door behind me. I spit the pill into my hand, toss it in the toilet, and flush it down.

No sleeping pills. Don't know who I can trust.

— —

The last of the uppers are fading from my system. My hands are shaking. So far, this hasn't been as bad as the doctor and Adam warned me about. I haven't thrown up, had insane sweating episodes, seizures, panic attacks, or attempted suicide yet.

— —

I throw up again, my body sweating so profusely that I feel like I'm cooking from the inside.

I swear I'll never touch another substance again if I can just get through this.

— —

Oh my God! I didn't know my stomach could hurt this bad.

I writhe in the blanket-less bed, the plastic mattress covered in sweat.

— —

I can't keep my eyes open.

I made it through three full days, but the lack of sleep is catching up now that the pills have worked their way out of my system.

Just before sleep carries me away, my heart pounds, knowing that the dark water is waiting, and a homicidal hospital employee may sneak up on me at any moment.

Sleep takes me.

— —

The dark water closes over my head, sloshing and reeling.

Adam isn't here to help me!

Darkness consumes me as the image of Joel floats closer in the water. I propel myself backward, pushing hard off nothing solid. Joel follows, getting closer and closer. Finally, he grabs me, and I scream before I'm hurled into the darkest part of the oily water abyss.

— —

I wake all at once, gasping. I glance frantically around the room, searching irrationally for Joel. I know it's not possible for him to follow me out of the dream, but so much has been crazy lately that I can't rule out the irrational.

Alone. I'm alone.

A moment of relief washes over me. I gaze out the window for the fifth night in a row, the half-moon shining bright on the other side of the glass. It looks close enough to touch. Tears fall, sliding into my hand that's resting under my head.

— —

. . . seven, eight, nine, ten.

My feet drop to the floor. I stretch my sore arms.

Another set.

I grab the upended bed rail and hoist myself up, my legs bent at the knees so they don't touch the floor. I'm short, and when tipped on its end like this, the bed is perfectly weighted to handle chin-ups. This is what it has come to without dance to keep me fit. I've resorted to creative exercise using what little I have to work with in this room.

One, two, three, four . . .

The door opens. It's Nurse Jacobs.

"Melanie, I told you that you can't turn your bed on its end like that."

I'm so sick of this. "Yes, ma'am. I apologize." I drop my feet to the floor and wipe the sweat from my forehead.

Nurse Jacobs smiles at me endearingly. "Between us, I don't care, but administration has all these rules."

"I'm not always good at following rules," I say with an apologetic smile, "but I'm trying. I just need something to keep me busy."

"I understand. I know it gets dull in here." She hands me a piece of paper. "Your one-week blood work is in. You're detoxed."

Hope rises. "Think I'll get out of here soon?"

Nurse Jacobs shakes her head. "We have a two-week minimum. So far, you're on track. It's not up to me, though."

Another week of this hell. I'm going to lose my mind. "I understand. Thank you for keeping me updated. I always look forward to your early morning shift."

She chuckles. "How are you getting along with the night-shift nurse?"

"Do you want the real answer or the proper answer?" I ask with an amused half smile.

"The real answer."

I pointedly inform, "She's a miserable troll who chooses to be nasty and rude to me. I pretend I'm asleep when she comes in to avoid any unnecessary chatter."

Nurse Jacobs grins. "That's about right." She squeezes my hand. "I have something else for you." She takes the plastic bag she'd hung on the doorknob and hands it to me. When I look quizzically at her, she laughs and explains, "I thought you might want a little piece of home. Your boyfriend . . . boyfriends?"

I huff and shake my head.

"Sounds complicated. Anyhow, they're both about to drive us nuts with calls for updates. I gave in and let the Trey boyfriend bring this by."

They haven't forgotten me! I smile. "What's in here?"

"The rules are no weapons, no food, no drugs. Everything else is fair game."

Nurse Jacobs leaves with a parting wave, the door closing behind her.

I turn, setting down the bag, and heft the bed off its end, down to its proper position. I return the plastic mattress to its spot on the frame and then pick up the sack and settle on the bed. I take a deep breath before opening the bag and looking in. On top is a notebook and pen. On the first page of the notebook, in my mom's loopy handwriting:

A journal. I know you love to write.
We love and miss you! Mom.

I tear up a touch as I trace my mom's writing with my finger. I set the notebook and pen on the bed.

Next out of the bag is a CD. Written with a Sharpie on the case is, *Happy music. One day at a time, Meley. Love, Demitri.*

I smile. Apparently, I'm now "Meley" to Demitri, and I love it.

Next come a Discman and headphones. A sticky note reads, *You need some music. Love, Hiram.* I grin and push the button to open the lid. Inside is a homemade CD with the names of our group's favorite songs.

A thick photocopied packet follows. The cover page reads, *The Pajama Game*. The sticky note on the bottom corner says, *You're Poopsie. Get your lines memorized. Sending good vibes. Ms. Ferry.*

I got the part!

Now that I'm not on the pills, I find myself caring about the show. Studying these lines will give me something to do in the coming days. I set the script down and reach into the bag again. Out comes another stack of papers in Trey's handwriting. I fan through the pages, and there's at least twenty of them. It looks like a letter.

He wrote me all this?

My heart races with conflict. It feels different from the pill-induced heart racing. I close my eyes, relieved to feel normal again, even if my current version of normal means being lonely, torn, and isolated.

I set the letter down and glance in the bag again. A sealed manila envelope. I open it to discover a smaller sealed envelope inside. Inside this one is another note. Adam's harsh, slanted, handwriting stares back at me.

I laugh. *He double sealed it so Trey couldn't read it.*

I set Adam's letter next to Trey's and stare at them with a racing heart. I start to pick up Trey's letter but can't bring myself to read it. *I'm not ready to face this. I have time, what with being locked up another week. I need to wait until I can handle all these conflicting emotions.* I stack the letters and shove them aside.

There's one more thing in the bag. I pull out a copy of the picture my friends and I posed for at homecoming. My vision blurs with a fresh bout of tears as my friends' grinning faces stare back at me. I set the picture aside, curl up, and sob.

———

The black water rises again. I battle the growing terror.

Remember what Adam said. When the dark water is scary, he's holding me in the ocean and it's all okay.

I float without fighting the push and pull, relinquishing control.

Melanie,

I love you. I want you to know how sorry I am for every-thing that's happened. I feel terrible about the Tiffany situation, and I'll do anything to make this better. I'm trying to get you out of there, but it's a mess.

I'm lost.

I promise I'll be there when you get out. We need to talk.

Adam told me that you explained everything. He's not doing well through this. I guess it's affecting our friends as much as it is me . . .

Melanie,

You have no clue how much I love you. It's hell not being there while you detox.

I haven't told Trey or Valerie yet. I thought long and hard about it and decided to wait until you're there to do it with me. You've said that Trey made a lot of the decisions in your relationship, and I don't want it to be like that with us. You're my equal, so I'm not going to wrap you in bubble wrap and tuck you away to protect you. You're stronger than he gives you credit for.

Look out your window on Saturday night at nine . . .

I set the letter aside and check the clock on the wall. It's 9:03. I stand from the bed and cross to the window. There, on the street below, is Adam leaning against the seat of his Harley, waiting. He looks up at me, so close but unreachable.

The dark-water distance has invaded my waking life.

The nearly full moon casts him in soft-blue shadows. He sends a pulse of love along the connection we share, and it faintly reaches me, even with the physical distance.

A sob nearly doubles me over. My chest is seizing up. I bend at the waist, trying to relearn how to breathe. Tears pour down my cheeks as I finally stand and look down at him again. I send a matching pulse back, but I know it's laced with desperation and fear because I'm not good at separating everything yet. Adam's shoulders slump as it reaches him, and I can tell even from this distance that he's fighting to breathe around it.

Adam rallies, stands up straight, and flashes devil horns my way. It's a sign my group shares when we need to kick ass. I smile through the tears and hold up my hand, returning the devil horns. Adam stares at me for another long moment before swinging his leg over the Harley. It revs, and he rumbles out of sight.

I lean against the wall by the window. Slowly, I slide down to the floor, curl into a ball, and cry.

⸺ ⸺

Movement!

I wake with an internal start but hold myself as still as possible in the pitch-black.

I let my guard down. Shouldn't have turned out the light.

To my left, a rustle of clothes moving stealthily in the dark alerts me. The slightest square of light from the hall filters through the tiny window on the door. I blink as my eyes adjust and faintly make out someone creeping slowly toward me. My blanket that I was finally granted lies over me, but I make a mental note that my left foot is free.

Don't get your other foot tangled in the blanket when the fight starts.

Adrenaline pumps through my veins. I welcome my dark-water side as it oozes up from within me.

The intruder gets close enough that I can faintly see her light-blue scrubs.

Curvy hips. Definitely female. Her body type fits Adam's description.

She reaches into her pocket and pulls something out. The familiar click of a cap pulled from the syringe follows.

This is it.

I wait, barely breathing, until she gets close enough. Silently, I lash out and grab her outstretched arm, yanking hard to throw her off-balance. I unintentionally use too much force. She flies over the bed, hitting my right side before she topples head over feet to the floor. She squeals. I jump up and rush to the light switch.

Light floods the room.

The woman blinks through her disorientation as she hops up. She smiles professionally as she smooths down her scrubs. "I'm so sorry I scared you. I'm the night nurse."

"Wrong. The night nurse is a cow with a surly attitude. She's lazy and doesn't come in here more than she has to." I appraise her. "You're an unwelcome new cow." I glance up at the clock. "It's two in the morning."

The lady looks unsure of herself. She moves her hand subtly behind her back.

"I know exactly who you are."

The nurse's eyes widen a touch.

"You're who the Stamp family hired to kill me." I gesture toward her arm behind her back. "Which metal is it you've got in that syringe? Mercury, I'd guess, since it stays in liquid form at room temperature."

Her mouth drops open.

My dark-water side shines from my eyes as I purr, "I've been stuck in here for eleven days . . . I'm boooored."

Doubt creeps into her eyes. "Melanie, let's talk about this."

Blasé, I shake my head. "I don't have any questions. Since it looks like I'm right about everything, let's have some fun."

She radiates fear as she starts slowly making her way toward the door.

I counter by darting over to block her exit. "Uh-uh-uh. You came in here for a reason." I grin. "What's the matter? It's not fun for you if I'm not helplessly asleep?"

"You're supposed to be on sleeping pills at night."

"There are a lot of things I'm supposed to do," I growl.

The nurse looks genuinely scared.

She should be. I look her up and down. "I've cleaned younger, stronger clocks than yours." I point up to the camera mounted in the corner of the room. "But I've never had it videotaped before."

She glances at the camera. Her face turns sheet white.

"You don't work in the detox ward, apparently, or you'd know they monitor us. Well, kind of. They never seem to check until later." I give a sadistic grin.

Her mouth opens and closes, but she doesn't produce a coherent thought.

"That little voice in your head that's telling you to talk, or walk, your way out of this . . . It's not serving your best interests. Pay attention to the other voice that's telling you that the money wasn't worth it. Sure, you're going to lose your career . . . that is, if you make it out of this room in one piece. That's what you need to be worried about right now."

Fear rolls off her in waves. I've spent the past few days shielding and working through my empathic issues. Adam put instructions in his letter on how to control the energy. Thanks to him, I've got my control back. Well, thanks to him and all the time on my hands. Being locked in a cinder block room with nothing but time has its perks.

Suddenly, she rushes me with the syringe over her head. I wait, playing chicken with her. She gets to me, and I grab her hand, slamming it against the wall. The syringe flies across the room, out of reach. She squeals.

What a moron. If she can't even fight, then why would she agree to this job? I spin her around and slam her face into the wall.

She drops to her knees and screams for help.

I grab her by the hair and yank her head back, forcing her to stare into my eyes. "They can't hear you. These rooms are sound-proof." I grin maniacally. "I paid attention as I was brought into this rehab ward. Each door requires a swipe with an ID badge. That means you have identification on you." I lean down and snarl in her face, "I highly recommend you fight like hell to get out of here, because if you lose, I'll know who you are."

She turns an even paler ghostly gray and gasps as I yank her to the side. With all my adrenaline-fueled strength, I send her sliding across the floor. I race to catch up to her, then give her a hard kick in the side. She grabs her rib cage and moans.

"Get up!"

She stares at me, her mouth hanging open. "Aren't you a teenager?"

A baffled expression contorts my face. "And?"

She glares at me. "Tiny teenagers shouldn't be this hard to take out."

I tip my head back, enjoying the giggle that escapes. Her eyes widen with fear at the sound of my teen laughter.

"The person who hired you forgot to clue you in. I've been through a lot. I didn't make it this far by hiding behind my mama, my daddy, or my boyfriend."

She puts her hands up in surrender. "If you'll let me go, I won't ever come back. I just needed the money. It was a mistake." She scampers back, attempting to flee.

I cross the distance to her, crooning, "A hustler's gotta hustle," before I hit her with a right hook that knocks her out cold. I shake the pain out of my throbbing hand and crouch down to collect her security badge. "Nice to meet you, Betty."

Nurse Jacobs comes through the door with my breakfast tray. She stops short and stares in shock at the nurse tied to the bars on the window with my bed sheets. It was only a few minutes ago that the nurse woke, yet again, and I knocked her out, yet again. The syringe, still full of the poison, is sitting at her feet.

"What happened here, Melanie?"

I push away from the wall. "Almost two months ago, I was admitted to this hospital for a nervous breakdown. I was released early because someone on the staff was trying to poison me, but we didn't know who." I hold up the sleeping nurse's security badge that I found in her pocket. "Now we do."

Nurse Jacobs's eyes widen, and she sets the breakfast tray down on my rolling table.

"Would you call Dr. Bryant on the second floor? He can confirm my story."

She looks from me to the unconscious intruder, unsure what to do.

I snort. "I'm good with a knot. She's not going anywhere. If she wakes up, believe me, I can handle it."

Nurse Jacobs practically flies out the door.

— —

Nurse Jacobs, Dr. Bryant, and two security officers rush through the door.

"Melanie, I'm so sorry." Dr. Bryant says once he's done surveying the situation. "No one told me you were in here." He mutters almost as if to himself, "If this hospital's wards ever communicated with each other, I could have . . ." He goes quiet, guilt sweeping across his face. "Are you okay?"

"I am." I jut a thumb at the still-unconscious nurse. "Can't say the same for Betty, though."

Security goes to the sagging nurse. One of them picks up the syringe and hands it to Dr. Bryant, who says, "I'll take this to the lab and have it tested. I'm going to get you out of here, Melanie. Hang tight."

The security officers haul the slowly reviving Nurse Betty up. She moans. She's rather unceremoniously dumped on a gurney, each of her wrists handcuffed to the rails on either side. One of the security officers takes the ID badge from me and snorts. "Betty Golbreth," he says to the other security guard. "If this is her actual badge, she's an idiot."

The second beefcake of a guard disdainfully glances down at Nurse Betty. "I guarantee she's an idiot. For the record, I've never seen anything like this in my fifteen years here." He gives his fellow guard a pointed look. "Lesson time, rookie. This ward has the tightest security in the hospital. She had to enter a code that coordinates with her badge at the first door, and the patient's door requires a thumbprint certification that matches the badge."

The security guards maneuver the gurney around. She's wheeled out, leaving Nurse Jacobs looking at me with her mouth hanging open.

"Let me get this straight," she says. "You were brought in here and locked up helplessly, knowing that someone on this staff was trying to kill you?"

I nod.

Nurse Jacobs crosses the room and hugs me. "I'm sorry, Melanie. Trey called and warned the staff that he was scared you'd end up dead, but we thought it was just a ploy to get you released." She grins, hitting me with an amused gaze. "Then Adam called and spoke with me later that day. He told me you were likely to kill the intruder, and I needed to know that it's self-defense instead of murder." She raises an eyebrow. "If you're struggling to decide between those two, I'd say Adam knows you better."

"I know," I respond softly.

She gestures to the items from my care package. "How about you gather your stuff? I'm going to get your clothes for you to change into." She grins. "Dr. Bryant is a force to be reckoned with. I suspect you're about to go home shortly."

I exhale, relieved to be almost free of this white room.

Nurse Jacobs turns on her heel and leaves briskly.

— —

My sweats, California Dreaming shirt, and flip-flops from the Monday I was carted here are a welcome relief. The shirt still smells like the ocean.

"You ready to bust out of this joint?" Nurse Jacobs asks.

I grab my bag full of the things my friends sent me during lockup. "Yes, ma'am."

She swings the door wide for me. I turn one last time to stare at the room that held me captive.

"What is it, Melanie?" Nurse Jacobs asks.

"This room's been hell, but it's also taught me a whole lot about myself." I send a silent pulse of positivity, leaving it in the room for the next person who's locked in these four walls.

We turn and walk down the hall together. Nurse Jacobs leads me to an elevator, and we descend two floors. She guides me off. We turn right instead of continuing the elevator ride to the ground floor. I glance at her quizzically.

"We're headed to the security viewing room," she explains.

We walk up to an open door, and I hear my voice from inside the room: "The person who hired you forgot to clue you in. I've been through a lot. I didn't make it this far by hiding behind my mama, my daddy, or my boyfriend."

Trey, Adam, Mom, and Rich are staring at a TV screen with their backs to me. I watch as my image slinks aggressively away from the camera toward Nurse Betty. I smile, knowing what's coming.

"A hustler's gotta hustle."

Rich cracks up. "That's my kid!"

The beefcake security officer hits a button on the VCR, and my image freezes mid-punch, just as Nurse Betty's about to hit the floor.

Trey rubs his face. "I love your daughter more than anything."

Adam inhales hard.

"I know you do," Rich says.

"I love you guys too," I say from the doorway.

They turn in unison, all smiles. Mom crosses the room to give me a hug.

Rich follows. "Are you okay?"

I nod and smile. "I'm legit good."

Now to face the boys and figure this out. I turn and survey the rest of my company. The guys both have dark circles under their eyes. They look like hell warmed over. The difficulty of the rehab ordeal is written all over their faces.

Adam raises an amused eyebrow. "A hustler's gotta hustle?"

I laugh. "I don't know where that came from, but I admit I enjoyed it at the time."

Trey laughs. He shakes his head as he crosses the room and pulls me in for a hug.

"Let's let Melanie catch up with Adam for a moment," Mom suggests. "We want to talk to you about something, Trey."

They leave the room, the door closing after them.

That's convenient.

Adam rushes to me, grabs my face, and kisses me. He slides his hands along my back, and my dark-water spark flares. I clamp down, shielding it off.

He slumps and whispers, "Don't shut it down."

I smile against his shoulder and whisper back, "You sure?"

"I'm sure."

I let my shield down, and the energy folds around both of us, but it's not manic anymore.

His eyebrows rise. "You've been working on what I wrote."

I nod and kiss him again. "Thank you, Adam." I send a pulse of love down the line we share, and he smiles, cupping my face and staring into my eyes.

He sends a pulse back, but it holds an uncertain edge. I give him a quizzical look as my eyes unfocus and I study the sentiment.

He clamps down tight, shutting off his side of the connection, but it's too late.

He's unsure about him and me. My heart starts racing, but there's no time to ask him if it's true.

We hear Dr. Bryant on the other side of the closed door. "We've got the evidence. The syringe had the exact same poison that was in Melanie's blood draw lab results. Nurse Betty is going to prison."

Adam opens the door, and we join everyone in the hall.

Trey exhales. "One problem down. Who knows how many more to go."

Mom smiles. "It's only ten in the morning. We asked Trey to take you for a nice day out."

No. This is the last thing I need right now. I need to talk to Adam. The flicker of uncertainty that I felt from him is nagging at me. "You sure?" I ask. "I know you and Rich probably want some time to catch up with me, and Trey needs to get to school."

Trey chuckles. "I'm not going to school today."

"We'll catch up with you tonight," Mom says.

I pulse down the line to Adam, telling him how much I don't want to do this, but he's so closed off that there's no response. He hugs me, slips a little paper in my hand discreetly, and turns to leave. I watch him walk down the hall and disappear through the door to a stairway. My heart nearly explodes.

Trey leads me down the hall. The moment the elevator door closes, Trey starts yammering desperately about how we need to fix things. I take the opportunity of his distraction to open the note next to my hip. I discreetly glance down and read it where he can't see it.

Midnight. Be ready.

I stuff the note in my pocket just as Trey unexpectedly leans down and kisses me.

CHAPTER 30

Exactly at midnight, Adam pulls up in his rarely seen vintage roadster. I push away from the railing and walk down the brick pathway.

"No Harley tonight?"

"No Harley. I needed to bring some things with me." He glances down at me and asks with a carefully controlled expression, "How did it go with Trey?"

"Awkward." *Just ask him. It's driven you bonkers all day.* "I felt your uncertainty about me earlier. It's driving me nuts."

"We'll discuss it."

I shake my head, my heart about to hammer out of my chest. "Just tell me, Adam. If you're breaking up with me, I need to know now."

Adam tips his head back and inhales. Finally, he wraps his arms around me and answers, "I'm not breaking up with you. I'm doubting myself."

"You're doubting us?"

"Yes and no. Anyway, I want to get out of sight in case your parents wake up."

He opens the passenger door, and I slide in.

Adam gets in, starts the engine, and pulls away from the curb. After a long silence, he finally says, "You were gone for nearly two weeks. I started to wonder if I'd made the connection up in my mind." He glances my way.

"What do you need?"

"I need to know how you feel about me."

"You already know, Adam."

"I know, but you being locked in detox screwed me up. It was too soon after we figured out what we had. I had to sit there and watch Trey spiral."

I laugh. "Sounds about right."

"Anyhow, he went on and on about your connection, and I started to doubt myself."

"What did you do when you doubted us?"

He sighs. "Can we skip this part?"

"No."

"I spent a lot of time with Valerie, exploring what I have with her."

I close my eyes, welcoming the dark water. My heart hurts. *I've lost him because I wasn't there.*

Dark-Water Melanie simmers under the surface. *Then get him back.*

"Say something," Adam says.

"What do you want me to say?"

"Be mad. Yell at me. Be *anything* but silent." He side-eyes me in the dark. "You're so closed off that I can't tell what you're feeling."

I say nothing, but I pulse love down the connection. I turn to watch his reaction. He closes his eyes, clearly forlorn.

Finding perfection with Adam, then having it slip away, is going to destroy me.

"I'm lost," he says.

"You're never lost, Adam."

"With you, I get lost."

Adam pulls to a stop at our beach spot.

"I was hoping we'd come here," I say appreciatively.

He smiles and gets out of the car, popping the trunk. I gather up my backpack and follow. He pulls a duffel bag and a boombox out of the trunk, and then I close the lid.

"Think you can get down the path in the dark?" he asks.

I nod.

We descend the dangerous pathway slowly and make it to the sand below. Our hidden little beach is exactly as I remember it, but in the dark, it holds an air of mystery. Adam sets everything down and spreads a blanket out on the sand. He takes candles from the duffel bag, lighting each one and setting them in the sand against the rocky walls. The soft glow makes my heart thud.

God, he's gorgeous by candlelight.

He turns after placing the furthest candle and starts crossing back to me. He stops halfway, radiating that he's unsure as he studies me.

I can't take it. *You need to resolve whatever this conflict is for him.* I cross the short distance and hop up, wrapping my legs around his waist.

He catches me easily. I lean in, our lips barely touching, and drop my carefully controlled connection between us, revealing everything I feel for him. I give him a second to absorb the emotions radiating from me. He inhales, and I kiss him softly. I wait for him to pull away, and when he does, I come up gasping.

When I drop my feet to the sand, he hugs me hard. His breath is ragged and shuddering.

I let him work through his thoughts, silently willing to be the thing he holds on to to keep his sanity. *Something's really off with him.*

After what feels like forever, he loosens his death grip on me and walks to the blanket, sitting down.

I follow. "What are you thinking?"

"That I made a mistake getting closer to Valerie while you were gone."

I lie down on the blanket and put my hands over my face. *I've lost him. Whatever's happening has him completely spun out.*

He shifts, lying down next to me as candlelight dances around us.

"I take it we're done?"

He shakes his head. "No. There's just some stuff you don't know."

"Tell me."

"Not now."

I demand a little harsher than I should, "Why?"

He really studies me before saying, "I need to know where you're at."

I sit up, unzip my backpack, and pull out the journal my mom sent in the care package when I was in detox. I stand and pick up the closest candle, carrying it back to the blanket. I settle back in my spot and wordlessly hand him the journal. He looks at me quizzically. I lie down before gently grabbing his arm and pulling him down with me. He rests his head on my stomach.

"Just read it."

Adam moves the candle closer and opens the notebook. I lie still, watching his profile while he reads through every thought, every experience, everything I wrote while locked away. I didn't think anyone would ever read it. It's raw, and honest.

Halfway through the pages, I feel tears, wet, on my side. I run my fingers through his hair, and he lets the notebook slip from his hand. Unexpectedly, he turns over and puts his forehead on my side.

I put my hand on his back, saying nothing. *He needs to work through whatever this is.*

After a time, he rolls over, picks up the journal, and settles back in his spot to read it again. Half an hour later, he gets to the end and closes the book. His gaze shifts to me.

I turn on my side, looking at him, and wait.

"You're the one," he whispers, "and I've screwed up . . . bad."

"Tell me."

He shakes his head and sits up. He pulls the boombox over. "We have a song."

I sit up, amused at the change of topic. "We have a song?"

He nods, pushing *play* on the CD player. Chris Isaak's "Wicked Game" drifts from the speakers. I close my eyes as the sultry song sends goosebumps up my arms.

Suddenly, Adam's fingers run slowly from my shoulders to the small of my back. I gasp.

He's there, inches from me, as he whispers, "I'll fix it. I'll find a chance to talk to Valerie. I promise."

"I don't know what you need to fix."

He kisses me, and everything disappears but him. He takes my hands and lifts me to my feet, his lips still on mine. He guides me off the blanket, and his arms slide around my back. Together, we slow dance to our song.

CHAPTER 31

"**W**e have a lot to do," Arch says, "but first, Melanie, welcome back."

I smile.

"Are you good?"

I take my time before saying, "I think so."

"How was it?" Presley asks. "Detox, I mean."

The dark water is calm as I close my eyes. That's both good and bad. Adam didn't get me home until five, literally twenty minutes before my parents woke up. I'm exhausted, and feisty Dark-Water Melanie would come in handy about how.

"I can sleep again, my heart isn't racing, and the dark water's manageable."

"Sounds like everything's better," Darren says.

My gaze catches Adam staring at me, and he looks away. He's so closed off that only his nervous expression clues me in.

Things definitely aren't better. "Better," I say absently. "Sure."

Adam's jaw tenses.

"Think you can handle getting down to some official student council business?" Arch asks.

I nod, and he calls the meeting to order. "Point one: Val, I need you to start figuring out the theme for the winter formal dance. We need something that's really going to sell some tickets. I want another full house for this one."

Valerie taps her pen on her notepad, contemplating. "Well, last year they called it 'Winter Wonderland,' and the whole thing was a snooze fest . . . Wait. I think I've got it. What if we call it the 'Snow Ball' and put up black lights all over the room? Everyone has to wear white and . . ."

I drift off, carried away on a wave of worry. *Why won't he tell me what's happening? It's obvious he still loves me.*

The ringing of the doorbell snaps me out of it. We all look at each other, and Kelsey checks her watch. "It's only ten-fifteen. Marcus's dad isn't supposed to be here yet."

Rich strides through our living room to get the door, pausing to ask us, "Any clue?"

We shake our heads.

"No chance this could be one of those death threats come to call?" he asks.

I get up and march recklessly to the door. "I hope it is. I need an outlet for all this pent-up irritation."

Trey, Adam, Isaac, and Demitri catch up with me, ready as I yank open the door.

Mr. Bentley, our student council faculty representative, grins at us as he steps inside. "Hi, kids. I heard Mel's mom's making lunch, so I thought I'd come for the meeting."

They all exhale and grin at him. I remain pensive.

Rich shakes his hand and invites him in. Bear brings a dining chair into the living room for Mr. Bentley to join us.

We settle back into our spots.

"I was just about to propose an idea," Arch says to Mr. B. "Your timing's perfect. I'm going to need your help with this one."

Apparently, I tuned out all the dance planning chatter.

Mr. B leans forward. "Can't wait. All the ideas that come out of this group are really popular with the student body. Hit me with it."

Arch looks down at his notes. "I want to do something new. Seems like the school focuses on the theater and dance side more, but we have a lot of talented musicians. I want to hold a battle-of-the-bands contest. I'm thinking we do sign-ups, and each . . ."

Blah, blah, blah! This inane teenage bullshit is mind-numbing.

". . . The winning band gets a cash prize, and student council makes the rest for our student activities account."

I missed most of that. Come on, Mel. Don't be cynical. You used to love this student council stuff. I attempt to pay attention as everyone plans some kind of Candygram sale, but I can't muster it up.

My attention is drawn back to the room as Valerie clears her throat, saying, "We have an announcement."

"Don't do this now," Adam says in a voice just above a whisper.

Valerie side-eyes him, confused. "I've been dying to tell them!"

Adam stares at the floor, his face slack with what looks like shock. His shields are clamped even tighter, giving me zero clue what's about to happen.

Valerie grins from ear to ear and pulls a little velvet jewelry box out of her pocket. She squeals, "Adam asked me to marry him! We're going to have the wedding this summer after graduation!" She opens the box, proudly displaying a gorgeous diamond ring.

The sound of a roaring jet engine fills my head. Shock reverberates. I push off the couch, crossing the room rapidly as everyone else moves in to hug Valerie and Adam. Suddenly, all my carefully held shields start cracking. I close my eyes in an effort to pull it together, but the dark water rushes in, busting through the walls. Earth-shattering heartbreak blasts out of me.

Darren, Demitri, Bear, and Trey all snap their gazes my way, shock playing across their faces as they feel my energy slamming out of control.

Damn it!

The girls swarm Valerie, dragging her across the room and grabbing her hand to ooooh and aaaah over the engagement ring she slides on her finger. This clears an open path between Adam and me. The less intuitive guys surround him, thumping him on the back and hugging him. I vaguely notice Isaac standing on his own, curiously watching Adam and me. Adam looks at me, his face a barely controlled mask of agony as the energy pounds and throbs from me unchecked. Luckily, only the select few notice.

Trey knows. Darren, Demitri, and Bear clearly know. Apparently, Isaac's enjoying the show.

Valerie bubbles over. "He took me late one night to this amazing little hidden beach with cliffs all around. He lit candles everywhere and asked me."

He proposed to Valerie on our beach.

Adam's control over the connection between us crashes down, and I'm hit with a blasting wave of everything he's feeling. It's chaos, but the message is clear. He regrets all of it.

Shock reverberates through my splintering mind. My mouth falls open and I shake my head, trying to find anything coherent to make sense of the overwhelming onslaught of emotions pouring from both of us. Tears stream down my cheeks. I watch Adam's face fall while he stares back at me. I hold out my hands in front of me, and they violently shake. *I'm going to lose it. I'm right on the edge of a seizure.*

Trey's expression morphs from fury to concern. He rushes to me, taking my face in his hands. "Breathe, Melanie."

He pulls me the short distance to Adam. Bear, Demitri, Isaac, and Darren step in to block the view from our happy friends, who are all surrounding Valerie across the room. Demitri puts his hands flat on my back, and my head drops as he uses his metaphysical gift to calm my panic.

"I don't know what the hell you've done to her," Trey hisses at Adam, "but it might kill her. This is how the seizures start."

My heart explodes, shattering into a million pieces as the celebration bubbles around me, but at least Demitri's made the shaking stop. Adam practically doubles over as my wave of emotion shoots down our connection.

Trey wraps me in his arms. "Let's go outside."

I nod against his chest.

We cross to the front door, and he guides me outside, leaving Adam staring at me, destroyed, while most of our friends celebrate obliviously. The shaking returns now that Demitri's not there to help.

Trey leads me around the corner, stopping by my bedroom window. He pulls me in, holding me. I close my eyes to the dark water in my mind, scared of what he's going to say.

"Tell me what's happening," he says, his tone calm and reassuring.

I shake my head and bury my face in his chest. A sob takes me by surprise, and I'm overcome with guilt and heartbreak all at once. I know we're not together anymore, but he deserves for me to have told him before now. Suddenly, I can't breathe. I gasp, and my knees go weak. Trey sits down in the grass. He crosses his legs and pulls me down to sit on his lap. I wrap my legs around him, and he holds me tight, exactly how Adam had done during our first visit to our beach.

Their beach.

My back convulses. I have to fight not to throw up. Shock whirls through my head. My arms shake violently against Trey's back.

I cry myself nearly sick, then finally, my head sags against Trey's shoulder. He smells like home. When I close my eyes, my dark-water side is nowhere to be found. Relief sweeps through me. "I'm sorry," I choke out.

"I have an idea of what's happening," Trey says, "but I need to tell you some things before we talk about that." He pauses, collecting his thoughts.

Oh, God, here it comes. He's about to blow up.

"I love you with everything in me," he says. "Part of loving you is being here while you deal with things. I've never been sorrier than I am about how I handled everything." He pauses as if to collect his thoughts. "I know there's something happening with you and Adam, and I'm not particularly surprised. You needed someone to lean on who would listen. I'm grateful that he could be that when I couldn't."

I can't believe what I'm hearing.

My tense muscles start relaxing one by one, until I'm finally completely limp against Trey. He waits patiently, holding me without saying anything.

When the shaking stops, he says, "I'm going to wait this out. I'll be here when it's over, although I suspect that the end of it may have just happened."

I lift my head from his shoulder and look up at him. There's love in his eyes.

After all this? "You aren't mad?" I whisper, baffled.

He frowns. "I'm mad at myself for letting things get so out of control that you slipped away. This was all my fault." He stares into my eyes as the silence stretches long.

Finally, I lace my fingers with his. I test the connection we've always had, but it's gone. "Our connection is gone," I say, looking sorrowfully into his eyes.

"I know."

"Do you have it with Tiffany?"

He looks baffled. "No. Tiffany was a fling."

"Then where did it go?"

He shakes his head. "After I screwed up over and over, I think you shut it down. I'm not an expert on this, though."

I put my head back on Trey's shoulder, exhausted. He holds me in silence for a long stretch.

When I finally open my eyes, Adam's on the brick walkway staring at me, radiating heartbreak.

CHAPTER 32

The night air is cold as I slip out of the house and walk with purpose to Adam's Harley. I look up into his hooded blue eyes in the dark, and there's heartbreak storming just under the surface.

"What, no duffel bag full of candles this time?" I quip. I narrow my eyes and seethe. "Let me tell ya, it's repulsive that you snagged your engagement candles and lit them with me days after you proposed to her."

He tips his head back, closes his eyes, and inhales sharply.

Before he can respond, I swing my leg over the Harley and get settled behind him, wrapping my arms around his chest. We're both so carefully closed off that neither of us have any clue what the other is feeling. He holds his breath as he thinks.

Suddenly, I say, "You know what? I have no interest in going to Valerie's beach." I get off the Harley and cross my yard, opening the back gate.

He follows. We stop by the pool, facing each other.

My insides churn, but I say nothing. *My silence always makes him uncomfortable, but I'm doing this my way.*

After the silence stretches beyond what he can stand, he doubles over, hands on his knees. I wait, watching, and finally he stands.

"You're doing this NOW?" I'd meant to rage at him, but I don't sound mad. *I sound desperate.*

He shakes his head, looking unsure of himself. Finally, he says, "I thought I was clear, but then you were gone."

I step closer, nearly touching him, my face contorted with agony from the conflicting emotions spilling from me in waves as my carefully constructed blockage drops between us. "You were crystal clear about us! You even planned what you were going to say to Valerie!"

"I don't know what happened."

The pool's water laps gently in the moonlight as the roving filter contraption drifts by. I watch it for a while. "You had to ask her at our beach spot?"

He's standing close enough beside me that I feel his breath on my cheek. "Where are you at with Trey?"

My dark-water side boils to the surface. "YOU HAVE GOT to be kidding! You haven't earned the right to ask me that right now."

Adam sinks down beside me on the pool deck.

I stare at the stars. "You're my other half. Unfortunately, I seem to be the only one who remembered that."

The storm in Adam's eyes has returned.

The eyes are windows to the soul. You're destroying his world. Just let him be happy with Valerie.

My dark-water side answers, *No. He's always said he wants brutal honesty.*

I let lose a firestorm of everything I'm feeling, projecting it out in blistering waves. "The engagement's what you refused to tell me about last night."

I take a few steps away, needing distance. But then an impulse catches me, and I whip around to growl, "I needed to hear it from you, not Valerie! We were in MY living room! Nowhere to hide IN MY OWN HOUSE while my heart exploded!"

He's holding his breath, lost in my rage. "I'm sorry, Melanie. I tried to talk to her before the meeting, but she was with her parents, and I couldn't reach her." He gasps, his head hanging while he tries to breathe. "I should have told you." He looks up with panic in his eyes. "You have *no idea* how sorry I am."

My hands start to shake again. "I would know if you weren't so closed down."

He says nothing.

In a brutally clipped tone, I ask again, "Why did you ask her at our beach?"

He stands and shakes his head. "I was lost. You have no idea how hard things were when you were in the hospital. I went to the beach every night, thinking about you. It was hell. Somehow, I convinced myself that I could be okay with Valerie. A big decision felt right at the time. I needed something to focus on."

"You still didn't answer my question, so I'm not asking any others."

He blinks rapidly, trying to keep up as this conversation derails out of his control.

I storm toward the waterfall at the deep end, needing some distance. "You wanted Valerie, and you've got her. She's an amazing person. At least we don't have to hurt her with this insanity."

When I smile maniacally and turn slowly to face him, his eyes widen a touch.

I take slow, menacing steps his way. "Good luck with that, though," I say. "You're going to be restless . . . and bored . . . and unfulfilled."

His eyes are tortured.

I put my lips so close to his that they're almost touching. "Tell me I'm wrong, Adam," I whisper. "With what we have, tell me that anything else will do. If that's the case, I'll walk my seething ass inside, and you can head to her house."

He closes his eyes, and his carefully held blockage collapses.

I'm hit with a tidal wave of his emotions.

"You already know you're right."

My hands are quaking as I turn from him and make my way toward the shallow end of the pool. He opens his eyes and watches as I take off my shirt and leggings and drop them in a pile. I walk down the steps in my underwear and bra and swim to the deep end. I feel him as he swims up behind me. He starts to speak, but I close my eyes and drop under the water. It closes over my head, and I feel safe.

Finally, after a long minute underwater, I break the surface and take a gasping breath.

Adam reaches for me, imploring. "I'll fix this."

"The dark water feels safer without you right now."

CHAPTER 33

"I feel like I'm in the movie *Groundhog Day*," Mom jokes, grinning at me. "Didn't we just do this yesterday?"

After the engagement celebration from hell disrupted yesterday's meeting, the student council decided it needed to get more done, so they scheduled another meeting for today to tie up the loose ends. Naturally, I wasn't consulted, and it chaps my ass. Here Mom is, cooking another huge lunch for everyone.

The doorbell rings, and Rich opens it. My heart races as everyone pours in with their usual excitement and babble.

I want to be left alone*! I don't want to deal with everyone today.*

Marcus peeks around the kitchen doorjamb. "We're BAAAACK."

Mom cracks up and gives him a hug.

Valerie's the last through the door. A huge stack of posterboards slide sideways from under her arm, scattering all over the floor. Adam rushes to help her get what's left in her arms situated while everyone but me helps pick up the rest.

"You guys need to plan one activity at a time!" Valerie says, exasperated. She looks at Rich and grins. "Hey, Pops. Thanks for having us over again!"

My temper rises as I glare at Valerie. None of this secret disaster is her fault, but I hate that she called my stepfather Pops. That's my thing. Trey, Demitri, and Adam are all watching me, wondering if I'm going to snap.

This is a disaster that could blow up all over our group. I can't hold it together through this meeting. As I move past Adam, I hiss in his ear, "If she calls him Pops again, I'll put her through the fucking floor."

Adam sharply inhales. Demitri follows me and subtly leans on the wall next to me with a calming hand on my back. It helps dissolve my irrational rage.

We have to get through the posters. I roll my eyes and sigh.

Arch stands up with a stack of posterboards in his hands. "We appreciate you, Val. I didn't think about what both events would do to your workload when I put so much on the agenda."

Valerie sets her stack of posterboards on the coffee table, and spreads out markers, gold star stickers, and musical note pages. "No problem. If you all help me, it'll go fast."

She starts giving out assignments like she owns the place. I roll my eyes. Apparently, we're going to be busy.

Wrong. They're *going to be busy. I'm over this.*

I turn and walk down the hall to my room, closing the door behind me. I pull my new black bikini out of the drawer and slip it on before throwing a tank dress over it and opening my door. I head down the hall and quietly slip out the front door while everyone's distracted with Valerie's never-ending instructions.

Around the house, I pass through the side gate to the backyard. I stop at the shallow end of the pool. My dress lands in a heap. I wade down the pool stairs into the cold water, continuing down the slope until my feet can't reach the bottom. I close my eyes and drift up, floating in the water so I can't hear sound or feel anything solid. I drift long enough to finally find contentment.

Unfortunately, I can still feel emotional energy. Adam's suddenly nearby, and I open my eyes. He's standing at the edge of the pool.

Kill me. I'm so over him right now. I swim to the shallow end where I can stand chest deep in the water. I'm intentionally closed off tight, giving him no emotional clue where I'm at with things. I stare at Adam, waiting for him to tell me what he wants.

Demitri comes out through the sliding door just as Adam says, "You threatening to beat the shit out of Valerie is a scary development."

"I didn't invite Valerie over, now did I?"

Adam sighs. "The whole council is here, Melanie. They were all invited by Arch."

I crinkle my nose and announce with over-the-top-gleeful sarcasm, "Fine. I quit the council. Run along and kick everyone out please." My gaze shifts, and I point playfully at Demitri. "Except you. You can stay."

Demitri's eyebrows rise as Adam turns a seething glare his way.

"Here to watch the show, Peter Pan?" Adam growls at him.

Demitri raises his hands innocently. "I just wanted to check on Melanie."

I hear Trey chuckle. We all turn to look toward the round courtyard across the way. Trey's leaning on the wall with an eyebrow raised in amusement.

He takes a few steps, rounding the corner, and looks at Adam with a grin before narrowing his eyes at Demitri. He whistles and says to Adam, "Oh man. You're waist deep in aaaall the shit with Mel right now."

"How long have you been standing there?" I ask Trey, amused.

"I watched you leave through the front door, and I came out to check on you." He clears his throat. "I got a little distracted while you were floating in the pool. Wasn't trying to eavesdrop." He gestures to Demitri. "With that said, Demitri isn't staying. I am. I'm in full support of kicking everyone out, though. This student council is a bunch of bullshit. We should be driving fast down PCH right now." He glares at Adam. "Your fiancé can eat my ass. I'm not gluing her glittery cardboard stars on shit." He grins my way. "I'm hoping Melanie stuffs them up her bossy ass sideways."

I laugh. "Drag her out here. Bring the stars, scissors, and the box they came in, and tell her to bend over."

Demitri laughs while he leans on the wall.

Trey snorts while he juts his thumb at Adam. "Numb Nuts over there didn't notice that you left. He was busy worshipping Princess Peach while she dictated arts and crafts instructions at Girl Scout camp."

I throw my head back, belting surprised laughter. It feels good to laugh, and this unexpected side of Trey has me rolling.

We both turn to Adam, but he doesn't share our sentiment. "Melanie, none of this is Valerie's . . ."

Trey flippantly interrupts, "Shut up, Adam." He strides to the edge of the pool, looking down at me.

"Melanie," Demitri cuts in, "I need to know whose side I'm taking if these two demons decide to throw blows."

I shrug playfully. "If they do, I vote you get in the pool and snuggle with me while we watch the death match."

Demitri chuckles.

"No Demitri for you, Mel," Trey admonishes. "You're mine."

I bite my tongue and give Demitri a playful look while I wiggle my shoulders. He glances to the side, clearly amused but aiming for neutral to avoid a fight.

"I love when you laugh," Trey says softly to me.

"I needed that."

"I know."

Trey turns to Adam. "How's your whole 'Love of Melanie's Life' plan going so far, Adam?" he asks with lighthearted sarcasm.

Adam glares at him.

Trey turns back to me. He holds my gaze, but he's speaking to Adam as he says, "I'll give you a little advice, jackass. When she won't speak, it's one of three things. She's either so mad she can't see straight, turned on to the point she can't think, or heartbroken." He looks at Adam. "I'm thinking it's two of the three right now."

I crack up.

Adam seethes as Demitri covers a chuckle with a quiet cough.

"That new swimsuit is everything," Trey says as he slides an appraising look my direction.

He crooks a finger at me and kneels by the edge of the pool. I swim to him, resting my arms on the pool deck. He puts his fingertips on my forehead. I close my eyes, knowing what's coming. This is my favorite thing he does. Slowly, he runs his fingertips from my forehead to my chin, featherlight.

I open my eyes and gaze up at him.

He whispers, "I love you."

We hold each other's gaze for a moment before he stands and tosses a towel near the stairs by the shallow end. "I brought you a towel." He turns on his heel and walks back to the house.

Just before he gets to the sliding door, I say, "Trey?"

He turns, looking back at me. "Yes, babe?"

I grin. "You won that round."

He winks at me before disappearing into the house.

CHAPTER 34

Bruce arrives just as the last of the decorated posters are stacked up. Inwardly, I groan. I just want today to be over.

"As you know," Bruce says, "I've taken over the role of acting district attorney. It's an insanely busy job, I've discovered, but you can believe that I'm concentrating on Joel's case. He's eighteen and being tried as an adult. There are witnesses on your side who can prove his guilt, and several of his friends took a plea deal to keep themselves out of hot water, admitting everything he told them. He's entered a not guilty plea. Frankly, I find his plea to be ludicrous. We offered him three years, with time off for good behavior if he entered a guilty plea, but his parents are convinced that the story he told them is true. It's the same story he tried to spread at the school about Melanie being suicidal and him trying to save her."

I grind my teeth, and a frustrated growl escapes my lips. "I'm getting really tired of that story of his."

"Most people don't believe the story," Isaac interjects. "When Joel heaped that pile of shit on me at a party, I found it to be insane."

When I narrow my eyes at him, he rushes to explain himself.

"It's one of the reasons I quit being friends with the Drones."

Bruce attempts to move the meeting along. "If we could, I'd like to go through some mock trial role play."

Everyone else exchanges pensive looks. The last thing any of them want to do is testify at the trial, but I'm over it.

"Just let him out of jail, "I say under my breath. "I'll deal with him myself."

Both Trey and Adam are standing close enough to hear me, and they grin at me before sneering at each other.

After riffling through some papers, Bruce clears his throat. "I want to double-check that Arch, Adam, Finley, Hiram, Darren, Presley, Bear, Melanie, and Trey are the kids that witnessed Joel's attack on the balcony."

We all nod.

"I'm scared," Finley says.

"That's precisely why we do these trial runs," Bruce offers. "Because you're all under eighteen, I'm working to get the judge to approve allowing your testimony through video depositions. If that route isn't approved, then you'll be expected to testify in person. The prosecution's questions will be asked by another member of the DA's office. Those will be to the point and professional, but the defense is guaranteed to do everything they can to throw you off. They'll work hard to intimidate, discredit, and confuse you. Some of you tend to be emotional. Others are hotheads. They'll dig up your darkest secrets, so I need you to be ready to handle the pressure."

Adam and I exchange a look across the room. *He's my darkest secret.*

Arch takes a deep breath. "All right. Let's give this a shot."

Bruce places a dining chair at the end of the room. "Since I'm the only lawyer here today, I'm going to play the role of the defense attorney. Everyone in?"

We nod.

"The defense calls Arch Terani to the stand."

Arch walks to the chair and takes a seat. Bruce swears him in, and Arch states that he'll answer honestly.

Bruce glances at his notes and starts pacing. "You witnessed the incident that happened between Joel Stamp and Melanie Slate?"

"Yes, sir."

Bruce grins at Arch and drops the defense attorney façade. "Excellent work, Arch." He turns to the rest of us. "Never give more information than the defense specifically asks for."

We all nod.

Bruce returns to the tough-guy act. "Describe what you witnessed."

"Please be more specific," Arch says.

Bruce nods at Arch, approving of his response. "What did you witness Joel do?"

"Stan rushed Melanie, and she fell over the balcony railing, three stories up. Joel caught her by one wrist, but then he intentionally let go. She was caught just in time by Trey Valdez."

I look at Trey, reliving how that moment went. He smiles the slightest bit and winks at me. I grin and glance away.

Adam's glaring at us.

"It's my understanding that Joel was trying to save Melanie Slate and had no intention of killing her. Is that true?"

Arch answers, "No."

"What happened after Joel supposedly let go of Melanie?"

"Trey Valdez caught her wrist and pulled her up as high as he could. I reached over, and we pulled her over the railing together. Then I hit Joel Stamp with a right hook."

Bruce takes on a look of surprise. "You were violent toward Joel Stamp?"

Arch looks baffled. "Absolutely."

"Why did you choose violence?"

"Because Joel tried to kill my friend, and he's an ass."

Bruce shakes his head. "No, Arch. Don't back yourself into a credibility corner. Less is more."

"Okay, okay," Arch says. "Do-over." He clears his throat. "Joel needed to be stopped so he couldn't hurt anyone else."

Bruce nods. "Better."

Arch grins. "Don't be me. Got it."

We all laugh.

"Trey, you're up next," Bruce says.

Trey makes his way to the chair and goes through the honesty declaration process.

A moment of silence passes as Bruce turns his back to Trey. Then, suddenly, he whips around and aggressively asks, "Is it true that you were dating Victoria Garcia at the time that you and Melanie started dating?"

"On and off."

"Do you regularly cheat on your girlfriends?"

Trey rubs his forehead. Finally, he says, "Yes and no."

Absently, I'm gritting my teeth.

Bruce switches gears, trying to take Trey off guard. "Instead of confronting Joel, you threw him through a window without saying a word."

"That's my version of confrontation," Trey answers.

"Clearly things weren't that bad. You and Melanie Slate were all over each other on the balcony after she was safely to the floor."

Trey looks at me. "Melanie kissed me."

"She kissed you, and you decided to lie down on top of her?"

Bruce asks incredulously.

"I fell on top of her."

You collapsed on me when your entire body buckled.

Bruce snaps me back to reality when he asks, "So, Melanie Slate's the kind of girl who lies down with guys in public?"

I glance at Adam, whose expression is blank.

Trey's eyebrows rise, and his jaw tightens. After a pause, he simply says, "No."

"It's our understanding that Melanie Slate was dating Adam Stone at the time that she started dating you."

Just kill me.

"He stood her up. She was suddenly available." He glances Adam's way, adding, "I never got a chance to thank you for being a player, by the way."

I glance at Adam. He's radiating irritation.

"Then it's true that Joel, Adam, and you were all fighting over Miss Slate's affections?" Bruce asks.

Trey's eyes narrow. "I'm not fighting with anyone for Melanie." He side-eyes Adam, who intentionally avoids his gaze.

Now's not the time, boys!

Bruce switches gears. "Three guys . . . Melanie was a busy girl."

Adam growls from his spot leaning against the wall next to Valerie, and his jaw tightens. Trey and Adam look at each other, both full of rage.

At least they agree on something.

Trey pointedly answers, "It's not Melanie's responsibility to control the hormones of male students."

Bruce nods, approving of his answer. Defense Attorney Bruce flashes a quick apologetic gaze my way before saying, "So, Melanie Slate's a slut?"

Trey comes up off the chair while Adam yells, "Watch it!"

Arch grabs Trey by the arm and thumps him back in the chair. Trey looks up at Bruce, who shakes his head.

"That's exactly what they want. The defense wants to prove that Joel was dealing with a pack of loose cannons, and frankly, this group's known for being scrappy. They also want to discredit Melanie. Don't give that to them."

"If they call Melanie a slut," Trey warns, "I'm gonna tear the courtroom apart."

"I'll help," Adam adds darkly.

Hooray, they're cooperating. I roll my eyes.

"No. You won't. Don't make this easy for them."

"Melanie's dating history is irrelevant to the case, Bruce," Trey admonishes.

Bruce's eyes narrow as he smiles. "What do you think court is, son? This question goes for all of you."

"Court, a trial, is about revealing the truth," Trey recites, likely remembering that tidbit from a history lecture.

Bruce shakes his head. "Wrong. The truth doesn't always prevail. Sometimes a good spin wins." He addresses all of us. "Don't get caught up in an idealistic fantasy where good conquers all. The court system is built on performance. Which attorney can weave the most convincing spin. The defense attorneys involved in this case are good. They will be prepared to create that convincing spin."

Trey mutters a cuss word that makes my mom blush and Rich grin. He glances at my parents. "I apologize. That was out of line."

"This joker just called your girl a slut," Rich says. "I'm good with it."

Everyone quietly chuckles as Trey grins at Rich.

"All right, Trey," Bruce says. "You need to take a break." He turns to me. "Melanie, you're up."

Yippee! I take a deep breath and walk to the stand.

Bruce guides me through the honesty oath. Then, immediately he hits me with a haughty defense attorney look. "Did you flirt with Joel Stamp the first day of school?"

"No. He helped me find a few of my classes."

"You had no interest in Joel?"

"He was questionable."

"How so?"

"He showed flashes of anger that were questionable."

"But he helped you?"

"Yes."

"If you felt he was questionable, why did you allow him to help you?"

"The school was new to me, and he was the only person I'd met at that point."

So far, this has been easy, but my palms start sweating and my heart rate picks up. The line of questioning is about to become more complicated. I can feel it.

Bruce smiles. "You went on a date with Adam Stone?"

"I did."

"Why did you go on a date with Adam Stone?"

"He's gorgeous, and the timing was right."

Trey side-eyes me aggressively. Adam smirks.

"So," Bruce says haltingly, "you regularly make impulsive decisions where gorgeous boys are concerned?"

Dark-Water Melanie peeks through and forces a giggle. "Sometimes."

Bruce gives me an exasperated look.

"Fine, fine, just a joke."

"Melanie, this is serious."

"I apologize."

"Do you think Joel's gorgeous?"

"I think Joel's a creep."

"But Adam Stone, a boy who's confirmed to have dated many at Hollywood High, was an acceptable choice?"

I glare at Bruce. "Adam Stone didn't try to rape me. Joel did."

"Good, Melanie. Let's move forward."

I nod and wipe my clammy hands on my leggings again.

"When the fight started, what happened?" Bruce asks.

"My friends lined up in the living room across from Joel and his group. Trey Valdez walked across the room, grabbed Joel, and threw him through a window."

"What did you do when that happened?"

"I listened to the sound of glass hitting the floor."

"Were you concerned about Joel's well-being?"

"No."

"Why?"

"Because Joel chose to put himself in that position."

Bruce nods, approving of my answer, and then switches back to defense attorney mode. "How many boys have you slept with at Hollywood High?"

I rattle my head, shocked, not expecting that particular topic. I stare at Bruce with my mouth hanging open. *Don't say a word.*

"There it is," Bruce says. "That's what you can expect, Melanie. They'll get you comfortable, and then they'll whammy you."

"Adam was my first kiss," I offer, attempting to steer us away from this. "My relationships are more innocent than you allude to."

Adam's mouth falls open, shock playing across his handsome face. "WAIT! Your first kiss was with me? In front of half the school while I dealt with Victoria?"

I nod, and he scrubs at his face hard with his hands. "I'm an ass. Unbelievable." He looks at me. "Melanie, I apologize. You deserve better than that." He turns to my parents, who are taking this surprisingly well. "Do you plan to throw me out?"

Rich laughs. "I think we can handle you kissing Melanie." He gives Trey an amused glance, adding, "We've caught Trey and Melanie up to more than that."

Trey snorts, shaking his head. "I'm an ass, also." He says to Adam, "We officially suck."

"Any chance two jackasses can have a smoke on your porch?" Adam asks my mom.

Mom laughs. "Make yourselves at home."

Adam motions to Trey, and the two of them head out the door.

"Wonderful," Trey says sarcastically just as the door closes behind him.

Bear looks at Darren. "We're up. Those two are about to shame spiral." Darren and Bear head outside to talk to the guys.

I need to get out there.

"We can continue your practice another time," Bruce mercifully says to me. "Finley, it's your turn to take the stand."

I head out, closing the door behind me. Adam, Trey, Bear, and Darren are on the sidewalk by Trey's car, and they're engaged in a heated hissing debate.

"You can't leave her alone, can you?" Trey snarls.

Adam responds with a warning. "Back off, Trey."

Bear interjects, "Hey! Guys, stop. What the hell is happening?"

When I walk up, all eyes shift to me.

"You want to fill us in?" Bear asks.

I answer with a deadpan tone. "Not particularly."

Silence stretches uncomfortably long.

"Bear and Darren," I say finally, "I need to speak with Trey and Adam alone."

Bear and Darren exchange a look.

"How deep are you in this with Adam?" Darren asks.

You don't want to know.

I don't answer, and after an extended silence, they exchange another look.

"Do you understand what a disaster this will be?" Bear exasperatedly asks. "The last thing we need are you and Valerie tearing each other limb from limb. A fight between you two would likely be a death match. It's a miracle Adam and Trey haven't killed each other."

Apart from my hard gaze, I don't respond.

"I give you two credit for your self-control," Bear says to the guys.

Trey growls Adam's way, "Give it a minute."

Adam snarls back, "Bring it the hell on, Trey."

I drop my shields, letting menacing warning vibes roll from me unchecked. They're laced with a touch of the seduction I can't seem to clamp down on lately. "You two, STOP!"

A matching energy rolls off Adam as the guys turn to me.

"Interesting," Darren says. He looks from Adam, to Trey, and finally to me. Baffled, he says to Bear, "I don't know who she belongs with anymore. Do you feel that?"

"Welcome to our hell, guys," I say.

Trey's mouth drops open as his gaze snaps to Adam.

Bear takes my hand before holding his other hand out to Adam. Adam hesitantly accepts it. Bear's eyes widen. He drops Adam's hand and holds his hand out to Trey, who takes it.

He's assessing who my energy works with now.

Bear drops our hands and turns to Adam. "Obviously, you know what's happening."

His face running pale, Adam nods.

Bear and Darren radiate calm, while Bear shifts by Trey and Darren subtly sidles up next to Adam.

Trey surveys our friends' cautious rearranging routine. "I'm not going to attack Adam," he says calmly. "Just say what you need to say."

Bear glances at Trey before turning back to Adam. "*Why* did you propose to Valerie? You've got a soulmate connection with Melanie!"

Adam's face contorts with something close to agony.

"Are you saying she's not my soulmate anymore?" Trey asks in an amused tone.

"Whatever has shifted in Melanie is a perfect match with Adam's energy," Darren offers. He turns back to Adam. "You know energy better than anyone. You should have cut things off with Valerie the day you figured this out. When was it?"

"The day we met you guys at Smokers' Corner and Melanie was taken back to county."

Darren rattles his head, baffled. "You had all that time to handle this, and instead, you lost your mind?"

"Why didn't you come to the two of us?" Bear asks him.

Adam breathes, "I don't know."

Bear and Darren glance at each other, then at me.

"This is beyond a disaster," Bear says.

I snort derisively.

"Mind if I say something?" Trey asks.

Everyone survey's Trey.

Bear nods. "The floor's yours."

Trey looks at me as he speaks to the others, "I assure you he's not her match. I know Adam and Melanie have the same throbbing energy. The problem is that they're both made of fire and chaos. There's heat, but no balance." He draws a long breath, taking his time. "Melanie's complicated."

All three guys chuckle at the same time. I laugh a bit.

"That's a given, I suppose," Trey says. "Anyhow, as I was saying, I know Melanie's complicated. That's what I'm for. I can think above the fray when she can't. Where Melanie is chaos and spontaneity, I'm reflection and anticipation." He looks Bear and Darren's way before adding, "We're not the same, because I'm her other half. What she lacks, I have. What I lack, she has. Together, we make a whole."

We all stand there, letting that sink in.

Trey levels Adam with a look. "Adam and Melanie are twin fires, but they both get bored and restless easily. They'll either burn each other out or drive each other mad. I think they're there already, and it hasn't even been a month."

Could that be true?

Stoically, Trey turns back to me. "I know you, Melanie. You thrive on chaos but regret the consequences every time. When you get chilled down to your bones, there's only one thing that fixes it." He turns me away from the guys. He lifts my hair and touches his lips to the base of my neck, exhaling.

The warm air makes my head loll forward. I close my eyes, basking as the warmth settles my frazzled nerves.

He turns me back around, saying, "Give me a second." He steps off the sidewalk and opens the driver's side door of his car. The car battery switches on. After a moment, the sultry guitar pull of my favorite song rises from the car as he rolls the windows down. "I was listening to this on the way over here," he explains as he gets out of the car. "Your favorite song is 'Blue Jean Blues,' but only the Jeff Healey version." He smiles. "It's about finding that person who makes you completely content in your own skin. I'm that person, Melanie. Adam makes you nearly vibrate out of your own psyche." He pauses, staring in my eyes. "Might I remind you about what you told me when we first got together? That you knew I was the one because love with me feels like how this song sounds."

My heart flutters. It's not the fiery, overwhelming feeling I get with Adam. This is purely Trey. He always remembers the little details that mean so much to me. I smile.

He steps to me and tips my chin up to look in my eyes. "I know it's made you insane that I haven't given in to the seductive chaos that rolls off of you in waves." He smiles. "I also know that you've questioned whether or not I'm interested, because I don't give in." He shakes his head. "That's not it." He puts his hand lightly against the side of my head. "Your mind loves the chaos and wants instant gratification. It thrives on it, but . . ." He moves his hand to rest over my heart. "Your heart wants to work for what you desire. It wants anticipation and complication. It wants to be sure, so your brain doesn't spiral."

I can feel Adam's frustrated energy.

Trey glances at him. "I work with her heart over her mind often because I want her to be content in her life. I recognize I got some of this wrong, but I had good intentions."

We all stand in silence while Trey and I gaze into each other's eyes. Energy rolls off me in waves, but it's not jagged and harsh this time. It's like my dark-water side is learning to breathe.

Suddenly, just as my favorite song hits a swell, Trey pulls me against him, raising my arms slowly over my head. He takes my hands, putting them over his shoulders, and starts to dance with me.

After a long moment, he takes my right hand and spins me around before pulling me against him. His hands slide seductively around my hips. He grips tight, making me gasp before swooping me around in a backbend. He grabs my hand and snaps me up, looking in my eyes. It's the exact same thing he did when we danced to this song together the first time.

My breath is gasping, my eyes unfocused. *He's absolutely right about all of what he said.*

His voice gravelly, he says, "I'm your soulmate. I assure you." He leans down, his lips barely touching mine.

My heart races as my dark-water side's signature energy starts thrumming.

He waits a long moment until my breath turns ragged and panting before saying, "I love you."

When he kisses me, fire shoots up my spine. Dark-Water Melanie gasps in my mind. My knees nearly buckle. He takes that moment to lace his fingers with mine, and our connection is blasted back open. Trey's energy wraps and melds with mine, spreading from my hand through my entire body. He laces his other hand in mine, and the energy meets, creating a perfect, synchronized hum that connects on both sides. I'm suddenly thrumming with relief because I'm whole again. He squeezes my hands and sends a pulse that everything's going to be okay.

He ends the kiss and lets me go.

Wait. He usually holds on to me. Weak-kneed, I sink to the sidewalk and smile through the haze. I can see what he's doing. He wants to leave me on my own so I'll get a chance to realize how much I need him.

Darren and Bear exchange a glance.

"Are two soulmate connections at the same time even possible?" Bear asks.

"Obviously," Darren says. "It's happening right in front of us."

I look up at Trey as my head spins.

"I'm going to leave you to Adam's rebuttal," he says. "I'm sure he has something charming to say." He struts back to his car as the final guitar riff of my favorite song hums through the air.

"Damn," Darren says. "He's good."

As Trey's Camaro rumbles away from the curb, Adam takes a breath to speak.

I put up a hand, completely sure where I stand. "Hush, Adam. You and I are done. You chose Valerie."

— —

Three taps on my window pull me from a fitful sleep. I cross the room, peeking past the curtain, and Trey motions for me to come outside.

I drop the curtain and let my head fall back with my eyes closed. *I'll sleep when I'm dead.* I grab the tank dress I'd worn by the pool and throw it on before slipping into my Converse. In the hall, I can faintly hear Rich snoring in my parents' room. Their door is closed.

I sneak quietly down the hall. *If this keeps up, I'm either going to get caught or die of exhaustion.*

Trey's waiting for me outside the front door. Without a word, he reaches around me and pulls the door shut. He backs me up slowly until my back presses against the door. I stare up at him in the dark as a slow, suggestive grin spreads across his face.

He leans down and kisses me softly. My breath catches, and my knees go weak. He gets an arm around me, holding me up as he ends the kiss. He lets me go and laces his fingers with mine. Our energy melds and braids.

I inhale, eyes closed, and study it to make sure I'm not making it up. *It's definitely back.* Relief surges through me as I exhale. I open my eyes to find Trey smiling suggestively.

He raises an eyebrow. "Are you sick of the anticipation yet?"

"Are you sure you're done with Tiffany?"

"Without question. Tiffany's not an issue."

I grin and nod.

He takes my hand and walks quickly to his car with me in tow. He opens the door, and I slide in. His car smells like home.

Trey slides into the driver's seat and starts the engine. Alice Cooper's "Poison" slinks through the speakers, making me laugh.

With just a touch of conviction, I say, "One request."

"Anything. Just ask."

"Don't take me where you took your bimbos."

Trey nods. "Done." After a moment of reflection, he says, "I'm truly sorry about Tiffany."

I wave my hand as if to clear his words from the air. "I'm sorry about Adam too." I meet his gaze. "Can we just forget it all happened and be back together?"

He murmurs, "Finally."

We pull away from the curb and head off into the night as "Poison" blasts through his speakers.

CHAPTER 35

Hiram arrives and hops on the table. He strings up a massive, hand-painted "Battle of the Bands" banner and hangs it from the awning in the Commons. He hands Adam another banner decorated with cartoon candy canes dancing and holding up quarters. Adam hefts himself on the other table and strings it up.

Finley laughs. "That's adorable."

My stomach flip-flops, and I wince and hang on to Demitri's arm.

"You good?" Demitri asks.

I look up at him pitifully. "My stomach's bubbling, yet again."

He scrunches up his face, concerned, and puts an arm around me.

"Nice work, Hiram," Arch says, gesturing to the custom banners.

He's interrupted by a booming, "HO, HO, HO," and here comes Bear marching through the quad in a Santa costume.

We all crack up.

"Have you finally lost your mind, Bear?" Arch calls across the distance.

Bear grins as he joins the group. "You can't have a holiday Candygram sale without Santa." He wipes sweat from his brow. "It's hotter than Satan's ass in this getup. Southern California doesn't lend itself well to a Santa suit, even in winter."

The bell rings, and the usual flood of students pours out of every building like ants fleeing their hills. A frighteningly long line quickly forms in front of the student council's battle-of-the-bands sign-up booth.

As each band signs up, Tanner announces, "Fifteen slots to go . . . Fourteen slots to go . . ."

Presley and I stand by the ropes and survey the line while we direct traffic.

"The line's getting shorter," I say, "but not short enough. Someone might get left out at this rate."

Presley nods. "Honestly, I didn't think we'd fill the slots." She wanders off to speak to Bear.

Meanwhile, the Candygram line is dead. Bear, Presley, and Isaac confer. Apparently, they hatch a plan. Isaac pulls the Candygram advertisement posters off the walls and passes them out to the student council members who are mingling with students. I'm hoping that helps. We've got two thousand candy canes that we don't want to get stuck with.

Bear starts boisterously working the crowd. I listen in with Demitri as Bear saunters up to a snuggly couple, smiles conspiratorially, and says, "My man! I see you have a lucky gal here. You don't want her to be the only girl in her class that doesn't get a Candygram, do you? Fifty cents and you'll win her heart!"

The boy grins and hops up, heading to the Candygram sales table as he pulls several dollar bills from his pocket.

When Bear flashes a triumphant expression our way, we crack up. The hijinks settle my stomach.

Bear turns to his next upsell victim. "What's up, Trudy! Santa knows all."

Trudy is a quiet, bookish type. She gives him a shy, bewildered look and shrinks in on herself. She pushes her glasses higher on the bridge of her nose before staring up at Bear like he's from another planet.

Bear guides Trudy our way. "I happen to have it on good authority that Lionel likes you," he's saying as they approach us.

Trudy's eyes light enthusiastically as she glances toward Demitri and me as if we could confirm this incredible news. Bear's handsome face splits with a bright grin aimed at us over the top of Trudy's head. Demitri and I smile at Trudy and nod encouragingly.

As Trudy turns her attention back to Bear, Demitri and I shrug at each other almost imperceptibly.

"He does?" Trudy whispers, looking dumbfounded at the possibility.

I glance across the quad at Lionel. I'm baffled about what Trudy would see in this guy, but then again, I prefer the bad-boy type. Lionel is wearing a button-down plaid dress shirt, and his corduroy slacks are a bit too short. He trips on nothing tangible and stumbles. Trudy swoons. I have to fight not to smile. They're rather charming, but I don't want her to think I'm making fun of them.

Demitri looks down at me, amused. When Trudy glances at him, he hits her with the puppy dog eyes that make girls melt.

Her breath catches, and she appears flummoxed.

He juts his chin Lionel's direction and says convincingly, "My buddy over there is a catch. He runs the science club." He says this last part with an edge of wonderment.

I drop my mouth open and give Trudy a girly look. "That's awesome," I say, feigning awe.

Trudy takes a faltering breath and stares at Lionel like he's the hottest guy on the planet. She looks back at Demitri and asks, starry-eyed, "He runs science club?"

Demitri crinkles his eyes at Trudy and nods. "Yup. He's really cool. You should get him a Candygram. You get to write a note and everything."

Trudy bounces on her toes, excited, but her resolve suddenly fades on a wave of insecurity.

I bite my lip and let my gaze slide alluringly toward Lionel. "Maybe I'll get Lionel a Candygram. Corduroy is hot." I wiggle my shoulders a little.

Trey and Adam sidle up to our little bunch just in time to hear this, and they're both staring at me like I'm insane.

"Yeah," Adam says with a deadpan tone. "Hot. So fuzzy."

Demitri turns his back, his shoulders shaking as he laughs silently.

The prospect of competition from me seems to spur on Trudy. She rushes to the Candygram table, anxiously joining the growing line.

I look up at Demitri and snort. "Lionel's your buddy?"

Demitri laughs. "I was in a few classes with him last year, but I don't know him. He's a nice guy, though." He shrugs. "Just using my powers for good instead of evil. Those two would be cute together."

Bear high-fives Demitri and me before "ho-ho-hoing" his way toward the next unsuspecting purchaser. After some spirited conversation, an overwhelming wave of students comes our way to join the Candygram line.

Presley whistles. "INCOMING," she yells to Valerie and Finley.

The last band in the line steps up to the table.

Tanner takes their form and money. "Fourteen out of fifteen slots are full," he says, standing up and gathering the stack. "We did it, guys."

Just then, Dante bolts up to the table. "Please don't close yet," he says, winded. "Is there another slot?" Dante is in a heavy metal band that's actually really good.

"One more slot. You're just in time." Tanner grins at the guy as he takes his form and money. "I was wondering where you were! I knew Diablo had to perform."

"Candygram sales are done," Valerie announces. "I think we killed it."

Principal Walker comes over. "Let's go to the conference room to check out the forms and get organized. I'm really excited about the turnout for both events."

We head to the conference room in the two-story building. Bear sheds his sweaty suit as soon as the door closes. He exhales hard.

Tanner claps him on the shoulder, grimacing as his hand is coated in Bear's sweat. "Nice work with the crowd, Bear."

Arch starts giving instructions. I intentionally move behind him, out of his line of sight, in the hopes of avoiding a mundane special-helper assignment. Adam's watching me, grinning because he can sense what I'm doing.

"Adam, please punch holes in the corner of the red papers," Arch says.

With a roll of his eyes in my direction, Adam takes the hole punch. I silently laugh. He holds my gaze and winks at me. I shake my head, looking down.

"Melanie," Valerie says, "would you start going through this box and separating the Candygrams into grade level?"

I give her a deadpan look. "No."

Valerie appears stunned. "You okay?"

"Quit telling me what to do, Valerie," I say in a clipped tone. "I'm not your bitch."

She stares at me like I'm nuts. "I never thought you were."

I gesture toward our friends. "Order one of them around. They like jumping through hoops."

Demitri gives me a "hold it together" look as he takes the box from Valerie. Valerie scoots closer to Adam and murmurs something to him. I ignore them.

I roll my neck, the tension in my muscles driving me bonkers. Adam's gaze is still warm on me from across the room. My pissy dark-water side stirs, but I shove it away.

"Let's try to figure out who's going up against who," Tanner suggests. "Okay, this one is 'Peewee and the Hermans.'" He looks at us with a raised eyebrow. "They're a ska band, and everyone dresses like Peewee Herman. I'm not so sure about this one. We might have some clunkers in the bunch."

Everyone laughs while Adam mutters, "This is going to be a freak show."

Arch picks up the next one. "This one's cool. They're called the 'Finish Line,' and it says they're a metal band. Who's next, Tanner?"

I tune the meeting out while they continue monotonously going through the bands. After last night, Trey remains forefront in my thoughts. I smile a touch just as I feel Trey's electric gaze on me. He smiles the slightest bit when I wink at him.

"I think we've got it." Finley sets the completed battle-of-the-bands list down on the table, and everyone leans in to look.

Marcus cautiously says, "Umm . . . guys?"

Everyone turns his way.

"There's a Candygram here for Presley. I think we have a problem."

"What does it say?" Principal Walker asks.

Marcus looks at Presley. "It says, 'Die, Bitch.'"

Everyone glances at each other, shocked.

"Let's pair up and take a box each," Mr. Bentley says. "We need to read through the notes."

We dig through piles of Candygrams. Most are standard love notes and friendly banter.

Darren holds up a Candygram. "Crap," he says. "Here's another one. It's for Finley. 'Don't testify, or else.'"

It hits us all at once what's happening.

Really? Candygram death threats? The Drones are pathetic. I groan out, "I don't know why you're all so shocked. It's from the Drones."

"This is worrisome," Mr. B says.

"No, it's ridiculous," I say.

CHAPTER 36

Sweat rolls down my back. I'm partnered with Demitri for the group dance numbers in *The Pajama Game*, and I'm convinced Mr. Isley is hell-bent on killing me. Because Demitri can do every lift on the planet, I'm learning stuff on the fly that I've never done.

Mr. Isley booms though the microphone, "Melanie, get it together."

I sigh and raise my head. Mr. Isley's at the back of the audience seating section, sporting a glare so ferocious that I can see it clearly from my spot on the stage.

"Yes, sir. I apologize."

"Everyone take five while Demitri and Melanie get that disaster worked out," Mr. Isley commands.

As the stage clears, I turn to Demitri. "Are you ever going to be willing to work with me again after this debacle?"

He grins down at me. "You're doing fine. Mr. Isley's just making a racket because he's got big plans for you. He's a trial-by-fire type."

Demitri grabs his flannel from his dance bag on the edge of the stage. He crosses back to me and wipes the sweat from my lower back. I'm wearing a sports bra, and the overhead arabesque lift fell apart a few minutes ago because I slipped out of his grasp. He tosses the flannel down and turns to me. He lifts the bottom of his tank top and uses it to wipe his sweaty face while he gives me instructions. He puts down his shirt and hits me with expectant eyes, waiting for a response. I shake my head and try not to laugh.

"What?" he asks.

I give in and decide to go with blunt honesty. We're close enough as friends that I figure I can get away with it. I wave my hand by my ear. "My brain leaked out my freaking ear, and I heard none of what you said."

Demitri looks confused. "Why?"

"You pulled up your shirt, and I got nothing. If you want me to pay attention, you can't show me your brain-liquifying abs."

Demitri laughs, surprised. He looks at me, radiating amusement. "So sorry. I'll just let sweat drip in my eyes next time."

I shake my head and giggle. "No, no, really. I'd hate for your eyes to sting. I'm good with not hearing what you have to say every once in a while."

"You're rather adorable when you're happy." Demitri gives me a charming smile.

"Being almost to the end of this horrific rehearsal definitely makes me happy," I say. "Plus, your abs."

He laughs. "I was asking you to prep that damn arabesque lift again now that you aren't slick."

With a grin, I get into place. I lift a leg and an arm, and he gets a decent grip, pressing me over his head.

He drops me into a cradle and nods. "Better."

Serious now, I gaze up at him. "I apologize for my inappropriate shenanigans a moment ago."

"First, we're friends," he says earnestly. "Second, my goal in these rehearsals is to make you laugh. You need that, Melanie.

Third, I'm flattered."

Just as Demitri sets me down, Mr. Isley booms into the microphone. "Reset. We're working through that mess again."

The cast gather back on stage.

"Thank you," I murmur to Demitri.

He grins and squeezes my shoulder before enthusiastically whispering, "Hey, do you think we could order pizza and choreograph some of that Wham! piece we talked about?"

I grin his way, whispering back, "I'm free after this rehearsal."

Demitri nods slightly. "I'll drive us to my house. Dad will love it. He won't have to cook, and he can get to know you better."

I bounce on my toes, excited, before following Demitri to places for the top of the piece.

CHAPTER *37*

I flip through the channels again, but Friday night TV is so terrible. *Uuuugh . . . I'm bored.*

The boys decided to have a guys-only night at a pool hall on Ventura Boulevard, and the girls all have other stuff to do. Even my parents are out enjoying a date night. So here I sit, alone. At first, I thought I wanted to be alone, but at this phase of the evening, it's lost its luster. I'm anxious and unsettled.

I turn off the TV and head to my bedroom, where I click on the reading lamp by my cozy upholstered chair and turn off the overhead light.

Trey and Adam are at the pool hall together. What if they finally come to blows in front of the guys?

All night, I've been consumed with nagging worry about the possibilities. We've managed to keep this mess from most of the group, and I'd like to keep it that way.

The sound of a car pulling up outside yanks me from my thoughts. I glance at the clock. *It's only eight . . . My parents can't be home yet. It's probably the neighbor.* I close my eyes, curling up for a catnap.

Then, all at once, my intuition blazes to life. My chest suddenly hurts. I sit up. With my overhead light off, the streetlight casts shadows of the tree in our front yard against my sheer white curtains. The unmistakable shape of a person is shadowed beside the tree.

My breath catches, and my heart pounds.

Maybe it's Adam or Trey. They've spent enough nights sneaking around my yard lately.

I click off my reading lamp, creep to the window in the dark, and carefully pull my curtain aside to peek out. There's a person out there, perfectly backlit by the streetlight. It's a full-moon night, so I can see his face and can hardly believe it. I blink twice, but the image doesn't change. Standing statue still in an aggressive wide-leg stance is Joel Stamp.

He's supposed to be in jail . . . How is this possible?

My heart pounds as I cross to my dresser and pick up the phone. Marcus is the only one of the guys with a cell phone, and I have his number memorized. It takes me two tries before my shaking hand manages to hit the right buttons.

On the second ring, he answers.

"Marcus, it's Melanie. I need to talk to Trey."

"You okay?"

"Just get him. Please!"

Through the receiver, I hear Marcus talking to the guys, but it's Adam's voice that comes on the line next.

"What's wrong?"

I don't have time to be annoyed at how Adam picked up instead of Trey. "Joel's standing in my front yard watching me through my bedroom window."

"Hang on a second, Mel," Adam says. "It's really loud in here." He takes the phone away from his mouth, and I hear him say to the rest of the guys, "Something's wrong. We need to go outside where I can hear better. I think I just misunderstood what she's saying."

"What do you mean something's wrong?" I hear Trey ask.

"If she said what I think she did, then something's very wrong."

The background noise slowly disappears.

"Okay, Melanie," Adam says. "We're outside. I'm putting you on speakerphone. Tell us what's happening."

"I'm home alone. I saw a shadow of a person standing in the front yard. I looked outside, and Joel Stamp is watching me."

"Are you sure someone's out there?" I recognize the voice as Demitri's. "It can't be Joel. He's in jail."

"Someone's there. He looks like Joel."

"Hang up and call the police," Marcus says. "I'm calling my dad to make sure Joel's still locked up. I'll call you back."

Before Marcus can hang up, Trey says, "We're coming to you. Are all the doors locked?"

"I don't know."

"Lock the doors. We'll be there in twenty minutes."

Adam's Harley revs in the background as they hang up.

I look out the curtains again. He's still there. I pick the phone up and dial 911.

"Nine-one-one, what's your emergency?"

"Someone's outside my window. I'm a teenager and home alone."

"I need your name and address."

Quickly, I give her the information.

"I'm dispatching a police unit," she says. "They should be there within an hour."

"An hour?" I gasp, baffled.

"We're a little backlogged this evening."

"If the person outside my window is who I think he is, I don't have an hour."

There's a pause. "Who do you think he is?"

"Joel Stamp. We've got a complicated history, but he's supposed to be in jail. He tried to rape and murder me."

"Are all the windows and doors locked?" the operator asks, with a little more urgency in her tone.

"I'm not sure." I make a mental note to do a better job checking these things when I'm home alone.

"Hang up and lock all the doors right now. Call us back if something else happens. The officers will be to you as soon as they can."

I thank her and hang up the phone. I take a deep breath, determined to be brave enough to leave my room and lock the doors. The phone rings, making me jump.

"Hello."

Marcus's distressed voice blisters through the receiver, "Melanie, I talked to my dad. He just got word that Joel was released into house arrest status this morning. Seems like his parents aren't following the rules. Lock your doors now! I'm in the car with Trey. We're on the way."

Before I can answer, I hear the front door crash against the wall as it's slammed open. I gasp and start to sweat. My hands start shaking.

Marcus hears the shift. "What's happening?"

"He's in the house," I whisper.

"He's in the house," Marcus says to Trey.

I hear Trey growl, "Put on your seat belt and hang on."

The line goes dead.

I hang up the phone and pick the receiver up to call Marcus again, but there's no dial tone. *Someone must have cut the phone line. If that's Joel inside the house, then he must not be alone.*

"Meeeelanie . . . Mellanieeee . . ." Joel singsongs my name from the living room.

My breath shallow, the terror rising up my spine, I look around for a weapon and spot one of Trey's baseball bats leaning against the wall in the corner. I rush across the room and grab the bat before backing into the middle of my dark room. My brain's running a million miles a minute. There's no point in hiding because Joel knows I'm in here.

I close my eyes, and my dark-water side is nowhere to be found. *Of all the times to lose the brazen new me!* Wheeling around in the darkness, I'm suddenly overtaken by a desire to run. *Maybe I can get out the window.* I turn the lock and try to push up the window, but it's painted shut. *Damn it!*

Suddenly, two hands slap the glass, palms flat. I gasp, and my weak knees go out from under me. I can barely breathe as I stare at the hands. Whoever they belong to is ducked below the windowsill where I can't see their face.

A boy's voice at the window sings, "Meeeellanieeee."

They're toying with me.

I glance at the clock. The guys are likely still fifteen minutes away. Tears roll steadily down my cheeks.

Come on, Melanie . . . You're better than this under pressure.

Joel sings my name again.

It sounds like he's still in the living room. My dark-water side roars to the surface. *About time!* My heartbeat gallops, and an evil grin spreads. *Let's have some fun!* "Jooooel," I sing, imitating his tone.

"Ballsy," Joel hollers. "I like it."

"Get the hell out of my house, Joel, and take your creepy friends with you."

He laughs. "Aren't you happy to see me?"

"How did you get out of jail? Let me guess, your mom pimped out her special sexy-time services with the warden?"

"Leave my mom out of this, bitch."

I laugh. "That wasn't a 'no,' Joel. It's okay. Her secret's safe with me." *Might as well go out with a bang.*

"Get out here, Melanie," Joel yells.

With the bat in my right hand, I turn the doorknob with my left. Carefully, I peek down the hall. It's empty, and the door at the end of the hall is closed. We usually keep it open, but it must have bounced shut when the front door slammed against the wall. The force of Joel's entry practically shook the whole house.

"Get out here, MELANIE!"

Quietly, I sneak down the hall and stop three feet from the closed door. I turn to the side, raising the bat, and get into the stance that Trey taught me once when we went to the batting cages.

"If you won't come out, then I'll come in," Joel announces.

He thinks I'm still in my room. This is my chance to take him by surprise.

When the doorknob starts to turn, time seems to slow down. The door swings open. I'm ready for him, but Joel doesn't expect me. The moment he steps into the darkness, I swing the bat as hard as I can. My arms jolt as the bat connects with his shoulder.

Joel falls sideways, out of view as the door hits the wall and swings back, closing between us. I wonder for a split second if I managed to knock him out. My hope dies when the door flies open and Joel rushes through. Flailing, I run backward down the hall. My back hits the wall, and I rush right into my dark bedroom.

I swing the bat wildly, but Joel catches it midmotion and yanks it out of my hand, throwing it behind him. The bat crashes into my bookshelf, shattering all my framed pictures.

Joels looks inhuman in the moonlight wash, his face a mask of rage. "You're going to pay for putting me in jail!"

He grabs me by the arms and slams me against my dresser. I get my legs up just in time to kick him in the chest with both feet. He flies backward, landing on my bed. He recovers faster than I expect, rushing across the room at me. Just before he's on me, there's a shattering sound to my right. A cinder block brick smashes through my window from the outside, hitting Joel hard in the arm. He grabs his elbow and bellows like a wild animal.

A crowbar comes through the window, sweeping from side to side, and glass falls in giant shards. Stan hefts himself through, tearing down my sheer curtains as he enters. I scream as Stan grabs me and shoves me out through the broken window. A guy wearing a ski mask grabs me on the other side and covers my mouth with his giant hand. I try to scream again, but his hand presses tight, blocking my nose and mouth.

Terror washes over me. I struggle to get free, but Stan and Joel have jumped out through the window and are helping the masked assailant carry me. My back's pressed against the masked man. He doesn't feel like a teenage boy. Something about the width of his shoulders tells me he's older. All at once, I know it's Joel's dad.

FIGHT BACK! Dark-Water Melanie screams in my head.

My attackers drag me across the front lawn and over the hedges that line the sidewalk. They're headed toward a blue van. I start fighting again, bucking and writhing.

My intuition rages, and I'm positive that the difference between life and death is that van. *If they get me in there, it's over.* I bite down hard on the masked man's hand, tasting blood.

He screams and lets go of me. "The little bitch just bit me!"

I hit Joel with a right hook. Joel stumbles back. Stan rushes me. I duck and spin out of the way. Stan whips around and makes another grab for me, but none of them have their hands on me for a split second. I turn and run as hard as I can down the street.

The sound behind me sends a chill running down my spine. My attackers have climbed back into the van and started the engine. They're going to run me down.

I hear Adam's Harley before I see it. He takes a sharp skidding left around the corner. He screeches to a halt, jumping off the motorcycle. I run to him, and he grabs me, pulling me behind him as if to shield me.

The van bears down on us, and at the last possible instant, jerks away and barrels past.

They're going to get away!

Trey's car screeches around the corner and slows down when he sees us. He looks past Marcus through the passenger window.

"I've got her!" Adam yells. "Go!"

Trey hits the gas, racing past me, following the van.

My entire body's shaking from head to toe, and I'm making a high-pitched repetitive squealing sound. Shock reverberates through me, making my teeth chatter. Adam pulls off his leather jacket and wraps it around me.

Arch's car pulls up, and he rolls down the window. "I'm going after them. I'll stop Trey."

It looks like Demitri has the same idea, because he races past us in his Jeep in pursuit of Trey. I see Isaac turn in the back seat, staring at us with wide eyes as they race past. Tanner's in the front seat, pointing the direction the van just turned.

"Never mind," Arch says. "D's got it."

"Trey's likely to kill them first and ask questions later," Adam says. "Let him handle it."

Arch shakes his head. "I just hope he doesn't do something to get himself thrown in prison. She okay?"

"I don't know yet, but I've got her."

Arch takes off down the street.

Adam turns down the hall, heading to my room. He stops at the door and flips on the light. His mouth falls open as he surveys the destruction. He pulls off the jacket and spins me around, looking me over. "Your shoulder has a shard of glass in it. Hold still."

I feel a tug, and the bloody glass shard is suddenly in Adam's hand. I'm surprised that it didn't hurt. "I'm okay."

He grabs my face and looks into my eyes. "You aren't okay. Your pupils are dilated. I think you're in shock." He pauses before adding, "I know this isn't the right time, but I need to talk to you soon."

I've had my side of our connection blocked since the night of the mock trial, so I have no clue what he's thinking.

He pulls me back through the hall to the kitchen, where he picks up the phone. There's a dial tone, so I guess my attackers only managed to cut the line to my room.

While he makes his call, I take a dishrag and wipe the blood out of Adam's jacket. I drift off, replaying the kidnapping attempt in my head.

Adam's raging growl drags me back to reality. "Why the *hell* didn't the police show up when she called earlier? . . . BUSY! You're too *busy*? . . . Fine. We'll wait here." He slams down the phone, and by the time he gets back to me, his hands are shaking with rage.

The second he wraps his arms around me, my usual post-trauma breakdown hits and I collapse in a fit of tears. He picks me up and holds me while I cry.

The side door opens. Oblivious, Mom and Rich come into the kitchen, laughing and talking. They stop short when they see me cradled in Adam's arms. His back's to them, so they don't know what's happening.

"Umm . . . ," Mom says hesitantly. "Hi, kids. Did Melanie and Trey break up, and you two are back together?"

Without answering, Adam turns around, and they see the condition I'm in.

Rich rushes over, takes me from Adam, and carries me into the living room. He sets me down on the couch. "What happened?"

I shake my head, unable to answer.

"Marcus got a call from Mel," Adam explains. "We raced over here as fast as we could."

"What happened, Adam?"

"Melanie saw Joel watching her while she was in her room. Apparently, he was released on bail, but Bruce wasn't notified by his staff until after it happened. We had no warning that he was being put on house arrest, or we would've never left her alone tonight. When we got here, Joel and two other people were attempting to kidnap Melanie. Somehow, she got away, and we pulled around the corner as she was running down the street."

"Who's 'we'?" My mom asks.

"Trey, Tanner, Demitri, Marcus, Isaac, and Arch went after Joel's van."

Rich's mouth falls open. "Call Marcus now. Get them back here!"

Adam heads to the kitchen to call Marcus. "You need to look in Melanie's room," he informs over his shoulder.

Rich leaves down the hall, and Mom sits next to me, putting her arms around me. We hear Rich whistle as he surveys the destruction.

The front door opens, and Trey strides through with the rest of the guys on his heels. He crosses the living room, headed to me.

"Guess I don't need to call anymore," Adam mutters.

Rich rushes back to the living room. "Did you hurt them?" he asks Trey.

Trey gets to me, leaning down to scoop me up off the couch. He sits down on the couch and cradles me like a scared toddler. "They got away," he says to Rich. "But I'm dealing Joel the next chance I get." He slides his other arm around me, his hand landing on my bloody shoulder. He examines his hand and then looks me over.

"Adam pulled a glass shard out of my shoulder," I explain.

Trey looks at Adam. "You and me. We're finishing this with Joel."

Adam nods, his jaw clenched.

"This is insane," Demitri breathes in exasperation.

Isaac sputters, "Melanie, are you okay?" He glances around the room at my friends and adds, "This is what goes on with her?"

Trey levels Demitri and Isaac with a serious look. "Welcome to Melanie's life. In all seriousness, since you're both with her for *The Pajama Game*, will you keep an eye on her in rehearsals and at the studio?"

Demitri nods. "I promise I will."

Isaac is too stunned to utter another coherent thought. He nods Trey's way before sinking down on the other couch with his hand over his mouth.

"It's gonna take a village, that's for sure," Arch says. "This girl's a magnet for intuitive nutcases."

"I just spoke to Joel's mother, and she stated that Joel and Mr. Stamp have been home all night." This from a police officer named Mitchell, who arrived some time ago to take a statement. He's proven to be a useless slug who couldn't find his ass with both hands and a map.

I give the officer a fierce look. Rage bubbles to the surface again. "You spoke to me, and I told you that he was here. Joel's facing attempted murder charges, and I'm an honors student. Your choice. Which story's it gonna be?"

"The Stamp family have no reason to lie to me," the officer says dimly.

"Are you kidding?" Adam says. "They have every reason to lie to you. Melanie's testifying against Joel. They've already tried, and failed, to kill her multiple times at the county hospital."

"You need to look deeper into this, Officer Mitchell," Mom says. "If Melanie says it happened, then it happened."

"How about I resolve this problem for you?" Trey asks. "Here's the license plate number for the van."

"Not to steal your thunder, Trey," Tanner says, "but I've got a few prizes to offer too." He opens his velvet suit jacket and reaches into the inside pocket, pulling out a stack of Polaroids. He hands the stack to Rich, and we all gather around.

It looks like Tanner managed to get close to the van, because he got clear pictures of Joel and Stan in the front seats, looking his way. He also managed to get full pictures of the van and another of the license plate.

Officer Mitchell raises his eyebrows. "You got Polaroids?"

Tanner shrugs. "Why of course. While Trey distracted them with a bunch of engine revving and fancy finger flashing, we pulled up next to them." He looks around at all of us and says to Officer Mitchell, "So, here you have it: proof that Melanie's telling the truth."

I grin. "Thank you."

Tanner hugs me. "We've got your back, girl."

CHAPTER 38

Even though I can see the evidence right in front of me, I still can't shake my disbelief. The caravan of my friends' cars has come to a stop, bathing the school in an ominous glow of headlights. There are squad cars parked along the curb that the buses usually use. The school looks different after dark, and I'm tempted not to get out of the car as soon as Trey cuts the engine.

He lets go of my hand and opens the driver's side door. Purpose in his step, he rounds the front of the car to let me out, but Adam gets to my door first and opens it for me.

Trey and Adam square off.

"Cool it, you two," Bear implores them. "Melanie made her choice, and we've got bigger things to worry about."

Our group gathers on the curb, everyone dressed for a night of fun, all the girls in neon, denim, and lace, and the guys in their denim jackets with the collars popped. Given the current dilemma, our outfits now seem way out of sync. We walk quickly together around the front of the school and up the steps at the front of the auditorium. Lights blaze from the lobby.

A police officer stops us as we enter.

Arch steps forward, putting out his hand. "Good evening, Officer. I'm Arch Terani, student council president, and this is the student council. Principal Walker called to ask us to come down here and survey the damage."

The officer shakes Arch's hand and waves us in.

We follow Arch through the lobby doors into the auditorium.

I gasp.

The set walls are full of giant holes that look like they were made with a sledgehammer, the two doors are busted off the hinges, and the pretty yellow walls are splashed with red paint.

Hiram flies down the audience aisle with all of us on his heels. We rush up the stairs on the side of the stage, and everyone stops dead in their tracks at the scene in front of us. Scrawled on the set wall to the right are the words *Die, Little Bitch*.

Joel's taunting me.

The officer turns to us. "Who do you think that message is intended for?"

All eyes turn to me, and I raise my hand. "I guarantee it's for me."

The officer nods. "I need to talk to you," he says, pointing at Arch. The officer leads him around the corner behind the back of the set and out of sight.

The rest of us look at each other, shock and horror playing across our faces. The set isn't salvageable. Hiram lost all that time and effort he put into it.

Arch walks back around the edge of the set wall. "Adam, come here."

With hesitation, Adam joins Arch and the officer. The rest of us are left wondering what's on the other side of that wall.

After a few moments, Adam comes back around the corner and says with exasperation, "I need Trey."

Trey glances at me before heading around the corner.

There's no point in delaying the inevitable. Whatever's over there is going to either scare me or piss me off, and either way, I might as well get on with it. My dark-water side is irritated. *They mean well protecting me, but this is ridiculous.* "For the love of . . ." I holler so they can hear me on the other side of the set. "You guys don't need to go through all of this."

The rest of the group follows close behind as I make my way around the set.

I hear a low whistle escape before Trey announces, "Joel's days are numbered," loud enough for the police to hear.

"Do you believe this is a message for the girl that raised her hand?" the lead detective asks.

"She's my girlfriend, Melanie," Trey answers just as I round the corner. "Yes, it's a message for her."

I take in the damage. A chair lies on its side on the floor, and it's covered in drying red paint. My eyes scan up to find a mannequin with a rope tied around its neck, hanging from the lighting rail overhead. The mannequin has a sign on it: *Watch your back, M. You're going to die.*

A laugh bursts from my mouth. The fact that the Drones were so childish that they thought this would scare me is hilarious.

"You think this is funny?" asks Officer-in-Charge.

"Yes and no. There's nothing funny about the destruction. Hiram's worked himself sick building the set, and all that work is lost. I realize that the threats are bad, but it's all so childish. A noose? A mannequin? Red paint? It's really stupid. I'm sick of dealing with the people who did this."

The police officer gives a pensive look. "Your reaction isn't what I expected. But I guess it's good that you're being rational about this."

I slide my gaze to Trey and then Adam. "What are you two thinking?"

They exchange a glance.

"We do what we can to help," Trey says. "Let's give the officer the info he needs for the investigation, and then we'll head back to Arch's house. It's only nine-thirty, so we can still salvage our evening."

Marcus snorts. "There's a big backstory here."

The officers listen intently while Marcus lays out the whole Joel-multiple-rape-attempts situation, the balcony nightmare, the Jessica knife arrest, the hospital poisoning attempts, and the attempted kidnapping at my house last night. The officers seem oddly intrigued by it all, but it probably helps that Marcus's version of the events is hilarious. He has us all in stitches, and even a few of the officers are quietly laughing. Officer-in-Charge's mouth is twitching, and he's rubbing his forehead as if it's all he can do to compose himself.

As he gestures in Trey's direction, Marcus ends the story with, "So, Victoria and Tiffany are likely in cahoots because they lost their Venezuelan playboy here. Joel's making the best of his bail time. Nurse Ratchet's in jail. A bunch of them are expelled. And it's all a spicy disaster."

The lead officer thanks us and tells us we're free to go. We head down the audience aisle and out the auditorium doors.

Bear crosses the street to his car. "I'm going to run to the store for more snacks. I'll meet you guys back at the house." He hops in his car.

I hear the starter click twice, but the engine doesn't turn over. My intuition blazes to life. "BEAAAAR!" I scream.

His window's down, so he hears me. His face is contorted with fear as he looks my way. We've been through enough rounds with my intuition that he doesn't question me. He opens his door and rushes away from the car. He's halfway across the street when it happens. A deafening explosion rocks the neighborhood.

Bear's thrown off his feet. The blast is so strong, my friends and I tumble backward. Car alarms are triggered up and down the road. We all duck and cover as shrapnel rains down. Bear hits the ground and rolls before clamoring to his feet and running to us as his car dances in flame.

CHAPTER 39

Dante is leaning over the railing on the balcony three stories up, the place where I almost lost my life. "Everything okay, guys?"

"Same old crap, different week," Arch answers. "Hang tight. We're on our way up."

We all get to the balcony, and Dante looks at us with barely restrained curiosity.

"The set's trashed," Hiram tells Dante, "but Principal Walker's giving us funds to replace it. We're going to have to work double time to rebuild it, but that's the least of the drama. After we toured the set destruction and finished with the police, we headed to the cars. Luckily, Melanie had one of her witchy psychic intuition moments, or Bear would have been dead. He turned the key in his ignition, and it went tick-tick. Melanie screamed, and he got out just before it went BOOM."

"BEAR'S CAR BLEW UP?" Dante screeches.

Arch nods. "It's charcoal."

Bear puts an arm around my shoulder. "I'm changing my nickname for Mel from Kitten Little to Lucky Charms."

"Was anyone hurt?" Dante asks.

"The police were still in the theater when Bear's car exploded," Arch says, "and they rushed out to investigate. They called in the bomb squad and found another bomb in my car's engine. They managed to safely remove it."

"Who did you all piss off? The mafia?"

Arch shakes his head. "We know it's Joel and the Drones, but it's still under investigation."

Dante rolls his eyes, then assumes a mischievous look. "You guys sound like you could use a drink. Isaac's blending up a fresh round of margaritas."

We all agree that this sounds like a great idea. I'm first through the door. Isaac hands me a margarita as the deejay fires up. C+C Music Factory's "Gonna Make You Sweat (Everybody Dance Now)" blasts from the speakers. The girls start dancing. Some of the guys head into the kitchen with Trey to fill cups and plates with nachos and drinks for themselves.

Presley and Arch wave me over, and we head out to the balcony to talk.

"Given the free-flowing margaritas and the late start," Arch says, "everyone needs to stay here tonight. Trey's not good to drive. Do you think your parents would be okay with it? The other girls have already called their parents."

I take the phone, about to dial my home number, just as Trey comes out to the balcony and stumbles a bit as he misjudges the step down from the door. He looks at me with an apologetic wince.

Prince Charming!

I roll my eyes at Presley, who snickers.

Rich picks up. "Hi, Rich. I've got a bit of a situation."

"Please tell me there wasn't another brawl." He sounds both amused and hesitant.

I better omit some details about our evening and keep this simple. "No. Everything's fine." I pause, trying to collect myself. "I'm going to be honest. The margaritas are a little strong tonight, and everyone has permission to crash here. I'm the last girl to call home, and I don't want to give you the wrong impression, but Trey's not exactly solid to drive."

Rich snorts. "Given how responsible he usually is, I'm a little surprised."

I hear Mom ask him what's going on, and he says, "Trey's drowning in a margarita trough and isn't good to drive Melanie home." He puts the receiver back to his mouth. "The other girls are staying there?"

"Yes, sir."

Arch gestures for the phone. "Rich, hi, it's Arch. I apologize. Bear and I'll be here all night with an eye on everyone." He nods, listening to Rich. "Sounds good. Thank you . . . Okay . . . Have a good night." He hangs up. "Rich sounds worried, but he says you can stay over."

Arch heads inside with Presley as Trey leans on the railing next to me.

Valerie comes out on the balcony with Adam, and they're loudly squabbling.

"You're so clueless sometimes!" Valerie slurs. "Seriously, Adam. You're an ass!"

She stumbles inside, leaving Adam standing there looking befuddled.

Trey raises his eyebrows. "Trouble in paradise?"

Adam shakes his head. Trey stumbles, a bit less steady from the drinks. I huff and Adam smirks.

I sigh and head inside, needing a breather from these two. My solo cup's empty, and I think I better eat something. My head suddenly feels like it's full of rainbow goo. The room's moving in waves, and it feels like the floor's spongy under my heel-clad feet. I stumble, nearly tripping over an invisible hazard before steadying myself on the wall.

"You okay, Mel?" Demitri asks.

I nod, pull off my heels, and toss them in the corner.

Hiram sweeps his arm over the top of the dining table, scattering empty cups, fast-food bags, and odds and ends on the floor. He sets up ten red plastic cups on each end of the table and loudly announces, "Beer pong tournament! The winner gets this *gorgeous* crown that my girlfriend made!"

Ugh, Hiram's girlfriend. Susan. I hate Susan. I hit her with a slightly inebriated death glare from across the room. My irritation is growing. *Something's wrong. I've only had one drink.*

Hiram holds up a crown made of cardboard and tinfoil, with Froot Loops "jewels" superglued all over it. Susan looks proud of herself, and Hiram gives her a sloppy kiss before putting the crown on her head for safekeeping. She obnoxiously giggles and swoons.

My dark-water side is reaching the end of her patience. *I'm so over this high school giggly teen crap.*

Finley claps her hands and heads to the table. "Crown is miii-ine!" She lives for beer pong and has a long history of winning every competition.

Demitri, Bear, Arch, and Tanner all announce that they also want to play, and Hiram sets them up for battle.

Bear and Demitri are first, and the two guys head to opposite ends of the table. They appraise each other before leaning over and shaking hands.

The first ping-pong ball is launched just as Trey steps up behind me and puts his arms around me, resting his chin on my shoulder. "Adam and Valerie are still mad at each other," he whispers.

"What's the fight about?"

"I don't know, but he snapped."

The deejay winds down, and the room goes silent just in time for the middle of an argument between Tanner and Finley to be revealed.

"Uh-oh . . ." Bear murmurs.

Finley smacks Tanner on the arm. "What the hell's wrong with you, Tanner?" She turns her back on him, crossing her arms over her chest.

Tanner slurs, "Babe, I'm sorry. I take it back! All the totally true things I said aren't true, I swear."

This is going downhill fast. Something's seriously not right. It's not just me. Everyone's off.

The guys crack up, and Finley hits him with a death glare. "You and me, Tanner! It's on . . . or is this game too manly for you?"

My jaw flops open. That's the first mean thing I've *ever* heard come out of Finley's mouth.

Presley cackles loudly from across the living room, having managed to untangle herself from the make-out session she's been lost in with Marcus for the better part of thirty minutes. They both look disheveled, and his mouth's smeared with her red lipstick.

"You tell him, Finley," she crows. "Guys suck!"

Marcus snaps his head around at Presley. "Hey! You take that back! You didn't think I sucked when you were latched onto me like an eight-legged sea monster a second ago."

Presley gasps and looks over-the-top offended. I laugh because drunk Presley's the last person I'd want to tango with.

"Did you just call me a SEA MONSTER?" Presley bellows.

Marcus sputters. "Ummm . . . I'm sorry . . . I think." He turns to Bear and asks, "I'm supposed to be sorry, right?"

Bear snickers. "Yes, you drunk jackass. You're supposed to be sorry!"

Marcus looks sheepish and makes a grab for Presley's hand, but she skirts him and marches over to sit next to Valerie on the couch.

Trey heads to the balcony, and the moment he's out of sight, Adam moves up next to me. We survey the quickly spiraling partiers.

Finally, I ask, "What's the fight about?"

Adam's jaw tightens. "She's talking about the wedding *again*. She's driving me nuts. We had an *hour*-long talk two days ago about flower colors. Her whole room is covered in wedding magazines, and I have to look through *every* SINGLE new magazine she buys. It's mind-numbing."

I snort. "Can't help you there. I've always thought big weddings are nothing but a logistical nightmare. I'm more of a 'spontaneously run off to Vegas' type."

Adam slides his gaze my way, radiating equal parts amusement and irritation. "Please don't be perfect right now."

I grin and glance at the balcony. Through the open door, I catch Trey stumbling again. Bear reaches out to steady him.

"Did we make the right decision?" Adam asks.

"I'm seriously questioning that," I say with a snarl.

"You have me blocked. Tell me what you're thinking."

"I'm a little drunk and a lot bored. My dark side's nagging at me to create a little chaos, and I'm attempting to ignore it."

Adam smiles.

"The only reason I don't do it, is it will add to Bear's workload." I grin and tip my chin in Bear's direction.

Adam and I watch while Bear scuttles here and there, sitting this person down, breaking up a squabble, picking up a spilled cup.

Adam chuckles and side-eyes me. "Triple-dog dare you."

I throw my head back, belting laughter. I glance at Adam and bite my lip with a mischievous snicker, considering it.

Bear sees the look I give Adam and pulls up briskly in front of us. "I need you two to hold it together. Tonight is a mess."

Playfully, I crinkle my nose at Bear. He rolls his eyes before walking away toward the sound of a crash in the kitchen.

Adam laughs quietly. "I love that about you." His expression is sad.

Trey drunkenly slurs, "Melanie," from the balcony.

"I need to talk to him about how wasted he is," I say to Adam. "It's revolting."

"A word of advice. Wait until he's sober. You're not going to get anywhere tonight, and it's just going to piss you off."

I consider his advice before saying, "I'm already pissed, Adam." I turn on my heel and head toward the balcony. "I need to talk to you, Trey."

Adam follows, leaning against the doorjamb.

Suddenly, my vision starts to go spotty, and just before my legs collapse, the dark water in my mind rages in a torrent. As it submerges me, I realize that there's a reason we've all been acting so off. We've been sedated.

My world goes black.

CHAPTER *40*

I wake up slowly, my head pounding in rhythm to the beating of my heart. *Oh no.*

I slowly open my eyes but close them tight as the bright morning sun blasts the east-facing balcony. Shielding my eyes with my hand, I turn away from the light. When I finally manage to peel my eyes open again, I notice that Hiram and Arch's balcony is littered with discarded solo cups and pizza boxes. An arm's lying heavy on my hip, and I shift to see who it is. Trey's asleep behind me. Adam's slumped by the door. Valerie and Demitri are splayed out in awkward positions next to Trey. Marcus and Tanner are sprawled on the other end of the balcony.

I slowly get up, stretching sore muscles and trying to clear my foggy head. Inside the house, I find Presley and Finley passed out on the couch. Bear's slumped over on one of the dining chairs, his head plunked down on the table at an awkward angle.

The kitchen brings another hilarious sight. Kenji's asleep, leaning in the doorjamb to Hiram's room on the far side of the kitchen.

I giggle about it as I get started making a pot of coffee. *How did he manage to sleep like that all night?*

Hiram's bedroom door opens, and I hear him groan out, "What the *hell*?"

I laugh. "Hiram, go through your other door and come around. I'm making coffee. I guess Kenji passed out there."

Hiram laughs and closes the door gently against Kenji's back. Soon after, he and Susan shuffle into the kitchen looking like death warmed over.

Ugh. Not Susan. My head's pounding.

Hiram gets out coffee mugs, sugar, and cream. With a flippant motion to the coffee maker, I invite him to take over the coffee situation, then slump to the floor and lean against the cabinet by the sink. My head's fuzzy. I don't remember anything after Adam dared me to cause trouble.

"You okay, Mel?" Hiram asks.

"Nope, nope, nope. It's so bad." I lie down on the floor, covering my head with my arm.

Hiram laughs. "Sit up. I've got coffee for you."

He hands me a cup, and I close my eyes, inhaling. I take a sip and feel a little bit better. Hiram and Susan sit down across from me on the floor.

"I don't even remember passing out," I say.

Hiram and Susan glance at each other.

"We were just talking about that," Susan says. "Neither of us remember going to sleep either. I woke up on the floor in Hiram's room, and he was out cold in the hall."

Slowly, everyone comes to and trudges into the kitchen for coffee, looking like zombies from *Night of the Living Dead*.

Adam yells from another room, "Everyone! Here, NOW!"

We exchange a worried glance before collecting ourselves enough to run through the townhouse.

"Bathroom!" Adam calls out.

We pile into the little room. Scrawled on the mirror in red lipstick are the words *Lights Out!*

"Does anyone remember passing out?" Adam asks.

They all shake their heads.

Something nags in the back of my mind. Suddenly, I remember. "Right before I fell over face-first, I realized something." I glance around. "I felt sedated, just like when I was in the hospital."

"Joel and the Drones are behind this," Adam snarls. "They somehow drugged us. I don't know how they did it, but this isn't a coincidence."

"Why didn't they do anything while we were unconscious?" Presley asks.

"Because they're toying with us," I growl.

My dark-water side starts roiling, and Trey and I side-eye each other.

"I'm not scared of the dark anymore," I say. "I'll show them 'Lights Out.'"

CHAPTER *41*

Trey rests his head back on his headrest, and I can feel the conflict within him reverberating down our connection.

Looks like we have another fight brewing. I gaze his way and raise my eyebrows expectantly.

After a long pause, he says, "I can't deal, Melanie."

"With what?"

He gives me a scathing look. "You and Adam."

My mouth drops open. "You're choosing *now* to fight about that?"

We're on Mulholland, parking in Trey's car.

He nods, and he's clearly pissed. "Why him? You chose *Adam* for your first time?"

Irritated laughter bubbles up. "Seriously? You pushed me away *how* many times? How many excuses did you make for why you and I couldn't go there? But *Tiffany* you could jump right in with?"

Trey reaches for the door handle and gets out of his car. I get out on my side.

He starts pacing. "Tiffany and I were a fling."

My face scrunches. "So that makes it okay?"

He turns to me, and there's genuine hurt in his eyes. "You knew it meant something to me to be your first."

I nod back, my face alight with cheerful sarcasm. "Sure did! Guess what? It meant something to me to be on my deathbed in the hospital and not have my soulmate screwing around behind my back! I guess we don't give a damn about that, so let's deal with the bullshit you're harping on instead! You're the one who chose to hold me off. Your excuse was always that I wasn't ready. I don't understand why you took it upon yourself to decide that for me. I was ready. I told you that, and you ignored me."

"We've been through this," Trey answers softly. "I was trying to do the right thing for you and wait."

"Instead, you drove me insane. I felt like I had zero say in my own decisions. Maybe it was you who wasn't ready, which is fine. But don't put your indecisive bullshit on me like it's somehow *my fault* that you suddenly discovered I was telling the truth about being ready!"

I turn my back to him.

"Melanie—"

"Let me clarify," I cut in, whipping around. I've had enough of this ongoing fight. "You weren't ready with me because apparently everything was on a fast track with Tiffany."

"I went there with Tiffany because the truth is, I didn't bother second-guessing myself with her. She said she was fine, and I took her at her word. I don't love her, and it wasn't my responsibility to protect her from her own rash decisions."

"Thank you for loving me right into a freaking nunnery, Trey! I appreciate it. It nearly drove me mad."

"Let me guess. You told Adam that I hadn't pulled the trigger, and he jumped at the chance."

I shake my head. "He had no idea. He trusted me to make my own decision. He didn't weigh me down with discussions. He let me be. It's exactly what I needed."

Trey closes his eyes. "Does he know now?"

I tip my head back, beyond sick of going round and round on this. He's been picking fights for days. I think this is what they've all been leading to, though. "Yes. He knows. It came up a couple hours later. He was shocked, but he accepted that I made my choice."

"How many times after that?" He looks down at his shoes as if dreading my answer.

"None. It was once." I narrow my eyes. "Your turn. How many times with Tiffany?"

Trey closes his eyes and rubs his face. He doesn't answer audibly, but he accidently sends through our connection that he feels like an ass.

"I'll take your silence as a clue that it was a three-week hump-alooza." I finally snap. "I've gotta tell you, Trey, that you treat me like a child. I don't need it. What I need is a soulmate who can trust me, and who I can trust. I'm sick to death of having to justify every little thing to you while you run rampant doing God only knows what behind my back."

Trey sighs. "I've obviously made mistakes. I apologize for them, but I didn't expect you to jump at the first chance you got."

"The first chance I got? I have a soulmate connection with Adam! I didn't hold a raffle at school and pick an entry from a bowl!" I hit him with a hard gaze. "Are you really going to shame me for being with Adam? YOU AND I WEREN'T TOGETHER! You cheated on me, and we broke up! I was free to do what I pleased, which is a lot more than I can say for you! You chose to cheat on me with literally the first girl that sidled up to you, the SECOND I was conveniently out of the way!"

Trey closes his eyes and shakes his head. He leans on his car and tries to explain. "Somehow, the fact that you were with someone you had a deeper connection with seems worse in my head than me coping with your life-and-death situation with a random."

Exasperated, I demand, "WHY?"

Trey's expression clamps down. "I don't know."

I'm close to tears. "I see. So, I'm free to take a ride down any random's road as long as I don't give a shit about them? Good to know."

Trey sighs. "It sounds ridiculous when you put it like that."

"It's ridiculous when you put it like that about Tiffany, Trey!"

When Trey says nothing, I finally can't take it anymore. "I'm not going round and round with you while you justify your double standards. Are we together or not?"

Trey closes his eyes and says, "Not. I can't handle the drama."

My heart hurts, but I'm relieved somehow. All we've done is fight since Adam left me. "Please take me home, then."

CHAPTER 42

Tanner steps up to the microphone. "Welcome to the final competition of Hollywood High's FIRST BATTLE OF THE BANDS!"

The crowd goes so nuts that it's deafening. I don't think we could stuff another person in the bleachers if we had a crowbar. At three bucks a pop for the entrance fee, we've made a fortune for our activities fund.

"We've had an incredible week," Tanner says, "and I'd like to thank our ten bands that didn't make the final round. You all fought hard."

The crowd cheers.

Tanner waits for the noise to die down. The crowd falls silent. Tanner leans into the microphone. "Introducing your five finalists. On riser one, Monday's champions . . . EL DIABLO!"

They killed the competition on Monday. The other two bands didn't have a shot. I clap and scream with the crowd as the members of Dante's band jog to their riser.

"Reporting to riser two, our Tuesday champions, HORIZONS!"

When Mr. B and the music teachers run out, the audience whistles and screams. The other two bands that day were okay, but Mr. B's band really is legit. They have a psychedelic jazz sound that's almost haunting. They were my favorite band from the whole week.

"Reporting to riser three, our Wednesday champions, FREEZE FRAME!"

"They surprised me," Trey says, trying too hard to talk to me. Things between us have been awkward all week. "I thought they'd suck, but they were great!"

He talked over the announcement of the Thursday winner. I'll have to piece it together later.

"Last, but certainly not least, reporting to riser five, our champion from lunch today, BEATS!"

Beats is a full drumline plus at least thirty dancers. The crowd goes berserk as they rhythmically march to their area in sparkly red-and-black outfits.

"All five bands are going to play," Tanner informs the crowd. "After, student council is going to pass out ballots, and the winner will be announced today! Now presenting the heavy metal grind of EL DIABLO!"

Looks like we're going to start with the loudest metal band that competed. The crowd jump to their feet, head banging and screaming as the lead singer growls.

It's too much noise for me. I skirt around Trey and wander down the track, turning under the bleachers to get away from everything.

Adam follows me into the relative calm. "You okay?" He lights up a smoke.

With dead eyes, I answer, "I'm so sick of all this high school jubilation."

Adam laughs. "You used to love this crap. I thought it was cute."

I hit him with a steely stare. "Are we seriously doing this weird small-talk thing? I've been dealing with the same thing with Trey. It's irritating."

After the first band finishes their song, Tanner's voice blasts from the speakers. "Your attention please."

A hush falls over the crowd.

"All right," Adam says to me. "Let's talk about something serious. What happened with you and Trey? The whole group is trying to figure it out. Bear and Darren feel like they have whiplash. They thought everything was fixed, and suddenly you two broke up again."

"He finally cracked under the pressure. He started overthinking everything once he didn't have the competition between the two of you to distract him."

Adam raises his eyebrows. "All he did that whole time was fight to get you back. What the hell?"

I sigh, tipping my head back with my eyes closed. *I feel dead inside.* "Human nature, I suppose. After the competitive need to win against you died down, jealousy got the best of him. He got mad, and it escalated to the point that all we did was fight about you and me. He finally broke things off because he 'doesn't like drama.'"

Adam snorts. "Really? *He* doesn't like drama? He started it with the Tiffany fiasco."

"Preaching to the choir. He justified the Tiffany mess as a 'distracting fling.'" I sarcastically inform, "Sex is acceptable as long as it's HIM with a bimbo."

Adam laughs.

"Don't get it twisted though." I jokingly imitate Trey during one of our fights. "'Sex between you and Adam is COMPLETELY unacceptable because it wasn't a fling.'"

"Good to know," Adam says with a thoughtful nod. "Naturally, that's different." He gets a mischievous look and raises his eyebrows. "I don't suppose you want to blow off this battle-of-the-bands mess and go have a totally unjustifiable fling instead?"

I crack up. "You're funny." I raise an eyebrow. "Tempting, though."

Adam ponders quietly, the mood shifting serious, and I avert my eyes. I don't need a reminder of how handsome he is when he's introspective.

"How are you taking it?" he asks.

"Well, with the two of you out of my life, I'm finally getting some sleep."

Adam smiles wistfully as he stares at the ground.

Tanner's voice blasts again. "It's been a great week. Right, HOLLYWOOD HIGH?"

The crowd goes wild.

I grin, amused.

"What are you thinking?" Adam asks. "You have me blocked."

"Just wondering what color flowers you picked, and if you're serving steak or chicken at your fancy country club wedding."

Adam laughs, and his shoulders relax. He looks at me and suddenly seems happier. "You're one of the few people who can tease me like that." He sighs deeply. "Honestly, it feels good to be amused for a second by the wedding mess. She's driving me insane. Don't get me wrong; she's not doing anything out of line. It's just that she's all in and I'm not."

"Not so sure Val's the one anymore, huh?" I quip.

His expression turns serious. "Asking her to marry me was never about being sure she's the one. It was about not having to face the fact that what you and I have terrifies me."

I shake my head. "Little did you know that in an attempt to

avoid one hell, you dropped right into another one." I smirk. "A rather expensive one, might I add."

"You're enjoying this, aren't you?" He breaks into a grin.

I crinkle up my nose at him. "You have no idea. I think your pain is hilarious."

After a laugh, we stand in silence. I gesture for his cigarette. He hands it to me, and I take a drag. When I'm done, he reaches for it, but I shake my head and pull my hand back. "Mine."

He smiles and pulls another one out of his pack. The flicker of his lighter illuminates his beautiful blue eyes. "There's more to us than I was willing to face. I buckled."

I ponder whether to say what I'm thinking.

As usual, Adam reads my expression. "Either say it or unblock your side of our connection and send it."

Finally, I meet his gaze. "I'm better off alone. I'm not weak and scared anymore. Honestly, I'm not even a teenager anymore in anything more than a number. I've accepted that I'm tough, always in danger, and have an evil streak. I was too dependent on you and Trey. I've had a lot of time to think lately, and I've come to terms that everything landed where it needed to."

"You're wrong," Adam breathes. "I need to tell you something." He pauses in thought. "Trey's theory that you and I are nothing but heat and we'll burn each other up . . . That sounded accurate at the time, but he's wrong. I've spent a lot of time with Bear and Darren, and I'm more clearheaded now. We don't burn each other up; we fuel each other. I know you're going to stand beside me and kick ass with the same brutality that lives in me. I'm sick of fighting alone. You're my match."

I roll my eyes and huff. "No offense, but I'm *so* sick of having these discussions with you and Trey. I'm off this hamster wheel. It never goes anywhere."

Thoughtfully, Adam nods. "I hear you on that, but I need to discuss this with you for my sanity's sake. If it helps, I'm not trying to start a fight."

I close my eyes. "I know you're not."

Adam rushes to say, "I screwed up, Melanie. It's haunted me from the moment I asked Valerie to marry me."

Apparently, he's not going to let this go. After an exhausted pause, I groan. "Then *why*, Adam?"

"Do you have any clue how terrifying it is to stare into your eyes knowing that you can destroy me?"

"Yeah. I do. Because that's exactly what you did to me."

He closes his eyes, letting my words sink in. "Melanie, I'm so sorry. I've screwed this up in every possible way. I've done absolutely everything that I asked you to never do when we were on the pier." He opens his eyes and pulls me in, wrapping his arms around me. "I'll leave her this weekend if you'll try for a fresh start with me. I'm supposed to have dinner with her on Sunday."

"Don't leave her for me. I never want that guilty nightmare on me again."

"I'm not. I'm leaving because it's not working. I want to start over with you."

"Let me stop you right there. I'm flat out not having this conversation. I learned a hard lesson with this mess. I'll *never* get tangled up with someone who's taken again. It's not right, and it nearly ate me alive. I owe it to Valerie not to discuss this. If you end up single, we can revisit the topic, but not before."

Adam nods. "I respect that. I'll talk to Bear to make sure I'm clearheaded and have a solid plan to break the news to Valerie. Do you promise you'll discuss this with me after I break it off with her?"

"I will discuss it if that happens, but I don't think it will. You had ample opportunity to end it with her before and you didn't."

Adam tips up my chin. "Trey and I both screwed up. Both times you were in the hospital, we cratered, and we each justified our poor decisions because things were so difficult for us. I fully grasp how unfair that was to you. You were the one going through the reality of everything. We were both selfish. I want you to know, though, that I was the worst between him and me. What he went through was horrific while you were sedated. It took the entire group to hold him together, and we didn't get the job done. That was my first mistake. He needed more help than anyone realized, and he used Tiffany as a crutch. I've been lectured at length by Michael on that." He takes a breath before continuing. "There's zero excuse for how I fell apart when you were in detox. I needed to hold it together. You trusted me, and I folded the first chance I got. I knew what I wanted all along. I apologize, and I mean it. I take full responsibility for this mess. Things were mixed up and complicated. I'm usually good at thinking above the chaos, and I failed this time. You have my word that it won't happen again. I'm going to leave Valerie, and if you give me another chance after that, it'll be you and me. No hesitation."

I say nothing.

Adam meets my conflicted gaze. "I won't destroy you again. What we have is right."

We stare at each other while Tanner's voice booms, "Now, our grand prize winner, with three hundred and seventy-four votes, receiving a FIVE-HUNDRED-DOLLAR cash prize, your battle of the bands grand champions . . . BEATS!"

The crowd screams at ear-splitting volume as I turn, heading back to our friends. I don't make it far. Deb bounces up to me with a jubilant smile. Her bubbly demeanor is completely out of place for her, not an ounce of sarcasm or brass knuckles to be found. Deb's a lot of things, but girlie isn't one of them.

I stare at her like she's lost her mind. "You okay there, buddy?" My tone is both amused and suspicious.

"Michael just asked me on a date," Deb says giddily. "Tomorrow night! We're going to dinner at Orlando's." She clasps her hands in front of her and wiggles her whole body like an excited puppy.

My eyes widen as my expression morphs amused. "That's awesome! Now embrace your inner chill. You look over-enthused. We'd hate to scare the nice twenty-one-year-old man away."

Deb goes rigid. "Damn! Did he see my happy outburst?"

I send a shy glance Michael's way. He's across the field, sitting on one of the risers. People pass by as everyone leaves the football field. He's watching Deb with a hawk's eye, a slight smirk of amusement gracing his face.

I curb a grin and meet Deb's gaze with big eyes. I shake my head a little too emphatically. "Definitely not."

She exhales, buying my lie. "What's he doing?" she hisses excitedly.

Subtly, I glance in his direction, finding him in a spirited conversation with Adam. The smile on Michael's face speaks volumes. Adam shoulder-pounds him. "Well, he's currently wiggling like a happy puppy while Adam congratulates him. If I were to guess, I think he's doing the same thing you are."

My enthused expression stills as Michael looks back our way, and he's suddenly a bit more stoic. I can't hear anything they're saying from this distance, but Adam's body language clearly communicates that Michael's asking if I'm back together with him. Adam shakes his head while he stuffs his hands into the pockets of his jeans.

Michael and Adam turn and walk toward the alley. Michael puts an arm around Adam and thump-thumps him on the shoulder. Either they're heading off to a private location where Michael can console his friend, or they're heading together to the set for the movie. Either way, Adam's leaving, and I feel both relieved and downtrodden.

"What's going on, Melanie?" Deb asks gently. She apparently saw Adam's reaction to Michael's question, and my reaction to Adam's reaction.

I quirk my mouth and take a breath but don't reply.

"I know our friendship is new," Deb says, "but I've got your back. I'll never betray your confidence."

I smile a tiny bit. "I know. I trust you and appreciate that. There's nothing going on. Literally. That's the issue."

Deb nods. "Do you want there to be something going on?"

I wobble my head. "It's complicated." My smile perks as I intentionally change the subject. There are already enough people aware of this mess with me and Adam. I don't need another. "You know what isn't complicated?"

Deb grins. "What?"

I gesture toward the alley. "Heading to Hollywood Boulevard to shop for your date outfit."

Deb's expression assumes a touch of bashfulness as she shakes her head. "I'd rather go to the mall and get a pretty dress."

My mouth falls open in mock horror. "The *mall*? Who are you, and what have you done with Deb? We *hate* the mall. You despise pretty dresses."

She shrugs and kind of melts all over. "I know, but he's so cute. I want to be pretty."

Amused and shocked, I tip my head to the side. "Well . . . all right. Let's go shopping for something girlie." I scrunch up my face. "Just don't pick anything pink or I'll have you admitted for insanity."

Deb hooks her arm under mine, and off we go to be whatever weird version of us that the afternoon has in store. I side-eye Deb and grin to myself. Maybe a girlie evening with an uncomplicated new friend is exactly what I need.

CHAPTER 43

It's a rare rainy day in Los Angeles. Rich turns the corner onto our street, the Grateful Dead's "Ripple" playing loudly from his van stereo. Mom looks back at me from the passenger seat and lightheartedly smiles. I grin back at her. I love these moments with Rich.

Rich's enthusiastic singing suddenly falters. "Mel, were you expecting Trey? He's parked in front of our house."

I look through the windshield and see his car.

Rich parks behind him, and we all gather on the sidewalk.

"Hi, guys," Trey says with a note of apology in his tone. "I'm sorry for showing up unannounced, but something weird is happening."

Rich and Mom look from Trey to each other.

"What's wrong?" Mom asks.

"I planned to spend the day working on my car, but Kenji called me an hour ago. He sounded bad." Trey looks down, and then at me. "Any chance you know what's happening, Mel?"

I shake my head. "We left early this morning to run errands. Haven't heard from anyone."

"What did Kenji say?" Rich asks.

"He was cryptic. He told me to get Melanie. He wants us to go to Hiram and Arch's house as soon as possible."

Rich looks worried. "You two head out. Let us know what happens."

I'm a nervous wreck as Trey leads me to his car and opens my door. Trey walks around quickly and slides into the driver's seat. The car roars to life, and we pull away from the curb.

"Did he say anything else? This is really strange."

Trey shakes his head, his lips pressed in a tight line. "Nope. I tried to find out more, but Kenji started crying and told me just to get there."

My mouth falls open. "KENJI WAS CRYING?"

Trey glances at me with worried eyes. "Yes. Whatever it is, it's bad, Mel."

My heart starts racing, and suddenly my intuition blazes to life. *Something's wrong with Adam.*

"Drive faster, Trey. We need to get there."

We find Darren slumped in the corner of the balcony, tears streaming down his face. He takes a drag off his cigarette and looks up at us with a mournful expression.

"What's wrong?" Trey demands with an edge of panic.

Darren shakes his head and points to the door without saying a word. Trey knocks on the door, and Arch answers it. He's pale, his eyes hollowed out, with a far-off expression on his face. We step inside, and I scan the room. Marcus and Presley are leaning against the wall. Presley is doubled over, clutching her stomach, with Marcus's hand on her back. He looks like he's seen a ghost.

Tanner's sitting on the smallest couch with Finley curled up on his lap. She's sobbing. Bear and Kenji are sitting on dining chairs next to Tanner, and Bear's cheeks are wet. Demitri's sitting on an upholstered chair across from the couch, calmly watching me with a pained expression. Val's lying on the couch, facedown with her head on Hiram's leg. She isn't moving, and Hiram has his eyes closed, his face scrunched up in agony.

My stomach knots with dread. No one's talking, but the tension is so thick it's hard to breathe.

"What happened?" Trey asks.

No one answers.

Valerie's muffled voice comes from the couch, "I'm going to throw up."

Trey grabs a waste basket and rushes to Val, putting it next to the couch just in time. Val loses her breakfast.

Trey kneels in front of her. "What happened, Valerie?"

She whispers, "Adam's dead."

Trey gasps, and it's the last sound I hear before the roar of the dark water rages in my ears. I close my eyes, and the water engulfs me. Shock reverberates through my sputtering brain, and everything moves in slow motion. Tears slide down my cheeks. My knees buckle, but I don't feel my hip hit the floor as I collapse. Trey picks me up, carrying me, then sets me down in someone's arms. I open my eyes to find that Demitri's holding me.

Valerie throws up again before slumping back into Hiram's lap.

Trey walks to the corner of the living room and falls to his knees. His back is to us, and his shoulders are shaking.

Arch takes a rattling breath. "Adam and I talked on the phone yesterday, and he said he planned to go out early this morning to race the canyon on his Harley. He wanted to spend some time at the beach and watch the sunrise. He was supposed to work all day, but he told me he needed to clear his head." He takes a long pause before continuing. "You all know how private Adam was, so I didn't ask a lot of questions. I feel bad about that because something was off."

"It's okay, Arch," Bear says. "I know what's been happening. It was better that you didn't ask."

No, no, no, no!

Valerie cuts in with a moan, and then shifts to throw up in the trash can again.

"Adam asked me to meet him at the beach at six this morning," Bear continues, "but he didn't show. I figured he was just running late because of the gloomy weather, but when he still wasn't there at seven, I decided to drive the route he would've taken. Halfway through the canyon, traffic was at a standstill. I pulled over and walked the rest of the way to where the police cars were. The officers told me that Adam must have taken the curve too fast, and his motorcycle skidded over the cliff edge. They found the motorcycle halfway down, hung up on trees."

Valerie slowly sits up. "Wait . . . so you didn't see him?" There's hope shining in her eyes, and my heart nearly explodes, because Bear seems sure that Adam is gone.

"I want him to be alive as much as you do, Val," he says, "but I was there when they pulled his motorcycle out of the canyon. The bike was so mangled that I had to check the license plate to make sure it was his. When I was leaving, someone radioed that they'd found a body. I didn't get details because I was so upset, but I'll talk to Adam's dad and find out."

Valerie gives him the most pitiful begging look, her eyes filling with tears.

"Adam shouldn't have been riding that fast on the canyon in the rain," Bear says sorrowfully.

Valerie's face goes slack, and she puts her head on her knees. She sobs for a moment, then inhales and throws her head back, letting out an anguished howl that sends shivers down my spine. Everyone rushes to Valerie to console her.

I turn my face into Demitri's neck and try to calm my racking sobs. Demitri wraps his arm around my head and whispers, "I need to get you out of here."

He stands, carrying me into Hiram's room. Bear follows and closes the door, locking it.

Demitri sets me down.

"We were meeting this morning so he could make a plan to break things off with Valerie tonight," Bear says. "He was hell-bent on being with you, but he filled me in on your terms. I'm proud of you for setting your boundaries until he ended things."

My knees buckle. *This is all my fault. If I had just avoided all of this with Adam, he'd still be alive!*

CHAPTER 44

Trey's car pulls into the student parking lot, the early morning sun blinding us as he wheels into a spot. He cuts the engine and slowly turns to look at me. "You've hardly said a word since yesterday."

I take a shuddering breath and look at him. My reflection stares back at me from his mirrored Oakley sunglasses. I look dead. I shake my head and stare down at my hands.

"Mel, talk to me."

"Thank you for picking me up this morning. I didn't want to ride the bus."

He gives me a wry smile. "It wasn't my idea. Your mom called me last night and asked me to pick you up. Apparently, you still haven't told them we broke up . . . again."

After a long pause, I say, "I don't want to do this."

Trey kisses me on the forehead. "We have to."

Tears slide down my cheeks for the millionth time since yesterday afternoon. I feel like I'm walking through a haze.

Trey reaches over and unbuckles my seat belt. Then, he gets out of the driver's side and comes around the car. He opens my door and puts his hand out, helping me stand. I look across the parking lot to where most of our group has gathered. We walk to them, and everyone silently hugs. We're all in black, we're all in shock, and we're all exhausted.

"I talked to Adam's dad last night," Bear says. "Adam's body was recovered from the canyon. As much as I knew it was a long shot, I was hoping maybe Valerie was right, but . . ."

I double over, gasping, and cross the parking lot to throw up behind a truck. Demitri follows and holds my hair.

"Will there be a viewing at the funeral?" I hear Hiram ask.

"His dad says he's so mangled from the accident that the funeral will have to be closed casket."

Tanner's car wheels into the parking lot with Valerie in the passenger seat. She looks like hell warmed over. I watch as Darren puts out his cigarette and goes to Valerie's car door, opening it and helping her stand. He puts his arm around her and guides her over to the group. Valerie's hands are shaking. Presley gives her a tissue, and Finley hugs her.

Bear looks at me from across the parking lot, then closes his eyes and starts rubbing his forehead.

Demitri pulls me against his chest and puts his hands on my back, trying to calm my racing heart. "How many people know about you and Adam?" he asks so only I can hear.

"Trey, Darren, Bear, Isaac, and you."

He nods. "I'll be here for you through this. Everyone else is going to rally with Valerie."

"Thank you, Demitri, but I don't deserve to have any of you with me."

"Bear mentioned that you had a soulmate connection with Adam. Bear trusts me because I'm an energy worker. You're going to need help, but your usual support system is a little distracted right now. Bear and Darren just lost their best friend, and you and Trey are a disaster. Isaac is clueless about how all this spirit connection stuff works. I'm on Team Mel through this."

The first bell rings. The group turns together, walking across the street and up the campus alley, with Valerie and Darren in the middle. Trey starts to approach me, but Bear stops him. They talk for a second before Trey nods.

Bear comes to me and hands me a piece of gum. "Do you have her, D?"

Demitri nods and puts his arm around me. We walk quickly to catch up.

"Make sure they don't ever tell Valerie, okay?" I whisper.

"I was hoping you would say that," Demitri says. "I'll talk to Bear and Darren."

As our group rounds the corner to Actors' Alley, dozens of heads turn, all eyes on us. Apparently, word about Adam's death has already spread through the student body.

A hush falls over the crowd as the loudspeaker clicks on.

Ms. Ferry's voice echoes through campus, all her usual flair drained. "Hollywood High, please report to the theater immediately."

Everyone waits to allow our group to climb the four-story staircase first, and then the crowd follows. The sound of marching feet clanging on the metal staircase casts an eerie pall. It's like the air's been sucked out of the school, replaced by a bizarre ritual of silence and respect for the dead.

Principal Walker greets us at the top of the stairs. "Good morning, kids. I'm so sorry." He pauses, his gaze shifting to Valerie. He puts out his elbow for her to take. "Valerie, may I escort you to your seat?"

She nods, taking his arm, and he walks down the aisle to the first row. Mr. Bentley steps up to the rest of us from a long row of teachers standing at attention. He hugs each of us one at a time, and then escorts our group to sit with Valerie. Bear takes the spot next to her, putting his arm around her. She deflates, looking small and frail, something I never thought I'd see from her. Trey sits on one side of me, and Demitri sits on the other.

We wait in heavy silence as all the students get settled. Adam's death has changed the school. His habit of brooding, watching, and saying little has enveloped us all.

As the last students are seated, Principal Walker walks up the stairs to the stage. The main curtain has been closed to block the students' view of the destroyed set. He steps up to the podium. "Today, I have the displeasure of announcing the death of one of our own. Adam Stone was involved in an accident yesterday morning. He died doing what he loved, riding his Harley through the canyon. I ask for your respect as we honor Adam this morning." He pauses, looking down at our group. "Darren, please join me."

Darren stands, smoothing the front of his suit jacket. He walks up the steps, nods at Principal Walker, and steps up to the podium. Trey looks my way and sighs, knowing I'm broken.

Just what Trey needs. Now he gets to deal with his ex-girlfriend being destroyed because her other-other half is gone.

My attention's brought back as Darren's debonaire voice rings out. "Adam Stone was my best friend. All of you knew him. Some of you feared him. Some of you envied him. A handful of us had the privilege of calling him our friend, and for one of us . . ." He looks at Valerie before continuing. "He was her future." His eyes flicker to me.

I'll always be Adam's dirty secret.

Valerie takes a shuddering breath, and half the students start crying quietly. Valerie's pain reverberates through the cavernous theater.

"Adam was a guy of few words," Darren continues, "but when he spoke, you were guaranteed one of three things . . . wise words, wit, or anger. The lines were clear for Adam, except when he chose to blur them." Darren looks down and smiles as everyone quietly chuckles. "Adam loved viciously . . ."

You have no idea.

"And he fought like a junkyard dog. No one liked a brawl more than Adam."

Heads nod knowingly all over the audience.

"Adam rebuilt motorcycles in his dad's garage, and in two years, he sold nine Harleys. He was brilliant in his way. We've all lost someone today, whether you liked him or not, because Adam silently protected and watched this school every day. I'm sure he will continue to watch over us." He pauses, taking a shaky breath, and slow tears fall down his cheeks. He looks back out at the audience. "Adam lived his life dedicated to the people he loved, and we were privileged to have him in our lives." Darren slowly scans down our two rows, making eye contact with each of us. "Our group has lost a leader, a protector, a best friend, a lover, and a rock. We're leaving now and heading to the beach Adam was driving to so that he could watch the sunrise with his other best friend, Bear. Thank you all for being here."

God no. Anywhere but there.

Darren leaves the podium, walking down the steps from the stage, and our group stands and follows up the aisle to the exit after him. The blazing sun blinds us as we exit the auditorium. We descend slowly down the long staircase, headed to the alley. The gate's open, and we cross the street to our cars.

"I can drive Mel," Demitri offers.

Trey shakes his head. "I'll do it." He opens the passenger door for me, and I slump into the seat. He walks around, opens his door, and slides in next to me. The car feels safe and smells familiar.

When he's situated in the driver's seat, he offers a sad smile. I don't know what to say. He pulls us around the parking lot, joining the line of our friends' cars waiting to exit. Looks like we're doing our own funeral procession, our way. He clicks on his hazard lights, and we wait.

"Adam told me once that packs of wolves put a leader at the front of the line when they travel," Trey says. "But the other leaders are at the back watching for trouble. That's why he always insisted that he, Arch, and I were the lead and trailing cars whenever we drove in a caravan."

We watch as Arch pulls out first with Valerie in the passenger seat, followed by Marcus's, Kenji's, Demitri's, and Hiram's cars, all packed with our friends. Trey turns left behind Hiram, and I hear a roar behind us. I look over my shoulder to find that Deb, Darren, and Bear are all riding Harleys side by side, bringing up the rear, their hazard lights flashing.

"Adam's dad gave Bear and Darren the two Harleys that Adam was about to sell," Trey explains.

My eyes fill with tears. "You, Arch, Bear, Darren, and Deb are all taking over Adam's role as protector of the group?"

A tear slips down Trey's cheek, his sunglasses masking any other sign that he's crying. "Adam was badass. It's going to take five of us to replace him." He looks at me and quietly says, "After the battle-of-the-bands assembly, Adam told me he loved you and he was ready to leave Valerie." He squeezes my hand. "I'm sorry, Melanie. The look in his eyes when he told me spoke volumes. Bear filled me in that they were going to the beach so he could help Adam work through all of this. I blame myself. If I'd stepped aside sooner, Adam would still be here, and you'd be okay."

I double over and cry silently as we make the long drive through the canyon where Adam died.

CHAPTER 45

I stare out at the ocean, standing away from everyone as the last of them make it off the treacherous path. My heart hurts, and my lungs are strained nearly to crushing. *Adam loved it here.*

Everyone forms a line. No one says a word, but slowly they start taking off their shoes, walking one at a time toward the water. I follow suit, and as my feet meet the wet line in the sand, we hear the screech of air brakes, one after the other. We look at each other, wondering what just disturbed our death ritual.

Valerie turns around to look at the bluff and gasps.

We all turn and see Mr. Isley, Ms. Ferry, Mr. Bentley, Ms. G, and Principal Walker standing statue still, looking down at us from the cliffside above.

"Would you look at that . . . ," Bear murmurs.

Suddenly, hundreds of teenagers step into view, covering the bluff from one end to the other. The sound we heard had to have been the screech of brakes as bus after bus pulled up.

We all look at each other.

"There are so many of them," Bear says. "It has to be all the Magnet students."

As if to confirm, Dante puts up devil horns. Trey returns the gesture.

Everyone looks at Valerie, worried that this is going to ruin the ocean service that she wanted with just our group, but she looks deeply grateful.

She smiles, and her eyes light up for the first time since Adam's death. "This is perfect," she says.

We watch as the students reach out, one at a time, grabbing hands, creating a chain across the cliff and down the pathway. They come down as far as the space will allow, standing one after the other in a line that reaches all the way to us. Dante's closest to our group, and he takes the person's hand next to him, then reaches out to me. I take his hand for a moment, but then the grief becomes too much to bear. I step out of the line and cross the short distance to lean on the rock wall. Demitri steps up behind me and puts his hands on my shoulders.

We wait in silence. After a few breaths, Valerie nods at Hiram. He carries a boombox to the middle of the little beach and hits *play*. The haunting violin intro of Val and Adam's song, "Never Tear Us Apart" by INXS, glides through the air. Everyone listens in silence as the song mixes with the crashing waves.

My heart can hardly take it. *He belongs to her, and that's okay. I need to let him be hers.*

Valerie's voice rings out, true and perfect as she sings the first line of the song. She falters, and Presley and Finley sing the next few lines with her.

On the drum section, the students instinctively stomp out the rhythm before they start to sing the chorus together.

My arms goosebump, and tears roll silently down my cheeks. The melody swells, everyone's voices taking over while Valerie breathes in the support of the school. She stands a little taller, her chest rising, her shoulders no longer slumped. Our Val—*Adam's Val*—is back.

The students all sing the first line of the final verse of the song, and then a hush falls over the crowd.

All eyes are on Valerie as she turns to face Adam's ocean and belts out the last line, her voice suddenly stronger.

Everyone slowly makes their way down the treacherous path after the song ends, crowding the little beach. I slip away alone, walking up the path to the cars parked above. I kneel by Trey's car, trying to cope.

After a few moments, I feel a hand slide on my shoulder. I look up, my vision blurry from a torrent of tears. Demitri's there. He helps me to my feet and leads me to the passenger door of his Jeep. I slide in and put my head on my knees. Demitri gets in on the driver's side and pulls me to his shoulder. I cry myself sick. When the tears stop, I look up at him.

His face is inches from mine.

"What's your motive in this?" I choke out.

Demitri looks surprised. "You have my word that I have no motive beyond helping my friend. Melanie, you've dealt with all the ulterior motives you can take lately. I'm not that guy."

I drop my head to his shoulder, radiating relief. "Thank you, Demitri."

He wraps his arm around my head, hugging me against his bicep. "You're welcome."

I can't help but laugh through the tears.

"What?" he asks.

"I just got snot all over your black dress shirt."

He laughs. "I'm not scared of Melanie snot. I've got a good dry cleaner." He tips up my chin to look in my eyes.

Softly, I smile, grateful for his ability to be the perfect friend.

CHAPTER 46

Ms. Ferry walks into the auditorium and crosses to the cast, all seated in the front few rows of the audience.

She takes a breath. "Hi, kids. It was important that we took Monday off for Adam's beach service, and I wanted to give everyone yesterday off to collect themselves. I know how hard the news has been on all of you, and I appreciate your being here this afternoon." She pauses before adding, "We have a hard decision to make. With the loss of Adam . . ." She shines a mournful look Valerie's way. "We need to decide if we're going to cancel the show or recast Adam's role and carry through."

Valerie raises her hand, her expression hard. Ms. Ferry calls on her, and Valerie stands addressing us with a serious tone, "The show must go on. Period. We perform for Adam."

Fantastic. Now I get to be Poopsie while I'm completely devastated. I sigh. I'm exhausted down to my soul.

I slide an irritable gaze Demitri's way, and he whispers in my ear, "You can do this."

He chuckles and shakes his head when I make a childish scrunchy face at him.

Valerie sits back down and nods once, hard and final, at Ms. Ferry.

"Ya'll heard the lady," Ms. Ferry says. "All in favor of doing the show still?"

At first, everyone's hand goes up except mine, but then despite my hesitation, I rally and join them.

Ms. Ferry grins. "Okay. We need to come up with a suitable replacement for Adam's character, Vernon Hines. Someone who can honor Adam the way he deserves." She looks around the room and asks, "Hiram, are you here?"

Hiram raises his hand.

"Are you up for playing Vernon?" Ms. Ferry asks him.

Hiram gives her a sad, wry smile. "I'll do it for Adam."

Ms. Ferry nods at him and looks us over. "For Adam. It's settled then. So that everyone understands the time frame, our show opens Friday night and runs for two weekends. That gives us today and tomorrow to finish preparations. With that said, we have a problem. Hiram, please open the main curtain."

He heads up the steps on the side of the stage and disappears behind the heavy main curtain.

After a moment, the red drape slowly opens.

"I don't have to remind you all what's been done to our set," Ms. Ferry says. "The police are still getting to the bottom of who did this. I want us all to take another look because I have some good news. New funding has been allocated and approved by the school board, and we've finally received a check for the replacement materials. This afternoon, we need to clean up what we can because tomorrow will have to be dedicated to rebuilding. This means we're losing even more of the precious little time we have remaining to polish our production." She sighs. "It also means that we won't be able to have a full rehearsal on the new set before

Friday's opening night. With that said, I think you guys can do it. We need to clear out everything we can to make it easier for them to run the rebuild."

The cast make their way up the stairs to the stage, surveying the damage and preparing themselves to start the cleanup effort.

Kendra shakes her head. "How is it that police are still trying to figure out who's behind this? Victoria's message for Melanie is spraypainted all over it. I'm sure the Drones were involved too."

Her best friend, Jayla, snorts. "We've got your back, Mel. Victoria's a nightmare."

I don't need backup. But I smile at them, appreciating that they care. I don't know Kendra and Jayla well, but they're the stars of the dance department. Having them on my side could be beneficial.

Demitri points to the set pieces that have the nasty message for me. "These come down first."

We all get started hauling broken pieces of the heavy set to a dumpster behind the loading dock as Hiram, Bear, and Demitri pull bolts and screws. It's hard work, but the cast doesn't complain.

Thirty minutes later, Ms. Ferry surveys our cleanup job. "Great work, kids. What do you say we try giving Hiram a run-through?"

Hiram gets his script out of his backpack, and we all go to our places for the top of the show. Hiram struggles at first, but he picks up steam after the second scene, and by the end, he's killing it.

At the close of the final song-and-dance number, we all gather around.

"We've got this," Ms. Ferry says proudly. "Hiram, you did great. Thank you for stepping up."

Everyone claps Hiram on the back.

He grins sheepishly at us. "I'm no Adam, but I promise to try. Anyone who has time tomorrow evening, please report here at six. I could use all the help I can get."

CHAPTER 47

"Hi, guys," Arch greets us. He lights up when he sees my stepdad. "Pops, you made it!"

Rich smiles. "I'd be here no matter what, but someone needs to fill in for Adam. We all know he would've done the job of two people. I'm going to do my best in honor of him."

Arch smiles, his expression soft. "Adam would've teamed up with you. He always wanted Pops on his team. Everyone's already on the stage getting started. Hiram will give you instructions."

We head through the audience and up the stairs to the stage. Hiram grins at us from across the way, sweat beading on his forehead while he strains to push up a newly built wall section. Rich and Trey run to help him.

Presley and Finley greet me.

"What's up, chickadee?" Finley says.

"Hey, guys. How's everything going so far?" I gesture toward the busy frenzy of our group, hard at work.

"Really good," Presley says. "Javier and Demitri both brought their dads. Now that Rich is here, I think we're going to get it done."

Demitri gestures me over, and Mr. Cantrell hugs me.

I smile softly up at his dad. Something about his presence always seems to calm me.

"It's nice to see you again, Melanie. I look forward to the show."

"It's nice to see you too, Mr. Cantrell. Demitri has tolerated my learning curve in rehearsals. Hopefully the show goes well."

Demitri shakes his head. "She underestimates herself," he tells his dad.

Mr. Cantrell beams at me. "Melanie, I've got to tell you that you blew me away while I watched you two choreograph that duet at my house. You're incredible."

I blush shyly. "Thank you."

Trey chooses that moment to join us. "Can I talk to you?" he asks me.

When I nod, he crosses to an empty area at the edge of the stage and waits there for me expectantly.

I huff and slide an irritable gaze at Demitri. "Please kill me."

Demitri laughs.

"See you later," I say to his dad with a smile.

"I'm here if you need to talk," Mr. Cantrell says.

I bark an ironic laugh. "I appreciate the offer, but I've exposed enough people to my crazy." I squeeze Demitri's dad's arm in a silent thank-you.

As I walk away, I hear his dad tell Demitri, "You need to snag that little gal as fast as you can. She's adorable."

"Trust me," Demitri says, "the last thing she needs is more guy drama. I'm better off in the friend zone."

His words spread warm gratitude over me just as I reach Trey.

Trey draws a breath to speak, but we're interrupted by an angry growl from Tanner.

"YOU'VE GOT TO BE KIDDING!" Tanner leaps off the stage, storming through the auditorium.

We all whip around to see what's happening. Of all people, Victoria is walking down the aisle toward the stage. Everyone stops what they're doing, dropping tools and leaping off the stage to confront her. Only the dads are left standing still, wondering what's happening. Rich crosses to Valerie and stands watch over her.

I jump off the stage and stalk toward our unwelcome guest. "I'm done, Victoria! LEAVE!"

My friends all scream at her, and the babble is deafening.

Victoria raises her hands, uncharacteristically quiet, and waits. When we calm down, she turns to me and says, "I'm not here to cause trouble."

"Of course not," Hiram barks. "You already caused enough trouble when you destroyed my set. We got your message for Melanie, loud and clear."

She meets his eyes, her usual cattiness absent. "I didn't destroy the set. I'll explain all of that later, but I had nothing to do with it. Right now, there's a bigger issue." She turns to Trey. "I need to talk to you. Now." She crosses her arms over her chest, not waiting for a reply, and walks into the lobby.

We all look at each other, baffled. Victoria seems dejected and scared, and scared Victoria is maybe the only thing worse than catty Victoria.

Trey follows her up the aisle, leaving the rest of us to stand together and wait for him to come back. My intuition is nagging at me as I look up at Darren. He glances down at me, nodding. He feels it too.

Trey comes back down the aisle in a hurry, his face pale. "I need to speak with Arch, Tanner, Deb, Marcus, and Darren. Everyone else, go back to building the set. I'll explain later."

We all exchange glances as Trey's chosen few head into the

lobby. After a minute, everyone hesitantly returns to the stage to work on the set.

I'm left standing alone. *Something's very wrong.*

After a moment, Arch runs back down the aisle with Tanner. I intercept them, hoping to find out what's happening.

Arch calls Rich and Hiram over. "We have to leave. I'll explain later. You guys finish the set. Hopefully, we'll be back before you're done."

Hiram frowns. "What's going on?"

Arch shakes his head. "I'm not sure yet."

"Is everything okay?" Rich asks.

"I hope so," Arch says. "We'll see."

Tanner goes to his girlfriend, Finley. I can't hear them from this distance, but she's nodding while he gives her instructions. She looks worried.

As he passes me, I grab Arch by the arm, running to keep up with him as he races down the stage steps and back up the aisle. He stops and draws a deep breath. "Go help with the set, Mel."

"Not a shot!"

He gives me a long, appraising look. "What we're headed to do is dangerous. Trey doesn't want you there."

I snort. "Screw that."

Arch sighs, closing his eyes, deciding my fate. Finally, he says, "All right, Mel. You're a beast, so you're in, but Trey's not going to like it." He grabs me by the elbow and pulls me into the lobby.

Trey sees us. "No way, Arch. I already told you that Melanie's not coming with us."

I gape at him and hiss, "*I* can't go, but *Victoria's* got what it takes to handle whatever's happening?"

Victoria meets my sharp gaze. "Truce, Melanie."

My dark-water side flares up for the first time since Adam

died. Welcoming the feeling, I give her a nasty look. "Go to hell, Victoria."

She takes a deep breath. "I'm serious, Melanie. I apologize. I've been terrible to you, and I'm truly sorry."

My eyebrows rise as I look around the group. That was shockingly sincere of her.

"We've got a serious problem," Victoria continues.

Trey holds up a hand. "The specific problem that we have isn't one Melanie needs to face," he says to Victoria.

"I agree," Darren says.

I glare at them. "I guarantee that whatever it is, I can handle it. I'm coming with you. Does someone want to fill me in?"

"Later," Arch says. "We need to roll."

CHAPTER 48

Trey hasn't said a word on the drive, so I still have no clue where we're going. We turn from Outpost Drive onto Mulholland, and it's oddly desolate for bustling Hollywood. The pitch-black, moonless night makes it difficult to figure out our surroundings. Arch's brake lights shine red and ominous in front of us as he stops in the middle of the quiet road. He jumps out and jogs back to us.

Trey rolls down his window.

"We need to stop here so that they don't hear the Harleys," Arch says. "Park, and I'll let the others know."

With a nod, Trey pulls to the right and parks on the side of the road next to a fence. He rolls his window up and cuts the engine.

The silence is deafening.

He looks at me, concern making his face look more angular in the darkness. "You shouldn't be here, Melanie."

"Tell me what's going on, Trey," I demand.

A knock on his window makes us both jump. Trey opens his door.

Darren leans in. "Mel, you need to come out this way. There's not enough room on your side."

I climb over, sliding out the driver's side, and we all start walking up the hill. There are a few houses spaced far apart and set back from the road.

What are we doing here?

Before I can demand for the hundredth time that someone tell me what's happening, Arch stops short and ducks behind a line of hedges. We all instinctively crouch down. My heart's racing. Victoria's on my right. She looks at me with big, scared eyes.

Arch turns to us and puts a finger to his lips. He waves us forward. We skitter along the hedge line and up a driveway, hugging the shadows as we trail behind Arch.

Whose house is this, and WHY are we trespassing? "This isn't some weird Charlie Manson shit you guys are pulling, right?" I hiss.

There's a sound to our right, and Victoria and I both jump. She reaches out, grabbing my arm, and hangs on. Though I have no desire to deal with Victoria, I secretly feel better having something to hold on to now that Trey isn't always holding my hand.

Arch snaps his fingers and motions for us to follow him. He slides between two hedges and hunkers down. We all race around the side of the hedge and duck out of sight just in time. Stan and a couple of the Drones come around the corner from behind the house. They're stumbling drunk, laughing, and talking loudly.

"You have a plan, right?" Isaac asks Stan.

Arch hisses to Victoria, "*Isaac's* in on this? That two-faced son of a . . ."

Victoria nods, clearly terrified. Her hands are shaking, and she inhales a wavering breath. I take her hand, figuring whatever we're dealing with is bigger than the issues she and I have. She looks at me with gratitude.

"Screw that guy," Stan says. "I don't care what happens."

He high-fives the third guy, who I vaguely remember from school, and the trio heads to the front door.

When the door opens, my blood runs cold. Joel's standing there in what looks like the soft glow of candlelight. Heavy metal music blasts so loudly from inside that I can't hear what he says to the others. The trio steps inside, the door closes, and it's quiet.

"Mystery solved," I snarl. "Isaac must be the one who drugged us that night."

"He totally played us. I'm gonna *kill* him!" Arch growls.

"Good," Trey hisses. "You deal with Isaac because Joel's mine." He looks at Victoria, his eyes huge. "You're serious, Tori? This is actually happening?"

Victoria nods, and everyone exchanges a look.

"We might solve a whole lot of problems in the next few minutes," Trey says.

"Yeah," Darren says, "but first we've gotta live through this."

"Will someone *please* fill me in on what's happening?" I hiss.

Arch ignores me. "Okay, here's the plan. Victoria says we need to go through the garage door and down a staircase that's hidden behind a big poster."

"The garage door's locked, though," Victoria says.

"Anyone have a bobby pin?" Tanner asks.

Deb pulls one out of the bun her curly hair is twisted in and hands it to him.

"You know how to pick locks?" Darren whispers.

Tanner grins and winks at him. "I have a seedy past and many talents."

"Tanner picks the lock, and we all slide in quick," Arch says. "Not a sound, guys. Victoria, be ready to lead everyone to the hidden door."

She nods.

"What's behind that door?" he asks.

"There's a stairway down to a basement storage room," Victoria explains. "We turn right at the bottom of the stairs, and there's a cellar across the room. That's where we're going."

Tanner glares at Victoria. "This better not be some insane trap you're luring us into. I swear I'll kill you!"

Victoria shakes her head rapidly, and with a raspy voice, whispers, "I swear. They still think I'm an ally, but when I found out about all this, I knew I had to come get you guys. I can be mean, but I'm not about to be a part of something this evil." She looks at Trey imploringly.

After a long pause, he whispers to us, "I trust her on this. She's telling the truth."

Arch nods his head once, hard and fast. "Then we move. Let's go." Bent at the waist, he sneaks out of our hiding spot and sticks to the shadows, skirting the edge of the driveway. We creep around the curve to the garage.

Tanner silently slinks up the three steps to the door hidden around the back side of the garage. Deb keeps watch, peeking around the garage to check for the Drones. Tanner pulls the little plastic ends from the hairpin with his teeth before snapping it in half at the middle. He makes quick work of the lock, and the door squeaks open. We all grimace at the sound and hold our breath. Music blares from the party in the house. There's a door across the way that must lead inside. We all watch it, but no one comes to investigate the sound. Arch gestures to us, and we pile into the dark garage. My heart is thudding out of my chest.

The poster is exactly where Victoria said it would be. Darren quickly lifts it, and Trey opens the door on the other side. Deb clicks on a flashlight, and we look in. The room's pitch-black except for what the beam of her flashlight catches. She takes point, quietly inching her way down the staircase. She turns and motions for us to come down. We follow, and my heart's pounding so loud I can hear it.

"Can you feel that?" I whisper to Darren. "The whole room feels off. It smells like incense and evil."

Darren nods. "These people are freaks."

I raise an eyebrow at him. "Coming from us?"

"You have a point."

We cross the room, and Victoria silently points to a big steel sliding door. Just like she promised, it's there.

Arch surveys the door before his head tips back dejectedly. "It's padlocked." He gestures to the lock. "What kind of cartoon ACME shit is this?"

We study it, and it really is comic overkill. You could hold elephants in a paddock with that lock.

"Who are these guys," Darren asks, "the fucking marines?"

Trey shrugs. "Have Tanner pick the lock."

"It doesn't use a key," Arch informs. "It's got number tumblers."

Everyone spreads out, searching through the odds and ends in the basement for clues or anything else we could use to get through the door.

Tanner's triumphant voice hisses out, "Boom!" He crosses to the door with a set of bolt cutters. He gets the cutters around the curved top of the metal lock and squeezes, but to no avail.

Trey and Arch join him, and they all stack up their hands. They grimace and grunt as they squeeze hard. Finally, with gritted teeth, they all stumble as the bolt cutters snap, doing nothing to break the metal lock.

I roll my eyes and strut forward. "For the love of all things holy, move."

The guys shift out of the way, and everyone watches as I pull the lock down. It clicks and releases. I crack up to myself.

Marcus asks, "How did you think to do that?"

"The Drones are idiots," I say as I remove the lock. "Joel knew there was no way all his morons could remember a five-number combination." I shrug as Arch pats me appreciatively on the shoulder.

"Who's going in first?" Darren asks.

I demand yet again, "What is *happening*?"

"They're holding Adam hostage," Victoria says sheepishly.

My mouth drops open, and I rapidly back up, plowing into Trey. My brain sputters. I instantly get hot sweats as the shock turns my hands to ice.

Trey catches me as I stumble. He wraps his arms around me and quietly says, "I didn't want you to know, Melanie. We have no idea what's on the other side of that door."

Fury roars up through me. I turn on Victoria, a fresh bout of rage erupting. "What the HELL is WRONG with you people?"

Victoria's eyes fill with tears. "I swear I didn't know before tonight! They were all joking around about some secret. They brought me out here to 'see a surprise,' and that's when I figured out what's happening. I'm horrified! I knew you guys were going to be at the school, so I snuck away and drove to the theater as fast as I could to get help. They think I was going out to buy a pack of cigarettes at the bowling alley vending machine. They haven't missed me yet, but we have to hurry. They're going to get suspicious that I'm not back."

I sneer at Victoria, my expression suddenly an inhumanly ferocious mask as I back her slowly across the room. She appears terrified.

In response to her expression, I snarl, "Be terrified, Victoria. I'm going to fuck you up once I rescue Adam."

Victoria's back hits the wall, and she turns her head to the side, squeezing her eyes closed. She whimpers as if begging.

I whip my gaze Deb's way. "You stick to this bitch like glue. If anything happens, knock her the hell out." I level everyone else with a steely glare. "I'll be the one who goes in that room. The rest of you fan out and be ready for an ambush. I don't trust this situation."

"Your intuition?" Darren asks.

I shake my head slowly before freezing Victoria with a deadly gaze. "I don't need intuition on this. I've got common sense. A rattlesnake's going to rattle. I'll be damned if we get bit."

"I agree with Melanie," Trey says. "I'm going in with her. We'll let you know what we find. Stand guard. If we're ambushed, drop anyone you have to."

"Why would you go in there?" Arch asks. "With your body-guard training, you should be out here on the front line with the rest of us!"

Trey shakes his head, his piercing eyes and steeled jaw set. "I'm going in with Melanie and Adam. There's either an ambush in that room, or one coming in here the way we just entered. Either way, if Adam's in there, I'll be the one to defend him. If they've been able to hold Adam, of all people, captive, then he's either dead or in bad shape. If what's coming gets through all of you, you have my word that they won't get through me."

Everyone spreads out.

Deb strides up to Victoria. She puts her hands on Victoria's shoulders and shoves her down to her knees. "Sit," she barks.

Victoria does.

Deb grins at her maliciously. "Good dog."

I grab the second, smaller flashlight that Deb pulls from her back pocket. Once everyone's in their defensive positions, I turn to Trey. "Let's do this."

Trey slides the heavy metal door. It opens partway before squealing to a stop. He holds his hand out for the flashlight, quietly saying, "I'm going in first, baby."

I take a wavering breath and shake my head. "We go in together."

Trey breathes back, "I don't know how you keep doing it, but you never back down to danger."

My expression is stark, my voice harsh as I ask, "You'll do this with me?"

Trey nods and holds a hand out to me. I take it, and we turn to face the narrow gap. Trey slides in first, shining the flashlight into the narrow space ahead. I squeeze through the gap after Trey, my heart pounding. There are empty shelves. My guess is that this was an earthquake shelter, a place where they stored food and supplies before Stan's family moved out. As I peer across the long, narrow space, at first all I see are some tarps and scattered beer cans. Trey sweeps the beam along the narrow space, and we spot something bizarre in the corner. It takes a moment for the horror to register . . . then my heart stops. I gasp, and my whole body starts shaking.

I try to speak, my mouth opening and closing. On the third attempt, I finally manage to croak out, "Oh my God, Trey! Is that a rope thrown over that ceiling joist?"

Trey points the flashlight up to the joist. "They've had Adam tied up. Holy shit!"

He hands me the flashlight before rushing to Adam, but I can't bring myself to cross the distance yet. I close my eyes and search for my soulmate connection with Adam. There's nothing there but a faint hum that I didn't notice before because we can only feel each other when we're close by.

"He's breathing," Trey says.

I rush across the space, needing to confirm it myself. Terrified, I reach to check his pulse, my heart screaming.

My hands shake as my fingers touch his neck. *He's alive, but barely!* Relief floods my body from head to toe. Tears stream down my cheeks.

He's unconscious and has obviously been here since Sunday when we thought he died. It's Thursday . . .

Five days of this torture!

His face is covered in old bruises that are turning a sickly green.

"Adam," I whisper, "it's Melanie. I need you to open your eyes."

There's nothing. He only takes occasional shallow breaths.

I touch his arm to find that his energy is nearly dead. Instead of his usual blasting vibrancy, there's just a faint, sluggish hum. I panic, my lungs seizing. Shock reverberates as I double over, silently screaming in my head.

I close my eyes, and Dark-Water Melanie is looking back at me. *Get it together or he's going to die in here.*

Trey quietly orders, "We have to get him out of here."

I pause for only a moment before I know what to do. "How did you do it?"

"Do what?"

"No offense, but if you could reach me in the dark water, then I know that I can also do the same for Adam. With my intuition, newfound energy control, and connection with Adam, I can do this. But only if you tell me how." I take a sobbing gasp. "He's completely broken inside and out."

Trey thinks hard for a moment. "Okay. At first, I could only get there in dreams, but after a while, I figured out how to drop into what I would compare to meditation. I'd sit, or lie down, and close my eyes. You have to slow your heart rate and focus on your breathing. It's like dropping into a trance. There are a lot of terms for it—trance, meditation—but the definition of astral projection was the one closest to how I would describe it."

I nod, reviewing what he's said. *It sounds like what I do with energy work when I try to gain control.* "I think I can do this."

"I know you can," Trey says. "I'm warning you, though, it's a wild ride. Things don't work in the mind in a sensical way. It's kind of like being in a dream where anything can happen, except you can control a bit more of your reactions and movements."

"Like being awake in a dream?"

He nods.

"What if something goes wrong? Will I be able to get back out?"

Trey looks at me earnestly. "I don't know."

"If I don't start to fix him now, he's going to die before we get him out of here. Not to mention we'll never be able to heft him out of here if he's unconscious."

"I'll try to help you," Trey says. "I always know when something's wrong with you. I'll yell for you if I know you need to open your eyes. But first, I need you to drop the blockage on your side of our connection."

I nod and close my eyes, dropping the blockage. Once Trey has access to my mind, I say, "Hold the flashlight and don't let anyone else through that door until I come back out. I don't really know what I'm doing, and he's running out of time. I've only got one shot at this."

Trey checks Adam's sluggish pulse and looks him over.

"Grab his hand. You'll feel the difference."

"You're right," he says after he's grabbed Adam's hand. "He feels kind of flat."

I nod.

"Do it fast before you're interrupted," Trey says.

I turn back to Adam, fighting to calm my sledgehammering heart. I close my eyes, and my dark-water side breaks the surface, rising slow and calm in my mind. My heart slows through my dark-water side's sheer will.

I step to Adam and slide my hands around to his back, placing them where I remember he put his when he calmed my panic at the beach. I lay my head on his chest and close my eyes. I start counting my breathing, even and slow. *This is so hard to do standing.*

Suddenly, Trey's arm slides under mine and he flexes, picking me up. I relax against Adam and attempt to slip into the meditation trance I learned from my energy work.

I gasp tearfully as dread creeps up my spine. I open my eyes and look pleadingly at Trey.

"Screw this," he snarls. "I know how to help you." He takes out his pocketknife, and I shift out of the way. He cuts the rope and holds Adam up. "Help me get him to the floor."

We ease Adam down to lie on the filthy floor. Without much room to work with, I decide that social decorum doesn't matter. I scoot in and straddle Adam.

"Lie down on him," Trey orders. "I'll ground you."

I lie down, careful not to cut off what little ability Adam has to breathe. I feel Trey's weight descend on me as he straddles the back of my legs.

Trey calmly says, "I need you to trust me. I'm going to launch you in."

"I can do this, Trey."

Trey hits me with a blistering look as he adjusts his weight on my legs. "Damn it, Mel! You aren't a one-woman army! If I help, it'll go quicker."

I take a deep breath, fighting to relax. *This is beyond awkward.* I close my eyes and focus on Adam's sluggish heartbeat against my chest. Steadied, I wrap my hands around Adam's head.

Trey puts his hands around the back of my head, radiating calm.

My protesting muscles release, and I exhale hard.

A thought bubble full of calm comes to me from Trey: *"Here we go."*

I suddenly feel him in my mind. He reaches under the dark water in my psyche and gathers me up. I feel a tug, and then I'm launched through the water at a lightning fast clip. I scream in my mind, and then I unexpectedly hit something hard.

"I'm watching," comes the sound of Trey's disembodied voice. *"I'll get you out. Open your eyes in your mind, Mel."*

I do as he says, opening my eyes only in my mind. I find myself in a dark, wide-open space. It's hard to tell exactly where I am. There's only the faintest light around me, and it gets darker the farther I look. *It feels like the big room at Carlsbad Caverns.* I smile to myself. *Leave it to Adam's mind to be something like a rocky cave.*

Panic chases up my spine. I don't know where to start. I send panic through my connection with Trey.

His distant voice responds, *"Focus, Melanie."*

You know exactly where to start, my dark-water side reminds me. *You've always been able to feel his energy before he even comes into a room.*

I close my eyes and search for the energy that's distinctly Adam's. I feel him in the distance to the left. *This is bizarre. Don't get distracted. You already knew it wouldn't make sense. You lived in your own trapped mind for three weeks. Focus!*

I hurry through a dark, narrow corridor to the left and wind through a complicated series of cave passages. Finally, I turn a corner and spot Adam. He's farther down, lying on the rock floor with his eyes closed.

I send to Trey, *"Found him!"*

Weird. Inside Adam's mind, I can think in actual words with Trey.

Trey's voice wafts through the caves, *"Good girl. Now do what you need to do."*

"Adam!" I rush to him, dropping to my knees.

His eyes snap open. *Melanie?*

"I'm here. I'm going to get you out."

You can hear me?

"I can hear your thoughts. You need to come with me now."

How are you here?

"Trey. He launched me into your mind."

Even in his horrifying state, Adam manages to think, *"Thanks, fucker."*

Trey's concerned chuckle wafts in. *"You're welcome, asshat."*

I roll my eyes. "Can you two knock it off?" I look in Adam's eyes. "Love, we're all here getting you out. We're worried about an ambush." I send the image of our friends in the basement together before we cut the bolt.

Adam panics as he realizes he's still trapped in the storage room. The earth quakes as he loses control of what little sanity he was hanging on to. Giant boulders fall, crashing and threatening to crush us.

"Adam, I need you to calm down. This is all in your mind. I know you feel trapped, but I need you to help me help you."

The shaking gets worse, and giant cracks start spreading in the low-hanging ceiling above.

I close my eyes. *What do I do?* Suddenly, I know. "Adam, look at me. Now, or you're going to die in here, and you might take me with you. We don't know exactly how this works."

He snaps open his eyes, madness raging from him.

"I know how to get you out of here, but I'm going to have to do this my way. I understand the dark water better than these caves."

He nods.

Trey's voice floats through. *"Do it, Mel. I can help pull you this way."*

Destruction rains down unchecked around us. *He's going to crush both of us to death.* "You need to trust me."

Adam nods, and for a moment, the rumbling stops. Dark water begins to seep through the cracks in the floor, filling the space. I speed up the torrent because Adam's mind is disintegrating fast. He flails in the water, unable to find solid ground as the floor collapses.

I wrap my arms around him in our minds. "I've got you," I say to reassure him, just before the water swells over our heads.

He calms, stilling, and stares in my eyes through the water. I grab his hand and swim, pulling him through the disintegrating corridor. I feel Trey lock onto my dark-water side. He wills the raging underwater current to pull us back through the twisting, winding series of cave corridors, until the expansive cave room opens up around us. The rumbling growl of a new round of earthquakes fills the water. Everything is dissolving around us.

I grab Adam, and he stares at me.

He thinks at me, *"I can't hold it together. It's over."*

I pulse back through our connection, *"Then we go out together."*

I wrap my arms around him, holding him, peaceful in the realization that Adam's about to destroy both of us in his failing psyche.

He whispers in my mind, *"I'm sorry."*

I send a pulse of love to Trey and say, *"I'm sorry for so much. I apologize to both of you."*

Just as I'm positive that time is up, I hear Trey's voice in my mind. *"Melanie, follow my voice. I'm going to pull."*

His voice gives me a direction. I swim toward it, seeing the blue water above. I kick hard, yanking Adam while pushing off against nothing solid. We shoot up, drawn by Trey's sheer force of will, and our heads break the surface of the water just as the cavern collapses below.

Adam and I gasp at the same time. My eyes snap open. Trey's still behind me, straddling my legs. He sags above me, his forehead coated in sweat. He groans out, "That was new . . . and shitty."

We're all laughing half-heartedly as Arch's, Tanner's, Marcus's, and Darren's heads pop around the doorjamb in a comical synchronicity. They study us skeptically.

Marcus chuckles. "Ooh, kinky."

Arch's face scrunches up, baffled. "You three chose *now* for a humparoo?"

Trey gives them a disgusted look. "I'm not even about to explain to you morons what just happened."

Darren scoots past the guys and helps Trey up. He steps over Adam and me. Tanner helps Trey steady himself as he sags against one of the empty shelving units. He's panting and closes his eyes.

Darren looks at me expectantly. "What did you just have to do?"

"Trey launched me into Adam's hardheaded noggin," I explain. "Then, he helped pull us out."

Tanner looks at Trey like he's nuts. "You helped save Adam?"

Trey chuckles quietly. He looks down at Adam and me, still in our prone position. "I love fighting with that asshole too much to let him die."

Adam chuckles hoarsely and retorts, "Ah, pumpkin, you say the sweetest things."

"I'll be damned if I die in this tomb while Adam and Trey sarcastically flirt with each other," Arch hisses. He scoots his feet on either side of Adam's shoulders. "Up you go."

I feel hands under my armpits as Arch awkwardly lifts me off Adam. He sets me on my feet next to Trey, and my knees buckle.

Trey tries to reach out to catch me, but his knees start to give too. "We're tapped," he gasps. "We need a minute."

Tanner gets an arm around Trey, helping him through the narrow door gap. Darren scoops me up, cradling me, and carries me out. I look over Darren's shoulder and watch as Arch and Marcus wrestle Adam up and awkwardly attempt to haul him to the door. Adam's still so weak that he isn't much help, but he's alert.

We all make it around the corner.

Deb stares at Adam in disbelief. "Holy shit," she murmurs. Her lips part into a brilliant smile. "Welcome back from the dead, He-Man."

Darren lowers Adam into a chair while Trey and I lean against the wall and relearn how to stand.

"Damn, girl," Adam says to Deb with an exhausted smile. "You really will go to bat for us."

Deb nods. "Hell yes, I will. Tonight's been a blast." We all look at her like she's insane, and she shrugs. "We got out of rebuilding that damn set. This is way better."

"I agree," Adam quips. "Saving me from death is way better than Hiram ordering you all around with screw guns and design schematics."

We all silently look at Adam. He's staring at me, his eyes a strange combination of hopeless love and the desperation that can only come from near-death. "You got me out," he says, beside himself.

I smile the slightest bit. "You didn't think I'd leave you in there, did you?"

Adam looks terrible. He's gaunt and half-starved. His clothes are filthy, and he's covered in injuries, but he's alive.

"We need to get out of here," Darren says. "Let's go."

Tanner and Trey help Adam up, and we follow Darren up the staircase and through the door into the garage. Arch heads to the door leading outside.

"Where are you going?" Adam croaks.

"Out this way and down the driveway," Arch whispers. "We're parked two blocks up the road."

Adam cracks his bruised and swollen knuckles and rubs his bloody wrists. He's come to life a bit more now that he's been rescued from that tomb. He shakes his head. "Do you hear what I hear?"

The music is still pulsing from the house.

Arch smiles, slow and vicious. "Yup."

We all exchange a look.

Adam looks at the door to the house where the Drones are partying, exhaustion radiating from him.

All at once, I know what he's thinking. *He needs to do this to start to heal.* I decide on a route on his behalf. "Adam, look at me."

He turns and stares into my eyes.

I close the distance between us. "You said you needed someone who could fight next to you because you were tired of doing it alone. I'm here, right here, right now."

I drop all the shields and radiate relief that he's alive. I send him earth-shattering love, fury, and everything that makes my dark-water side tick.

Adam stares into my eyes, shattered.

He's utterly broken.

"I'm not going to be able to be what you need anymore," he says. "I'm so broken and lost."

"It's my turn to be what you need," I whisper back.

Adam looks at Trey standing behind me. I turn, and Trey nods.

"Let Melanie do this," he says.

"Clearly we've missed some things," Tanner says.

Darren mutters, "You have no idea."

Trey, Adam, and I turn and appraise our confused friends before chuckling quietly and glancing at each other.

"Could you handle this, Darren?" Adam requests.

"You're about to hear and see some things that never leave this room," Darren quickly informs our captive audience. "Bear and I have worked with these three tirelessly to keep a complete shitstorm from destroying everything our group holds dear. Melanie and Adam are both energy workers, and their energy is largely the same . . ." He glances at Adam, adding, "At least usually. He's not where he used to be." He turns back to our friends and implores, "Do you understand the gravity of what I'm saying?"

They all nod but are clearly confused.

"I'll be honest," Marcus says, "I've got *zero* clue what you're talking about, but we all know you guys, and we've seen some of the freaky witchy spiritual stuff that happens . . . so, I guess I get it."

"That'll work." Darren says before becoming serious again. "It's going to get weird, and I guarantee it'll be a story you want to tell. You can't. Got it?"

"I've got your back," Arch says. "All of you." He makes eye contact with Adam, Trey, and me in turn before shifting his focus back on Darren.

Darren nods and turns to Deb.

"Absolutely," Deb says. "Your secret's safe with me, whatever it is."

Next, Darren looks to Marcus.

"Always," Marcus says.

"Without question," Tanner agrees when it's his turn.

Finally, we all turn to Victoria. She glances from Trey to me and hits me with sincere eyes. "I've got your back, Melanie. My lips are sealed."

I nod. "Thank you, Victoria." *I can trust her.* I turn to Adam and put out my hands. "Time to give you what you need."

Adam grabs my hands, and I step up to him, dropping the shields that I've learned to keep tight. He leans down and kisses me. The slightest energetic fire tingles up my spine.

Even half-dead, he's so captivating.

He pulls away. "This is going to take forever, Melanie. I usually meet you halfway energetically."

I can't help but laugh and raise an eyebrow. I step behind him and put my fingers, featherlight, on his shoulders before running them down his back. His back tenses, and I close my eyes, unleashing my dark-water side completely. Seductive waves crash into him, nearly tearing him apart because there's little left that made Adam, Adam.

Suddenly, he grabs my arm, and my eyes snap open. He pulls me against him so hard it nearly knocks the air out of me. He leans down, kissing me with almost excruciating force. Fire laces and crackles up both our backs, spreading through us. My heart pounds out of control, and my hands shake. He moans as I hop up and wrap my legs around his waist. My dark-water side thrives in both of us.

Finally, the kiss slows, and we both pull away, staring at each other.

"One last time?" Adam asks. "We do this our way?"

He's back, at least temporarily.

Dark-Water Melanie shines vicious through my eyes.

Adam's expression morphs to match. "Let's rain hell down on them," he growls.

Adam sets me down, and Trey steps up next to me.

Battle rage rises in Trey, but it's *for* us instead of against us. "You two need to get through what's waiting on the other side of that door," he says. He turns to me. "I'm right behind you."

I nod.

Trey turns to Adam. "You got Melanie through hell when I couldn't. I want you to know how much that means to me. Now it's her turn to get you through hell."

"Thank you," Adam says.

A look of mutual respect passes between them.

"Well, all right," Tanner says.

The three of us turn and scan our friends' shocked faces.

"Told you," Darren says.

The quip loosens the tension for only a moment. We're ready for battle.

Adam turns to face the door. "Let's do this."

I step up next to him, and Trey takes his place behind the two of us.

Radiating the dark-water fury I lent him, Adam drops all his shields. He rolls his neck and says, "God, that fits. It feels exactly like what my energy used to feel like."

"I know."

He tries the knob, and it's locked.

A new song blasts from the house, and we all grin evilly at each other. Stone Temple Pilots' "Crackerman" vibrates the door at ear-shattering volume.

I grin back at my friends gathered behind me. They feel it too.

"God help them," Deb says.

Adam kicks the door with all the rage he's borrowed. It flies open, bouncing with a loud crack off the refrigerator next to it. We pour into the kitchen, fueled by white-hot fury. The Drones in the living room look shocked as we storm in. There's no hesitation. Every Drone that comes into our path gets the brunt of everything Adam, Trey, and I have been through.

Stan makes the mistake of stumbling into my path in his attempt to avoid Tanner, and I hit him with a right hook so hard that he drops, out cold. Adam takes two Drones by the back of their heads and smashes them together. They drop in a heap. Trey grabs another Drone as he tries to run out the front door and smashes his face into the wall, dropping him to his knees. His eyes roll into the back of his head, and he face-plants on the floor. Adam gut punches Isaac, dropping him flat.

Tanner headbutts a tall, muscular Drone, who moans and tries to crawl away. Darren pummels him, and he's out cold. Arch flattens Dan with a punch to the temple.

The song ends, and the silence that descends disorients me briefly. Joel rushes up out of nowhere and grabs me. He hefts me up and throws me. I hit the wall and bounce off, smacking face-first into the polished hardwood floor. I see stars, and when they clear, I look up at the sound of a combined roar from Adam and Trey.

Trey and Adam malevolently circle Joel, radiating fury. Trey feints a rush forward, and Joel runs back.

"Don't ever touch Melanie again!" Adam snarls in his face.

Adam lunges at Joel, and Joel jumps back, terrified. Adam smiles maliciously, his eyes alite with evil amusement. Joel wheels around, searching for an escape route, but Trey's got him boxed in. The devil's in Trey's eyes. He's capable of morphing demonic in a way that sends his enemies screaming. I grin maniacally, enjoying the sight of my guys toying with Joel.

Trey and Adam step in and block all potential exit routes. Joel's eyes widen. His lower lip quivers. I lean on the wall behind him, reveling in the show. Trey grabs Joel around the neck, choking him with his forearm. I chuckle as Joel flails helplessly while he turns an odd shade of purple. Trey squeezes harder.

"Sir, you may do the honors," Trey says politely to Adam.

Adam chuckles darkly as Trey releases Joel and shoves him hard in Adam's direction. Adam gets a vise grip on Joel's neck with his right hand and shoves Joel to his knees. With a deadly expression leveled on Joel, Adam politely responds to Trey. "No, no, old chap. I insist that you go first."

Trey grabs Joel by his hair and drags him back toward him. He whips Joel around, his expression wicked. Totally out of sync with the look on his face, Trey shakes his head and replies with overly polite sarcasm, "It would be rude of me to go first. You've earned the first crack at him."

Adam busts up laughing, along with all our friends who are watching this nonsense.

I tip my head back and smile. *Looks like my guys are getting along again.*

Trey's expression lights with amusement as he shoves a now-cowering Joel between him and Adam. "I think it's high time we work together. Do you prefer the dome or the jewels?"

Adam smiles congenially. "I'll take jewels. My legs work better than my arms right now."

Trey grins Joel's way. "That okay with you, Joel?"

Joel crab-crawls back, bumping into me.

I peek around him and say, "Boo!"

He squeals, and we all crack up.

I hit him with big, girly eyes. "This is about to hurt."

Joel's terrified gaze snaps back to Trey and Adam as they rush forward in unison. Trey grabs Joel around the neck and pulls the struggling guy to his feet while Adam kicks him so hard in the crotch that Joel starts throwing up. Trey lets go of him, and Joel sags to his knees. His face is red and contorted. I almost feel sorry for him . . . almost.

Marcus surveys the gooey sludge pile. "I see that psychotic hostage takers enjoy pizza."

Tanner winces. "Absolutely vile!" he complains flamboyantly. He glares down at Joel. "What kind of host are you? You didn't offer *us* any pizza."

Joel manages to gasp out, "Fuck you."

Tanner struts up to Joel and tips his chin up with the toe of his stiletto boot. He sasses back, "No, no. Fuck *you*."

Adam reaches down and grabs a fistful of Joel's hair. He holds his head back and says to Trey, "Your turn."

Trey gives Adam a disgusted look. "He's pathetic. This is so beneath me."

Adam grins. "We could always let Tanner sarcasm him to death."

"It would be my *pleasure*." Tanner luxuriates in the thought.

When Trey shrugs, Joel exhales, relieved. Without warning, Trey draws back his arm and punches Joel so hard that his eyes roll into the back of his head. Adam lets go, and Joel falls face-first into his own sludge puddle.

"Well, that's done," Trey announces. He exhales hard. "Finally!"

Adam shakes his head. "Nope. Melanie gets the final crack at him."

Trey gestures toward a pitifully moaning Joel. "Melanie doesn't need to sink to this. That's what she's got us for."

Adam shakes his head. "You can't wrap Melanie in bubble wrap to keep her safe. She needs to do this."

After a moment of silence, Trey nods.

Adam grabs a handful of Joel's hair, and as he pulls him to his knees, I singsong at him, "Upsy-daisy."

I step into Joel's view, and he stares at me slack-jawed, barely hanging on to consciousness.

I smirk down at him and tip my head. "You're cute on your knees," I say coyly.

Joel's eyes snap wide, his expression reading terror.

I nod knowingly. "How does it feel, Joel?" I lean in and snarl at him, "What you're feeling now is what every girl you attempted to rape felt like." When I smile, he takes a rattling half breath. "Let your dad know that I'm not the 'little bitch.' *You* are!"

Slowly, I wrap my hands around Joel's head and feel my dark-water side flare maniacally. I bare my teeth as I hear Arch gasp out, "Holy shit," from behind us.

Trey yelps, "Melanie, no!"

I slide my gaze Trey's way, and his expression snaps shocked as he frantically shakes his head.

"Melanie," Adam says calmly. "Look at me."

I shift my demonic gaze to him, and his eyes widen a touch. To his credit, he doesn't show panic.

"Baby," Adam says, "you can't snap his neck. Let the court system deal with him. Fuck him up, but don't kill him."

My gaze drifts down to meet Joel's eyes. Joel cowers, and I can feel his pulse thudding under my fingers.

I squeeze his head a touch harder. "If you ever come for us again," I say darkly, "I'll kill you with my bare hands." I smile. "And I'll enjoy it."

Joel makes a high-pitched keening sound.

Without warning, I drop to one knee, facing away from Joel. I use all my adrenaline-fueled rage to yank Joel by his head, up and over my shoulder, dumping him on his back on the hardwood floor like Trey trained me to do. There's a sickening crack.

Marcus rushes forward, putting two fingers on a now unconscious Joel's neck. He exhales with relief. "He's still alive."

Trey and Adam are grinning down at me. Trey holds out a hand, helping me up.

"Feel better?" Adam asks.

I nod, feeling the first wave of post-trauma shock bubbling up from my gut. I shove it harshly aside.

Tanner yodels out, "Well, hot damn and giddy-up. We now know who the deadliest psycho in our posse is."

Our chuckling is cut short as five girls come in from the back hallway, surveying the scene before aggressively rushing up to Victoria.

"Hooray, there's more!" Tanner squeals.

One of the girls screams, "You're a traitor," over the driving beat of the music.

I stalk, my dark-water malevolence blasting again. I'm radiating soul-bending rage. My dark-water side is loving the chance at another round.

Victoria reaches out, grabbing the girl by her ponytail, yanking her head back, and hitting her with an uppercut that rattles her teeth.

Deb, Victoria, and I each take on one of the other girls, working in synchrony.

I turn to the last one, a girl I know as Cathy Gregor. She's a snotty wannabe who not even the Drones really like.

She doesn't wait for me to attack. Instead, she drops to her knees at my feet, cowering in a puddle of her own urine. "Please, no! Please, no!"

My lips part into a malicious grin. "Lights out," I growl before kicking her in the face with my Doc Marten boot. She drops.

As calm spreads through the room, we all exchange glances. Arch opens the front door wide.

"We need to call the police," Darren says as we're leaving.

Adam and Trey step up on either side of me, and together, we stalk down the street, battle rage still roaring. I reach out my hands, and they lace their fingers in mine. We let the others worry about the rational logistics.

Our friends rush to keep up.

"Principal Walker was supposed to show up to the school at seven," Tanner says. "If we hurry, we can get there before he leaves. Maybe he can help us figure this out."

"Did we kill any of them?" Victoria asks.

"I checked," Marcus says. "They're all alive."

We get to our vehicles.

Darren tosses the keys to his Harley at Adam. "Think you're good to drive?"

Adam grins at him. "Hell yes."

"I'll ride with Arch," Darren says.

Trey grabs a bottle of water from his car and opens it, handing it to Adam. Adam guzzles the whole thing, then tosses the empty bottle back at Trey.

Adam turns to me. Everything and everyone stops as he stares down at me. His ocean-blue eyes hold pain that the others can't even begin to comprehend. Whatever he went through during this ordeal has left him broken in a way that only I can understand—not just because of our connection, but because I've been through a similar ordeal.

He's got a long road ahead, but he can do this.

He traces my jaw lightly. I close my eyes, and he pulls me in, hugging me. He whispers, "Thank you."

I whisper back, "You're welcome." I send a pulse of love through the connection. Tears fill my eyes, and my lungs tighten. "I can't breathe."

He tips my face up and stares tearfully into my eyes. "I can't either." He kisses me delicately, then whispers, "I love you."

I sob, knowing this is it for us. It's over. He's radiating erratic, broken, jagged energy, and it's going to take someone with less intense energy than I have to fix him. My chest folds in on itself as my deflated lungs scream for air but won't inflate. Adam puts an arm around me, pulling me against his chest before reaching his other hand over my shoulder. I feel Trey step up behind me.

Adam takes Trey's hand and pulls it over my shoulder. He whispers to me, "You're going to be okay," while tears stream down my cheeks. He turns me around and puts Trey's arm around me. Trey wraps his other arm around me and holds me against him as Adam lets go.

Over my shoulder, I watch Adam lean over the hood of Trey's car, his head in his hands. His back racks with sobs.

Darren steps up next to him and puts his hands on Adam's back. "It's going to be okay," he says. "We're going to get you through the trauma."

Everyone stands, silent but present, letting everything unfold how it needs to.

Finally, Adam gets his arms under him, his head hanging dejectedly. "I've got a rough road ahead," he says to Trey, "but I need to make sure Melanie's okay before I'll be able to focus on me." He takes a ragged breath, before continuing. "Trey, you need to get over this whole issue that you have about her and me. I'm telling you now that you're screwing up. You need to take care of her. Be everything she needs. I know you understand her because you're her soulmate, but I'm telling you that I am also. There are things you don't understand about her. I'm asking you to really hear what I'm about to say."

When Trey nods, Adam takes a shaking breath. I turn in Trey's arms, facing Adam as I lean my back against Trey's chest.

Adam stares into my eyes as he talks to Trey. "You have to listen to her, but I want you to really hear her, even when what she says makes no sense to you. She knows what she wants, and she's capable of making her own decisions. You have to let her fight like a demon instead of protecting her. You have to love her with the heat that fuels her but hold her when she cries." He closes his eyes as if it pains him to say this. "You MUST balance her life. When there's pain, balance it with joy. If you can do that, she can be whole." He pauses, trying to pull himself together enough to finish. "I'm completely broken inside. You have no idea. I can't be any of that for her, and her energy is going to make healing harder for me. My energy that used to match hers is gone."

He feels it too.

Adam turns and swings his leg over the Harley. The engine roars to life. He stares at the ground, waiting.

I spin around in Trey's arms.

He slides his hands to my cheeks and looks into my eyes. "I've got you," he whispers. "I promise. Give me a second."

He lets go of me and walks to Adam. Trey puts a hand on Adam's shoulder and says something I can't hear over the rumbling Harley. Adam's head drops, and Trey stays with him while Adam completely breaks down.

I sob uncontrollably. Darren crosses to me, pulling me in and holding me while the guys get through their moment. I feel hands on my back as my friends gather around, there for me while I'm both lost and found.

CHAPTER 49

In the hospital parking lot, Trey cuts the engine. We sit in the pitch-black, parked in the odd glare of an overhead light. Trey allows the silence to pass until I finally exhale and open my eyes.

"I heard everything Adam said," he tells me. "I promise I absorbed it all."

We look at each other. I grapple for something to say, but he puts a finger to my lips, quieting my sputtering brain.

"Melanie, just listen . . . After I got over my misguided need to make things how they used to be before the sedation issues, I started really trying to pay attention." He pauses, gathering his thoughts. "I can't apologize for taking so long to grasp the situation, because I had to grow and learn. I think we all did."

I smile the tiniest bit.

He returns the smile with an edge of hope. "I know you're reeling from all this," he continues. "I'm not mad or hurt by how deeply you love Adam." He looks down. "I think we're past that. I'm grateful to him because as hard as this has all been, if it weren't for him stepping in, I wouldn't have a shot at getting you back." He looks at me. "I want you to truly understand that I'm not mad.

We're not going to have a 'How could you?' series of exhausting discussions anymore." He takes my hand. "If you'll allow it, I want to move forward, starting this moment, and build from a new place. Fresh start. Together."

Completely content, I close my eyes and my dark-water side recedes. I take a moment to float in the dark water in my mind without fear or confusion, just being. It's calm and safe.

I open my eyes to find Trey waiting patiently. "Everything you just said was exactly right," I whisper.

He waits silently while I gather my thoughts.

Finally, I say, "I know that I've asked more of you than anyone ever should. I know this has been impossibly difficult. I've hurt you. You feel betrayed. I changed dramatically while you struggled to keep up. I'm sorry for all of that, but I want you to understand that at the time, I couldn't do better."

Trey shakes his head. "I want you to know that Tiffany was the biggest mistake I've made to date. It will *never* happen again."

I nod, my expression completely content. He opens the armrest compartment and pulls out my promise ring. He takes my hand while he gazes in my eyes and slides the ring on my finger.

"I love you, Trey."

He rests his fingertips on my forehead and runs his hand slowly down my face, featherlight, to my chin.

I close my eyes. "That's my favorite thing you do."

"I know."

We turn down another hall in this bright white maze that smells antiseptic.

I glance at Trey. "Hospitals and airports give me the creeps. It's something about how they're temporary places that people pass through on a journey. They always smell strange." My eyes dart right and left, and fear travels up my spine. "I hate this place."

Trey puts his arm around me. "I don't like it either. I'll never be comfortable here after everything we went through."

A pang about how difficult these past few months have been shoots through me. I swallow hard. "You and me, right?"

Trey nods. "You and me." He considers this briefly before adding, "Let's see how Adam's doing, and then we can leave so he can rest. I'll let my parents know I'm not coming home so I can stay at your house tonight."

Not expecting this, I smile up at him.

"Self-preservation," he jokes, raising an eyebrow. "I'd rather stay on your couch than have you wonder all night if I went off the deep end and backslid into Tiffany again."

I can't help but giggle. "I was literally just worrying about that." I glance at him. "Our soulmate connection is blocked on my side. How did you know?"

He squeezes my shoulders. "I know you, Mel." He looks at me adoringly. "Never again. I've got my girl back, and I'm not screwing this up."

I smile at him appreciatively, and his expression softens around the edges.

We scan the room numbers on the brown plaques next to each door, finding room 318. Trey squeezes my hand and grins at me. He knocks softly.

Arch opens the door, peeking around us and glancing in each direction. "Adam's technically only allowed to have four visitors," he whispers. "Get in here quick."

We slip through the door and squeeze into the crowded room. Adam's in his hospital bed, propped up on pillows with a dinner tray covered in foul-looking globs in front of him. He grins at us and reaches for my hand. I cross the room, edging past Hiram, Valerie, and Adam's dad, Mr. Stone. I take Adam's hand.

"Hi," he says.

Trey smiles at him. "Damn, Adam! Way to make things dramatic this week!"

Adam's laugh causes him to wince and grab his side. "It hurts to laugh, but I'm so happy to be here with you guys that I can't help it."

A knock at the door interrupts us. Arch hurries Tanner, Darren, Victoria, Demitri, and Bruce inside.

"Everyone needs to keep it down or we're going to get in trouble," Valerie says with a grin.

Bruce crosses the room and shakes hands with Adam's dad. "I can't tell you how relieved I am that Adam's okay."

"Me too," Adam's dad says. "Are the kids in legal trouble for hurting everyone during the escape?"

"I just finished speaking with an officer," Bruce says. "I think they're in the clear. Joel and the Drones are in custody, and Adam's alive because of the rescue attempt. I think they're cutting our pack of brawlers some slack."

Trey side-eyes Adam with a sly grin. "The school threw you a beautiful memorial service."

Adam looks baffled. "You're kidding."

"Clearly, we all have a lot to catch up on," Arch says. "Darren gave a heck of a eulogy. He made you sound a hell of a lot cooler than you are."

Darren snorts and grins at Adam.

"Okay," Valerie says. "One thing at a time. I need to ask a question or I'm not going to be able to focus on anything else we discuss." She looks across the crowded room at Victoria. "Why the hell is she standing here like we're all friends?"

Victoria looks uncomfortable. "I'm sorry, Valerie," she says sheepishly. "I'll leave."

Arch stops her. "Not a chance. You pulled through for us today, and you're not going anywhere." He turns to Valerie. "Victoria figured out that Adam was being held hostage, and she came to the school to get help. He's alive because of her."

Valerie huffs as she looks at Victoria. "Damn it! That means I have to like you." She breaks into a grin that Victoria returns.

"There's so much for everyone to tell," Adam says. "I don't even know where to start."

Bruce clears his throat. "How about we start with Adam telling us what happened to him?"

Adam nods and shifts in his hospital bed, trying to get comfortable. "Okay. Damn, this bed's awful." He grimaces, shifting again.

We all settle in, sitting on the floor and leaning against the walls, waiting with bated breath to hear Adam's story.

Adam clears his throat. "I was supposed to meet Bear at Leo Carrillo to watch the sunrise on Sunday morning. I woke up and saw that it was drizzling. I try not to take the Harley out in the rain, but I wanted to head that way, and I had the transmission taken apart in my roadster. I left my house at five and fired up the bike, backing out of my driveway. Suddenly, three cars came speeding up and blocked my way. Isaac and a bunch of the Drones leaped out of the cars and jumped me. Isaac went with me to Bear's house the night before and knew when I was leaving. He was playing both sides. I fought back, but there were too many of them. They surrounded me, and eventually, I guess I was out cold. I woke up in that dark space you guys found me in with my arms tied over my head. I fought to get free, but they did a good job tying the knots. They'd show up on occasion to throw stuff at me, but twice, Isaac snuck in and gave me a few bites of pizza and some water. He kept apologizing."

Trey growls, "Isaac's a lying sack of shit. He infiltrated our group, and it's my fault. He used to be on the baseball team. I thought we were friends. Looks like he had it out for us the whole time."

"Yeah," Adam says. "He definitely fooled us, but I probably wouldn't have made it if he hadn't fed me."

"I should've put a stop to all of this when I started to figure out that they had dangerous plans," Victoria says. "I just didn't think they'd actually go through with it. That group's usually all talk and no action."

I glare at her. "Really, Victoria? Really? Joel tried to rape me twice, murder me, and he attempted to kidnap me! That's what you call all talk and no action?"

Victoria grimaces.

Bruce saves her from the discomfort. "Victoria, why don't you fill us in on what you knew?"

She looks down and takes a hesitant breath. "They got drunk one night and started hatching a plan to silence all of you who were supposed to testify. It started out as a joke, but things became more sinister pretty quickly. The guys were planning on dealing with Melanie, Adam, Arch, Hiram, Darren, and Trey. The girls were assigned to Finley and Presley. I told them they were idiots because you'd all figure it out right away, but they didn't listen. I intended to go to Principal Walker, but I got the flu and my parents had me in bed, under lock and key."

After we've had a chance to process all this, Bruce turns to Arch. "All right, you tell your group's side of things."

Arch nods. "Bear should go next."

Bear tells his whole sad tale of finding the police on the canyon and watching as Adam's mangled bike was hoisted up. He looks at Adam. "I'm sorry, brother, but not even you have a shot at fixing that bike."

Adam winces. "I'll build a new one."

Darren grins. "Your dad gave me one of the ones that you were going to sell to pay for the wedding. It's yours."

"It didn't take you long to give stuff away, huh?" Adam quips to his dad.

His dad laughs. "The only two things I gave away were a Harley to Darren and another to Bear."

Adam smiles appreciatively. "You guys can keep them. I have two more that are almost done being restored. Unless you gave those away too, Dad."

His dad beams and shakes his head.

"I still have my car," Darren says dismissively, "and my Harley's yours. Bear, though . . . Well, his car exploded, so he might need the bike for a while until he can get a new car."

Adam's dad snaps his head around to look at Bear, his eyes huge. "Your car *exploded*?"

Everyone hisses, "Shhhh."

"Yeah," Bear says sorrowfully. "It seems that the Drones have some skill in the explosives area. We'll get to that, but first . . . A body was recovered from the canyon. The person was so mangled that he was unrecognizable. Adam, your dad identified the body because he was wearing your leather jacket."

Adam winces. "Damn, I love that jacket. The Drones must have taken it off me before they tied me up in their freaky little dungeon. The question I've got is, whose body was in the canyon?"

We all look at each other with questions in our eyes.

Mr. Stone inhales sharply and says, "No! Please no." He tips back his head, clearly forlorn.

"What is it?" Adam asks.

Mr. Stone looks from Adam to Bruce. "I got a call early Sunday morning when I woke up. It was Michael's father. Michael didn't come home Saturday night. He didn't think much of it, given that Michael's an adult, but he was scheduled to be on set at five in the morning and didn't show."

Deb squeezes her eyes closed. "He was supposed to take me to dinner Saturday night. He didn't show, but I didn't think much of it either." She looks down sorrowfully and shrugs. "Guys bail all the time."

"What happened?" Bruce asks.

"I got so caught up in the news of Adam's death that I wasn't much help," Mr. Stone says dejectedly. "Police refused to do anything because Michael's an adult, and they assumed he just cut out of town. But the whole neighborhood is tight, so they rallied together and formed a search party."

Adam glances at Deb. "There's no way he'd miss a date with you, Deb. Your whole tough-girl vibe had him revved up." He rubs his face. "There's also zero chance he'd miss a call time. He's been at this acting business a long time, and he was unshakably professional."

"I'll talk to the investigators," Bruce mutters. "What is *wrong* with those Drone kids?"

We all contemplate this question for a long second.

"I have some news you might all like," Bruce adds, breaking the silence.

We turn hopeful gazes on him.

"I got a call this morning. I've been trying to avoid the situation where any of you have to be in the courtroom at Joel's trial. Due to your ages and the violent nature of the accusations against Joel and the Drones, the judge granted my request to allow you all to testify by deposition."

We all look at each other as relief washes through me.

"The depositions are scheduled for Tuesday. Those of you who are on the witness list need to plan to miss school."

Just as we all start celebrating this news, a man in a cheap suit slogs through the door unannounced. He looks exhausted.

Bruce recognizes him. "Detective Torrez, what brings you by?"

The disheveled Detective Torrez surveys the room before glancing down at the paper in his hand. In a clipped tone, he says, "I need anyone who's extraneous to leave." He looks up at Bruce. "Only those who are a part of the case against Joel Stamp can be here."

All our friends who aren't on the witness list say goodbye to Adam before scooting out the door. Mr. Stone and Bruce stay with us. We watch the detective curiously.

"Son," Detective Torrez says to Adam, "do you know a Michael Gramely?"

Adam's face falls. He shakes his head dejectedly. "No! Don't tell me . . ."

The detective's expression is suddenly compassionate as he nods. "I'm sorry, Adam. Michael was reported missing on the Sunday we thought we'd found your body. We had DNA samples from what we thought was your autopsy still in storage. When we learned that you're alive, we tested the samples against Michael's father."

Adam squeezes his eyes closed. His dad steps up to his bedside and takes his hand.

"Damn it," Adam murmurs. "Michael was one of the most solid guys I've ever known."

My heart breaks as I watch Adam absorb the news that what he has feared has come true. "I'm so sorry," I whisper.

He opens his eyes and glares at Bruce. "What the fuck do we need to do to lock those psychos up forever?"

Bruce meets Adam's harsh gaze unflinchingly. "We take all your depositions. We'll schedule them for Tuesday. I need perfect control, nothing but facts, and I need each of you to tell it all."

We all nod our agreement.

"We'll get them locked away," Trey promises Adam. "For Michael, for you, and for Melanie."

CHAPTER 50

The next day, we're all interviewed by the police about what they found at Stan's house. Between the blood and vomit, Adam's DNA was all over the room in the cellar, but they also found his wallet just for extra confirmation. Every one of the Drones had left some piece of evidence of their involvement in the room as well. Maybe it was the gruesome nature of the crime, but the police had no trouble believing our cobbled-together story that we'd just come to the house to confront the Drones about Adam's death, and they'd been the ones to start the fight.

We all recognize that there's still a ton of dust to settle on this saga, but for now, with the officers off doing their investigative work and those of us involved in the play gathered at the school auditorium, we shift our focus to more immediate matters.

"This has been the most insane few months of my life," I say to our group, who've all gathered in the stage-right wing.

Arch scoffs. "Isn't high school supposed to be boring?"

We're all laughing as Ms. Ferry comes around the corner. "Okay, everyone, let's gather on stage to have a discussion."

After everyone gathers, Ms. Ferry calls for Hiram.

Hiram holds up his hand from the back of our circle.

Ms. Ferry smiles at him. "Are you ready for this? I know you only had a few runs as Vernon."

Presley drapes her arm around my shoulder and says, "Umm . . . Ms. Ferry? I think there's something you don't know."

We all grin at her expectantly.

"Give him a second," Bear says. "He's moving a little slower than usual."

Most of the cast look confused, and Ms. Ferry scrunches up her face. "Who is?"

Our group points to the lobby across the auditorium, and everyone looks that way.

"I am," Adam says from the lobby doors.

Valerie helps Adam make his way down the auditorium aisle, grinning. Val throws a fist up in the air, and Arch raises up devil horns, greeting the pair from across the distance. Adam beams, returning the gesture, his left hand a little lower than usual because of his shoulder damage.

Everyone gasps, and we smile at Ms. Ferry's expression.

"It's a long story," Arch says, "but as you can see, Adam's alive. We rescued him last night."

Ms. Ferry's eyes practically bulge out of her head as Adam makes his way up the steps on the side of the stage. He crosses to her, and she gives him a hug.

"You think our makeup crew can fix this face of mine so I can do the show?" Adam asks.

"Forget that," Tanner says. "I've got you!"

They exchange a grin. The whole cast rushes over to hug Adam and pound him on the back.

Adam winces. "Easy, easy. I'm a little torn up. I'm glad to see you guys too."

"Everyone take a seat," Ms. Ferry says, still beaming about the incredible surprise. "We've got an hour and a half before places. We need to hear this."

We all sit in a circle.

Ms. Ferry says to Adam, "We had a memorial service for you. You were dead."

Adam looks down pensively. "Yeah. Fortunately, I was only *almost* dead. They didn't manage to take me out so easy."

"Who did this to you?"

"Joel, Isaac, Stan, and the Drones."

Ms. Ferry looks around the circle. "Isaac isn't here?"

Adam shakes his head. "Isaac and friends are currently locked up on more charges than I have the energy to list. Long story short, those maniacs kidnapped me, faked my death using the body of one of my best friends, and held me hostage in a bizarre little basement dungeon. Victoria, of all people, figured it out and decided to be a human being, for once."

"Victoria showed up here during our set rebuild last night with a shocking secret," Arch chimes in. "A select few went to Stan's old house. There Adam was, tied up in this creepy cellar. We got him out, and he was taken to the hospital."

Ms. Ferry's eyes go wide. "So, you managed to build the set *and* be superheroes last night?"

We laugh.

"I managed to argue for an early release from the hospital this morning," Adam says. "The doctor said I'm doing surprisingly well given the trauma, dehydration, and lack of food." He sighs, looking deeply pained. "The investigators needed to meet about my friend Michael's death, and I refused to miss that. I'll do whatever's necessary to help the case against the Drones."

Ms. Ferry looks baffled. "So, you're here? At opening night?

Wouldn't you rather go home and rest?" She motions behind her, toward Hiram. "I think you've earned it. Hiram's prepared to play Vernon tonight."

Adam looks to Hiram. "Are you going to be upset if I play Vernon?"

"The part's yours," Hiram says. "Besides, I know all of the chorus dance numbers and someone's gonna have to replace Isaac."

Ms. Ferry's eyes widen. "I guess you have a point. Okay, then Adam's back in as Vernon. I'll need to do an announcement before the show, so people don't think the theater's haunted when Adam comes strolling out."

Marcus cracks up. "I triple-dog dare you not to warn them. It'll be hilarious!"

Ms. Ferry grins mischievously, considering it, but then shakes her head. "As much as I'd love to, I think our community's had enough shock."

Susan checks her watch. "The show starts in an hour and fifteen minutes. I think the cast needs to walk the new set, test the doorknobs and working parts, and we need to run Hiram through the three big chorus dance numbers."

Ms. Ferry nods. "I agree! Well, Hiram, welcome to the chorus. And Adam . . . welcome back to the land of the living!"

We're gathered backstage behind the closed main curtain in our costumes, the lights at a dim glow. The murmur of our waiting audience drifts from the auditorium into the backstage area, adding to the usual preshow jitters. From the sounds of it, we have a full house.

"Adam, you look fantastic," Finley says. She turns to Tanner. "You really should become a makeup artist. I can't believe the job you did covering those bruises."

Tanner smiles. "I must admit that I gave myself a pat on the back when I finished with him."

"You guys ready for this?" Adam asks.

We all nod.

Looks like we're all embracing the normalcy.

"Let's have the time of our lives out there tonight!" Demitri says.

The lights fade backstage, and Susan quietly announces, "Places."

She's been put in the incredibly stressful job of stage manager, and as hesitant as I am to admit it, she's killing it. I watch as she heads to her podium at stage right and settles in, putting on her headset. Hiram walks over and kisses her on the forehead. They gaze at each other for a moment, and Hiram looks happier than I've ever seen him.

Maybe Susan's not so bad after all. I grin at her, and she smiles back.

Susan says into her headset, "House lights fade to black." We wait, and then she says, "Microphone hot."

She cues Ms. Ferry, who heads out in front of the curtain.

Ms. Ferry's voice rings clear over the speakers. "Good evening, and welcome to our winter production of *The Pajama Game*."

The audience applauds enthusiastically, and Ms. Ferry waits patiently for them to quiet down.

"Our productions are always special, but this year will be one for the record books. You see, there's been a holiday miracle, and it's mind-blowing." She pauses, letting her message sink in. "As most of you know, we recently suffered news of the devastating loss of Adam Stone. Adam was cast as the lead, Vernon Hines. We were prepared to perform in honor of him, because, as they say, 'The show must go on.' But . . . we got the surprise of our lives an hour and a half ago. It's a long, complicated story that can't be told due to an active police investigation, but . . ." She pauses, allowing the anticipation to build again. "I present to you *The Pajama Game*, featuring a very alive Adam Stone."

The crowd erupts in joyful disbelief.

"Microphone out," Susan says. "Go cue two. Stand by on main curtain . . . Main curtain go."

The curtain opens, and after a pause, the set door stage right opens. Adam strolls out the door, and the audience gasps at the confirmation that it's all true. Adam grins at them, raising an eyebrow.

Adam, as Vernon Hines, speaks the first lines of *The Pajama Game*. "This is a very serious drama. It's kind of a problem play."

The whole audience spontaneously cheers, whooping and hollering. The cast all cheers with them from the wings on the side of the stage. Adam grins, and I tear up.

He's in the spotlight, surviving and thriving, right where he belongs.

Presley and Finley put their arms around Valerie while she watches Adam. Darren and Bear step up next to me and hold my hands while I watch Valerie gaze at Adam.

Demitri slides his arms around my shoulders and squeezes me affectionately. "You okay, Meley?" he whispers.

I nod and tear up a bit as a grin spreads across my face.

So, how did it go? Well . . .

The show sold out every performance. Word spread that Adam was alive, and the whole school—hell, most of the town—showed up to lend their support. It was a raging success, and naturally, we were all marvelous.

Now, for the bad news. Bruce called us in for a long meeting with the lead investigator on the case of Michael's death. We were questioned about Michael's disappearance, and we explained that Isaac was likely the common link. Isaac had met Michael several times, and so he was well acquainted with how much Michael looked like Adam.

After the interviews, the police showed us surveillance footage they had recovered from a security camera at a gas station. They warned that the footage was difficult to watch, and that Adam in particular didn't need to see it, but Adam refused to leave the room. He needed to understand what happened. It haunted him, and still haunts him, to know that one of his oldest friends was murdered just because he bore a resemblance to Adam.

As we all stood around Adam, wanting to be there for him, Deb took it especially hard when the footage began, and she realized that the gas station was just around the corner from her house. It seemed that Michael was heading to their date, after all. The video showed Joel sneaking up behind Michael, then suddenly surging up behind him just as he was closing his gas tank. Joel pressed a rag over Michael's mouth and nose. The police believed that the rag was doused with chloroform. Michael struggled for only a second before he slumped unconscious and was dragged into the same van the Drones used during my own attempted kidnapping.

Michael's funeral was tough. Adam was destroyed. We all

went to lend our support. I was blown away by how many people were there. The funeral was held in the community center where Michael, Adam, and all their neighborhood friends used to play, and it was packed from one end to the other. It turned out to be a big reunion for the kids who grew up together, but that was one of the only bright spots. I'd never seen so many guys in their twenties sobbing. It was gut-wrenching. In life, Michael had been something of a leader for their group, and he was so loved.

A stream of people kept coming up to the front of the assembly to speak about Michael. The stories were mostly hilarious, and we collectively laughed through our tears. Adam's speech was especially heartfelt and gut-wrenching to listen to. He can be a very soft guy when it boils down . . . In truth, I miss being with him.

Joel's trial was held the Wednesday after Michael's funeral. By chance, it was a half day at school, and Darren, Bear, Trey, and I made plans to leave together. Marcus got a call from his dad just before we left. Thanks to the work of his prosecutorial team—with a strong assist from the new charges about the many crimes they committed in kidnapping Adam and staging his death—Joel was sentenced to twenty-five years in prison.

That same day, Joel's accomplices faced their bail hearing. Their judge ruled that they were too dangerous to release, even going so far as to promise to fast-track their cases. For the first time since the day I met Joel, we all breathed a little easier, knowing that there isn't anyone out there trying to threaten, rape, kill, or kidnap any of us.

Our little group decided to spend our half day off school at Adam's hidden beach. When we arrived, we found Adam sitting alone in the sand.

I squeezed Trey's hand. "Give me a minute."

Trey nodded and stood with Bear and Darren while I crossed the short distance to Adam.

"This seat taken?"

He looked up and smiled. Sincerity radiated from his cracked and failing shields. He was still broken from the kidnapping, but every day, he seemed to get a little better.

I sat and leaned my shoulder against his. "You okay?"

"No," he said, "but I'm working on it. I'm getting a little closer to normal."

"I'm here for you."

"I know."

"How are things with Valerie?"

"I guess they're good. She never found out everything. Our friends kept their mouths shut." He glanced at me and smirked. "But I'm bored."

I chuckled quietly. "I told you so."

A surprised laugh bubbled up from Adam. "You can always do that."

"I don't know what to say."

"I might be able to help with that," Trey said, joining us. He set down the boombox he'd thought to bring. "I've got a Nine Inch Nails song that I think sums up everything the three of us went through."

Adam chuckled. "It isn't Melanie's red-light Nine Inch Nails song, is it?"

Trey raised an eyebrow my way. "No. That song's mine."

"Looks like Trey's finally found some fire," Adam whispered for only me to hear.

I grinned and whispered back, "Definitely."

Trey pushed *play* on the boombox, and the pounding rhythm of Nine Inch Nails' "Sin" blasted from the speakers. The three of us stood in the sand looking at each other while Bear and Darren watched over us. The story of this insane chapter rode through the air on the dark-water wave of the lyrics.

When the song ended, I said, "That about sums it up."

Everyone laughed.

They all turned to leave to get some stuff out of Darren's car, and as they made their way up the cliffside path, Adam side-eyed me. He reached over and rubbed the inside of my wrist, featherlight.

I gasped silently as my dark-water side roared to the surface, held tight behind my shields that I only let Adam see through. *Uh-oh.*

We stared at each other for longer than we should have—right up until we heard, "Melanie!"

We looked up to find Trey at the top of the cliff by the path, slowly shaking his head at me. To his credit, he was smiling.

Adam threw back his head, laughing, the sound exuberant.

"Are you good?" I asked him.

He looked down at me and smiled. "I'm legit good."

I laughed. "That's usually my line."

"Go to your guy, Mel."

I nodded and practically ran up the treacherous path. I got to Trey, winded, and looked into his eyes. He put his fingertips on my forehead, featherlight, and ran them from my forehead to my chin.

Special thanks to the incredible team of models that keep pulling through for me over and over. Thank you to Deidre Michelle for her endless ability to find the right people to depict these characters. Thank you to Anna Hall, Kyle Fager, and Stephen Knezovich for making this series magic. Thank you to Jordan, Bear, and Carol for their endless conceptual support.

MELISSA VELASCO is a true explorer of the arts. With a well-rounded background as a choreographer, professor, dance teacher, stage manager, author, and Crystal Grid teacher, she thrives in creation. At her core, she believes that the arts save lives and provide a route for passion and connection. The artistic ride makes life a whole lot brighter.

With a quick wit, often edgy mouth, and loud laugh, Melissa exuberantly embraces life. To find balance from the mental cacophony in her head, she enjoys expansive views in her mountain home. Her ideal day involves a mug of hot tea, music playing, and a whole day to write. Her greatest loves are her three children and husband. The four pillars of her ultimate happiness include her family, friends, dance, and laughter.